The Chosen Novel

Rise of the One

THE CHOSEN NOVEL

Rise of the One

Second Edition

Kyla Noble

TATE PUBLISHING
AND ENTERPRISES, LLC

Published by Tate Publishing & Enterprises, LLC
127 E. Trade Center Terrace | Mustang, Oklahoma 73064 USA
1.888.361.9473 | www.tatepublishing.com

Tate Publishing is committed to excellence in the publishing industry. The company reflects the philosophy established by the founders, based on Psalm 68:11,
"The Lord gave the word and great was the company of those who published it."

Published in the United States of America

ISBN: 978-1-63122-313-6
1. Fiction / Science Fiction / General
2. Fiction / Fantasy / Dark Fantasy
14.03.17

Table of Contents

CHAPTER ONE
This is where it all began; this is the beginning of the end

Dear Diary,

Tonight is the first night I've had this journal. My mom said it'd bring me good luck and change. Hopefully she's right. I've gone through so much recently and I've been getting this feeling that it's only going to escalate from here on. I don't know. I'm probably just being paranoid... ~~Jost~~ like always. UHH wow! Did I really just spell "Just" Incorrectly? I'm really not much of a diary person. I don't really know what to talk about with you. I'm really only doing this because my big brother asked me to... He agrees with my mom and says it'll also help me get though school better. I'd do anything he asked me to. Is that bad? I don't even know that he'd do the same for me. I know he loves me, but... I don't know. I'm just rambling. But anyway, that's just the person I am; too prone to forgiving, too willing to love. Well, I'm really just rambling on. I suppose it's better to just go to bed before you combust or something along those lines and all my writing goes up in flames. Good night.

-Elaina
8/8/10

It was a dark and stormy night. I was in my old backyard, tied up. I wasn't on the ground, but on some man's cold, hard shoulder. I tried to scream but then I realized that I was gagged. I started struggling, trying to make the man drop me.

"Girl." He spoke. "You woke up, huh."

I couldn't struggle my way free of him and every time I tried to get loose, he tightened his grasp. I noticed my brother Jason kneeling on the ground, bound and gagged helplessly looking up at me.

As the man watched my brother struggle against his bonds he taunted, "Oh, is big brother going to try and protect his little sister?"

The man pulled out a gun from his pocket, and pointed it at Jason holding it steady no matter how hard I kicked. I was so... *imperfect*. I didn't have much muscle. I was weak. I was powerless.

Desperate to kick the gun from the man's hand, I did all that was humanly possible to get away from the man or at least affect his aim so I could aid my brother but the man was just too strong for me.

"Say your goodbyes to him, little girl!" He laughed as he pulled the trigger.

Shocked, I woke up throwing myself off the couch.

My vision blurred slightly and then recovered after a few moments of rubbing my eyes. "Jason!" I yelled, but my brother never answered. "Jason? Where are you?" I called out. Still, Jason never answered.

I walked to the window at the front of my house to see if his car was parked outside. The mixture of the rain and fog outside combined with the darkness made it difficult to see and the tree that he liked for its shade cast a dim shadow where his car should be, making it even more difficult to tell, but I finally had to admit to myself that Jason's car was gone.

With a sense of relief, I realized that it was just a dream and that I wanted to call him to see where he was and tell him all about my idiotic dream for both a good laugh and a good counseling method.

As I walked to the kitchen and picked up the phone I didn't even get a chance to dial when a man whispered from behind, "I wouldn't do that if I were you." as he gently placed his hand firmly over my mouth.

My heart skipped a beat and I tried to let out a scream.

From the hard object thrust against my back, it also felt like he had a gun pointed in my back.

"Now, be a good girl," He commanded "and put the phone back down."

Startled, I dropped the phone back down on the marble counter.

"That's a good girl." He continued, "Now, I'm going to release my hand from your mouth and I want you to be real quiet. You're going to be good and do that for me... right?"

I quickly nodded my head not knowing what else I could do.

"Now walk over to the couch, sit down and keep quiet."

I didn't know how to respond. I was really, really scared. I just couldn't move.

"Why aren't you moving?" He asked impatiently. "What do you do when I give you an order?"

"I-I don't know." I replied. "I'm scared."

"You don't need to be scared right now. As long as you do as I tell you, I promise you'll be fine. I'll give you a simple hint that even you should

4

understand. When I tell you to do something you say, 'Yes sir.' in that pathetic girly voice. Now. Get. Over. To. The. Couch." He said.

He seemed to control his temper perfectly... when and if he wanted to.

"Y-yes sir..." I said quietly.

I couldn't even control my legs. They were just walking on their own even though I was still too terrified to move. I fought the incredibly strong urge to look back at my tormentor fearing that he would kill me for sure if I looked at him.

My eyes were closed when I sat on the couch. I knew I wanted to keep this man as happy as possible if I had any hope of surviving. He sat down beside me and I tried to move farther away to the end of the couch.

"Elaina," he began. He noticed that I flinched at the sound of my name. "Yes Elaina, I know your name. You may open your eyes. Just so that you know, I appreciate the extra effort to keep me happy."

He's too smart for this... He's not letting me go if I see his face. If I see him, he'll either take me or he'll kill me. That ensures his safety.

"I've come here to take you with me and I *want* to leave without any trouble. You'll be good and help me out with that, right? Answer this, will you come with or without a fight?"

I opened my eyes and stared blankly at him. *Did he ask me a question?* It didn't sound like a question but it was one... However, the two choices he gave me didn't include the option I wanted which was him leaving *without* me.

"U-uhm mister, is there any option that doesn't include me going with you? *Please*? We have tons of stuff. You can take it all. We won't call the cops. Please, just take what you want and go!" I asked.

"Yes, there is, plenty of stuff but what I want is you so I intend to leave with what I want. Besides, if I were to leave without you, it would make me responsible for having to kill more people. And as for your pathetic cops," He smiled gently. "I will never be worrying about them, I promise."

Therapeutically, I began imagining how I could describe him to the police. I didn't want to be one of those victims that could claim "It all happened so quickly!" but then it backfired. I looked at him for half a second and after looking away immediately, knew he was not going to let me live. With the very first glance, you could tell that all he consisted of was violence. His eyes just lit up as he talked about him being able to kill people and the way that he looked at me when he spoke about the police... he wanted to kill them too. He hoped I would choose to stay and allow him to kill more people. He was a blood thirsty son of a bitch.

Knowing that, I kept telling myself I wouldn't go without a fight. Ignorance is bliss, after all. I still believed that crap that they told us in school: "You can do anything you set yourself to!" Bull. I definitely didn't want anyone to die, but I knew there was no way I was going to go easily.

The thing was I knew he was stronger than I was by a lot. He managed to come into my house without setting off my alarm, without alerting my dog, and without me hearing. How could that possibly be normal?

"Hello? Is anyone there? I want my answer Elaina!"

He was angry now.

"SHUT UP!" *Oh god, oh holy god.* "Uhm, I mean... Give me time to think... Please?"

I really had to be more polite to people that enjoy killing.

"Five minutes." He agreed glaring at me.

I thought that was good. I really needed time to think of a decent escape plan. "Uhm, thank you." I said.

How could I not be upset with myself for that lack of any form of thought and as that crazy man stared at me, I could see that he was too. He wanted to see what I could come up with in five minutes. I wouldn't leave him disappointed. While he was waiting, I'd thought of a somewhat good plan... sort of... not really... I'd agree to go with him without a fight, and then when I was close to the phone I could run and get it.

"I-I'll go without a fuss..." He didn't seem pleased with my answer. He was looking forward to beating me up.

He got up and started to lead the way out of the room but when I didn't follow quickly enough, he got tired of waiting and he grabbed me to get me on my feet. I could feel his muscles. They weren't just for show. The smartest choice would have been to discard my escape plan knowing that it wouldn't work for the life of me and go without a fight but obviously, I really just wasn't that smart.

As we were walking, he seemed distracted, so I figured that then must be the best time to make a run for it. He might have known what I was planning on doing before I even did. As I was making a run for the phone, he just turned around and smiled. I got the phone, and began dialing, except, it didn't dial.

The line was dead.

No wonder he was smiling. He knew I was going to run for the phone! I just stared at the phone and when I looked up, the man was gone.

I heard a bitter laugh right behind me, and it grew into, not a chuckle, but bawling laughter. I spun around and fell to the ground in sheer terror. That was the first time I ever got a good look at him. He had, it was... well, hard to explain. He had medium length dark brown -- almost chocolate colored --

hair, almost like it was dyed, very dark brown eyes, really muscular and average clothes: a T-shirt and jeans.

He was surprisingly pretty good looking. For a psychopath. Actually, he was better than pretty good for *anyone*. It was more like godly looks, but still really scary looking. I just didn't understand how he had gotten over to me so quickly. I was petrified with fear.

"Tell me," He snarled taking another step towards me. "Did you really think I would let you get away that easily?"

I moved back pleading, "STAY AWAY FROM ME!"

"No," he replied keeping up with my movements. "I don't think so."

I screamed at the top of my lungs. The front door barged open. It was another man. "Did I hear a scream?" He asked.

I smirked at my kidnapper and screamed "HELP ME!" I should have realized that this man couldn't have heard me unless he was on my doorstep and so he had to be helping the man to kidnap me.

My kidnapper whispered, "You just sprung the trap and when I get a chance you'll get a real good beating from me."

The second man that walked slowly into the kitchen and sweetly said, "Hello Elaina." My smirk disappeared.

"You aren't here to help me, are you?" I whispered helplessly. That wasn't a question, it sounded like one but it wasn't. I already knew the answer. I suppose I just asked in all hopes that he was a good person ready to rescue me from this nightmare I refer to as life.

"No. I'm here to help him in case you decided you wanted to go with a fight. Now, walk." He told me. He grabbed my hair and yanked me to my feet.

"Let go of my- let go of me and I'll walk quietly." Once he released his hold on my hair, I started walking slowly and then tried once more to run. It was just no good. I didn't even manage to set my foot on the ground when he wrapped his arm around me and slammed me into the wall. "NO! NO!" I screamed.

Ignoring my screams of desperation, he tightly grabbed my arm, and this time, without letting go, shoved me down the hallway and into my room. He let go of my arm and shoved me to the middle of my room. With my amazing, award winning clumsiness; I fell down as he shoved me though the doorway.

I was sitting, stunned in the middle of my bed room and asked, "Who are you?"

See, most people in this situation would be screaming or whatever people do. My way of dealing with bad situations is by asking questions; it helps me keep my mind straight and allows me to devise a plan along with buys me a little bit of time before the next phase of the situation comes along.

"My name is Dylan." He looked to be about thirty years old; he was much older than my previous tormentor.

"Who is the other guy with you?"

"His name is Alec." He continued.

"Andrew," he called out. "Come here I want you to meet Elaina."

Another man sauntered into the room. He looked to be about twenty-three.

He had bleach blonde, longer length hair, and was also very muscular. Not as much as Alec, but still strong. He wore sunglasses and casual clothes – a long sleeve collared shirt and jeans with those high top basketball shoes. His clothes were a little outdated for him. They looked as if they belonged to a surfer boy in the 9th grade.

He had this amusing aura about him. His hair was... I'll try to describe this: He had hair that he constantly had to shake his head to one side so that every piece of hair on his head followed that direction. It looked like he had a tic or something...

"Hello Elaina, it's nice to meet you." He smiled. "Hey guys, let's give Elaina another chance to come peacefully. She looks terrified. Would you like that, Elaina? One last chance?" Andrew asked in a charming, soothing voice, waiting until he saw my reaction of pure happiness, just to tear it apart saying, "Just kidding. In fact let's beat her up *more* than we planned just to see her squirm." he laughed.

Andrew took a step towards me and I, without thinking, moved backwards. Amused, they all began to slowly close in surrounding me almost like sharks getting ready to feed.

"Come-on" I pleaded desperately. "I'll go with you without a fight. I don't want any trouble. Let's just go."

"Why would we give you one more chance," Alec mused. "When that offer has already expired?"

I blinked and they were all gone. I blinked again and they were next to me! Andrew and Dylan grabbed my arms and lifted me off the ground just holding me there like I weighed nothing at all. At first I didn't know what they were planning until Alec came towards me rubbing his fist. They were going to hold me while Alec used me as his new punching bag. I tried to stop him with everything in me. I pleaded, I screamed, I kicked, and I struggled pointlessly against their overpowering strength... What more was there to do?

"Wait!" I stammered. "Please stop! Please don't hurt me! What do you want from me?" I was getting hysterical and began kicking and screaming, but it didn't matter, I was held too tight.

Tears began streaming down my face before they had time to throw a single blow. These men were psychotic. With normal people, they would have just accepted my surrender and taken me without all the pain.

These men, on the other hand, let my hysteria be an assurance that I really was terrified of them and their amusement with me only grew. They all let out a small chuckle, mocking my torment. Without a second thought Alec began hitting me. Every time Alec punched me, it felt like a truck hit me. That wasn't human strength. And my being able to withstand it? A miracle in itself.

He punched me four times before another man came. "That's enough! Let her down, now!"

Something happened when that new man walked in. The edges of my vision for a very brief moment became blurry.

He was younger than everyone else but he looked very dapper, wearing a white dress shirt and a tie –very classy, very good looking. It was just enough to say he doesn't just think that he's all that; he really is all that.-, tousled chocolate hair with natural lighter brown and blonde highlights and beautiful crystal blue eyes. Not the average appearance of someone that looked as though they were only eighteen years old. In fact, all of these people looked amazing with godly beauty.

They just dropped me. I fell like a sack of bricks unable to move, gasping for air and in severe pain. I struggled to sit up.

"Please," I gasped. "Help me."

He completely ignored me. Who does that? "I gave you orders to make sure she would remain under control. I didn't tell you to kill her!" He said furiously.

"You did this?" I asked, still trying to catch my breath.

He offered me a hand to help get up but I just shoved his hand away. He grabbed my arm and pulled me up without showing signs of being discouraged.

He admitted slowly so that even an idiot would understand, "Now, now kiddo, I didn't deliberately do this. I just receive the orders, carry them out and make my Lord a very happy man."

"And what are your orders?" I asked curiously.

The interesting thing was I wasn't nearly as afraid of him as I was for Alec. I definitely had feelings for James from the moment I laid eyes on him. Now the only thing I needed to decide is if those feelings were positive or negative.

"One was –"

He was interrupted by Alec, "James, stop saying things to that girl! She has no right to know *anything*! It's our job to *torture* her, not protect her from your allies. Your –"

"That's enough Alec," said James. "Last time I checked I still outranked you and I believe that makes you under my command."

This time I saved you from a world of pain, but next time … well, let's just hope there isn't a next time.

I heard a voice in my head. It sounded like James. I looked up at him, confused. His lips hadn't moved. *How did I hear that?*

James simply smiled and said, "Team, we need to talk to her about the reason for our visit." The three men lined up looking incredibly bored like they have done this hundreds of times before.

"Elaina, I need you to do something for me."

"What is it that you think I can do?" I asked. "You're holding me captive."

"You need to choose one of us to be your master and –"

"*What*? Why? Why would I want to choose one of you to be my master?"

My vision momentarily blurred again. It wasn't random that had happened. It was a sign that a door to my future had been unlocked.

Almost immediately after I said that, I realized that I would really regret it. It seemed as though I made a mistake by saying that to him.

His complexion and demeanor changed completely. His beautiful eyes turned to something that looked blood red like they were taken from a demon. His hair began to move and became very messy. His skin, nicely tanned, turned a reddish hue.

He slapped me. In fact, he slapped me so hard I flew across the room and hit the wall before I hit the ground.

Stunned, I looked at him. His sweetness and sanity had returned. At least it looked like it had. He bent down and with his deceiving smile made it look as though he was about to kiss me and make it all better. Instead he grabbed my throat and with his sweet smile still on his face and lifted me off the ground strangling me.

I looked around helplessly as the edges of my vision grew darker and darker. I actually accepted my fate thinking it would be the end of my suffering so I closed my eyes. I was ready to die.

Just as I thought I was done for, I heard someone yelling. I couldn't make out what was said but whatever it was it made James drop me.

I caught myself on the ground, on my hands and knees, desperately gasping for air. As my sight and hearing gradually returned, I found out that Alec was the one yelling at James.

"Are you *insane*?" Alec yelled. "Don't kill her, not yet!"

Perfect.

"Now you're protecting her?" James asked taunting Alec.

Alec warned, "You know He will be very angry if he hears about this, James."

"Yes," James murmured looking down at me. "I suppose I shouldn't kill her just yet."

There was something missing about him. I just couldn't put my finger on what it was that was off.

"J-just yet?" I repeated.

"That is what I said, wasn't it?" James spat harshly.

His face hardened showing more signs of fierceness. That was when I noticed it. His eyes. That was what was so off. His eyes were gorgeous, yes, but they were missing the thing that made him show emotion. That shine in people's eyes to allow others to know what emotion you're feeling, that shine that shows life was gone.

"W-well, yes, but..." I was interrupted.

"Shut up. You're probably going to die anyway." James pointed out. "I doubt that you'll be the one from billions that will live. You're just another life. You're *nothing*! Don't even fight it."

Alec chimed in, laughing gently. "Just think of us as population control."

We ignored him.

"B-billions?" I questioned. "But, if you killed them all, wouldn't there be billions of people missing?"

"Yes. Yes, there would," James said playfully. "But you see, that's where mind control comes in. Humans are so easy to manipulate."

Alec glared at James; they were having a silent conversation.

17

"Oh, you're right Alec. Please Excuse my earlier rudeness, Elaina." He said kneeling down, planning to caress my face.

I was scared that he was going to try and strangle me again so I began to move away.

James made a disappointed and sad expression and then looked at Alec who then moved behind me preventing me from moving out of the way again.

James squatted gently in front of me. He once again reached out but this time, grabbed the back of my head, entangling a chunk of my hair in his grip and forcefully yanked my head forward so he could whisper, "You do as I say. You don't do anything without my order. When I want to do something, you allow me to do it. No matter what it is. You're just lucky you're not dead yet."

His eyes gently shut and once they opened, that shine was there.

I know this must seem so frightening. Your world is falling apart right under your shoes. Even if you make it through this, it won't end there.

You're so young. Too young to be broken like this. You're too young. It's just better we start now. Just believe me, I'm not the one that wants to hurt you.

The cold, hard truth is that you've just been given the unlucky draw. This is your destiny. From the moment your heart began beating, this life was assigned to you. If this is you, I'm so sorry that I'm doing this again. Last time, it left me broken. This time, I won't make the same mistake.

This will go one way or another. I will either be your friend or foe. I will be loyal once again though. Fate will take me wherever it takes me. Or should I say, our goddess will lead me. Then again, I guess that means that YOU will decide that. I don't want to lose you again. I don't want to see you go again.

If you can hear this, I promise you, it will not end here. It won't end soon. All they say is how much you would have changed: how much weaker you are, how much younger, more human, *less you... But there's just something about you. You're not like the others we've killed. You're different. And that's bad. I feel like I'm looking at you again. You're just so... not you. It pisses me off. You're so pathetic now... you're just so* human.

That was James. I looked up at him showing every possible emotion there was to show. I was *so* confused.

His eyes widened in disbelief. *Oh my god.*

"James, today!" Alec glared.

James squeezed his eyes together and that shine was gone.

"Huh? I mean, excuse me?"

That caught Alec's attention, the word "huh". There was something behind what was happening here. I just needed to figure out what the hell that was.

Andrew laughed out loud, "What are we doing next, hot shot."

"Get her to the car." He said as he began to move away. "By the way Elaina, I still expect your answer when you wake up."

"W-wake up? What does he mean wa-," I asked but was cut off by something wrapping itself around my neck, forcing me to lose consciousness in just a matter of moments. I whipped my body in the direction of James, making sure that the man who just ordered my demise would be the last person I saw except James wasn't there anymore. He disappeared.

My eyes, desperately searching the room for this mysterious man were quickly dimming along with the rest of my senses. The last thing I remember sensing was Andrew saying, "I'm sorry."

CHAPTER TWO
Some people just don't get the concept of LEAVE ME ALONE

The next morning I woke up in a large room fit for a king. The bed I was laying on was soft, the duvet was silk, the windows were stained glass and the drapes were silk. Even the floor felt soft as though it were made of silk.... in short, the room looked expensive.

My notebook was here beside me. I couldn't help myself; I had to write in it.

Dear Diary,

There's something wrong here. I don't know why... but something's just so very off.

When I see James, I don't see hatred. I just see desperation.

Actually, I really don't know what I'm feeling, but I'm sure it's not hatred. These people...UGH!

I don't know what to say...I really have nothing to say. I don't even know why I'm making this diary entry. I don't know what's going through my head. I've been acting so different recently. I don't even know who I am anymore.....

-Elaina
8/9/10

Suddenly it seemed James was there staring at me.

"Ah, good you're finally awake. I told you I would expect an answer to my question, didn't I?" He asked.

"Yes," I yawned rubbing the sore part of my neck. "I suppose you did."

"Now," He began in a bored tone. "Who do you choose?" It sounded like he had to done this multiple times; his eyes were barely open showing no interest in what he was saying. I wondered, how many times did he say this line?

"You. I choose you. That's okay, isn't it?" I asked.

I took a moment to examine his reaction. It was anxious but amused, angry but relived. I continued talking.

"What is it, James? You have so many emotions on your face I can't tell if you're happy or angry that I chose you." I asked "Would you care to explain?"

He took a moment to answer. "Well Elaina, I'm just surprised you said that. You're the first that has chosen me as her leader. Not only are you the first to choose me as her leader but you're the only one other than my team that has seen me like...well, you know...and lived." he explained. "Then, to top it all off you have lived longer than anyone else so far even though we have treated you the worst."

He paused for a moment and then shouted in excitement "Oh. Of course! There's one more test to see if you die!"

I wasn't exactly happy to hear those words from his mouth. It was like he wanted me to die. No, I was sure that he wanted me to die.

"What's the test?" I asked.

"May I ask why you chose me?"

I thought he was kidding. Every other test included how badly I could get hurt before I pass out but this was a legitimate question.

I answered, "You seem to be the most polite and gentlemanly person. But, the biggest reason is that it's like I have armor on when I'm around you. No one can touch me unless they have your permission. So, as long as I keep you happy, I should be safe." I've always been somewhat of a strategist. I always think so far ahead that I don't think about "the now" unless emotions get involved. That's when things really start going downhill.

And because there's something about you: something that really makes you stand out from the others. Something about you astounds me. I added silently.

He let out a small chuckle and then called his team.

"Guys, come here!" James yelled. "We have found 'The One'! She is The One!"

"The One?" I asked totally lost now. "The one what?"

I really didn't understand. I heard footsteps running towards the door. They came to a sudden stop right in front of the door and began to whisper.

"Is it really her? That girl is the one?"

The door opened slowly showing all of the captors from the night before.

"Inform him," James ordered. "Tell him we have found his precious gem."

I asked in slight fear, "What's happening? Whose gem am I? What do you mean 'a gem'?"

"What would you like us to do with the brat?" Dylan asked.

"Are you seriously asking that?" Alec asked. "We take the brat as proof."

Why am I always called everything BUT Elaina? Yeah, I'm pretty sure I was given a name for a reason. But seriously, Brat, Kiddo, Kid. I'd much rather be called Kiddo than Brat any day if I had to be called one of those, but still!!

James shoved me towards Alec.

Alec whispered in my ear, "I really pity you, kid. I'd hate to be in your place right now." Then he gently pushed me out the door.

From their expressions, it seemed as though everyone here pitied me.

"You're our Lord's kid. You're very...very special to him." Andrew explained quietly.

That struck a nerve. "No! *My* dad is at my house worrying about me with the rest of my family, wondering where I am! Who does this poser think he is? No one has the right to call me his child except *my* dad! Who is this man to call me his child?"

Everyone closed their eyes momentarily as if they were shaking something off.

"You dare call him a poser?" Dylan asked angrily.

Dylan seemed to transform before me. His eyes started to turn blood red. His hair began to move forming a wavy pattern. It looked like Dylan was beginning to turn all demonic, like James had the night before.

"Stop! I-I'm sorry! It just slipped out. I-I didn't mean it. Please calm down." I pleaded hiding behind Andrew.

Andrew and Alec were trying to calm him down but were unsuccessful. Dylan's sweet geeky voice turned scratchy and hollow.

"NO ONE INSULTS MY MASTER! I'LL MAKE SURE YOU PAY! YOU DESERVE TO BE PUNISHED!" Dylan yelled.

Master? That's a bit of a strong word. His expression was angry but almost empty. Was this a form of hypnosis as well?

"W-what's happening? Why does he look like that?" I asked terrified.

"Elaina," Andrew ordered. "Get back!"

I slowly stepped backwards too scared to look away from Dylan. He suddenly disappeared then reappeared in front of me.

Dylan slashed my chest and plunged his hand into my abdomen. He was about to slash my face until someone's hand went through him, not into him, but ALL THE WAY THROUGH.

Dylan collapsed to the floor.

"Andrew," James said wiping the blood other liquids off his arm. "Will you take this traitor out of here?"

"Yes sir." Andrew replied with a hint of sarcasm in his voice.

James sighed. "Damn it. He ruined a perfectly nice shirt."

"You killed him!" I yelled. "I thought he was your friend!"

James made a weird expression, "Calm down. He isn't dead. Look at your stomach. If you're smart you'll thank me for doing what I did." And pointed at my stomach.

There was a gaping hole in my shirt and a growing stain of blood rapidly spreading across my outfit. *Oh my god. I'm not dead.* I thought.

"OH GOD! I-I didn't feel a thing..." I said just staring at my wound in shock.

"Yes, I know." James said pausing to chuckle. "I will fix you up. Then you can talk to your daddy."

"Yeah...Okay...Why can't I feel the pain?" I asked shaking myself out of shock and avoiding the thought that I'll talk to my 'Daddy'.

"You can't feel it because you humans are too idiotic and your nerves don't feel pain as fast as ours do." James said. "Oh and don't worry. You'll feel the pain soon enough."

"Can you fix my wound before I fe-" I was cut off by a screaming sound.

They all just laughed.

The screaming was me. All the pain came on at one time. It didn't just build up like I expected; it appeared all at one time. The pain was unbearable.

"Let's take her to the healing room and fix her now." James said.

They laid me down in water and a female apparition appeared above me. She spoke some unfamiliar language that I was too dazed to pay much attention to and then touched my stomach and chest. After she finished her chant and made some peculiar movements with her arms my wounds were healed and the pain gone. My vision blurred once again.

I wished they didn't heal so fast. They vanished way too quickly for me since I wasn't looking forward to meeting this supposed father of mine and hoped that they would take longer to heal.

James walked into the room and yanked me to my feet. "Are you excited?" James laughed. "You get to meet the man who is fit to be even *your* worst nightmare."

I just looked away. I didn't want to be rude and say something close to *I'd rather die than meet this poser.*

James grabbed my jaw and yanked it, forcing me to look at him with my undivided attention.

"When I ask you a question, I *expect* an answer; when I say something, I *expect* you to look at me," He spat impatiently.

"I'm sorry." I said with the most sweet and innocent smile I could force out painted on my face. "I didn't know how to answer that question without being rude to your precious Lord."

Actually, now that I think about it, it was the most smug and sarcastic smile painted on my face just to piss him off.

He grabbed my arm and pulled me with him to a room. It was like nothing I'd ever seen before. The walls were lined with monitors, buttons, and knobs.

It all looked extremely high tech. "Are you aliens or something? We don't have this stuff for sale..."

Ignoring me he asked coldly, "You so much as breathe the wrong way in here and your dead! Got it?"

"Yeah, I got it." I said.

He yanked at my arm to move me to a certain spot in the room, told me which direction to face and even how to stand properly. He got out something that looked like a remote and some buttons on it. The main monitor in the room turned on and a pitch black screen popped up.

A silhouette of a man was all I could see on the monitor. He had a very deep voice and a massive body. And apparently didn't know how to use a light bulb. "Yes," he told James. "This is definitely that brat for a kid I told you about."

"You, girl." He snarled at me.

"Yes?" I asked.

This man looked as though he was definitely not someone to mess with...none of these guys were...but this guy was in a whole different league.

"What is your name, girl?" he asked.

There was no kindness or compassion in this man's voice. It was very hard to believe that he was my dad.

"My name is Elaina Martin. I-it's very nice to meet you." I lied.

"Welcome, my child. I would have chosen a better name than Elaina if I were your human parent."

"Human..." I repeated quietly. He was trying to get the point across that he was not human and that I was a little more than human as well.

"Oh, Elaina," the man thought aloud. "When will you turn back into one of us?"

If I wasn't completely lost before, now I was. "Turn back into one of us?" I repeated.

I continued on, "What exactly is "one of us"? If you're my dad then... what are my real parents?"

"You'll find out soon enough, Elaina." He said.

It seemed like he was done talking to me. He was now facing James.

"James," He ordered. "Let her go. She still has yet to learn some very important things. Erase her memory and set her free."

James stared at the screen briefly and muttered respectfully, "Yes sir." putting an obvious amount of effort into not breaking everything in the room.

The screen flipped off and James looked back at me desperately.

I paid no mind. Really, how could I say that I wasn't happy? I was going to be released with no worries. I could go back to being a normal kid. No kidnapping, no demon people, just me, my family, and my friends. I was excited to get on with my boring, ordinary life.

He laughed halfheartedly, "And after all that we went through to find you, I'm just supposed to set you free. Cool."

CHAPTER THREE
Lesson learned: Pay attention to your gut

My alarm went off. I remember thinking every morning as I moaned, tossing my arm on the snooze button, *God, that's loud!* I breathed a sigh of relief. It was all just a dream. But, of course the first thing I *had* to do was write in my Diary. Except there was a diary entry already in there for that day. Something about some boy named James? There were thoughts flying through my head. I didn't know anyone named James.

Who wrote this? It looks like my handwriting. This is definitely strange. Even for me.

Dear Diary,

I had a really weird dream last night about a guy named James. I'm must have woken up in the middle of the night and written about him because there is already and entry for today and I just woke up. The thing is I have no recollection of waking up and writing in my diary. Wait a second, I'm looking at my phone and today isn't the ninth. Today is the tenth. And yesterday, yesterday was the eighth. Almost two days of my memory ~~is~~ ARE missing. Gosh, things are just getting a bit weird... Well, as weird as my life can really get.

You know what? It's... this is all probably just caused by my fear of the first day of high school after summer break, right? I'm...

knock, knock-knock, knock, knock.

It was my brother saying "Hey Ellie. Hurry up. Let's go."

"Okay Jason, I'll be out in a second." I said.

... I'm glad I know it was just a dream. Otherwise, well, wouldn't people have said something if I was gone?

-Elaina
And I guess today is the 10th... so...
8/10/10

Jason drove me to school every day since he got his license. That day, it seemed like everything was in such a rush. I didn't get to enjoy his company and I didn't even get to eat breakfast with the rest of my family. It seemed so small at the time, I didn't care. I had every day for the rest of my life to do stupid family stuff. Why would I give a damn?

I got into his car feeling both uneasy and relieved. I felt like I was missing something really important that I needed to remember but there was something in the back of my head thinking that maybe, just maybe, it was better that I forgot.

"What's the matter Ellie?" Jason asked.

"Huh? Oh it's nothing," I said. "I just have a lot on my mind."

For whatever reason, I knew that this was the day that my life was going to change forever but I didn't know why.

"Oh... Okay... I'll see you after school." He smiled reassuringly dropping me off.

I was fourteen years old. So innocent, so ignorant. I was a just a freshman. It was my first day in high school and I thought that I was all grown up.

"Bye," I said waving good bye. "I'll see you after school!"

If I knew that this was going to be my last drive with my big brother, I would have tried to have more fun and not have been so distracted with my dreams....

There were two guys in suits standing in front of school's doors. Other than them, there was no one else around which was kind of strange for the first day of school. Was I late? I wasn't early. I kind of expected to see security guards, but not men in suits.

"Elaina," The taller of the two men said. They both had very pale skin and reddish tint to their eyes.

"What?" I asked rudely. "I just got here! What did I do? How do you know my name?" That was my defensive mode. If I felt threatened, I'd get rude and obnoxious. Which now that I think about it, my defensive mode failed so hard… My defensive mode made people want to punch my face in.

I think maybe somewhere inside of me I thought these people were some seriously bad news. Normally, I'm decently delightful and easy to get along with but also, I've always been an exceptional judge of character.

"Look kid," The shorter one said grabbing my shirt and tossing me against the wall hard enough to make a noticeable thud. "We work for the president himself so I'd advise you to answer all of our questions truthfully and respectfully, that is, of course if you know what's good for you. Now come along with us."

Not thinking, I responded, "Okay, okay, I'll go." And later added, "What does the president want from me?"

I should have known someone working for the government wouldn't touch me unless I'd done something really wrong or illegal. It'd be political suicide. They'd lose everything if word got out and I pressed charges.

I wouldn't have cooperated with them if I had merely thought. It. Through. But c'mon, that's just not the way I roll.

"You aren't in a position to ask questions, Miss Martin. Now, are you ready to go?" The taller man asked.

For some reason they seemed really familiar... like, I've known them all my life but somehow forgotten them completely.

"After you answer my one question, what are your names?" I asked. I was so excellent with names. I almost always remembered names after I'd heard them the first time.

The taller one replied, "My name is Alec and this is my partner Andrew." I've never met anyone by those names... yet, they seemed so familiar.

They just started walking away, periodically turning back to see if I was still following closely behind them. They walked me to a helicopter with the supposed president inside.

"Ah! Elaina, it's so nice to see you again!" The "president" said in a cheery voice.

I ignored the questions that suddenly popped into my head like, *where did I ever meet you?* And just replied, "Hello Mr. President, it's nice to see you too." With a nice smile on my face.

"Will you do me a favor?" He asked me.

"Well Mr. President, I suppose that depends on the favor." I said. It was too good to be true that the president of the most powerful nation in the world needed *my* help.

I have learned in past experiences that you should never agree to something before you know what it is or before you have all the details or unless you have no choice... and this was, of course, one of those times.

"Well kiddo, you don't really have a choice. You have to accept the job." The president said.

Weird way to ask for help... "Alright then, if I have no choice... what is it?" I asked.

"Go fetch these boys, and then I'll tell you." He said giving me a list of people.

The list said Jean Night, Jake Austen, Eric Night, and Sean Power.

I've been going to school with these boys since the first grade... Why would he care for these boys? Why does he need them? Why does he need ME?

Before I knew it I was out of the helicopter with Alec shutting the door behind me. I couldn't help but wonder as I walked back to my school,

I discarded any ideas of just leaving without any return just because I'd get dragged back here and the boys on the list would end up getting contacted anyway so I just walked back to school, got my late pass for being an hour late to school and walked to class. Luckily all the boys on the list were in my first class so I didn't have to go searching for them.

I handed the president's list to my teacher and convinced her after another twenty minutes that I really needed those boys to come with me. The teacher gave us permission to leave the school campus to go meet with the president. That's something I had always been good at convincing people to let me do outrageous things. My friends joked about I was the group's attorney and I could win any argument the world had to offer me.

We walked a little ways from the door leading to the outside when Jean asked, "Why do you need us? I thought we agreed, you leave us alone and we won't hurt you." Oh yeah I forgot to mention these boys all despised me from the moment we met.

I sighed dramatically, "Oh please, you think I actually volunteered you for anything? Ha, that's funny! If you want the truth then you should know the president made me come get you. Don't ask me why. He told me he'd tell me when I retrieve you boys."

We walked silently, avoiding any further confrontation for the rest of the time before we went inside the helicopter.

"Ah! Good! You got the boys!" the president said.

"Yes, now tell me exactly what's going on," I demanded.

"Okay Elaina. I suppose you deserve to know. I need you to test a procedure." He explained.

"What exactly is the procedure?" I asked.

"Well I believe all brats should be imprisoned but as you know I can't do that. So I decided to see if I could… fix you." He told me having us sit then continued. "Basically I want to see how force works on kids like you." He said.

"What are you talking about?" I asked.

"I'm talking about my plans for the future." He growled.

I received a look from the president that basically told me that he believed I had just asked the dumbest question in the world.

I'm screwed. I thought nervously. My eyes blurred momentarily.

"Yes." He answered chuckling.

"And if I refuse?" I asked. I regretted and still regret ever asking that idiotic question.

"You'll re-live that nightmare you had last night. Yes Elaina, I know all about your dream and I have the power to make it come true." He said.

My eyes widened as a shiver surged my body. If he knew about the dream then that either meant that it had happened already and it was going to happen again, or he somehow knew I would have that dream. I stood up to have Alec appear behind me and push me down again. *I could swear he was across the room…* I thought.

The president smiled sweetly at me then I realized that Alec was actually holding me down.

Why? I asked myself. *Why would he hold me down?*

"This is only a small taste of what may come to be if you disobey me." He turned all demon like, just like the men in my "dream" but his skin turned darker almost like it was decaying in the most a rapid paces.

"Wha-" I began but was interrupted by my own screaming. He was smiling so sweetly but was causing so much pain, nothing physical but all mental. How was he doing it? I didn't have the slightest clue. I felt so helpless.

All I could do was scream. Alec and Andrew just laughed and cheered the president on. Jean, Jake, Eric, and Sean were actually freaked out by the whole demonized thing. They looked at the president until he stopped and looked back at them.

They were just as clueless as I was in the beginning of this new way of life. They were scared and the president saw that; he used that against them.

"Don't worry boys. I won't do that to you as long as you obey me." he said.

What kind of person is capable of using that kind of fear against kids to make them obey? I couldn't understand what these boys had anything to do with the presidents' plan.

We were almost to the middle of the grassy field; where the president told us to be until the clouds where getting very dark. Lightning kept striking the field that we were on almost as if it were trying to hit us. We found out after it actually hit Sean that it *was* trying to hit us.

I ran... I can't say I was proud of the choice I had made out of fear... but I thought I would have died if I stayed. I thought I was safe at home. No one bothered me except my over protective brother who was worried because of my abnormal behavior. I was alone.

CHAPTER FOUR
You can t escape fate

Dear Diary,

Me again. I've been hiding in the house for a couple months. I'm scared. I don't know what to do; I know don't what to think. What am I supposed to do? The president of the United States threatened me! How the hell do I get away from that? Actually, it's bothering me even more than I HAVE gotten away. The president should be perfectly capable of figuring out where I live. If he wanted to find me (which I know he does) he would have done it by now! What is he waiting for? Maybe he lost interest? No... He wouldn't have. I'm scared... I just don't know what to do.

-Elaina
10/15/10

For days, I was completely isolated from everyone until the doorbell rang... I was out of my room getting a drink so I figured; what could possibly go wrong by answering the door? Biggest mistake I have *ever* made. It was Jean, Jake, Eric, and Sean.

"Help us... please, people are injured... He is chasing us." Jean said.

"He? Who's He?" I asked.

"Please, just let us in and we'll tell you anything you want." Sean said.

Obviously, I wasn't thinking when I let those boys into my house. "Yeah, sure. Come on in." I said.

No one was home so I figured it could be safe for everyone. My family wouldn't be in danger. The only reason I had let them in was because they had seen what happened. It's logical; I didn't really trust anyone other than them anymore. "What is happening?" I asked.

"He is chasing us. He murdered people in front of us without a second thought. He's not human. I don't think humans are capable of what he's done." Jake zoned out in the middle of his sentence and was talking subconsciously as if he was trying oh so hard to *not* remember something terrible, etched into his mind.

"Oh, so you just lead a murder to my house." I asked furiously.

"Yes… but you have to understand, he has held us captive for the last month! We just managed to get away and if it makes you feel better we are almost sure that we lost him." Eric said.

And for some reason *almost sure* that they lost the serial killer wasn't good enough for me.

My mom came in through the garage door with my brother and dad. My mom walked through the hall and her happy smile broke into anger or rage.

"Elaina Martin, what did you do to these poor boys?" She asked.

We all looked at each other, not knowing what to say. We all knew that we couldn't involve her. The less she knew, the better. It had to be that way, we had to be on our own.

"Mrs. Martin! We, uhm… It's my mom's make-up. We're just playing a simple game and her make-up got all over us so Elaina offered to help us clean it up." Jake smiled.

That was a pathetic lie. It wasn't told properly, and it wasn't anywhere near believable but she bought it anyway. At the time, I really thought that she probably really thought we were playing some game. She was normally just one of those people that really thought nothing bad happened in the world.

Her face turned expressionless while her voice turned monotone. At the time, I really thought nothing of it. Maybe I thought that she was just happy I was talking again. "Oh, okay then. Don't let us disturb you." My mom sounded like she was in a trance. "Elaina, will you take these boys to the bathroom and take care of the makeup you put on them?" My mom asked.

She *really* thought that their wounds were makeup… "Yes of course mom, that's what we were just about to do." I nodded.

I kept telling myself a pathetic lie, *It will all be over soon. I will just bandage them up and then they will leave.* Incidentally, that did happen, just not in the way I imagined it would. I sat them all on the bathroom floor.

"I'll be right back I just have to go get some cotton rap for the cuts you have on you." I said going to the laundry room then coming back.

"Here you go. This may sting a little…" I whispered dumping alcohol on the cotton wrap. Maybe I wasn't the most careful or gentle with my application of the alchohol, but for the most part, that was because my vision was a little cloudy at this point and I began fighting what felt like the beginning of passing out. But doing that for them triggered something inside me something that eventually comes back to change me forever.

I put the cotton wrap on Sean's leg first. "*Ouch!*" He shouted as he kicked me. "That hurt!"

"That hurt *you*? You weren't the one who was kicked in the face… Look, don't hit me this time okay?" I said approaching slowly.

I put it on him again. He made a small squeak in pain but that's all. All the boys had scratches in the exact spots: A thick scratch on the shoulder, across the back, down their arms, down the bottom of their legs, with the exception of Sean with a burn on his rib where a chunk of his shirt was missing.

"He was whipping you… wasn't he?" I asked.

Jean spoke, "Apparently he's doing a test.. Something was supposed to happen but it wouldn't."

It was supposed to be one of those rhetorical questions. I didn't *want* to know what happened.

It almost seemed like a fortunate coincidence for a moment because the doorbell rang, allowing us to avoid the awkward silence that surely would have followed my question. And then, it suddenly struck. Coincidences are *not* real.

I looked up immediately at the boys. The same fear that shot through them shot right through. I screamed, "*No*, Mom, don't answer it!" But it was too late… my mom answered the door. Sean grabbed my arm preventing me from leaving the bathroom so all I could do is watch the reflection from the bathroom mirror.

The man at the door didn't say anything, she didn't do anything. That man grabbed a gun faster than anything I'd ever seen and just raised his arm and shot her through the head. She didn't *need* to die.

My dad ran to my mom's corps and was shot through the heart and my brother, I didn't even know what happened. That man was outside my house and then he appeared a good thirty feet from where he stood. That spot he reappeared just happened to be behind my brother.

His last words: "Elaina, *run!*" I heard my brother's body hitting the ground after the man tapped my brother on the head, followed by him shouting in a booming, deep voice, "Haunt this place forever. You are trapped here *forever!*"

Why? How did my brother just die? What just happened? And I have heard that voice before! But where? Naïve: It's usually a human trait. *My* kind grows out of that weakness before they reach age ten. I hoped against everything that I just heard, that my family wasn't dead. I tiptoed quickly toward my already long gone family and started screaming when I was entirely sure they weren't going to get back up. And why? Was that going to help anything? No. Was it going to bring any of them back? No. Another human trait.

I started freaking out. I was literally going insane in a matter of moments. I was terrified, shaking. "No. Jason. Mom. Dad. No. Don't leave me. Don't go! This can't be happening, please, *please* don't go!" My eyes blurred for a longer period of time: almost thirty seconds.

And why was I begging dead people to not be dead? None of it made sense. Emotions suck.

My worst nightmare realized. My entire family was dead. Selfishly, I couldn't help but think, *where does this leave me? What do I do now that they're gone? How will I live?* And most selfishly, *why couldn't he kill me FIRST?*

The boys, seeing my reaction, exited the bathroom to see just what was going on and when they saw that man they trembled and moved back towards the end of the hall way.

"Will you choose to come peacefully?" He asked emotionlessly.

"Elaina, we all know that we will go without a fight but you may be a bit angry at the moment and so we want to advise you to go with him peacefully too. Please, Elaina I-" Eric was interrupted.

"You don't need to advise me to do anything. I know this guy is... I'm only going to mess with this guy unless I'm planning on dying or something." I whispered.

"Answer the question, Elaina Martin." He said.

It was like his voice was the earth itself. His voice was so deep and sinister it was somewhat hard to comprehend.

He concerned me. "You know my name? How?"

He laughed, dismissing my question as stupid. "I know everything about you." He began walking towards us, hand extended outwards as though we were supposed to hold hands and go on some merry adventure.

"Why?" I asked ignoring his almost friendly gesture.

This time, his reply became fiercer and well, scary. "Because you are *mine*."

"What the hell is that-"

"Shut up. Now, Answer. Me."

"I'll go."

He seemed like the impatient *you do one thing wrong and you're dead* type of guy.

"Good, now come, all of you." He said walking out the door. Even if I thought I could take this guy on, I was too stunned to argue. Nothing seemed right. I kept telling myself it has to be a dream.

We walked with him and he shoved us in the back of his truck. Inside (not including those of us captured) sat Alec, Andrew, and the president. The president wasn't moving and he looked like there was no blood circulating in his body. I made sure He shut the door to the truck before I started talking.

"How did they get…? How did they kill the president?" Questions were how I kept my mind in check. The more questions I asked, the more sane I became.

"Shut up… You don't want to get us all whipped do you? *Whoa*, did you just say the *president* was in the front seat?" Sean asked crawling towards the window I was sitting next to.

"No idiot! Get down! We can't be seen looking! We need to act scared and like we move only when they te-" I was interrupted by a man slamming his fist against the window, inches from my head.

I stared shook as I stared upwards to see the new threat to our existence. More frightening was the fact that I recognized him. *Where do I recognize him from?* I kept asking myself. He opened up the window.

Even more frightening? He recognized me too.

"You are all going to sit down silently and not move anymore got it? Oh, and Elaina it's nice to see you again." He said.

"Elaina, do you know these people? 'Cause they all seem to know you." Jean growled furiously (failing to hide his fuming personality) probably because he expected me to be able to tell them something about these strange people. He was just as scared as I was. This was just his defensive mode.

"I- I don't understand. I don't know any of you from anywhere. You must be mistaking me with someone else because honestly I don't know what you guys are planning or anything, honest! I won't even tell anyone about you guys being responsible for the president's death. Please, just let me – I mean us go." I pleaded.

It wasn't intentional lying. I honestly didn't remember anything that had to do with those freaks.

"Oh that's right. We wiped out your memory. Here's what going on: you were kidnapped, then were stabbed, our Lord, your father," *He's my dad?* "had us erase your memory and now here we are all over again. Oh and the president you met earlier was me taking over a corpse feeding on his soul." He summed up my life story in a matter of seconds. Props.

I stayed silent. What could I say? *I don't remember being brain washed so it must not be true? Oh and it's not nice to feed on people's souls.* I don't quite think it works like that. Actually, I'm pretty sure he said that *just* so I would get confused.

"You kids are in a load of trouble. You can thank Elaina for getting you into it though." James said closing the window and locking it.

"I-I'm sorry. I didn't mean to..." I said.

I knew it wasn't my fault; I knew I shouldn't have needed to apologize. I just wanted to get rid of at least some of the guilt that was stored up inside me.

"Yeah, I don't think that will do anything for us." Jake said.

I growled. "Well please, tell me any brilliant ideas you have, Jake."

"Wing it. That's all we can do right? None of us have any idea what is going on, we are outnumbered, much weaker, and definitely not as smart as any of them so all we can do is wait and see what happens." Jean said.

"Shut up back there. Next person to talk is going to get the VIP seat next to me and the president here." Alec said. No one talked anymore.

It was then that I realized that my memory had never been wiped. That "Dream" was nothing more than a memory my brain defensively dismissed as a dream to protect me. The memory that they supposedly wiped was the same as the diary entry that I couldn't figure out.

Honestly, I'm not sure if I was more scared of the president's dead body or the men up in the front seat. James, the leader, and Alec definitely scare me the most and are the cruelest and they seem to hold a grudge or something on me.

The truck stopped. There were no windows in the back of his truck so none of us could see where we were until we got out of the car. When the truck doors opened no one moved. I'm not totally sure if the boys' reasons were the same as mine but I know that I was too scared to move.

"Come on out. We won't hurt you." Andrew smiled.

Everyone stared at me as if to say "go first please" and right on cue, I listened. I got out of the truck and as expected Andrew kicked me. I didn't know where these men got their strength but every time one of them tends to hit me I fly across somewhere until I hit something and in this case, I flew across a street until I hit someone's garage.

"Ok, ok, I lied. But I really dislike her and she was right there so I couldn't pass up that opportunity. I won't do it to anyone else." Andrew promised.

I stared at the garage. *I was down the driveway from this place and he kicked me and now I'm here. And it didn't hurt that badly. Or at least, for whatever just happened, it didn't hurt that bad. Actually, what just happened?*

I waited for everyone to get out of the truck and to get told to go into the house before I moved from the spot I was thrown to. Andrew was having everyone line up to go inside and beckoned me with this look on his face like, *hurry up, idiot!* I jogged to the line and began walking towards the house. The architecture surrounding the house looked like a mix of Italian and Greek, the plants out front caressed the house's beauty and the sun beaming down, made the house glow and stand out from every other house on the planet. And the inside was truly the most gorgeous of it all.

The massive medieval style archway lead us to the very middle of the house where strange, sci-fi art filled the room. It was like that entire horrific experience the boys and I were going through appeared almost worth it. I felt like a piece of me had been filled; I knew I was supposed to be there. From the air I breathed to the pictures and vases surrounding the room, every single aspect of the house *meant* something far more to me and I just couldn't explain it.

I was attracted to a specific painting on the wall. The picture was called "The Power" and it looked like a sweet family portrait with two grown men (one looked like the leader of the psycho group) one woman, one older boy of maybe eighteen years of age, and two girls, one near the outside between the woman and the blonde man, and the other girl in the middle of the family was holding some... I don't know. Triquetra type artifact the size of her head in her arms. It was actually really cool looking and ancient. The ring that weaved around the actual three black, marble loops seemed old and tarnished but the symbols etched on it revealed a layer of crimson beauty and light.

As I came to think more of it, I realized that the photo was of a royal family. Each and every one of the family members had crowns and was dressed like futuristic-ish medieval royalty.

Wow, this stuff is truly amazing. This art is... Out of this world. It's so mystical but so real. Who is this guy? I thought.

Is she kidding? She is the reason that we are here and all she can say is "I like your art?" this is repulsive! Eric thought.

I responded in fury, "Oh that's nice! I'm going through just as much as you Eric! Don't you *dare* try and put this on me! I'm sorry that you are going through this but I obviously can't do anything!"

"How did you-" Eric paused.

"And from what I understand, that is out of character for you, yes?" Alec asked calmly. "You're much more of a speak calmly with very insulting words type of girl. Are you losing that control?"

He was aiming for a specific response but before I got a chance to retort, He responded.

"You can read minds? Then surely you are my Princess." The real leader smiled just for a moment until everything began to get dark. I didn't know why or what was happening. But it was like I just faded out of the world.

The very last thing I heard was that man talking to someone about me waking up then getting led him and then said something about a gift. It's hard to understand when you're half unconscious.

I was woken up by a loud *bang*. It was Jake stomping on the ground.

"Oh good, your awake!" Jake said kneeling down. "Your dad wants you."

Dad?

"Yeah, that was a completely natural awakening." I laughed bitterly. "What does he want?" I mumbled half asleep.

Yeah, not a morning person. Actually, I don't know that it was even the morning. The windows were covered completely, keeping all the sunlight out.

"What was that?" Jake asked. He was giving me a second chance to let me talk nicely.

"Go away." I said.

Jake mused. "Umm, no, I don't think so."

"You are such a jerk. *leave!*" I said.

I definitely regretted that.

"What? Okay let's see… who has the upper hand here? Oh that's right, me. Now I will see just what this can do." Jake said putting on this glove. I got a pretty good look at it. It was Brass knuckled glove that was colored black with the knuckles painted red and there wasn't any part of the glove that covered the top of the finger. He picked me up and punched me one time in the rib and one of my ribs actually snapped, like, in half.

"Where's that strong talk now?" He laughed watching me as I whimpered, dropping to the ground as I grasped my rib.

What else could or should I do? I tried to get away. I didn't run. I couldn't even walk so I crawled. To stop me from moving he slammed his foot on my back.

Every time I attempted to move he just pushed harder on my back making me hurt even more. I learned my lesson. I stopped moving hoping he would stop pressing on me.

That wasn't the Jake I knew. I've known him for forever and, yeah, we didn't like each other but, the pranks we pulled were school kid stuff, not... this. This was criminal and *not* like any of these boys.

"Ah! That's more like it! Good girl." He said finally getting his foot off.

It was then that it actually clicked that it was *actually* Jake dong this to me. That wasn't a dream. There was no waking up from this. That was when the full impact of this situation slapped me across the face. "Jake, why? You're on the same boat I am." I whispered. "He took everything from you too. Don't do this."

"Get up." He replied, looking emotionlessly into my eyes.

"I- I can't move." I pleaded hysterically.

"You can't or won't? Maybe I should give you a little motivation." He said putting the glove back on. "This time I'll break every bone in your body." He raised his hand.

"N-no! I'm sorry! I'll get up." I trembled to a standing position.

"Well, ok. This time I'll let you off with a warning." He said putting his hand down.

I struggled to look at him and began glaring. I couldn't believe what was happening.

"Think about what I could do if I really decided to hurt you. I will tell you what, I'll give you time to get out of my sight 5-4-3" He began counting.

By one I was long gone. I ran nonstop up to the second story until I collapsed on the stairs. I wondered how in the world I was able to breathe after he broke my rib when just a couple months before this all occurred I'd have a mini-nervous breakdown if I even got something as minor as a paper cut.

Motivation is a powerful tool. *I have to get up or who knows what will happen.* I told myself. You know, the only thing that was keeping me going was my fear. I was ready to just go home and sleep. I was even willing to go home and die. I figured *anything* was better than this house. I didn't, in my wildest dreams assume that it would only get worse.

I was so tired and in so much pain. I finally convinced myself it would be better for me to just get up and go to see the man who kidnapped me. I walked through the door leading to his room only to get lectured on how to be on time.

"Ahh, Rissa. Finally you have arrived. I have been waiting five minutes. Why are you late?" He asked looking concerned.

What, five minutes? Grow up.

"I- I was delayed by something... it was hard to get here." I answered.

He "What was that something?" He asked with a cruel smile.

"I was hurt accidentally. It's nothing really." It got harder and harder for me to speak.

He sighed. *Why would he sigh? Was he worried about me?* I asked myself.

"I -is something wrong? I –I" I couldn't find the words to tell him.

He snapped at me. "Did I ask you if it was a big deal? You *only* speak when spoken to!"

I thought I was scared but really, I was hurt by that for some reason. I felt as if he really was my dad and against my will, began whimpering.

NO! NO! Why does this man matter to me? He should mean nothing to me and he won't! Maybe I'm just scared. Yeah, I'm just scared, that's all. I thought.

"I'm sorry, Rissa. Did I scare you? Daddy's just in a bad mood, okay?" He said.

What the hell is a Rissa? That's not my name! HE ISN'T MY DAD! Why is he trying to take his place? I thought.

This man gave me so many emotions I didn't even know I had. I've never been so angry at anyone, so filled with hate...

"... May I ask you something?" I asked cautiously.

"Of course, my dear." He said.

"Will you stop calling me Rissa? My name is Elaina. And also… Please stop acting like you're my dad… because you're not… and you remind me of my dad, you know, that man you killed, and that makes me sad."

This man pretended to be my dad so why not act like a little girl, his little girl. "Elaina, Rissa is your real name. You can't run away from your fate. I *am* your dad."

What you are is a delusional psychopath.

"That man I killed was a fake. He deserved to die a horrible, painful death, Ri… are… are you crying?" He asked.

I didn't realize until he said that how badly I hated the way he just had the nerve to tell me that my dad deserved to die.

I glared, "You *so* did not just say that!"

I turned away from him not daring to look at his stupid face. I didn't get a good look at his face but I could swear that he actually smirked at me. My hands clenched, trembling with tremendous rage and hatred.

"Rissa, come here." He ordered.

"No! Leave me alone!" I yelled beginning to walk away. I was now acting like a little girl, *his* little girl. But this wasn't on purpose; this was instinctive. I knew that some part of me was attached to this insane psychopath and I hated it. And that only made me more angry.

"What? Did you just disobey me? No. I must have heard wrong. I'll give you one more chance, Rissa, come here or you'll be brought here. You don't want to turn out like your human pets." He said.

PETS? And he was referring to my *parents*. Although I turned to face him again and stopped walking away, I screamed, "Stay the hell away from me!" I should have just taken that second chance I had to go back to him.

My life would have been *so* much easier if I just learned to suck up once in a while.

He walked up to me turned me around and smiled. "Now, don't be like this, Ri."

"Don't be like *what*?" I hissed. "You *killed* them. You killed my parents! Don't be like that my ass, man! Just drop dead you stupid son of a-" He hugged me.

WHAT? Did I miss something?

"Get away from me you disgusting cockroach! I hate you! I hate you with everything I have!" I was on fire.

"Which isn't much, now is it." He whispered almost soothingly.

Stupid prick.

There are no amount of words to describe how pissed off I was. I was swinging at him and the cocky ass hole didn't even bother blocking or dodging my hits. I screamed, cried, and nothing I did would affect him.

He let this go on for a matter of seconds then swiftly spun me around to face the door, grabbing both of my arms, pinning them across my chest like an X. The boys walked through the door looking all high and mighty. He pushed me at them as he spun me around to face him.

It was then that Sean caught me and put my arms behind my back like *I* was the criminal here. Really? Me? I didn't know their story of how they really got involved with Scorn. I don't know what happened to their families and I don't care. There is nothing that could have happened to excuse them for doing this to me.

"Boys, please take Rissa to her room." He ordered. "I'm done seeing her today."

Like I was his pet, he wanted me taken away because he got bored with me.

Jean stepped in front of me. "Right away."

I looked away from Jean and Sean stepped up, sharply turned me around.

"Let's go, princess." He grabbed my wrist, pushed and twisted it until we heard this *CRACK*. My wrist bone was cracked. "Sorry, I'm just getting used to this whole thing."

I whimpered quietly, "Liar."

That was one of the few bones I didn't damage in my short lifetime. As I looked back, for a split moment, he seemed confused or startled but then a smug grin grew on it expressing his fascination with breaking my feeble bones.

"Sean, stop!" Jake said. Sean looked deliberately at him then twisted more until we heard another crack. He popped my shoulder out of place.

"Jake, it's amazing. Look at how easy this is!" He grinned in surprise.

"You need to *stop,* Sean. Leave it alone." Jake repeated.

And then another crack. "Ooh I like that sound. Let's hear it again." He was about to start toying with it until Eric slammed Sean into a wall.

"You care for that girl?" He asked Eric. "No, I don't care. Why the hell would I? She's irrelevant to the situation." Eric said.

How nice of him... By the way, I *was* the situation.

Sean shoved Eric's hands off of his shirt. Immediately Sean glared at me. Scared I flinched back and well, my natural reaction is to throw some insult out there to try and look a bit less scared than I am.

"You know, at least I know which side I'm on. I don't switch to an evil man's side just because he's winning and it'd be easier. He's going to throw each and every one of you away and you are *so* going to regret all of this." Sean, without me even noticing lifted up then thrown down the stairs. Then he jumped off the top of the stairs and landed on me.

At this point I'm sure many of my poor little bones were dislocated, shattered, broken, or cracked. When he got off, I ran as fast as I could down the stairs hoping for the slightest chance that none of them knew I was crying.

The last thing I heard was someone yelling at Sean about... something... for breaking so many rules.

I just kept running ignoring everything around me until I got to the dungeon. Yeah I know what you're thinking. Why the hell would anyone need a dungeon in their home? Well it turned out that it was in his basement. No it *was* his basement. He was waiting in the dungeon for me to arrive. He asked me an odd question.

"Who do you want to die? It is your choice who dies and how they die. So who do you choose?"

"Do I have to choose someone to die? I really don't want anyone to die or to be responsible for their death... it's not something I really want to happen, sir. Please respect my decision." I said carefully.

"You either choose who dies, or they all die and you watch. Those are your *only* two options." He said with a smile in his voice.

I didn't think he was serious. How could someone be so cruel?

"I will ask once more, Rissa, who do you choose to die?" He asked again impatiently. The boys all came in just in time to hear him ask that. With fear in their faces they looked at He then at me.

"Elaina, you're going to kill one of us?" Jake asked me.

I love how he thought he could talk to me like I was doing the bad thing after they switched sides after I risked and lost *everything* for them.

"She won't pick one of us. You'll see. She'll chicken out." Sean said. "She doesn't have the balls to kill."

"He's wrong. I can do anything I want... However, I really don't want anyone to die." I said. He looked at Sean with a cruel smile then looked at me then back at Sean. I knew exactly what he was going to do. But once again, I couldn't do anything.

I screamed *stop* but it was too late. Sean had died and his body quickly disappeared into the air. I dropped to my knees and started crying. With no sympathy He looked at me with that same cruel smile and asked,

"Now, will you answer my question? Or shall I kill the next one?"

I was terrified. I had practically just killed someone. All because I couldn't make a decision fast enough.

"Would you care to compromise?" I asked.

Part of me knew this was the only way it could be.

"What is your proposal?" He asked me.

"You let all of them go and I'll stay here… with you… would that work? I mean, all that you have done had something to do with me." I said. "Besides, we both know they're just your puppets. They'll only get in your way."

I was working on instinct alone. If I actually thought about what I was doing I wouldn't have done anything.

"You have a point, my dear. See, I knew you would catch on quickly."

"No, Elaina think about what you're doing. You'd be throwing your life away! You wouldn't want this! How about all of us stay and Elaina goes and you never go near her again?" Jean suggested.

"No, boy. Everyone on this pathetic planet isn't worth my precious little girl here. Rissa, I accept your proposal." He said.

"*NO*! *ELAINA*! There's more at stake here than you know!" Jean yelled.

I didn't understand what he was screaming about. He hated me last time I checked. Maybe not even those selfish boys are completely heartless. Slowly, they faded away trying to say something that I couldn't hear. Maybe their voice had faded first or something. I looked at Him and as soon as I saw the smile in his eyes, I knew I just made a giant mistake.

CHAPTER FIVE
My stupid agreement

The president is dead. And I know who did it. In fact, the people that killed the president kidnapped me just yesterday... As you could obviously imagine, I'm feeling this serious sense of security now that I've been captured by a mass freak'n murder. AND he killed my family too. Just thought I'd mention that. FML.

This man happens to have some very advanced technology that I've never seen before. Also, he's like, a psychic. Unless he's using technology to make me think he's a psychic... I don't know. But all his accomplices seem to have these same abilities. And don't worry. That's not even the best of it yet. The man that killed my family and the president also thinks that HE'S my real dad and I'm his daughter from some parallel dimension. WEIRD MUCH.

-Elaina
...I don't know the date...

His smirk was bigger than ever, like the HAHA I JUST SET THE TRAP AND WON THE WAR look. All my courage left with those boys. I was alone with this man and I don't think anything could be scarier. He stuck out his hand towards me closed it like he was grabbing something, and then hurled it towards one of the open cages. Almost immediately after, my entire body followed exactly where he threw the air. I didn't know what to think then but now I know that those types of people can, levitate, read minds, and just about every other thing psychics can do except they have super strength too.

I was trying to keep my logic in check. I didn't have an open mind when I was experiencing any of this. It was all just so weird. I was raised to believe nothing like this is possible. Reality slapped me across the face though and set me on the right state of mind.

"Good bye, Rissa. I appreciate your cooperation." He said slamming the cage door in my face. He left the room but left the door out of the dungeon unlocked and open. Then James came in.

He moved a chair in front of my cage. "Hello, Elaina. How are you?"

He sat facing the back of the chair and placed his arms gracefully on the back support of the chair and rested his head on his arms.

"Well James, I'm not doing so well. I'm stuck in a cage, still in this house, and all of you guys are still living. I honestly don't know what could make things worse." I spat angrily.

James smirked lightly, "Hey, Elaina, maybe you should treat us all with more respect. Any one of us could make your life much worse or much better and that's all up to you." James said. Now, was that the real reason that he wanted me to be nice?

"Yes, James. Thanks for the heads up. Will you leave me alone now? I'm tired and I need to get my sleep or I'll bite someone's head off." I said pointing to the door.

"You humans are weird. You bite others heads off when you're tired? That's really odd. Well, I wouldn't want to be the one you bite so I'll be on my way, I'll just send my Lord in here..." He said heading towards the door.

Obviously he was playing me to force me to let him stay in the room. He seemed a lot more at ease when he was with me than when he was with the rest of his comrades. "Umm, no you can stay... just let me sl... sleep..." I said passing out on the hard, damp, stone floor.

I can honestly say before that time, I've never fallen asleep while I was wet or on the floor or while

I was cold *or* while I wasn't on some kind of cushion. First time for everything, I suppose. I wasn't really even tired before I passed out. It just kind of hit me.

I woke up to a small sound. It was the sound of the straw outside of my small cell. *Someone was in here.* I thought getting up from the floor. It was a miracle I didn't catch a cold. Being around these people set me *so* on edge. I looked around and Andrew appeared like, an inch in front of face scaring me out of my skin.

"Whoops! My bad. Did I scare you?" He asked playfully laughing a little.

I simply nodded. Each and every one of these boys destroyed me inside. I hated all of them but I also... had this feeling that maybe I didn't know all of it. Maybe I didn't really hate them for what they did. Maybe they were friends instead of enemies.

"Well, there are these men at the door who want to see you. I got Lord' approval for you to see them." He said opening the cage door. I discarded any ideas of running even before I saw that I was chained to the cell.

How did I not notice that?

He continued chatting away as if I really cared about what he had to say. "You know, I'm surprised. I didn't know he allowed anyone to know you were here. Nothing happens without his approval, you know He controls everything It's amazing. And they asked for you by name which is why I know they knew you were here. Maybe we messed up when we were taking you here and someone saw you and got worried when I kicked you earlier... but that doesn't really explain how they knew your name. Were you carrying an ID with you or something when I kicked you? No... I definitely would have noticed it. That's just so weird. But anyway, I'm sure he has some plan or something with those humans at the door."

Andrew..." I began. *SHUT UP*.

"Shh, don't interrupt me."

"But Andrew," I repeated.

He turned around so quickly and ferociously it took me by beyond surprise and he *lightly,* using his definition, shoved me backwards into the far wall of the room. "Shut the hell up. I was speaking, girl. You don't speak while one of us is talking to you. Got it?"

"Y-yeah," I stuttered. "But-"

"He told me to leave you there alone with them too. Maybe they're going to run tests for Him or something. You're not sick or anything, right? No, I don't think so. You can't get sick. Not anymore. Unless you were sick before... were you sick before?" He rambled.

Overly talkative psychotic prick.

"Have you been hurt? Yeah! You've been hurt. They're probably going to check out your bones for us. But we could do that on our own... that's just really weird, I suppose... and I..." He walked out the door without realizing that he didn't have me behind them. And he didn't SHUT UP long enough for me to say anything.

He walked back into the room, a little annoyed. "Why aren't you behind me?"

"Uhm... Andrew." I said pointing to the cuffs.

"Oh, my bad. I guess I should get rid of that." He said clapping twice. I started walking right next to him. I didn't want him to even get the slightest thought that I was even thinking of escaping. He led me to these men. Then he just left.

"Hello. May I help you?" I asked.

A bag flew over my head, knocking me out within seconds and once again, I was too weak to fight back. *Disgusting*.

CHAPTER SIX
Outrageous, I was kidnapped by humans!

Dear Diary,

Sorry, I know I haven't really informed you on what's been up for a while... I don't really know where I am right now. I'm being held captive. Again. But this time, by my own race. They're holding me in this dungeon because... I don't know why. They won't tell me. They also won't feed me. I'm starving. I have no idea when I got here or when I'll be leaving. Yet, I like it so much more here than with that man and his people. That entire group survives off of hatred and evil. I'm too much of a coward to fight back to my people or to... Whatever they are. I need help.

-Elaina

??/??/????
--(I completely lost track of the date and it's just way too hard to actually try to keep up)—

Without answering then men just put some cloth over my nose and mouth and after moments of struggling, I passed out. I woke up on a bed or more like a stone table. My wrists were cuffed so that I wouldn't be able to move them. My feet were cuffed the same way.

There was someone who looked like a scientist beside me typing on a computer. I could see what the monitor had on it. On it was some kind of graph measuring my power. I blinked a couple times.

"Why are you measuring that?" I asked.

"To see if you are useful. If your power is below average then we'll kill you, and if it is normal you will be kept alive, and if you're above average then you will be kept alive but just barely. God help you if you are above average, kid." The scientist said stroking my.

"Have you started testing yet?" I asked.

"No, but we will once we get all the wires hooked up. And... now they are all hooked up... this will only hurt for a moment." He said grinning through his mask.

"How much will it hurt?" I asked.

"It will only hurt... a lot." He said flipping the switch next to him.

It only felt like I was hit with a tooth pick. Here I was, prepared to get a pain worthy of what at least Sean did and I could have inflicted that much pain with a feather. I looked at the monitor and it gave a description of me... or more like a description of Rissa.

Rissa Zemnas
Age: 16
Height: 5,7
Power: Psychic, Time, Destiny, Strength, Speed.
Family: Zenon (sister): age 17
Neva (Mother): age 30310
Cloud (Step) Father: age 30310
Scorn (Father): age 30310,
Status: IMMORTAL
Weapon: Mind, Sword, Fist, Magic
Power LVL: ERROR—ERROR

…. Boom….

They had information on my "real" race. How they got that? I don't know. I'm assuming someone from my race had either decided to exchange our secrets with the humans for something in their benefit or maybe one of our people had actually been killed with this information on them. Those seem like the only two really logical reasons that made sense.

Then the power chart computer program broke. The entire computer shattered, and caught fire. How was I strong? I never have fought back successfully even once. I thought I was really weak. The doctor looked at me stunned. He pushed a button that was hooked to what was left of his desk.

"Please get someone to escort our guest to our dungeon. Code thirty three." He said taking his hand off the button.

"God sucks." I sighed.

"Don't talk, kid. Be as respectful as you can or you won't be able to talk. Period." He said releasing me from the table, then restraining my hands. I nodded knowing he, by no means, was exaggerating and waited for the person the doctor paged to come get me. The man that had come to escort me was very large and muscular. I was blindfolded, gagged, and my arms were tied together and I think that they were being too cautious.

Nothing is going right! I do as I'm told and get kidnapped. I make a deal that I will stay if he lets my... well, I want to say friends, but I know that's not right. He let my very mean acquaintances go and I get kidnapped again! How many times do I get kidnapped?

He brought me to a cage that was fairly small. I was in there with there was no light unless the door leading to the outside was opened. I think I got night vision while I was in there. I received no food at all in my time there so I probably lost all my excess weight. I was totally alone for months with skeletons in other cells. I realized as long as they had me I was going to live without any food, water, or "human" rights. Then again from what I have heard from... all over, I'm not human; I'm a freak.

One day, the door was opened for the first time since I was brought in here. I think I was there for maybe... six months. The light was like looking at the sun to me. It HURT. I flipped myself onto my stomach and covered my head ensuring that no light would escape past my arms and into my eyes.

Once the light dimmed, I could see two boys were bought in blindfolded, gagged and hands tied just like mine were. The blindfolds were taken off along with the gags.

"Isn't it a little dark in here?" one of the boys asked.

"Shut up, brat." The tall man said kicking him into the cell before quickly hurrying himself out of our darkened dungeon. The doors shut, we were all blinded by the shadows.

"Are you okay?" I asked feeling for the boy that was tossed into the cell.

"Are you a girl?" The boy asked feeling around for me.

"Isn't that a breach of privacy?" the other boy asked.

One of the boys found and tugged on my hair. "Ah, yeah, dude. It's a girl."

"Yeah, I'm a girl; we're all going to be okay." I tugged his hand out of my entangled hair. "Christ, you freaking weirdo."

Now, there really weren't many rules to be followed. You just sat in a cage and tried not to make too much noise for them.

"Well, I'm Elaina. Charmed. So what's your name?" I asked.

"My name is Eric and this is my brother Jean." The taller of the two said.

"Jean and Eric. Hmmm, where do I know those names fro- Oh of course! Jean and Eric, I was held captive by that man and you were kind of… You were on his side. But you're in here. Why? Were you forced to? You do remember right?" I asked.

For some reason I was relieved that I found them. I probably only wanted to make sure that they were alive.

"Elaina? Elaina Martin? Yeah, that's it. And yeah I remember you! *cool!*" Jean said happily. *Except we weren't forced. It was by choice.*

Ignoring that. "Oh… yea… have you guys been tested yet?" I asked.

"Tested? What are you talking about? We were just brought straight here from the streets." Eric said.

"Well, they are probably trying to rebuild their machine that I kind of… exploded. Once they do that they will test how strong you are and if you're immortal or what. If you're weak then the shock of the entire testing will kill you. If you're average then the shock will probably hurt you but not kill you and depending on how you act they may keep you alive. If you're over average then you will be kept alive but in the worst circumstances. If you're over average but immortal, like me, then you will be kept alive but you will not receive food, water, or light. Okay, seriously though. There really aren't rules if you're an immortal like me. They don't feed me and honestly this is the first time I've ever seen these people other than when they first brought me in. You're just meant to keep out of their way." I explained softly.

"Okay Elaina." Jean said. The steel door opened. The tall man stepped through, slowly walking down the stairs then walked to our cage, unlocked it, walked straight in and grabbed my shirt, lifted me up then said something.

"You did tell them the rules, right?"

"Oh, yes sir." I said. "And you should let me down now like the good little henchmen you are." I was dropped but next thing I knew I felt something very hard *slam* into my body. I flew across the small cage until I hit the metal bars that were maybe two feet away from where I was originally. How was everyone so strong?

"You are *going* to treat me with more respect! Got it?" He asked standing over me.

Something flashed through my head. That wasn't human strength. He was our leak. He destroyed our secrets in exchange for... I don't even know.

"Or you'll what? Kill me? Oh that's right, I can't die! Dying would be a blessing for me right now but we both know that's not going to happen. Traitor." I spat.

"THAT'S IT! I'VE HAD IT WITH YOU!" He said dropping me and next thing I knew I was knocked out. I didn't have enough food or strength to fight back or even stand any pain without fainting.

Next thing I heard was someone calling me.

"Elaina! Is that you? Where are we? I'm scared."
It was my mom. We were just floating in this empty
space.

"You knew, didn't you? You knew that I wasn't
human and you never told me." I said.

"Yes but it was for your own good, sweetie. If I
told you, this would have happened sooner than you
were ready for." My mom said. "Besides, I wasn't
allowed to interfere."

I started crying and finally I managed to in
between breaths say, "I am not ready for it NOW,
mom."

"Don't worry sweetie, you can stay here forever."
She told me.

"No mom, I have to go back to help these people.
They're depending on me. I feel like it's something I
HAVE to do." I told her.

"Now you're making excuses! Like always. Why
won't you just for ONCE LISTEN TO ME?" She started
screaming.

That was NOT my mom. There was a light
appearing behind me. "What?" I replied.

"Stupid, stupid girl!"

My mom never behaved like that. "I- I'm sorry
mom... I'm so sorry... good bye." I cried running into
the light. I slowly started disappearing into the light.

"You'll have to come visit us, you know. You will
in the future. And we'll be there waiting for you." I

heard distantly "Just wait." as I woke up from that dream and slowly opened my eyes.

"Elaina? You're awake?" Jean asked. I wiped the tears from my face.

"Yeah…" I replied.

Jean punched my arm. "You're such an idiot! We were really worried about you, Elaina. You really could have gotten yourself killed!" Jean shouted.

"Jean, quiet." Eric said.

"But, Elaina-" Jean was interrupted.

"Don't you remember what she told that man? 'Or you'll what kill me? Oh wait, *I can't die'* but Elaina is that true? Can you really not die?" Eric asked.

"I can't die. That's what the test told me along with what I'll become when I am Rissa." I said.

This black hole appeared and He stepped out of it. "Ah there you are Elaina. I've been looking everywhere for you. I didn't realize that you would be able to be captured by those *humans."* He said the word human with such disgust; with such hate I couldn't comprehend.

"No, no! Leave me alone! I want to stay here!" I screamed kicking.

"Oh, my dear Rissa. What have these humans done to you? You have the strength of a human child." He said dragging me towards the portal.

"*No*! I don't want to go back with you! Go away!" I screamed.

"Say good bye to your friends, sweetie." He mused paying no mind to my screaming.

I needed them. I knew that. They knew that. We all needed each other. It's good vs. evil and we needed all the friends we could have.

"Be careful. Don't die in here, please." I pleaded disappearing into the black hole.

We were back in his house, in his room. He set me on his bed, kneeled down and in his very sweetest voice told me, "You're home, sweetie. Everything's going to be okay."

"What's your name?" I asked. "I don't even know who you are."

"My name is Scorn." He replied.

"I know you knew where I was. You just kept me in there for... some reason. What was that reason?" I asked furiously.

His response: "Look Rissa, I didn't want to kill your parents but I had to... the... humans made me do it."

He used his fingers to comb back his long, shoulder length midnight hair to reveal his icy *eyes*... they had this aura about them; one I couldn't ignore. They shaded smoothly from blue to a more yellow color and I don't even know what took over me. Manipulation plus idiocy and hunger equal bad. "Why don't you help me get revenge? Starting with the leak you met; our wondrous little traitor. Why don't you just allow yourself to be free?"

I don't know how it happened but I began to get all demonic. My teeth all got sharper, my nails grew, my hair grew and got messier, my eyes turned red. My eyes saw everything. I could see the very essence of a person's soul. My speed increased ten full and… I got a sudden taste for human blood.

I didn't know what came over me… that wasn't like me at all. He laughed like this was his entire plan. Step by step, everything that he had planned came true up until the point that I began to kill.

I blacked out with just a few memories from while I was a demon was that and killing children, parents, and elders. I killed a good forty percent of the human population in my demon form and as you can imagine, that was a major guilt bomb. That day was the last time people actually saw the blue sky that in my time, we all knew and loved.

From that day, the sky always seemed to have a reddish, cloudy hue and lightning would always be present. It was terrible. Like, how a sky in Hell would look. And of course, there was the inevitable truth: It was all my fault.

CHAPTER SEVEN
After the blackout

Dear Diary,

I wish there was really a way to spread the blame for my parent's death. But I guess there really isn't. I know that they'd be alive if it weren't for me. I kind of just need to figure out how to fix it. Or if it's fixable. Cuz I'm the one, right? So I can do anything. Yeah. I can do anything.

-Elaina

I woke up in a familiar environment.

A hard bed that was a bit too small with springs sticking into my back (which beat sleeping on hard straw on the cold, damp, stone floor any day), thin drapes that the sunlight would beam through like nothing was in the way at all, pillows sinking into my face with cotton clumps sticking out, and the incredible lack of furniture allowed me to realize that I was sleeping in my room again.

I was all alone in the place I had slept in all my life, the place I felt safest.

I kept my eyes closed, praying that it really was all just a dream and I would never need to hear another word about it again. I heard my family's voice.

"Elaina come here! We have a surprise for you."

Oh my god. That's Jason. Jason's alive!

"Elaina, honey, hurry please!"

Mom. She was shot in the head. This isn't possible. I thought.

"Elaina! C'mon, I have our shows recorded, let's all watch. It'll be our time like always."

Dad.

I thought before I opened my eyes, *Was that all a dream? Is it really possible to go through all that pain and suffering in a dream?* I had to have known it was all a trick; I should have known better by that point, but I had to try. I had to hope that everything was okay.

"Oh, good you're awake. It's so fun manipulating you now that you know everything. You assume that you'd be told the truth and everyone's good at heart and that's what makes it so fun to torment you." Scorn's voice echoed off of the walls. "You are incapable of learning."

Figures. Too good to be true. "SHUT UP! You killed my family, you killed so many people... You tortured me and those boys then threw them out when they had nowhere to go! Their families, my family, everyone is dead because of you!"

"Have you forgotten, my dear, that it was *you* that did all of that?"

"But... you did it! You made me do it like the manipulative scum bag you are!"

Silence... Then a roar shook the few objects I had in my room, "Have you forgotten your place? Do you remember what I will do to you if you continue to act in such ignorance?"

I begged, "SHUT UP! Just shut up... Just leave me alone." Because obviously, pleading with a sociopath could have no negative effects on my current absolutely irreversible situation.

"No Elaina, I'm afraid I can't do that. You see, you can never leave me without breaking the rules. I'm afraid that this world is much more difficult to undersrtnad than you could possible understand." He began to laugh quietly but then stopped to let me know that he wasn't going to tell me what he'd do to me; he told me that he would let me find out as we go and then he simply disappeared.

Laughs and chuckles echoed around me like Scorn was invisibly circling me and closing in for his first and final attack.

"What? G-get away from me! Get the hell away!" I screamed hysterically.

I looked around frantically searching for the source of the sounds of his voice, but nothing was there. No speakers, no televisions, no Scorn. How could it be possible I fight something I can't see or even comprehend?

Scorn then momentarily appeared, "No, not a chance... My dear." He then raised his hand then swinging it towards the ground revealing my house for what it truly was.

There were eternal flames: the house looked like it was burned down mostly but the blue flames still continued burning with power.

"What happened here?" I asked.

I was trembling in sheer fear; I didn't want to move but I also didn't want to stay where I was. Scorn had never actually hit me before but there had to be a reason that everyone listened to him, right? He was the leader because he obtained the most power so if everyone else was more powerful than anyone on this planet, then what would that make him?

Laughing, he lifted up his hand and made some stupid, cocky smile and I was getting shocked. About a half hour later the shocking stopped.

It hurt to even breathe. At first, I didn't really care to move; I rolled around not even knowing what to grasp in pain. Even then I knew he wasn't through with me. He wasn't the type to know when to stop. He liked pushing past the limit just to see the reaction given.

I struggled to stand up. Sharp, unbearable pains kept surging through my weak, defenseless body. I ignored the pain and sprinted for the door. As I ran closer to the door, I heard laughing. I slid to a stop and took a step back. The laughing grew and Scorn walked around the corner with an intimidating smirk on his face.

I cried, "Why won't you just leave me alone?"

"I can't, sweetie. You see if I let you go now, my plan will fail, and we wouldn't want that now would we?" He said.

"I won't ruin your plan, I promise!" I said.

"Well as long as you promise that you won't ruin my plan, then you may leave." He said stepping to the side of the door.

To be realistic, it was a bit late for leaving me alone. I had nothing to live for; nothing but revenge. So knowing this, I would in fact do everything in my power to ruin any plan he may have had.

I was stunned. "Thank you." I said. I couldn't believe it.

Is he actually letting me go? I ran towards the door until I felt a painful jerk against my neck. He grabbed my forehead and smiled as if he were mentally mocking my intelligence.

"Are you empty in the head? I lied. Why would you even consider that was the truth when it's obvious that… girl, you *are* my plan." He said.

He started squeezing my head and messing up my hair even more. Apparently he was trying to reach a certain part of my unconscious. "OUCH! Let go of me, Scorn!" I whimpered in pain.

"No complaining, now. Even you have to admit, that was deserved. My dear… Why in the world would I let you go after all this?"

He squeezed my head with so much power; I would have thought my head would explode. And then I saw a flash back. He was showing my families death, examining their body's, and explaining what they are going through this very second through my mind.

It was like I was getting stabbed with little daggers through my skull a million times a second… It hurt to the point that I couldn't comprehend the pain. My body immediately shut down preventing me from moving or breathing regularly giving me hands down the worst feeling I had had in my entire life.

"NO! NO! Stop! Don't show me this!" I was hysterical. I was screaming and crying. "Please! Please…" I knew it was all my fault. If I never existed, none of those people would have died.

"Do you see that?" He tossed me to the back of the room. "Do you see what you've done? This was all you. You're the bad guy here! You have killed everyone that you have come into contact with. You killed your parents. Not me."

"You're a liar..."

"We both know I'm telling you the truth. There is a move that I would like to show you in dear time that is supposed to kill anyone in an instant or in an immortal's case, it will last until you give up on everything: be praying to die, be willing to do anything. The thing is you're so incredibly unreasonably obstinate. So in the end, if I used it on you, your immortality plus you're stubborn personality result in a never ending series of pain. Don't worry though, I'm not that god awful. I'll just show you on someone else, but like I said, all in good time."

He raised his hand and I realized what he was about to do.

"Don't worry, child. You only need to go through it all one more time. This has to be done. It unlocks a piece of you that you have locked away for the right time. And my dear, the right time is now."

"Scorn stop!" I yelled. But it was too late. He shot a thing at my head. Some black and purple ball just slapped me across the face and began to sink into my skull. I managed to say in a very frail voice right before I fainted, "I want to die..."

I don't know why I decided to tell him that. I guess that maybe it was to show that I wasn't what he thought I was, to show that he could use his special move on me and it wouldn't be a never ending series of pain. Or maybe I noticed that he was really describing himself and I needed him to know that I, the girl that he apparently is a parent of am nothing like him; I was nothing like he wanted me to be.

CHAPTER EIGHT
Valley of Septima

Dear Diary,

My house was on fire, so I didn't really have time to write in you as soon as I woke. Something's weird. For starters, I'm pretty sure I've grown quite a bit since before the fire. Like, I've literally grown like 6 inches. My parents are dead too. What the hell happened to my home? What happened to my life?

-Elaina

I was out cold for some time. When I woke up, my memory of anything... supernatural was gone. I woke up surrounded by blue flames. I think I was more startled than scared of the flames. I sprinted towards the exit to my room.

I never took a second to wonder something like, *why am I on the floor?* No, that would make life easy and we can't have that. When I bolted out of my room and around the corner that leads into the hallway I ran into Scorn.

"Who are you? Did you start this fire?" I asked.

"Yes, yes I did." He said. Before I could even get out another question he began attacking me. I couldn't dodge even one of his attacks. I didn't know why at the moment, but I was crying and bleeding.

"Why did you do this?" I shouted looking up at him.

He disappeared after I asked that. I got off the floor and ran towards the front door with a million questions in my head until I saw my family lying lifeless on the floor. I stopped dead in my tracks. I stared at them momentarily. The mix of emotions clouded me: Regret, pain, sorrow, sadness, fear, and anger all were surging for me.

I turned around and ran into our family room quickly opened the old, broken cabinet in the far corner of the room hoping I wouldn't get burned and took the only picture that was unharmed by the flames that was small enough to fit in my pocket. At this time, I didn't care if the house was burning down. I didn't care if I died right there. But I needed them. Even if it was in the form of a picture, I needed my family in my life.

"You will never be dead to me. As long as I live on, you will all be alive. I'm so sorry I couldn't save you. I love you all. Rest in peace." I whispered running back to the front door, opening the door and leaving.

The funny thing is the outside of my house looked fine. There was no sign that a fire occurred. As I was staring at my house wondering what the hell just happened, a giant rock was thrown at me. I barely dodged it.

The friends of mine that were still alive were being held captive by these people that were dressed like they had just survived a world war: Ripped camouflage clothing.

"What is happening? Why are you doing this?" I asked. They never responded. Instead, they decided to shoot at me. With a gun. Which is bad.

"NO STOP!" I screamed. I didn't exactly mean that literally. The bullet was literally half a centimeter away from my face when everything stopped. Yea, I know what you're thinking. I wasn't really aware that time could stop on command like that either.

For normal people it isn't possible... but for me, that's a whole different story. I fell to the ground and blinked multiple times trying to come up with some logical explanation for why time stopped and why I wasn't dead.

I blinked away my tears thinking that I had to be strong, if not for me, than for my two best friends, Ally and Anna. I thought that it had to be some kind of miracle that they were both kept alive when everyone else I cared about was gone but I had to be strong, I had to make sure that no one else I cared about would disappear.

"Ally, Anna! WAKE UP!" I screamed. I suppose I didn't really expect that screaming at a statue would accomplish anything but it did.

"Ellie, what's happening?" Anna asked.

I stepped back, surprise struck when time was frozen but I could still have a conversation with my friend.

"I don't.." I thought for moment, trying to come up with any type of answer, but then realized, "We need to go now. I don't know how long this freeze might last and I'd love to be long gone by the time they recover."

Ally almost objectively, "Where to?"

Good question, Ally. How was I supposed to know? All I knew was that I woke up in some abandoned, burning house with my dead family and some absolutely *insane* man only to come outside and find angry psychotic people who shot at me. I thought that if anything, they should be telling *me* where to go.

I stared blankly at Ally, nothing I could have said would make any sense and I didn't want to just pull an answer out of a hat and seeing that, Anna suggested that maybe we should just run *somewhere* so if the hurtful people awoke, we wouldn't still just be standing there waiting to be seen.

The three of us began running at such a quick pace, probably quicker than most humans. Maybe it was because of the fear we were all harboring; maybe it was because we were about to be inhuman.

Ally asked again, "Where are you going to go, Ellie?" I didn't notice that she said "you" instead of "we".

"I don't know…"

"For nothing is hidden that will not be made manifest, nor is anything secret that will not be known and come to light."

"What?"

"It's a Biblical quote, Elaina… Didn't you read that Bible I gave to you for Christmas?"

"No. I didn't, my bad."

"So, where are you going?"

"I *still* don't know, Ally. I really don't-" But then a vision passed through me along with an overly rude suggestion from a young girly voice *Piece your shit together, girl. I won't always help you when you're too stupid to know where you're going.*

"We are going to an abandoned factory that has been locked for years. I've been there a couple times when I was younger but that place kind of freaks me out so I don't go there unless I really need to and I believe this is a *need* situation. It'll be hard for anyone to follow us there so we should be safe. Everyone agree?" I asked.

They both nodded. We ran out of my neighborhood and down into one of the nearest, no longer used, waterways.

Ally asked me, "How far are we from the factory, Elaina?"

"It's just over that hill. Don't worry it won't be long till we arrive there." I told her pointing ahead.

She turned, and started running in the opposite direction. "Ally, where are you going?" I yelled out at her.

"I'll be back soon Ellie! I… Promise!" She yelled.

"Wait, what?" I shouted but it seemed that she was already too far away to hear my objections "Okay wait." I took off my grossly undersized tennis shoes, took my laces, and tied them to my foot, creating my very own, incredibly uncomfortable sandals. "Let's go."

The way there was rough on us. There were a ton of cacti and our shoes were all wearing down to the point that we felt every rock and prick that we came to pass in the dead landscape of the desert and the two of us were out of energy.

"Ellie… Do you think Ally will make it back here okay? She isn't very fast or strong… What if they hurt her?" Anna asked. I think she was more asking something along the lines of: "What if they catch her and tell the psychopaths where we are going?"

"Yes. I *know* that she will be okay." I lied. She was always very weak but I trusted that she would come back more so because I needed her than for unselfish reasons. That's probably always been my downfall; I will never do something for others unless there is something that I get in return.

"How can you know? I'm worried about her." Anna asked. The real unselfish one, Anna, she cares about Ally's wellbeing for no reason.

I turned my own uneasiness on her, "Because she promised and friends have faith in each other."

Anna nodded. For whatever reason, that was enough to allow her to rest. Because nobody *ever* breaks promises, right?

Along with her gift of selflessness, she also can read people like picture books, "I think you know the odds are against her. You can only *hope* she will be okay but you pray deep in your heart that she returns."

I knew that she was right.

"I never said that." I argued.

"Ellie, you never really share your feelings… it's sad in a way. You need to stop pretending to be who you're not."

"Look, Anna, people can't change. It's simply not possible. I act how I act and that's *exactly* who I am." I said.

"You changed." Anna said.

"What are you talking about?" I said.

"Since the last time I've seen you. It's been over three years and somehow... I don't know how to explain it. You're stronger and... Colder. It's almost like you don't seem to care about anyone. It's really worrying me. What happened in those years? Where did you go?"

Here we go. Why can't you just shut up?

I stopped running and stared at her both confused and annoyed, "What are you talking about? Three years? That's a bit of an over exaggeration, don't you think? I saw you just before summer break. No, I even saw you over summer break. It's been like, a week since I saw you last."

"The last time I'd seen you was over eighth grade summer break. No one remembered you either. You simply disappeared."

"No way. What year is it?"

"December 2012..." She replied.

"You're joking! Where the hell would I have been the last two years? There's no way-" I was interrupted. Something was rattling in the bushes. "Come out." I commanded.

"Elaina? Is that you?" A familiar voice asked.

Oh god. "Come out *now*!" I commanded.

"Elaina, it's me. It's Drake." He surrendered stepping out of the bushes. "Where... Have you been?"

"Oh my, are you... Drake... what *happened* to you?" I asked examining his person. Comparing that boy three and a half years ago to now; he was a different person entirely. His once childish face which was at this point tainted with hate and damaged by scars along with the rest of his body which was covered in filth, his clothes were shredded, and his once soft and tidy hands, stomach and knees were stained red with blood. A shoulder length, dreaded, mop-like mess now took the place of his chin length hair that always used to be styled in such a way that we could go outside and play but it would never be damaged by our stupid games.

"They took me… they said I was over powerful and no longer human… no longer a servant of god… What does that even mean?" He asked, trying to fight the tears coming to his eyes. "I've been to church! I don't even work out!"

"I don't know Drake. Look your hurt, we need to get you to the factory." I said.

"I- I…" He stuttered falling over.

I walked over to his unconscious body to see if he was breathing, "Carry him I'm going to go ahead and unlock the gates."

I jogged toward the factory, passing every disarmed rock-hurling trap Drake and I mindlessly set up trying to "protect" people by not letting them get to the factory. To actually get into the factory, I simply had to climb a wall and manually pushed the main gate down into the moat so I could get through to the second and final wall to then, push a switch which would then open the first gate that I needed to hop over and unlock the first lock on the door to get inside the factory. After doing that, all I needed was a password to type into the keypad next to the door.

The password was "In the land of power." I didn't have the slightest clue what that meant at the moment.

It was a cotton factory. All of us had cuts everywhere on our bodies now along with shredded clothes. There were clothes a couple yards from the door where there was a table with three outfits. Under the three outfits was a note saying, *"IF YOU WISH TO PROCEED THROUGH THE DOOR TO DARKNESS YOU MUST KNOW YOUR PAST LIFE. CHOOSE YOUR POISON; CHOOSE YOUR SYMBOL."*

Along the walls was a cloth with writing on it.

"LONG AGO THERE EXISTED A KINGDOM WHERE AN AMAZING POWER LAY HIDDEN. IT WAS A PROSPEROUS LAND WITH LOVELY VEGETATION, TALL MOUNTAINS, AND PEACE. BUT ONE DAY THERE CAME A TERRIBLE, POWERFUL DARKNESS. SHE HAD NO DESIRE FOR PEACE, NO DESIRE FOR LIFE. SHE ONLY DESIRED TO WATCH THE PAIN OF OTHERS.

SHE HAD BROUGHT THREE CHILDREN SOON AFTER. SHE USED HER POWERS TO MANIPULATE THOSE CHILDREN TO SPREAD HIS DARKNESS ACROSS THE KINGDOM. IN THE END, THOSE CHILDREN HAD DEFEATED THE DARKNESS BUT WERE OVERCOME WITH EVIL. TOGETHER, THEY TOOK OVER THE KINGDOM AND SOUGHT ONLY REVENGE AND SEARCHED FOR THE GOD THAT BROUGHT THEM INTO THE WORLD AFTER REALIZING THEY COULD NEVER LEAVE THE LAND OF DARKNESS. OF THE THREE, ONE HAD BEEN CHOSEN TO RULE THE LAND AND THE SEARCH FOR THE EVIL ONE: HIS DAUGHTER.

HE HAD ENSLAVED AND CAPTURED HIS PEOPLE SHOWING NO MERCY TO ALL WHO DEFY HIM. WHEN ALL HOPE HAD DIED FIVE YOUNG PRODIGIES, ALONG WITH WONDROUS WARRIORS THAT THEY THEMSELVES HAD TRAINED, CAME FROM A DISTANT PLANET, THEY DESTROYED THE MAN ALONG WITH HIS FOLLOWERS AND SAVED THIS KINGDOM. THESE CHILDREN WERE KNOWN AS THE SAVIORS OF DESTINY. THE CHILDREN'S TALE WAS PASSED DOWN FOR GENERATIONS UNTIL IT BECAME LEGEND, THEN MYTH, UNTIL IT WAS EVENTUALLY LOST.

A DAY CAME WHERE A TIME ITSELF HAD RESET. THE EVIL THAT ALL THOUGHT HAD DIED, HAD RETURNED. PEOPLE BELIEVED THAT THE HEROES WOULD ONCE AGAIN COME TO SAVE THEM... BUT THE HEROES NEVER RETURNED. FACED BY EVIL THEY DID NOTHING BUT APPEAL TO THEIR GODDESS. IN THEIR LAST HOUR THE PEOPLE LEFT THEIR FATES IN THE HAND OF DESTINY. WHAT BECAME OF THE KINGDOM? ALL WHO KNOW HAVE DISAPPEARED. THE MEMORY OF THE KINGDOM HAD VANISHED, BUT ITS LEGEND SURVIVED ON THE WINDS BREATH."

Then below the cloth was a giant tapestry that same triquetra that the girl in Scorn's family portrait had. Then,

"HERE LIES THE MEMORY OF THE CRESCENT MOON."

I knew from the very beginning that I was missing a major piece of the puzzle. After all, the first half of the legend is speaking of completely different people who I was not associated with at the time. I only get mentioned near the end where my apparent destiny is stated.

Anna soon after walked into the room I waited to see a reaction from my friends before I began explaining what this was all about. "Ellie... what is this?"

Then I remembered we only have a certain number of minutes until the strange people came for us. "Check to see if Drake is alive. We can't afford to waste any time asking and answering questions. Please get the bucket and cloth that will appear in the corner of the room in a few minutes." I said pointing to the corner. In about twenty seconds the bucket and cloth was in the corner.

"How did you know..." Her voice faded as she began to ask her question.

"I told you this place freaked me out. Now, please go get the items that I asked for." I said.

She nodded silently observing our surroundings as she retrieved the bucket.

"Thank you. Now get the cloth wet and wipe it once on each of his cuts."

"His cuts are healing. How did you know?" She asked.

"Hand me the cloth and water and I'll tell you." I told her.

As I was wiping my many cuts with the cloth I explained, "A few years ago, I came to this place with Drake. We were into doing things we weren't allowed to do and once we found out about this factory that was said to be haunted and closed down since 1865 due to some kind of magic, death, and... this was a devil warship hideout... they were forced to shut this place down when devils began to show up and once this place was deserted this was made into a devil hideout. The rumor was that those devils were still hidden in this factory but only a select few may enter their underground hideout to see them. Drake and I found the hatch and... and the rumors... they were correct. Another rumor was that on the other side of this tunnel is a portal to another dimension that is described on the walls here. Those select few have been chosen before they were even born and are to find this place and reach that wall, have it open, and reach the other side... That part has not yet been confirmed but will be proven true or false today by you Drake and me. Here you wipe your cuts now." I said giving her the towel. "I broke my leg trying to get here and got a few burns so when we saw the bucket; we tried cooling the burns with the water which now that I think about it is a terrible idea... I could have gotten infected from the water but I was too young to know any better. But long story short, my leg and burns were healed."

"Why wasn't the door to a different dimension confirmed?" She asked me.

"Because, when we reached the end of the tunnel, there was a wall. When I tried to open it, we were caught by the devils. We were taken to a dark dungeon and kept there until we swore to never come back until the prophecy has been for filled. In other words one of us had to be… awaken, whatever that means. Whatever happens on the other side of that tunnel will change our lives and I'm one-hundred percent sure about that." I told her.

"What happens now? Will they try to stop us?" Anna asked.

"Yes, they will try to stop us but they won't."

She asked again. "What if they do?"

"They won't." I assured her.

"What if they do though, Elaina? What will they do to us?"

"… They'll kill us. But as I said they will *not* get us. You have my word." I told her.

"Here, I'm done wiping my cuts. What should I do with the rag?" Anna asked.

"Dip it in the water then put it on Drakes head." I told her.

"So, remind me. Why are risking our lives going into a devil infested tunnel?" Anna asked. I walked to the window showing the front gates. My eyes widened in rage. Ally had betrayed us to the humans.

"Because of Ally. She betrayed us and brought the weird people here. Quick, take the stones and give the figure of the blacked out six thing to me and give the fire one to Drake and you take the last stone and please don't let go of it. I guess you need it to get through the tunnel. Go to the door hidden in the

ground under the table and hide. I'll be there soon."
I said.

On the table, there were three different symbols.
A blacked out number six: mine, a warm stone with a
fire inside: Drake's, and a stone full of water, which
was anna's.

"Are you going to be okay?" Anna asked peaking
down into the tunnel.

"Yes, I will. Now get down there before we get
caught!" I hissed, hiding on the second story of the
factory. I needed to make them think that we had
already left or they would get suspicious and destroy
the factory, and that would unleash the devils, which
wouldn't be good. As the freaky humans were
coming in the factory I heard Ally talking to
someone.

"You said that the demon spawns were coming in
here right?" a man asked.

"Yes, master. Ellie- The head monster told me
herself." Ally said.

*They think I'm some kind of DEMON spawn?.. I
knew Ally's dad didn't ever like me very much but
when my best friend thinks of me as a demon... that's
cool.*

"Do not think of them as humans, Alice. They are
its not she's or he's." He told her. "Remember, *And
for your cattle and for the wild animals that are in
your land: all its yield shall be for food.*"

Dogs and cats can have genders, why can't I? And why are they speaking in bible verses all of a sudden...

Now they were visible.

"Yes master. *It* is not worthy of life. God will show no mercy when we send it to the devil." Ally said.

I stood up automatically in protest. Ally's "master" saw me. I did almost exactly as planned but in the wrong order. I was planning on hearing their plans then "accidentally" revealing myself but this works too.

"Go get her Alice." Ally's "master" told her.

"Yes, master." She said running up the stairs.

"Ally, think of what you're doing. Remember all the good times we had. We're best friends. Forever and always, right? Come on, I trusted you and that's why I let you go away all alone. Don't do this." I said

"Obviously, you haven't had good luck with trust, E- *monster*. You have been born in hell and now, you need to go back." Ally whispered walking closer with a knife.

"Funny, I'm the ungodly one here and I would *never* try to hurt you. You're the more "godly" species and you're betraying me and trying to kill me." I laughed bitterly. "And I'm the demon spawn."

"SHUT UP!" She screamed trying to jab me.

When I dodged I fell off the second story and landed on the hard floor down below. Ally's master started reaching onto his belt for something.

"Oh crap." I breathed running out the door. He was reaching for his gun. I ran for the tree near one of the windows. I climbed the tree and unlocked the window. When I tried to jump for the window the branch that I was standing on broke! Luckily I grabbed the edge of the window and blearily hoisted myself in. Apparently Ally saw me.

"Master, it is going back into the factory!" she screamed.

"No way! We would have seen it!" Some men said coming out of the bushes. I was lucky they were arguing otherwise I probably wouldn't have made it to the trap door in time.

"Master, you must believe me! It'll get away if we don't capture it!" Ally said.

"Alright Alice, but know that if you are wrong there will be punishment." Ally's master said. "*Blows that would cleanse away evil; strokes make clean the inner most part.*"

I'm sorry Ally… but as long as you're on their side you're my enemy. I thought.

I climbed down into the tunnel softly calling my friends names until I heard, "Tell us where she is!" a man said.

"She'll be here soon! She'll come to find us and when that happens, you can talk to her!" It sounded like Anna said that.

"She had better or you'll die." The man said. He was walking out of the room.

CRAP! This hallway is a straight line with nothing to hide behind! What do I do? I thought. His electric yellow eyes locked with mine as soon as I walked out of the room. His eyes, of course were the only identifiable thing about him: he wore a suit of armor that covered every inch of skin but left his bright, almost flashlight like eyes open for everyone to see.

"Perfect timing, Rissa. We were just about to kill your friends here... but you're here so I can't kill them... bummer. Well we are here to stop you from entering the other side so... you can stay with us as long as you like." He said. "And I'm really quite surprised you have returned. I didn't realize your memory would ever come back."

The memory that was "locked away" that Scorn was talking about is what that man was referring to.

"Rissa? What's a Rissa? Oh, never mind! Let me and my friends pass." I said.

"No. You may join us or leave for the human world." He corrected.

"We can't do either of those. The humans want us dead and you people are... well, not the people we need to be with. We need to enter the other side. You need to let us pass."

"You are Rissa. We cannot let you pass or our location may be at risk." He said. "You understand that, right? Do you understand where you are? This is Septima; named for its part in separating the two worlds! You Cannot leave Septima for the next world, Elaina. You *must* understand."

"I don't! Why can't we just go? Why does it matter if we leave?"

"You're staying here will decide fate. It either ends here or it *never* will."

"We'll force our way and you don't want to mess with us. Let. Us. Through." I growled. I was bluffing or *trying* to bluff anyway. I'm sure he knew the three of us were mere humans, incapable of doing anything worth talking about."

"Typical." He scoffed. "So what's your human name, girl?"

Way to avoid the topic. "I believe its common courtesy to say your own name before asking for others." I replied.

"Fine, my name is Grant. Now address your old name please. How old are you?"

"Elaina Martin. But again, it's always polite to address the information about yourself before asking for other people's information." I smiled.

"I turned twenty." He said.

"Well then I assume you used to be human. And I don't know how old I am... Apparently, I disappeared for three years before I woke up in my bedroom." I told him.

"Interesting..." He told me.

"What's under that mask and armor?"

"We are never permitted to take our second skin off in Septima."

"Take off your mask and armor. I want to see what you really look like."

"I'm sure..." his voice trailed off.

"Do it. It's mandatory for me to make my decision." I told him.

Lie after lie spat out of my mouth. I just wanted to see what he looked like. It's so much easier to tell who your enemies were when you knew what they looked like.

"Well then I will be right back, Elaina Martin." He left the room.

The way he said my name was odd. I thought that he already forgot *how* to be human. You don't address people by first and last name. Little did I know this was all a ploy.

He left the room and allowed me to be alone with my friends who were tied together in the corner.

"Are you guys okay?" I asked picking up the knife on the desk on the opposite side of the room.

"We're fine, Ellie. What are we going to do? He said he wouldn't let us pass." Anna said.

I cut the rope. "We're going to make a break for it." I told her.

"How do we do that? Elaina, he won't show any mercy on us." Drake coughed.

"Drake, you're awake!" I said hugging him.

"Elaina, how do we do it?" He asked again. "You know he won't give us another chance; he is the same man that turned us away last time."

"How fast can you run in your state?" I asked.

"Fast enough." He told me.

"Then we run now. And that's how we do it." I said.

I didn't give them time to disagree: I just turned around and started running. We ran through the tunnel until we reached a man in armor guarding the hallway that lead to the special wall.

"What business might thy hold Elaina Martin?" He asked.

"Grant asked us to meet him at the wall." I said. I thought I was working on becoming a natural liar and making such wonderful progress.

"For what business?" He asked skeptically.

"Uhm," I stammered. Okay, maybe not such a natural liar.

Fortunately, Drake came to the rescue. "He didn't really tell us. He told us to meet him there and then he'd explain."

"Tha'd be Grant... Thou might pass." He said.

Thee, thou? How old is this guy? I thought.

"To answer thy question Elaina Martin, five centuries have passed since I entered my thirty-seventh year." He said.

"They can read minds?" Anna asked.

"Yeah we'll have to ask Grant about that when we see him at the wall." I said.

We walked around the corner to the wall. "I command you, Wall of Mystery to open!" I said touching the wall's center.

"As you wish, Lady ." It said opening.

"Ellie w-" Drake began.

"I have *no* idea. But we need to go now. I'd bet that Grant will be informed soon and we need to leave before we get caught." As soon as the "wall of mystery" opened, there was a rope that quickly materialized to climb up into the "New World." We were in some kind of burned down house up above. There was no front door and half of the walls on the north and west side of the house was gone.

"Thank you Wall of Mystery. You may... conceal the door again." I said peaking down the hole where we climbed up.

"Elaina, can we rest? I'm really tired." Anna pleaded. "Drake is too."

I almost wanted to get a little upset with her for asking for a *rest* at such a terrible time but then I got thinking and realized that it was completely understandable. She carried Drake all the way to the factory after running however many miles only to get confronted by these strange beings under a secret passage way to another world. Like I said, understandable.

I replied, "Just tell me when you're ready to go again."

CHAPTER NINE
Things Never Change

Dear Diary,

We seem to be capable of making enemies wherever we go. Humans want us dead, the in-between-crossover-world demons probably want to kill us after crossing them, and of course the world we are in now is that man's world and no one really knows what he wants but... he's just bad news. Anything he does is bad. And everything he does has something to do with me. FML.

-Elaina

"I think she's ready. Now where do we go?" Drake asked in between coughs. "We can't stay here, can we?"

He was so pale. I thought he was catching a serious cold or something. I didn't know then that our newly discovered race didn't get sick. We were genetically perfect. And now that we had opened that part of us, we shouldn't have been able to get sick.

"I can answer that. You'll be coming with us." Jean said.

When did he get here?

Anna replied threatened, "No way! We will never go with you! Isn't that right Elaina?"

I took a moment to think. "...Wrong... We need them. Who knows how long it will be until the freaks show up. We need them to get us to safety. You will get us away from the freaks right?" I asked.

I was speaking like a leader. And I sucked at it. Any good leader would be a little more charismatic than I was and more friendly... I had no qualities that a good leader should possess. I tried to seem so confident I tried to make it seem like I knew what I was doing... I needed my friends to think that. More importantly, I needed to think that.

"Yes. We will take you to our Lord's home. You will be safe from the humans when you are with our Lord." James said walking around the corner of the burned house. "No one can touch you while you are with our Lord; you will be safe from all outside parties."

"Who are you?" I asked.

"Well third times the charm... maybe this time your memory won't be erased. My name is James." James said.

"Okay... So... How was my memory erased?" I asked.

"Scorn erased it because he... wanted to keep you on the right path. Now let's go." He said.

Scorn... I know that name...

"Elaina, I don't trust them. Let's not go. We can run and-" Anna was interrupted.

"And what? Run forever? That won't work. Look at your friend there; do you really think he can make it anywhere? I don't know about you but I think that's out of the question." James laughed.

"I agree. We at least have a small chance of freedom. I'm going to take that small chance. I'm going to take that small chance." I said looking at James. "Besides, don't you want to know what's going on? These people can provide *answers* which is something we are in desperate need of. Take me to your home." I finished.

"Yes Ma'am." James said.

"Stop. Don't call her that." Jean spat. "She doesn't deserve it."

"Yeah, don't call me that. Just treat me like... I don't want to say how you treat everyone else but... how you treat your friend." I said.

James didn't respond. He just turned around and started walking away. I immediately started following.

"You coming?" Jean asked Drake and Anna. Drake and Anna looked at each other then looked back at Jean then nodded hesitantly.

On our way to Scorn, we passed nothing that was alive... The brown, lifeless hills to the side of us covered the sunset, the crunchy dead grass under our feet was withering away with even the smallest amount of wind, and the sky carried no hope. The scene was depressing. To put it in a nutshell, it was like Arizona, my home, but worse.

The combination of taps and crunches on the half paved road as we walked made us all grow uneasy. I figured that any civilized society could afford nicer roads to say the least. And the amount of *dead* around us practically screamed GO BACK. It was a small town that we were walking through though. I figured at the time that the town's lack of finance was the reason that the roads weren't up to par with anything civilized.

But our saviors spotted something we didn't. I was looking at what was missing, the ground, the people, the noise, the life. Jean, however, was looking at something I would have never thought of as bad. There was a single ball laying across the street from the row of houses that laid to our right. The houses themselves seemed so empty and uninhabitable. They almost resembled gingerbread houses in the way that it seemed so endlessly cheerful that it had to be fake, but more so resembled a haunted or abandoned gingerbread houses in the way that what was once obviously great and happy was now completely broken down, dirty, and depressed.

Jean picked up the ball stared at it unhappily for a few moments and then looked at James as if expecting an answer but no facial reaction was given.

So Jean tossed the ball up into the air and then kicked it through the front window of one of the houses. As Jean began walking up to the front door of the house I asked James, "What's happening? Why is he doing this?"

Jean then kicked the door open and stomped in. Ten seconds later, he began to leave the house with a child being dragged behind him screaming desperately for his mom as the boys mom was running behind him crying and pleading with Jean, "Please! He's just a boy, don't take him too! Sully!"

"You were allowed to live out here on one god damn condition! All you had to do was stay the hell off of the streets when we are walking through! Is that *really* so difficult?"

She begged for forgiveness and tried to block his way back to James. Jean back handed her, knocking the poor lady to the ground. I stared at what was happening, too afraid to speak up. Just like always.

He stared at me, thinking deeply about something. "Jean, there's a time and place. Maybe they just lucked out today. We have to get these to

Scorn." He referred to us as *these,* like we were items.

The little boy broke free, took off his shoe and threw it at Jean. "You're a bad man!"

James and Jean stared at the boy furiously taking him back into their grasp. But that gave me the opening I needed. I then stared at Anna, knowing that she was right all along. "There were three of us, two of them..." I mouthed to Anna, "Run in three different directions. Just worry about you."

In thought, at least one of us could get away... but that was before we knew who and what we were dealing with. Anna made the first step and at the *sound* of it, Jean tossed the boy at his mom warning, "Get lost before I change my mind!" and almost instantly appeared in front of Anna.

Drake didn't even run, and when I picked up my foot, James already had a hold of my arm and jerked me back in front of him. "Stop, just stop." There was no escape; there never was an option of escape.

"How could you do that?" I growled.

"You aren't going to say a word about what you just saw." Jean told Anna.

She repeated, "I'm not going to say a word about what I've seen."

"And you are going to forget what you just saw. Do you understand?" James looked into my eyes, and I stared blankly back at him.

"Oh Jesus, I'm so sorry. I totally zoned out... What were we talking about?"

"You were telling me about how much you loved... Puppies."

And I really talked about puppies until we arrived at the fortress.

As we arrived at the painstakingly dark and depressing home to the most evil man on the planet, the sky slowly darkened and the wind stopped. Each step we took, slowly began to seem more and more unbecoming and creepier. I knew that I shouldn't have kept going. I knew the risk that I was putting us through but it was just too late to change my mind because we were mindlessly stepping toward the automatic, shining, white-marble-like-metal doors that were most certainly not from my world that were twice as tall as my house and practically screaming evil. Anna grabbed me, pulled me close and whispered, "For the record, you are making a mistake."

I began thinking at that... *Jean disappeared without a trace. So did I... but he never came back. I did.*

That made me think and it *really* worried me. We walked into the fortress it was silent until the doors were shut tight while the rhinestone windows and the floors were made of this diamond-like silver metal, and the walls were eight to fifteen feet tall maybe taller shook.

"Wow! This place is giant!" Anna whispered in awe.

That was when it hit me. If Jean disappeared and never reappeared until now, then he had to be with whoever took us for those three years: the man that erased my memory. I realized it was a *bad* idea to have followed these boys.

"Good then you won't mind staying in the dungeon for... the rest of your life. Scorn, the Prisoners have arrived!" James called. The diamond chandelier shook like there was a strong wind but it was just James voice... dang.

"Prisoner? We trusted you! Why did you betray us? Why the hell would that benefit you *at all*?" I screamed.

I wasn't so much angry that he betrayed us, I was more upset that he did it without reason.

Without saying a word he swung his hand up grabbed the air then swung it down towards me. Immediately after a small cage a little shorter than I was slammed down on me. Luckily I bent down at the very last second or it would have broken my head open. Instead it just slammed down on my back making me slam onto the ground.

"Ouch..." I breathed. Then Jean did the same except over my friends. Theirs was about twice as wide as mine and about a foot taller than they were.

"Why... Why would you do this to us?" I asked. Both James and Jean never answered.

A dark whirlwind slowly formed two meters from my cage. Inside it was Scorn. It took me a few seconds to realize that he was the man who killed my family.

"You!" I growled. "Jean, you don't know who you're dealing with!"

"Ah so you remember me! Good! It's so nice to see you Rissa!" He said.

"Let us go!" I cried out.

"No. You will not be treated as you have in the past, my child. No, you do anything I do not approve of and you will suffer the consequences!" He said.

"Oh my god, Jean! He killed my family; this guy is bad news!"

"Elaina, he was there." James replied for Jean. "He watched them die with you."

"What shall we do with the... her friends?" Jean asked.

"Kill them." Scorn said looking at me with obvious satisfaction with himself. He had set a trap and I fell right into it.

I grasped the cell bars ferociously, "NO! No! I swear to god, if you hurt anyone else!"

They humored me. "Okay Rissa. But you do anything that I do not approve of and they will die." Scorn agreed halfheartedly.

"Fine." I agreed quickly. I wasn't exactly in a position to debate. He sighed.

"This is going to take some work..." He just walked away! What was that supposed to mean?

"Sir, what do we do with group two?" Jean asked.

"Take them to the dungeon."

"Hey!.. Wait? Couldn't you make them more... comfortable?" I asked carefully.

"Shut up! You are such a *human*!" James said saying the word human in disgust.

Is that supposed to be an insult? I thought.

"James, take her to her room. What are you waiting for?" Scorn said.

"Yes, Scorn. My apologies. Eric, take them to their cell!" James shouted. Eric appeared.

"Hello Elaina. How are you?" Eric asked.

"Oh, you're here too! I should have figured" I laughed bitterly.

"Nice to see you too, Elaina. I know deep down you're glad to see me!" Eric said smiling playfully.

"No, Not re-" I was interrupted.

"I wouldn't say what you think if you think you're going to regret it in the future. If you know what's good for you you'll just say what everyone wants you to say." James whispered appearing behind me.

"O-Okay. Yes, of course I'm glad to see you! You know that you're just my *favorite* person ever!" I said.

The word favorite was incredibly difficult to say. "You know what; I think we should take her friends to the T-Chamber. I think that's a good idea, how about you Elaina?" James smirked as though I had a single idea what the T-chamber was.

I suppose that I figured out all I needed to just by seeing his overly cruel and satisfied expression. "No! Don't you dare lay even one finger on them!" I screamed.

Now glaring at me James muttered, "Hmm? Did you say something? I hope not... for your friends sake."

"My apologies for interrupting but, what shall I do with the prisoners when they get to the dungeon?" Eric asked.

"Maybe we should just kill them. Elaina has yet again caused someone's suffering." James said looking deliberately at me just to make my skin crawl.

I didn't even do anything. Everything that was happening was to get a reaction out of me.

"NO!" I screamed.

"Shut the hell *up*! Do you really think that annoying us will really accomplish anything?" Jean said.

"Don't hurt my friends... please..." I dropped to my knees. "I'm begging you... I'll do anything to keep my friends safe, so please, don't hurt them." I pleaded. My eyes blurred for a moment.

James smiled. "Anything, eh? Well, we'll discuss that proposal later, but for now, get them into the smallest dungeon cell, and give them enough *only* enough to keep them alive, nothing more."

"Umm… if it's possible… can you please make my friends more… comfortable? I-I'm just asking… Please?" I asked. It was obvious I was putting a tremendous effort to be polite. James seemed to pity my pathetic attempt and decided to discuss his terms with me.

"I will tell you what, Elaina. They will live in a cage with three rooms two bedroom and one restroom. They will be as children, who are simply grounded, not allowed to leave their room but able to eat and drink when they want… but, if you do *anything* wrong then they will get punished along with you. Understand?" James explained.

"Yeah… Yes… I understand." I said.

"Good. Alec, will you come here please?" James called out.

"Wha- Elaina. Nice to meet you… again… Oh, you want me to… Okay." Alec said.

"What?.. " Then I took a moment to ponder my memories and hopefully come up with how I knew him. "Yeah, what?"

"Alec, let's speed this up. I don't plan to babysit a human for the next eight months."

What?

"Okay. I'd be happy to oblige." Alec said walking towards me.

"G-get away from me!" I screamed.

"It's up to me how much it hurts, so be a good girl, get on your knees, and say 'Please Alec, be merciful to me and I will please you in every way I can.' Say it now." Alec said putting his pointer finger under my chin lifting my head so that I looked straight at him. I pulled away from him violently but obediently got on my knees to say,

"Please... what was the rest? Oh, right. Get the hell away from me." I spat angrily.

"Okay, I guess we'll just have to do this the painful way." Alec said.

I began thinking hysterically, *I can't believe I just said that to him! I'm such an idiot! I really need to learn to SHUT UP! God, what's he doing? That look on his face... What's he thinking? What's going to happen? Ugh, I'm WAY too terrified of all these people and something always takes over me and makes me rude! Oh shoot! What is he going to do to me? Or worse what's he going to do to my friends.*

I took a deep breath followed by a sigh. *What is he going to do to make sure I pay?*

"Really? Well no shit you're scared of us. I don't think you realize how incredibly pathetic you are! However, it will be a lot more fun now that you can even admit to yourself that you are an afraid, useless, punk. I'll just go get Scorn and tell him to come up with a fun game for you and your friends... unless you have something in exchange for the secrecy of your rudeness." Alec said.

He was trying to intimidate me into doing something really stupid... and it worked... Not that that's really surprising. After all, I was only human.

"Well, I guess I'm at your mercy... again... what would you like me to do in exchange you don't tattle on me?" I asked.

Alec gave James a short, disappointed look then realized that he was visibly disapproving of my reaction and straightened out his face. "At the moment I'm not sure. But for now you will be sure to follow all my orders. Understand?"

What kind of question is that? Stupid asshole is just trying his hardest to get me to yell at him. I thought.

"Do you have something to say? Say it! Unless, of course, you think you might regret saying it later. In which case... Do not think those thoughts! I can read your thoughts you *human* brain!" Alec said.

Was that an insult?

He closed his eyes put his hand on my head. Suddenly a bubble appeared around me that was skin tight. "Wh-what is this?" I asked.

"Shut up!" Alec shouted.

The cage around me began to disappear. "What's happening?" I asked.

"SHUT UP!" Alec roared hurling my bubble covered body towards the wall. I figured that the worst part would be the impact of me hitting the wall, I mean, that would only make sense, after all.

"This isn't it Elaina. You'll feel the real pain in just a moment." Alec said taking a small step forward. Just that small step caused my... I didn't even know what.. Everything, I suppose, a ton of pain.

"A- ou-ch... s-stop... it... wh-a-ts... happening? What are you... doing to me?" I asked.

"I'm speeding up your transformation, Elaina. What does it look like? When I'm done with this bubble exercise then you will have lost consciousness and will be just weeks away from full transformation." Alec said taking another small step forward.

James looked away as I screamed in pain but Alec showed nothing in his expressions. To Alec, that was just something that had to be done; nothing could matter to him more than Scorn's missions.

"Oh, I guess I forgot to mention that this bubble reacts to me. If I step further it's another step to force your human soul out." And after every step he took my vision blurred and then regained its perfection. I didn't know what that was supposed to mean at the time. I probably just assumed it was from the pain. I assumed wrong.

"S-so exa-exactly how could you make this painless?" I asked.

"I normally would just run towards you and by the time you realized that you were being hurt you would be out cold."

He took another step towards me; I couldn't speak anymore. He started walking slowly towards me while I was trembling as a reaction to the pain. He put his hand onto my head and the other with the pointer finger and middle finger up and the rest closed into a fist then dropped his middle finger and pressed his pointer finger to his lips as a silent signal to shut up. He muttered something to himself, probably some kind of chant to speed up the "process" and after he finished his chant, he slammed his palm into my stomach causing the bubble to pop, releasing me from its bubbly grasp. I landed on the marble floor, first on my knees; then my hands landed allowing me to look up at Alec and Scorn. "What... Are... You?" and then passed out.

I heard a few voices in the darkness of my sleep. "Oh, the poor little kid fainted. Come on, we've done what we needed to." I think that voice was Alec's.

Then I felt a firm grip on my neck line and I was dragged across the floor. That was definitely Alec. You could tell that the next one was James. A soft hand lightly touched my head and then I heard James say, "It's really too bad, don't you think? She's nothing but a kid."

"We both know the stakes. This *has* to be done."

I felt something. It was almost like wind whirled around me, but it was warmer and it didn't actually blow; it was almost like a warm aura that surrounded me.

I woke up in my new room but didn't want to open my eyes. I figured that if they thought I was asleep, they wouldn't attack me and also they would speak freely.

"I can't believe that Scorn would want this girl here. This place is better than *our* rooms!" Alec pointed out, obviously pissed at the world.

"She is Scorns jewel. Wouldn't you want your kid to have the best? All she has in her closet is dresses. It almost makes me feel under dressed..." James said.

"Shut up, James." Alec laughed. "You're *never* underdressed. That's why you get all the ladies!"

James began to laugh but then he noticed... My heart beat quickened and began thumping harder. The happy-as-it-got aura turned to anger. "Our little princess brat finally woke up, huh?"

I kept my eyes closed hoping he was just trying to scare me. Next thing I knew something jabbed into my abdomen sending me flying off the ground and into the air. Then something caught me right before my feet touched the ground. That would have been nice if, well, he didn't catch me by my neck.

"So, Elaina, exactly how long were you listening? Did you honestly think we wouldn't find out? Did you *really* think we were that stupid?" James asked.

I tried to say something but I couldn't due the crushing of my neck. I tried to tell him I couldn't breathe using what little sign language I knew. He just dropped me. Something fell out of my pocket. It was a picture of my family back when they were alive. I forgot that I had it with me. I couldn't believe that it hadn't fallen out of my pocket already. I tried to reach out for it, and grab it but when my hand was over it James's dress shoe slammed on my hand. Normally I would be worried about my hand but this time...

"Ouch! James you're going to break it! NO! You can't take this away!" I screamed. His foot pressed harder on my hand.

"I'm not going to be the one to break it Elaina. It's your hand and so it's not me." The picture was starting to crack.

"*No*! Stop! This is really precious! This is the only thing I have left. I *need* them, James. Please... James..." I pleaded looking desperately up at him.

He raised an eyebrow, surprised I begged him for something so stupid as a picture. "I'm sorry but I really do have to do this for that reason."

He kicked my hand off of it and then crushed my picture and watched it burst into flame.

I didn't know how it caught fire and I really didn't care at the moment. "*No*! Why? Why did you have to do that? That was all I had left of them! You've taken everything from me! I have nothing left now, is that what you wanted? Why did you have to take away everything I lived for?" I screamed.

James gave me excuses. "It brought you another step closer to being one of us... Scorn wants you to be back as one of us as soon as possible... It really did need to be done."

He felt remorse for destroying me. He felt something for me at that time. It was written all over his... Everything. His body movements were more sporadic and exaggerated, his facial expression was sad and concerned. I didn't know why; I didn't care.

My vision blurred once again but for a longer period of time. I blinked the blurriness away, "No... you... why? Don't you get it? I don't *want* to be like you! There's nothing good about you. You all should be dead!" I cried out.

James looked quickly at Alec. Alec stared, confused with James's new found concern for me and James stared back, afraid of everything that Alec had to judge him for. Within half of a second, James and Alec exchanged secondary, regular and cruel expressions; whatever happened in their heads for that worrisome moment was now gone and done for. Together, they disappeared; I looked around the room and both James and Alec were gone.

"W-where are you guys?" I asked out loud. *I... didn't see them leave... so where are they?*

Next thing I knew something smashed against my face sending me flying across the room then something smashed against my chest slamming me against the wall. I grunted in pain. "That'll teach you to talk about him that way. Normally we would do much, *much* worse but because you are in your human form we can't push it or you'll die." Alec said helping me up by grabbing my shirt and yanking me off the ground. I just fell down when he put me back on the ground.

I almost wanted to ask why they wouldn't kill me. I was, at that point, ready to beg to die, but instead, I asked, "You're not planning on killing me?"

Ironically, I was shaking. I would rather be dead and with everyone I cared for, but they still scared me to the point that I shook.

"What's the matter? You're shaking like a cold little puppy. Is something wrong? I hope you feel comfortable around us." James said squatting next to me. Immediately I moved away.

I know that was rude and all but … I'm scared… of them… Scorn, James, Jean, and Alec all give off the same aura. It's so strong and scary… like a warning… I thought.

"You have no idea how right you are, Elaina. Aura tells exactly how strong you are or can be, but enough talking. Scorn said something about your friends…" James exclaimed standing up.

Alec disappeared and reappeared next to James. James put his right hand on Alec's shoulder and used the other to wave.

"Bye, Bye, Elaina." James said.

I started sprinting towards him and then tried to tackle him screaming, "*No!* Why can't you just stay out of our lives?" and at the last second he teleported out of there which made me slam into the floor.

I started punching the spot on the floor they were standing on, uselessly. Now I was pissed *and* my knuckles hurt. "NO! No! Leave them alone... why?.." I whispered.

I looked at my outfit. If it could still be considered that... everything was shredded beyond belief... Splatters of dry rust colored liquid covered my... what used to be jeans.

Is that blood or mud? You know what? I don't even want to know. I thought as I examined the stains closer.

I looked up from the mirror and noticed my hair was as messy as always but on a much larger scale, almost like I hadn't brushed it in years.

I walked away from the mirror and sat on the floor in a corner behind the bed motionless until Jean came to my room.

"Elaina? Are you here?" He asked.

"Yes, Jean... I'm here." I whispered.

He wasn't nearly as strong as James or Alec... his aura didn't bother me in the slightest but there had to be some reason Scorn kept him.

"What, not calling me an idiot? What's that about?" Jean asked.

"As long as I'm here, Alec made me promise to be polite and all that so he wouldn't kill my friends...." I said.

"Oh, that sucks." Yeah, he definitely didn't pay any mind to what I had to say. "Okay, well, anyway, Scorn wants to dine with you." Jean said.

"Why?" I asked.

"Just go take your hair down from that ponytail and I'll do the rest." Jean said.

I took my hair down from the messy ponytail my hair was in since I was knocked out. My hair was now layered, with side bangs, back how it used to be years before they ruined my life.

My sorry excuse for cloths was now a shorter dining dress. My gold dangling necklace THAT MY GRANDMA GAVE TO ME turned into a wide cloth choke necklace with that same triquetra figure that was found in the factory.

"Wow you look like her... I mean, like, her as in a loser. could you look any weirder?" Jean asked.

Was he referring to Rissa? Who the hell is that chick and why am I continuously being referred and compared to her? I thought.

"Alright, let's go, princess." He smiled holding his arm out to me like he were about to escort Cinderella to the ball as a sarcastic gesture but I played along. I took his arm and waited to appear in the dining room.

"Scorn... It's nice to see you..." I said.

"Ah, I see we have made progress with that politeness issue. Why have you come?" He asked.

"Jean told me to come here because you wanted to eat with me... if that's not true I can go back to my room..." I was interrupted by my stomach growling.

"It was true. I just wanted to see your reaction. When was the last time you ate?" He asked me.

"I don't know. A few hours ago I guess." I said.

"No. it was actually about a year ago. Don't you... oh never mind... from what you remember it only has been exactly nine hours. You poor child. You must be starving. Here, eat up." He said having Jean pull a chair out.

I sat in the chair Jean pulled out then all of a sudden all these exotic types of foods appeared on the table. I waited for Scorn to give the okay before I almost started eating.

"Can I ask you something?" I asked.

"What is it?" He asked.

"What's a Unashi and what's a Cheuva?" I asked. I saw those words under every picture in Scorn's house.

"Cheuva is a planet and Unashi is the Imperial city. You're Cheuva's princess. Unashi has two princesses but only one is royal by blood." He explained.

"W-what? Is that why everyone is trying to take me? Because I'm Unashi's princess?" I asked.

"Yes, that is correct." He told me.

"Wh-what? No. I've got to get out of here! This is just too crazy for me. This sounds like a bad plot for a Disney movie. Just let me and all of my friends go." I pleaded.

"Now, my dear. I couldn't do that even if I cared to. You're way too important to let free and your friends are the only things keeping you in check." He said making a gesture for me to eat.

Should I refuse? I thought foolishly. *What if it's poisoned?*

"You do as I tell you without any questions asked. But to put your stupid mind at ease, it's not poisoned and it can never be poisoned because you are far too important to kill." Scorn said.

"Y-yes sir. I'll try my best Scorn. Thank you, Scorn." I said. *I just hope my best is good enough...*

"Good. Take her back to her room James and Alec." He said that in a soft voice and Alec and James were there in an instant using teleportation.

"How in the *world* did they hear that?" I asked aloud.

"Yes sir." They said together. They disappeared then reappeared next to me.

"W-wait! I didn't get to eat... can I eat before I go? Please, Scorn?" I asked.

"Oh, yes, I almost forgot. Eat as much as you want." Scorn said.

Holy sweet god, yes! "Thank you!" I was really excited to eat.

"Tell me, do you *taste* the food when you inhale it like that?" Scorn asked when I stopped shoving my face in my food.

I stared at him blankly realizing he just called me out on the fact that I was eating like a savage. Because he *obviously* had oh so much to judge.

"Good, now wipe your face. No daughter of mine will be titled princess and still eat like that. Understand?" Scorn asked.

"Yes, of course Scorn. Oh, one more question. If I'm your daughter why do you treat me like I'm nothing to you? And *am* I human?" I asked taking the napkin that Scorn threw at my face.

"That's two. Yes, right now you are human, but soon you will go back to being a Cheuvean. I just really don't like it when people are disrespectful and... well, that seems to be all you consist of... but your existence is unnatural, you were never supposed to live, not in this world, not in the last. No more questions for the evening." He said.

What? "Thank you, Scorn. James, Alec, will you please take me to my friends? I haven't talked to them or seen how they're doing... I'm just asking. You don't have to do it...." I said.

"Yeah sure, Elaina. But you'll only have a few minutes." Alec said.

"Okay, that's fine with me. Thank you." I said. James grabbed my right shoulder and Alec's left shoulder and at the blink of an eye, we appeared in

Scorn's dungeon and it was terrible in there. The place reeked like people died in here and like mold was gathering for years.

I took my first step further into the dungeon but everything went black.

My dear, can you hear me?

That was a woman's voice. *Yes I can hear you. What is this blackout thing that keeps happening to me? Who are you?* I thought.

Good you figured out how to use telepathy. My name is Neva. I am your true mother. What that "blackout thing" you experience is called a time hollow. Now listen and listen well. You need to get away from your father and come, stay with me and Zane. She told me.

Who's Zane? I asked.

Your other father. Please get your sister Zenon and come! She told me.

Who is Zenon? What about the rest of my friends? I asked.

Zenon is mine and Zane's daughter. She is the pre incarnation of your friends. Forget about your other friend. Family comes first! Just bring Zenon! Get to safety." She told me.

Why do you want me to get away from Scorn? What's happening? I asked.

None of your business.

I blinked away the darkness from my sight. "Elaina, you okay? You blacked out." James asked helping me up.

He stopped me from hitting the ground. He caught me.

"Yes. Where are my friends?" I asked.

"Right over there, Are you sure you're-" Alec began.

"Thanks."

Drake and Anna walked to the front of their cage and stared at me with rage.

"Guys, you're okay!" I said walking up to the cage. "How's everything going?"

"Shut up, monster! Stay away from us!" Anna screamed.

"Wh- what? I don't understand. Why-" I began

"SHUT UP! You are the reason everything bad has happened to us. Why can't you just leave us alone?" Anna spat throwing her food at me. "You even have the nerve to walk up to us dressed like *that?* You've obviously been treated well, don't you think? While Drake and I are prisoners under the same stupid roof?"

I was too shocked to move out of the way of the flying food so the noodles were on my head and on my newly found outfit with spaghetti sauce stains. Smiling, I looked at Anna and looked at Drake. Something about Drake caught my eyes though. He was pale, and he seemed incredibly sick.

"Leave, Elaina. We don't want you here. You ruined our lives and took away our freedom." Drake coughed grabbing Anna's hand and helping her up. He was even more pale now, coughing after everything he said.

Drake coughed, "Come on, Anna. Let's leave that monster to die."

"Wait! How did I ruin your lives?" I asked.

"If it weren't for you we would be somewhere other than here... free... not animals in a cage." Drake said.

"No... you guys would have died if you weren't brought here." I said.

"We wouldn't have been caught at all. Even if we were caught... I'd rather be dead than here." Drake said. I opened my mouth to say something but nothing came out.

"Save it Elaina. We don't care for your lies." He coughed uncontrollably for a few moments. "Go die, monster. You're worse than they are. You're such a brat: You really only think about yourself. Everything always turns in your favor in the end. Go to hell."

I began thinking to myself about how they had no right to behave like that towards me. That cage had four rooms, they ate whatever they requested, what they had was hardly imprisonment at all. The more I made excuses, the more I realized that they had every right to be angry with me. I ended their freedom with my stupid decision to come with

James and Jean to see Scorn. Then again, though, was it ever really a choice? If we declined the boy's offer to see Scorn, they could have easily taken us against our will.

"Okay times up!" Alec said as he and James ran to me. James quickly teleported us out of there and back into my room.

"Why?.." I asked.

"Why what?" Alec asked.

"Why would you get me out of there?"

"Because you don't need to go through that. I don't think you get it, we only do what's necessary to get you to go through the change." James said putting his and on my head.

"Was it true?" I asked still bawling.

"Yes, it was true. You are a brat." James smiled letting out a small chuckle.

"Was it really my fault, James." I asked once more with the harshest tone I could force out.

There it was. That face that made him look like he really cared for me. So compassionate, so sweet, so beautiful. "No, it's really wasn't your fault. There are many groups of us and if they got caught by the wrong group they would be *much* worse off than they are now. Trust me."

If I really am hated here then why are you being nice to me? I thought looking up at James.

And just like that, his compassion disappeared and his look of dapper heartlessness re appeared. "As I said earlier, I pity you."

After I gave him a grief filled look, his compassion returned. "Oh, you know what I just noticed? You're being polite! Good girl!" James quickly said smiling.

It was a weird smile. Like, a desperate one, his smile was trying to accomplish a goal and force a smile out of me.

I wonder if I'm cheering her up... I always hated it when she cried this bad.

That was James I looked up at James and thought *You thought something like that?* I actually hugged him.

I can't believe I did that now that I look back at the event. Actually, to be truthful, something took over me. In my right mind, I wouldn't have hugged him but it wasn't *my* right mind. It was hers.

At the time, I figured that the reason I did that was probably just because I needed someone to be my friend and the only person that was anything close to that was James. "Thank you..." I said quietly.

"James, we need to talk." Alec grabbed James's shoulder and next thing I knew, I was hugging air. I decided to look around the room to see if I could find my *normal* clothes and I found a small window just two feet from my reach.

Maybe I have some kind of flying power... I could fly up to that window and fly out... I thought.

I started to concentrate on flying... now when I opened my eyes I was flying the level of the window.

Wow that worked. I thought.

Suddenly my body shot out of the window and then stopped flying! I was heading straight for the ground thinking that I was done for and right before I smacked against the ground something smacked the back of my head and I was out cold. At this point, I was far passed being annoyed with the amount of times I had no idea what was going on because I was unconscious and needed to stop getting knocked out! It's annoying and incredibly confusing. I woke up in a small cage. Well, I wouldn't call it a cage... more of a steel box with a steel door. I started looking around the door and then I noticed that behind me was Ally.

"Good, you're awake. I am your superior now." Ally announced like she was all high and mighty. She always was like that though, pretending to be strong, pretending to be above everyone. *"Remind them to be submissive to rulers and authorities, to be obedient, to be ready for every good work."*

"Shut up, Ally." I moaned rubbing the back of my head.

The best way to get in her head was to act more confident than she is.

Okay that didn't work but I just need to intimidate her with some ordering around. Ally thought.

"Don't you order me around! Or if you'd rather I could have the guards come in here..." Ally threatened.

I got up off the floor and charged at her expecting to maybe just tackle her enough to scare her but chains flew from the ground that stopped me from actually hitting her but I still had accomplished what I was aiming for. She showed her fear when I stopped just a couple of inches away from her forcing her to fearfully jump back, terrified of the damage she thought I could inflict. That was when I noticed it, her aura, she wasn't human. When I scared her, her defensive aura spiked past normal human possibilities.

"You can't hurt me! Good always defeats evil, Elaina. You'll never be able to hurt me! *Do not be overcome by evil, but overcome evil with good.*"

I laughed, "It's ironic that you say that, Ally. Especially since she stared back at me, completely fear struck. "Don't."

"Don't what? Don't tell your psychopaths that you're not who they think you are? Or should I say *what* you are?"

"Lock her up and begin experimenting!" Ally yelled beginning to walk out of the room.

"I know your secret. I know you're one of us."

"*NO!* I don't know what you're talking about, Elaina! God won't like-"

I interrupted her, laughing my head off. "I don't know if you're lucky you still have something to believe in or just too naive to realize that the god you know isn't real, Ally! Your god wouldn't let ether of us be here if he were real unless he had some *really* good plan." I said.

"I'll kill you!" Ally screamed charging at me with a knife she pulled out of her pocket.

I heard a voice coming out of speakers at the top of the box, "No, Alice. We'll kill you. We will experiment on you, just as we will Elaina, until you die. Traitors must endure punishment after all."

"Dad, that's not it! I didn't mean to betray-"

"*If we say we have no sin, we deceive ourselves and the truth is not in us*." He replied.

The gravity in the room became noticeably more intense and unbearable. Just before Ally came within arm's length of me she slammed onto the ground.

I was able to sit up for a few seconds longer than Ally, then I couldn't hold my weight up any longer and I fell to the ground too. A man came into the room with a remote in his hand I couldn't see his face at the time. He walked over to Ally and took away her knife. He drew a dot in the dirt of the cell on both sides of Ally's wrists, ankles, thighs, and waist. Then he clapped his hands and some metal came out of the ground bounding Ally's body parts to the ground then the gravity lifted up and I could move again.

"Come, Elaina. Follow me if you want to eat."

When I gained mobility I looked at his face to see if I knew him… It was Ally's dad… I stood up and started following him until something tripped me. I looked back at my ankle and I found I had a blue glowing cuff around it.

"What's the hold up?" He asked.

I rattled the chain attached to my ankle, "Can you get rid of my ankle cuff?"

"I seemed to have lost the key, see?" He said turning his pocket inside out… The key flopped out of his pocket.

"Oh there it is!" He faked excitement as he picked it up off the ground. Then put it back in his pocket.

"Oops I seem to have lost it again… oh I guess that means no food until next time… too bad… for you, of course." He chuckled gently.

Once he left, the room was silent so I attempted to start a conversation with Ally.

I began, "So…"

"Shut up!" Ally screamed.

"Hey, we're both here, so why not get along?" I asked.

"Elaina, I hate you."

I smiled, "Hate is a very strong word."

"Because of you most of the world's population is gone. Because of you, people quit believing in my god, and most importantly - thanks to you -

Cheuveans were discovered! Innocent children died because of you! *I'm* going to die because of you. Hate describes my feeling perfectly."

Because *all* of that was completely *my* fault.

"Okay, you were part of the organization that killed those kids, its people's choice to believe in your god or not, and Scorn was the one to kill the world's population. Not me." I told her.

"Who is Scorn?" Ally asked.

"It's the leader of the people who kidnapped me for the last three years. Your dad seems *nice* when you compare the two."

Ally laughed gently but then remembering how I exaggerated everything in my human youth, asked, "He can't be that bad, can he?"

I suppose that was the time that I was supposed to assure her that everything was going to be alright. But the truth was that it really wasn't going to be alright. "Yes, he can... Are we really going to die here?" I asked.

"And the Lord relented from the disaster that he had spoken of bringing on his people."

"Stop with the bible verses. Are you even using them properly?"

"You won't, of course, but me on the other hand... I will."

"Why won't I die here?" I asked.

"You really don't remember? Elaina, you can't die. You're immortal." She explained.

151

"Since when? I was perfectly capable of dying a few years ago!"

"That was *before* your change started, Ellie. There is no stopping it and you're already on your way." She explained gently.

"Kay, Screw it." I took my diary out of my back pocket.

She raised an eyebrow in disapproval. "You're writing in your journal?"

"Yeah." I smiled.

"Why?" She was confused. "Jason isn't here anymore. He won't care if you don't write."

"I can't stop myself."

CHAPTER TEN
Cheers to new friends

Dear Diary,

I have weird feelings for my "dad". It's like, I have this feeling of hatred and love mixed together. But there's a lot-a-bit more hate than love mixed in there. He fed me too which was great.

Apparently, nothing's really as it seems, which I really can't get over. I have this whole new identity with a step dad, biological dad, mom, sister (AKA my best friend who now seems to have this new found deep hatred for me), and my second personality.

My other besty is a pretty good friend of my other personality too which is a bit ironic considering that she's the daughter of the lead investigator of the non-humans. Even more ironic that her daddy would totally be willing to kill her just because of what she is. Not like she wasn't that for the other like, 16 years of her life, you know? ... wait... I don't know how old she is now. keep that on hold.

Ugh! WHAT. THE. HELL. This seems like a bad plot line for one of those stupid sappy movies my dad (Real/human dad) used to watch with me on Sunday nights. You know something? I made fun of him every single Sunday when he started watching those sap fests. I used to tell him that they were cast for sad old cat ladies without men in their lives. Ironically, I'm really, really going to miss watching those with him. Hell, I'm going to miss HIM in general. Actually, I already do miss him along with the rest of my entire life.

-Elaina

Alec stormed into the room, shouting at me, "Elaina! There you are! You stupid girl! I have been searching everywhere for you! Just like you to sneak out a crack in the wall and abandon both of your friends with us. You know that Scorn would kill us if he found out we lost track of his stupid jewel!"

"I'm sorry... I just wanted my friends to be safe... So I thought that if I weren't there... I couldn't do anything wrong... I'm sorry..."

"Really? Don't you understand that he thinks that the only things that keep you in check are your stupid friends? Once he realizes that they don't, what do you think will happen to them? Or to us? You will be all alone with him and I don't think you can comprehend how much worse he can be than we are." Alec growled dragging me away from the wall until I was tugged away from Alec's grip. It was that same cuff.

"How did I *not* see that?" Alec asked.

James now appeared, "Is that a spirit cuff? How did these inferior *humans* get the technology to make spirit cuffs?"

Alec's now furious undivided attention was given to James, "I thought I told you to stay back home!"

"Alec, this isn't appropriate. She is my responsibility just as much as yours."

"You want to know what isn't appropriate, asshole? Your emotions in regards to the past. You get that she's gone, right? The stupid girl that you are still persuing is gone and dead."

What?

"We can talk about this later, right? We need to take her home. I can be impartial."

"Well, what are you waiting for? Get the girl out of the spirit cuff." Alec told James. James walked over to me and pulled out a sword. Then pushed the tip of it to my neck.

I pulled away fiercely, "Ouch, that burns. What did you do to that? Soak it in lava?"

"This is what you can call a fire sword. Unlike your inferior human steel sword, this gives out a fire aura that makes it *very hot* and when I actually take it out for a hurtful intent catches fire and next time you ever, *ever* attempt to escape again, this sword will go straight through your neck. Understand, Elaina?" James asked.

Nervously, I replied "Y-yeah."

He took it from my neck but then the sword caught fire and he stood up. He rose the sword up then swung it down at me. He just got finished telling me that it caught fire when it was being used for hurtful intent so I was thinking that I was about to lose my leg. I closed my eyes tightly, bracing for impact when I heard the sound of a clean slice followed by the shaking of the ground around me.

When I build up enough courage to look at my leg I found out he cut the spirit cuff.

"And god forbid you leave your stupid non-friend here to die." Alec knew me well.

I nodded once.

"Fine, James, go unlock the friend." Alec said. James sneered and went to go unlock Ally.

I had an idea. It was the only way to make sure no one got hurt. "Okay, bye guys." I said.

"Bye? What are you talking about? You're coming with us." Alec said.

This is SUCH a bad idea... "What makes you think I'll go without a fight?" I asked. "I'm much better off here."

Alec and James looked at each other, and then nodded.

"If it's a fight you want, it's a beating you'll get." James informed me.

Alec and James smirked as they turned all demonic, you know, the usual really pale skin, fangs, messier hair, eyes turn red. That type of stuff still scares me after all this time... I was totally lost through the fight. It was like I'm in the air then smashed against something then flown across the room smashed against something then clawed at, and so on. It was just too fast for me to understand. All the pain started when they finished killing me. I tried to hold in a scream unsuccessfully. It hurt so badly when it all came rushing on you like that.

"I hope you've learned your lesson from all this, Elaina. This shouldn't happen, all you have to do is listen and everything should move fairly smoothly." James said kneeling down offering a hand to help me up but he was still in his scary looking so I moved away. James disappeared when I did that, then all of a sudden something like a shoe smashed into the bottom of my rib that sent me flying into the steel walls of the cage. When my body slid out of the new dent James had just made with my body, I landed on my hands and knees but started coughing.

I stared down at the back of my hands that were now covered in my own blood, and began reacting almost in an embarrassed manor. I looked up at Ally and tried cleaning any trace of blood from my face and hands, franticly wiping it on my dress. To Alec, my overly worrisome reaction was because of fear and because of that, this was a victory to him. With the approval of Alec, James appeared in front of me kneeling once again.

He looked like he was going to caress my face; his face looked so pure and sweet... if you haven't guessed he was out of his demon form. Instead he grabbed my neck and lifted me off the ground. He started morphing back into the demon again. I was shivering too petrified to do anything more than shiver.

"What's the matter? You aren't *scared* of me *are* you?" James hissed.

Yeah, that? That scared me. "Y-y-y-y..." I couldn't say yes.

"Come on, Elaina! Spit it out!" He growled.

"y-y- yes... I am scared o-of you..." I said.

"Really?" James asked as he pushed harder.

He was just toying with me. God forbid James just backed off after a simple surrender. He had to push it a good five steps past that.

He knew I was scared of him, and he knew what he did hurt. I tried to hold back any sound that indicated pain but as I have been this entire time unsuccessful of doing anything right and sadly enough, with every failed attempt to hold back pain, I made it just that much better for my tormentor.

"Am I hurting you, Elaina?" James asked.

I didn't reply. I refused to let out any further sign of weakness.

"Elaina, I've told you once to just simply oblige. Don't make me tell you again."

"Yes."

Why does that even matter to him? Why does he always feel the need to toy with me? It's so inconvenient for everyone. He is toying with me, right? That just seems so... wrong to do. I asked myself.

"Impartial enough for you Alec? Is this good enough for you?"

"James," Alec began.

"I hope you'll forgive me at some point of your timeless life." James mocked tossing me to Alec as If I was some kind of rag doll. "Tell me I can't do my job again, *Alec*." Then James took his time walking over and then we were teleported away, back to Scorn's fortress.

"Hello, James, Elaina, Alec... Human. Where were you all?" Scorn asked as we stepped out of the black hole.

"S-S-S-S-Scorn... we- we..." James stuttered.

Scorn even scares James!

"This will take too long. Elaina, tell me what happened." Scorn ordered.

What, Elaina? She'll do worse than rat us out! She'll lie to get us in more trouble! Alec thought.

I glared at Alec then told him telepathically *You'd deserve that, wouldn't you.* Alec then, looked away shamefully. "Scorn, it was my fault... When my friends treated me as they did, James and Alec took me back to my room. To make sure that nothing bad could happen they sealed the room... when they left I couldn't hold in my rage anymore and I turned all demon like...

I started banging myself around until the seal broke... then I... grew wings and flew out the window... James and Alec knew immediately that I was gone and came after me... Ally's human team caught up with me before James and Alec did and used spirit cuffs to stop me from being in demon form and they used the spirit cuffs to tie me to a wall and left me there to die...

Soon after wards I accidentally revealed Ally for a Cheuvean and they left her to die with me... Then Alec and James came to rescue us from dying where I discovered that I am immortal... I told them that I wouldn't go without a fight and so they… well that's why I'm so… messed up. Please don't punish them, Scorn it wasn't their fa-" I was interrupted.

I made up every piece of that story… it was obvious too. Cheuveans don't have wings and I said I grew wings. And now that I'm thinking about it, I probably should have just come up with the story that after I thought I lost my friends, I went to go retrieve Ally. It would have been shorter, sweeter, and a lot more believable.

"Did I ask whose fault it was? No, I didn't. I hope you realized you will be punished tonight." Scorn said.

"Yes, Scorn." I replied.

"No, I'm not talking to you, sweetie. James and Alec, you're going to die tonight."

"What?" Alec blurted out. "How is she *our* fault? She's your kid!"

"Alec, stop." James whispered under his breath.

"James is right, Alec. Hey, you both broke many rules today… Let's throw Eric into your shit. Closed discussion. Any more talking about the topic will result in more severe consequences. Now James, Alec, go with Elaina up to her room and stay there." Scorn said.

"Yes, Scorn." James said.

We were teleported to my room in the next few seconds… it was completely silent for a while until I said, "James, Alec, I'm so-" I was cut off by Alec.

"Shut up! It's your fault we're in this mess! It always is! You're lucky I don't destroy you where you stand!" Alec said beginning to get into his demon form. But then James sprang into action pouncing on Alec until he calmed down.

"Alec, she saved us from a life of torture. She could have told him a lie, and she could have told him the truth, but she chose to make a story to make us look good." James glanced at me. "Even if we don't grow wings..."

"Okay, Brother..." Alec said.

"Is there anything I can do before..?" It was so hard to say the word *die* now; I guess death was almost incomprehensible to me after knowing that I could never experience it.

"No, you have done enough," Alec spat coldly. "Don't you think?"

James rephrased what Alec had said, "No, thank you though. You put yourself in danger for us which came in a big surprise. That's all you needed to do for me... you tried." James said helping me up.

"Not like you really have anything to give anyways, Elaina."

"Are you done?" James asked. "Or are you honestly going to spend the remainder of your life sulking in the corner?"

He can be so nice but in an instant become so cruel...

My head began pounding; I dropped to the floor grasping my head, trying to protect it from the world's worst headache.

"Elaina, what's the problem?" James asked and then he dropped and we both blacked out.

<u>World Beyond</u>
"Elaina?" James called. "Where did we go?"

I sat there and watched James from a far. I couldn't go closer no matter how hard I tried. And then I saw my body appear in front of James.

"Hey, Blazin'." My body spoke.

"Oh... My god, Rissa!"

I got ejected from my own body so Rissa could speak to James. "Yeah, it's all me! So... This is what being human feels like. It's different. I like it."

"I've missed you."

"I miss you."

"We can be together soon." James laughed. "Scorn's going to kill us."

"No!" My body turned sharply to face him, "You can't leave her. Don't do to her what you did to me."

"I don't care about her though."

"You hear that, incarnate? He says he cares not for you." She was speaking to me. "But James, my essence will be erased soon. Once my Dad tries to kill you, I'll have to protect you. You know that. And when I do, I'll leave Lady Incarnate."

"Don't do it then!" James shouted.

163

"Do you think she won't do it? She's got pieces of me in her. James, don't deny your feelings just because we've spoken."

"That's... not the case."

"C'mon, Blazin'. Get a grip! You need to wake up now anyways. And girly, you know what I mean when I talk about feelings, don't you? Don't mess with fate." My body smiled, sitting back carelessly. "I'm pretty happy it's you taking me over, Cheeks. I've been watchin' you and you seem pretty cool. But hey, when you release me, make sure you don't let HER take over. There are three of us now, ya know. And girly, don't you be afraid to use me just because my existence will cease to exist. We'll both die if you don't. It's part of your transformation. The sacrifice of a piece of you needs to be made."

James and I sprung up at the sounds of Scorn's voice echoing off of the walls in my room, demanding that we come down for the execution. James and Alec began fading away and then it hit me. My fate slapped me in the face and I ran up to James, who was still in shock, struggling to stand, and cried, "Don't leave me again!"

The missing light came into his eyes, he looked down at me and said, "I wouldn't think of it."

My room faded in our visions until it could unnoticeably morph into Scorn's room of death.

Eric was waiting for us in the far corner of the completely empty, large room, "How... how are we going to die?"

"It will be a slow process of my specialty." Scorn explained.

"Oh... I see..."

James's spine disintegrated at the sight of Scorn. They were expected to take their demise in what they would consider "honorable". I called it cowardly. They were just too afraid to fight for their life!

I asked in a disgusting manor, "No... No! How can you all just give up?"

James just looked at me and shook his head in disappointment. He felt I should take their demise with "honor" too.

It's just easier this way. He thought.

"You need to shut up, Rissa." Scorn turned to me. "Or you will share their fate."

"It's like you think I'm scared or something. Bring it! I have someone awesome backing me."

"James?"

"What? No."

"Let's see then!" Scorn laughed. He shot this darkened whip at me. I was prepared to guard myself, but James jumped in front of me.

"You aren't doing this, Elaina." James shouted.

"This is easily fixable..." Scorn mused, having his whip wrap around James, flinging him across the room.

The yelling in terror began. Eric dropped and was being killed. Soon after, Alec began to wail in pain but James wasn't crying out in pain. He dropped to his knees, using every bit of his strength to not cry out. I couldn't just sit there; it was too hard to just watch and listen. "Come now, Eliana. No more distractions. Show me what you got." On sheer instinct I was charging at Scorn and somehow my anger and fear was enough to turn me into what I hated most.

I momentarily stepped out of my body allowing... someone else to take over. She quietly murmured to herself, "Scorn... Long time no see. But this time you will die tonight; *this time* I will make sure of it!"

Some white light shaped like the triquetra with black lights twisting around the figure was shot at Scorn. I suppose that the attack was really in my benefit but what I found was that I was struggling to keep hold of my humanity.

Elaina, you have to stop it! Don't let her take hold of you! Rissa shouted in my head. *It's time for me to peace out, 'kay Cheeks? You've got this.*

I didn't want this thing taking hold of me because of the feeling I got; I felt nothing. Nothing mattered to me anymore except his suffering and after being destroyed by a guy whose prime activity consisted of making people suffer, why would I want to *become* that? It was a struggle to break free from such power that held in its palms around every thought in your mind, every muscle in your body, and also had the key to unlocking every last drop of your power. I had to keep my own hold of the situation in any way possible but I wasn't quite expecting that once I kicked the demon out it would be such an issue for me to spontaneously stop an attack.

I suppose I expected everything to be easy like it seemed in movies. I figured it would be more of an if I think it, it'll happen type of deal. But it was then that I realized that your mind is connected to your power and the amount of trained mental power that goes into everything Cheuveans were *supposed* to be able to do completely surpassed my ability.

I started concentrating to make it stop and my power exploded wounding both me and Scorn. It all happened so fast. It hurt me, it hurt Scorn (I think) and then, somehow, something happened to Scorns attack to make it all of its magnitude go on Eric.

"How do I make that stop?"

I glanced at Alec and James were beginning to get up, struggling to live by the looks of it. *They're no help...*

Thank god for creativity: I thought that *maybe* if I made my power stop I could at least change the target of Scorn's attack... so I started concentrating on making Scorn's attack go against him and all of a sudden, after a massive headache, I felt relived.

Scorn's attack turned on him! Scorn began fighting against his own attack with all his strength giving me a chance to escape with everything I could scavenge. Alec and James were up now just staring at what I had just done.

"What are you waiting for? Get Eric and let's *go*!" I shouted hastily heading for the hole in the wall my explosion created.

Alec ran to get Eric, "Got it!"

James appeared at my side, "Elaina, you aren't looking so awesome. Everything alright?"

I looked him in the eyes and told him, "Catch me when I fall."

I fell into another time hollow which took me back to a forest where I saw a girl that looked just like me but younger and you could tell she was a Cheuvean; she was far too beautiful to be human. That must be Rissa. I decided glancing at her frilly, oversized, outdated pink frilly dress that looked as though it were from the seventeen hundreds. She was attempting to make something come out of the ground, trying being the key word.

Another older girl, Zenon, sat in a vine throne off to the Rissa's side overseeing her every movement with a jealous, judgmental glare.

"Come on little sister, I know you can do it! Just do it as I told you."

"But, Seenon, it's too harwd! I'm supposou learn that when I am older like you." Rissa wasn't very good at talking. I suppose that even though she was obviously very young, I expected her to be perfect. After all, she was a full blood Cheuvean.

Zenon leaned forward in fake, forced disbelief. "Oh, please. Don't play this game, Rissa. You're the Chosen, right? You can do anything apparently... or should I tell Mother about that little mishap in the village with Nearo."

"But Seenon... it was an asident; you know it was an asident, you were there." Rissa pleaded in fear, "What was I espected to do? I didn't mean to kiwl him... Peez don't tell Mazar."

"ZE-NON. The chosen one can't even speak properly. It should have been me, you know. I was born first; I'm better than you. Maybe you should give me Yuna, you can't concentrate with that thing here."

Funny... *I thought aloud,* I didn't see that stuffed animal in her arms earlier.

"Yuna, run! Hide!" Rissa tossed Yuna off as far as she could and Yuna tried to take off but Zenon was too good for that. Vines shot from the ground, pinning Yuna on the ground. "Did you think you could hide her? When a rax is dominantly florescent pink

with black paws and a black tipped tail, where do you think she could go in a GREEN forest that I control?"

"No! Seenon, you're howrting Yuna! Let her go Seenon! Pease!" The little girl screamed.

"Hush! Unless you want someone to hear us in the forbidden woods and tell our mother! Look, Rissa your big sister is telling you to do something so you need to do it. I'll take real good care of this thing for you… don't worry." Zenon hissed unwinding the vines that held Yuna, and picking her up by the back of her neck.

"Yes, Siser… I'm sorry Yuna… Don't worry. We can play together when my sister gives you back. I'll work extra hard so big Siser won't keep you wong." Rissa said.

"No, Ria." Yuna growled sticking her midnight black retractable claws into Zenon's arm as her hot pink fox-like tail wrapped around her chest and cat-like body viciously twisted and turned trying to break free of Zenon. "This isn't fair. She isn't fair to you!"

Ooh my god. That isn't a stuffed animal.

"Get this stupid thing to shut up or I'll lock it in the dungeon."

Yuna stared at Rissa fiercely, "Ria!"

"Gib me one more chance, Seenon. If I can't do it, you can take Yuna."

"Listen, Rissa, recite the lesson, steps, and what you're making." Zenon said sitting on a stump. "You'll be able to do it." How helpful for me.

"Yes, Siser. To make a spirit cuff you need to put your hand to whatever substance you are holding the person to, pointer finer one side of the pesons wist or ankle with da west of your finers and tumb on the uder side of the wist or ankol. Dis teneek can awso be oosed for howlding anyting still. So you make your spirit go to your hand, ten into de gwound. Den once a chunk of your spirit is in the gwound you use your spirit to form an infisable supstace that can hold any object or living being still for wong pewiods of time depending on how stwong dey are. Den you make de spirit shoot out of the ground and awound your supstace. White Siser?" Rissa asked.

"Yes, that is correct now show me how to do it." Zenon said.

"Okay Siser. I'll get you back, Yuna." Rissa whispered performing the technique flawlessly.

"...I didn't think you would do it." Zenon admitted quietly.

Rissa glanced at her sister briefly, "What can I say? I'm the chosen; I can appalently do anything. Pease give Yuna back to me." Rissa said.

"Rissa, you need to know something. Unfortunately, you are part of the spirit affinity. It heals as it attacks. It can cure someone if they are being possessed just by even touching them much

171

less attacking them. It's the most pure of all the elements but if you use it too much... It affects you in the opposite way. No one with this affinity has a good future in store for them."

CHAPTER ELEVEN
It s now or never. Escape now or stay forever

Dear Diary,

Right now I don't know who my friends are or who my enemies are. The line has been blurred. Right now, I'm just saving everyone and hopefully, if all goes well, my enemies will then become my friends leaving me with only one jackass to deal with.

-Elaina

The vision ended during Zenon's statement. I realized why I had that vision. I had to tie Scorn up, duh. Was that vision also a warning though?

"James, will you get my friends? Alec, take Eric and wait outside. I think I need to try out a technique I remembered." I started reciting what Rissa had said while I was doing the technique and it worked perfectly almost like the vision was specifically orchestrated for me to be able to use it then.

You have *no idea* how proud of myself I was. I looked at Scorn. He lost years to him. He looked as if he went from thirty to twenty five just because I attacked him. Funny, that was definitely the most calm I'd ever seen him. My attack probably helped that guy more than it hurt him.

I tied the spirit cuff to Scorns joints, upper arms and legs, and lower arms and legs. Then I remembered it only lasted a little while. I knew that once Scorn and began struggling, the spirit cuff would only hold him for a very limited amount of time if I was lucky.

"Look I know you guys are pissed and whatever and all but I'm going to take care of that now. Please hold hands." I spoke walking up to Drake and Anna, "You too, Ally."

She looked up surprised then cautiously walked over to my Anna while periodically looking back at me to see if I really planned on rescuing her after she tried to end me. If I wasn't desperate for allies, I don't know if I would have but no one needs to know that. Anna smiled at her and told her, "You're okay now." which caused Ally to smile back.

"Where did you go?" Anna whispered.

No one wanted to answer that. No one wanted to remember the mistakes that we've all made in regards to the past.

A massive headache then hit me. *Do as I say, I'm helping you.* A voice echoed through my head followed by a screech turning my vision black. I fell to my knees grasping my head; I wasn't knocked out. A kid, Rissa was in the darkness waiting for me. "Take them here."

"Elaina?" James's voice now echoed.

"This isn't a time hollow, get me out!" I screamed frantically. "Where are you?"

She showed me a crumbled up map of the forest in my vision with two circled areas, one being a safe haven, one was our current location.

This is where you used to be safe. Take them. You need to make sure you walk. Your stronger auras are too easily traceable. You'll remember how to get here. I don't want everything to end here; it's just getting interesting. She laughed, fading into the dark.

"What? Who?" I asked looking up at her.

Now go. The darkness instantly cleared leaving my shocked, kneeling on Scorn's floor, grasping my head.

"What just happened, Elaina?"

Rissa told me, *Forget seeing me.* and I forgot.

"I don't... James, get ready to teleport them we can provide a nice location for them to land if we do it together." I told James.

"You can teleport?" James asked.

"Maybe... well we'll just have to find out." I said.

175

We grabbed my friends but in the middle of the teleportation, something was thrown at us. It was like a small thin knife covered in some kind of green slime and went through Drake and jabbed right into Alec's back. Good news, my humans made it to the safe haven. Bad news, Drake died.

"Jean, *why*?" Alec growled tearing the knife out of his own back like a badass.

"Oh, please. As if you two couldn't tell that he was dying. His body was rejecting the change and we all know it." Jean laughed.

He was the most bitter person I've ever met. He could be in the best mood ever and he'd still be pissed at the world.

"Jean, stop! He tried to kill your brother and all of his other workers are running away! Don't you want to be on our side? Aren't you worried that Scorn will turn on *you* next?" I asked.

"No. he told me I was special! He would never betray me!" Jean said.

Laughable. "So you won't come with us?" I asked.

"No." Jean said walking towards Scorn. I looked at James as he disappeared. I don't know if I was hoping for him to do something amazing or protect us or anything. I depended on him then. I *trusted* him. James reappeared behind Jean and I didn't know what happened next because I looked away... but I knew Jean was knocked out due to the sound of a whoosh, then a yell in pain, followed by a bang, then something that sounded like a water balloon popped and all its water splattered all over the ground.

Everything was going black and I knew I was having another vision of the past. Another time hollow. This flashback was a little different though mostly because I was still in my body, I wasn't watching a recording like before. "

"Who does this poser think he is? No one has the right to call me his child except MY dad! Who is this man to call me his child?" I asked angrily.

My flashback skipped forward.

"What's happening?"

"Elaina," Andrew ordered. "Get back!"

I turned my back and ran for dear life, trying to get away but something stopped me and held me still. I had to follow the exact path of the flashback; I didn't have a choice.

Dylan slashed my chest and plunged his hand into my abdomen.

Another skip forward, James's hand was sticking through him, covered in blood and organs.

A smaller skip this time, just to where Dylan collapsed to the floor.

After that I knew what James had done to Jean… he jabbed through his stomach just like before. Then sent him flying into the broken wall sending his blood everywhere.

"What ever happened to Dylan and Andrew?" I asked.

"You remember them? Well, Scorn sent them to one of the more private prisons in Unashi as guards." Alec said.

James appeared in front of me, blood dripping from his arm.

My eyes locked on his arms, completely mesmerized in… I'm not sure if it was fear or disgust. He hid his blood covered arm behind his back, trying desperately to wipe off all remains of his violence realizing how uncomfortable it all made me "Elaina." He waited for me to look directly at his eyes, "Are you okay? You seem to be getting some… bad memories back…"

There's nothing that got to me more than James's compassionate looks. When he looked at me, it was like, he really saw me. He really cared; he really knew me.

"Yeah… We need to take Drake." I whispered.

"We can't take him, you know that." Alec argued.

"Why not? He deserves a burial."

Alec changed his approach to something more gentle, "We can't carry him away, Elaina. We don't have the time. And we have Dylan to take care of. Drake's dead, we need to move on."

"No, that's not o-"

"Elaina, look at me." I obediently stared at James fighting the urge to begin screaming. "You're going to leave Drake and never think about him again. He died, it's okay."

He made me forget Drake.

"You... you did it." James laughed continuing on a different subject. "I can't believe you beat the most powerful man in all of our worlds."

He was relieved for the first time in his life.

"Wow, wait a second. What about us? Why are we still here?" Alec asked.

"We have to walk. I think it's because we all have very distinct aura and Scorn will be specifically looking for us so if we don't use our Spirit, he can't track it, right?"

"Where exactly are we going?" James asked.

I told him "You'll see." Because I didn't know the answer. I led them towards where Rissa told me would lead us to the right place and if they knew that, I figured they'd probably kill me.

We were walking for a while and then I whispered to Alec, "Did Scorn tell you about his relationship with my mom? Or about my childhood?" I asked.

Random, but I had to know about her. She apparently knew all about me, after all.

"No. Go ask James. He, if anyone would know." Alec said pushing me a couple inches towards James.

"Why would he know and not you?" I asked.

"We all figured that James was his favorite. He was trained separately from the rest of us and got bumped to the top of the ranks faster than anyone else. Scorn trusted him." He then grabbed me and threw me at James.

I almost caught myself before I hit James but I knocked him over then Alec... pushed me on top of him. I was dazed for a moment but then entirely embarrassed as I tossed myself off James.

This was the first time we all behaved like *people* again. As Alec stared at us laughing hysterically, I grabbed some mud off the ground and threw it at Alec's face. Alec almost looked angry and began to seer but that was soon overcome by laughter and the happiness we had long forgotten. We laughed and joked like the children we were instead of fought like the robots we were raised to become.

Once we began walking again, we came to a fork in the road. *This wasn't here in the vision.*

"You look confused." James finally asked, "Where are we going? Don't say 'You'll see.' I want to know where we are going."

"It's a safe haven." I said. "I can't explain how I would know, but I just know that it's safe."

James humored me, "Okay... Wouldn't Scorn know its location?"

"No. I don't think even Scorn knows." I said. "Rissa found that to be a safe place once upon a time... I think we should go right. Let's go right."

We knew that we were on the right track when we passed by plants that weren't dead. The closer we got to a safe place, the happier things seemed to look until we reached a giant trench that was pinned up against a canyon wall.

I stared uneasily at the trench until I could force out any form of verbal communication. "Well, here we are."

"*What?* You're nuts! You just brought us here to push us into a trench and *kill* us?" Alec yelled grabbing the neck of my shirt.

"Alec, take a second to think. Why I would have taken the trouble to walk you all the way down here if I was planning on killing you? Why I wouldn't have tried to kill you or just have chained you to the ground with Scorn. I don't care if you come, I really don't; stay here if you'd like. Now, before you toss me into the trench, ask yourself one last question. Would you rather have certain death, or would you rather have a chance of freedom?"

Alec and James looked at each other momentarily, having another silent conversation. Alec replied, "That's what you told your friends when you convinced them to go to Scorn and look how that turned out."

"I still stand by my decision. They would have died if they were sent to the humans. Now let me go. I actually *want* my freedom." I said. "Besides, you guys would have found us anyway. My decision would have had the same end result."

"Can we trust you?" James asked.

I turned to James and looked straight into his eyes, working for the most sincere look I could possibly force out. "Why wouldn't you?" Then turned back towards the trench and jumped.

"Shit, Elaina!" I heard Alec shout from above.

That was what got me thinking. I don't float; I don't have Cheuvean bones. I would go splat at the end of the trench but I wasn't all that worried. Alec's shout meant that one of the two would be waiting at the bottom for me because they realized that I'm not built for cliff diving off of the top of a trench where we couldn't even see the bottom.

I closed my eyes, waiting for them to rescue me. I didn't have a doubt in my mind that I wouldn't be caught at the bottom and just like I suspected, James was there for me. "You're an idiot. You could have been hurt."

I replied, "I thought about that after I jumped." As though that was going to make me sound any less idiotic.

James laughed gently and set me on the floor. I expected it to be a little darker at the bottom of a trench, but the walls were lit up with scattered gems. "They're pretty, aren't they?" James asked.

"Yeah, they are. What are they?"

"No one really knows. Some things are better left undiscovered, don't you think?"

He was referring to something that just went straight over my head; he was referring to something he'd done with Rissa long before. "Did Alec decide not to come?" I asked changing the subject to something I could understand. "I thought he jumped."

"He's scouting the path ahead. We don't want to run into trouble with two handicaps."

"Which we will be." Alec appeared at in the hall that lead into the labyrinth . "Where are we?"

"I think it's some sort of a short cut portal from the human world to Cheuva. I doubt it's been used for a few thousand years so I suppose the *trouble* should have been expected." I said.

"These in-between worlds, Elaina are referred to as Septima. They're one dimension that is separated by our Human and Cheuvean worlds." James informed me.

"How fast can you two run with Eric on you?" I asked. "Can we make it?"

"We can run but not as fast as we normally can." Alec said.

"Great. Can I see him really quick?" I said. James and Alec looked at each other.

"Okay, seriously? *Why* would I kill him after all this time?" I said. They handed Eric over to me, needless to say.

"His pulse is not as good as it should be. He's cold too. Is he going to die?" I remember how in like, third grade my school taught us how to check a pulse. Who knew that would ever come in handy?

"Be careful. There's something really big in there... or actually a lot of big some things." Alec warned leading the way as James and I followed closely behind.

I was about to move a branch sticking out of one of the vine covered, stone walls that was blocking the pathway when James's hand wrapped around mine. "Don't touch *anything*, Elaina." James warned.

"Why? It's just a branch."

"This place is not as sweet as it looks. It's cursed; it's dangerous... Watch." Alec stopped moving, picked up a rock from the floor and dropped it on the branch and at the moment the rock grazed it, the branch wrapped itself around the rock and pulled it into the vines. That rock was long gone. "We can't save you if you touch that."

"But this place looks so peaceful..." I murmured glancing around my surroundings. The vines, with scattered flowers of all colors that covered the marble walls that created this maze and the crystals on the walls lit the room with a glowing, dim bliss. How could anything so gorgeous be so dangerous?

I passed by Alec and turned the corner, "WHAT IN THE-" I began. James slammed his hand onto my mouth.

"Shut up." James hissed.

"What is that?" I asked "It's... sort of like a minotaur but... different."

"It's bigger, faster, instead of horns on its head it has razor sharp teeth, and... by the looks of it a lot stronger. Instead of being half bull and half man its half... half wolf and half man. It's a lot smarter too." James explained.

And this was the point that I realized that everything from human history, no matter how absurd, is part true like these things that resembled the minotaur from Greek mythology. Just one thing I wished that the Greeks would have mentioned... They were armed with swords and spears.

"Behind the wall. Go." Alec shoved me behind them. "Stay here."

CHAPTER TWELVE
Blind leading blind

Dear Diary,

Right now I'm stuck in another in-between-worlds passage and it's FILLED with monsters. Weird. Makes me wonder what else is real that my kind always dismissed as myth or rumor or even just lies. I suppose I'm feeling alright about it all though. James and Alec are here with me and I'm sure that they're going to protect me. I mean, they have to. I'm their only way out.

I'm kind of seeing them in a new light. As I'm sitting here on a rock, writing in the memory of my brother, they're standing a few feet away from me just... chatting. Nothing weird or violent like what I'd usually expect. The ground's shaking a bit. I don't know what's going on. I should go.

-Elaina

"What's happening?" I asked tossing my journal on the floor. What was the use of keeping it on my person? It followed me everywhere I slept anyways.

"It's just moving. It's heavy enough to make the ground shake. Alec, how do we get around it?"

"It?" I wondered aloud.

"We have to take a different path. Maybe we missed something on the way here?" I thought out loud.

"Well, no harm in checking it out." James laughed quietly.

I turned and stared at what stood behind me both scared and intrigued. As the closest one to it, I could see every incredibly intimidating feature perfectly. It's grey, thick as needle fur, stood on end with fury as his rotting breath visibly clouded the air in front of him with a ferocious snarl but not to worry, it's glowing, blood red eyes made it easy to spot through the fog that the monster creates. "Back isn't an option, guys." Alec whispered.

James sighed quietly, "Thanks, man. I don't know where we'd be without 'cha."

Alec and James disappeared leaving me to stare down the beast. Not to worry, though. In half a moment I heard James hiss "Elaina! Damn, it, keep up!" and began being tugged at a much faster speed than I could keep up with through the maze hoping James had a decent idea of where he was going.

"James, I'm human! I can't do this; I can't keep up with you!"

You'll do what needs to be done and if you can't do it on your own, I'll help.

We stopped for a moment; I turned to him, confused. "What?"

"You're impossible! UGH!" He grunted grabbing my hand and tugging me with him again.

Unfortunately, we ran straight into two of the beasts and it was perfectly apparent they were aware of our presence and neither intended to allow us to leave this mid-world in one piece. We had to go through one of two minotaurs which were both staring at us ready to kill us. "Can't go around it, can't go over or under it... Let's go through it." Alec smiled at James.

"A-V-J?" James replied.

Alec nodded. "You know it."

"Don't move." James told me. He disappeared and Alec began charging straight at the smaller of the two. He held the minotaur still while James came from behind slicing it in half, watching it burn into ash.

The larger one, after seeing his... friend, comrade, fellow monster get attacked and killed seem to only infuriate him further, pushing him to charge straight at me. I shouted in fear, "Stay back!"

and put my arms up to block him. A transparent wall appeared in front of me, protecting us from it.

Aggravated, the minotaur began ramming the wall. After every hit the minotaur did, the wall changed to a redder color which meant that the wall was getting weaker after every hit. Finally, the minotaur saw the pattern. It backed up and prepared for a charge. "Elaina, let's *go!*" Alec shouted.

I turned to Alec and began running behind his slowed pace while trying to avoid any direction that there may be any signs of things that would want to kill us until we hit a fork in the road. "Which way?" I asked.

"Wait, weren't *you* leading *us*?" James asked.

"I knew we were supposed to jump in the ditch, nothing more." I laughed nervously.

Alec sighed. "Wonderful. Left." He began running down the left path while James and I followed.

Alec turned a corner and found an overly massive minotaur. *Shoot.* I thought looking up at it. Immediately, James and Alec turned around and sprinted in the opposite direction and James, instinctively grabbed me and soared me along. That one, however was smarter than the rest.

Instead of chasing after us, he roared to alert all the other monsters in the area that they had intruders and they needed to eliminate of the problem. We were running for our lives from things that were even faster than James and Alec were and to James and Alec, that was incredibly unusual. They were struggling to keep ahead and keep two handicaps safe. I only saw blurs of people running: the moment James let go of my hand, I was lost and left far behind. I was just too slow to keep up with it all; after all, I was only human. How could I keep up with their speed?

One of the minotaurs ran at me with every intent of killing me. I ran in the opposite direction, trying to... I don't even know what. I knew I wasn't fast enough to escape. There was no way out but just before the minotaur hit me, James ran by and knocked me out of the way.

"Stay with us!" He hissed.

"You guys are too fast! And I'm tired, James."

He picked me up and ran to find Alec. Within moments of what seemed like light speed blurs of colors, we were next to Alec, standing in plain sight, no longer worried about anything. "You are such dead weight..." Alec muttered.

"Sorry, I'm human. I can't do what you guys do."

"Where are we supposed to go?" James asked.

"I don't know..." I replied.

"You lead us here without knowing where to go?" Alec growled.

I smiled, "Yes." I looked around and noticed that this area of the maze was circular which, in my experience, usually meant something important was here. "Where are we?"

"The middle of the maze." Alec said. "Why?"

I looked around for a little more and noticed the only thing in the circle other than the three of us was a well. "What's that well for?"

"To get water?" James replied.

"For *what*? There's nothing else in here."

James got up to inspect the well. "Elaina, c'mere."

"What's up?"

James grabbed my hand, placing it on the well in a hand imprint that was just a touch too large for mine and now covered in vines. Everything around me became black like when I talked to Rissa but less painful. "James! What the hell is this?"

"Wait through it, I'm not there with you, I don't know what it is." James responded.

An illusion of Zenon appeared, touching the well where my hand now laid. "Rissa, if you're listening to this, then I didn't make it. I can't handle this anymore. I'm too tired of running, too tired of hiding. Scorn gave me an alternative, you know? I can be human. It's not ideal, I know. But he'd never have an excuse to come after me again. I'm sorry I left you. I'm taking the easy way out just like always. I suggest you do the same. There is no winning this war." She sighed and walked away from the well momentarily. *"You won't give up, will you? The exit is in the well. I hope you get everything you've worked for, Rissa. I'm done."*

I wished I could feel something emotional from that. It was like I was obligated to be sad but really, I didn't care. I got the information I needed. "The exit's at the bottom of the well."

"Do you know how to swim in our water in this realm?" Alec said.

"Isn't it like normal water?" I asked.

"All you have to do is let out spirit and you'll sink under water and if you stop letting out spirit then… you'll crystalize." Alec explained.

"Oh that's good. Now I feel safe." I laughed bitterly, sitting on the well.

"Well let's go. Scorn can still sense us until we get to the other side of Lake Leta." James urged me gently.

"Lake Leta?" I asked.

"The lake this particular portal will lead to is going to lead us through Lake Leta. This was once a sacred place before Zenon disappeared."

"You knew her?"

"Well enough." James smiled weakly. "Go. I need you in front of me in case you need us."

I was the first to get to the bottom of the well and I noticed that there was a hole in the side of the well that was large enough to swim through.

I knew that was our ticket out. And by that, I mean I really hoped that was our way out and if it wasn't we were doomed. I swam through the hole blindly, praying this was our way out. *You're smallest, Elaina. I can't fit through here with him on me.* Alec thought giving me Eric under water. *Do not let go of him, okay? If you let go, he dies.* No pressure.

When I was letting out my spirit, it was going through Eric and then got let out through him. Confusing, but that's how James explained it to me. We could breathe under this water, see perfectly, and hear each other's thoughts at the price of being able to speak out loud. As time passed, I noticed it was beginning to get more and more difficult to breathe but I said nothing assuming that it was my own imagination.

Eric is draining our spirit; I'm sure of it. If this keeps up we'll all die! Alec thought. That would be the reason that it was getting more difficult to swim.

WHAT? Why? How? I thought.

Let him go. We can't risk our own lives for this one. Alec decided.

You're kidding, right? We'll get through this. I... I'll think of a plan. I thought.

Is that so? Because you've obviously mastered this world in the little time you've been here!

I'm telling you, I'll take care of it.

Yeah, okay but if I die I will have my ghost come after you. Alec thought.

James intervened, *Well it won't come to that, now will it, Elaina.*

I hope not... I thought.

Things began getting dark. *OH YES! Perfect timing.*

"Rissa you're doing wrong! You let out your power too early. You KNOW that hurts your soul every time you do that. Hold it in longer." Zenon told her.

"But Zenon, I don't want it to explode when I hold it too long." Rissa said. *She could talk much better but still wouldn't let go of the animal that seemed to always have with me as Rissa.*

Rissa, I know that you can do it! You can do anything! I believe in you. *Yuna cheered through Rissa's mind. Now even Yuna could talk... think better.*

"Come on Rissa, you're eleven years old now. I know you can do it."

"Okay Zenon. I'll do it for you." Rissa said.

She inhaled deeply, stuck out her hand and concentrated briefly as a ball formed in her hand she held it for a few seconds and then shot it then it exploded four yards away from her. Though it wasn't perfect, it was good enough for Zenon.

Zenon picked Rissa up and began hugging her. "You did it Rissa! I told you could do it!"

"I'm happy you pushed me to do that Zenon. I really am." She said hugging her back.

"Now, what else can you do that technique with?" Zenon asked.

Rissa replied, "Fire, Water, Air, and the most amazing: spirit."

"Good job, little Sister. Soon you'll even be able to master it." Said Zenon with a sweet smile on her face. Rissa smiled back but soon her smile turned into a frown.

"I'm sorry, Zenon."

"Why, Rissa? You did excellent. I'm proud of you." Zenon said.

"No, not because of that... I know how you really wanted to be the chosen one... and I took that from you. That's why you were so mean to me all those years ago, right? Why are you so nice now? I know you STILL want to be the chosen one." She said.

"I've grown up, Rissa. I got over the fact that you are the chosen. All I can do is help you for fill your destiny and cheer from the sidelines. Maybe that was my destiny all along..." Normally I would call bull on Zenon but she had changed since the last time I'd seen her; she cared less about her unnatural appearance like she accepted herself more for who she was instead of who she was by birth right expected to become. "Now tell me, what will happen

if you put too much spirit in the Spirit Ball then hold the spirit Ball too long?" Zenon asked continuing her lesson.

"It will blow up, hurt you really bad, and send you flying far away from where you are?" She asked.

"Yes, very good little sister. I'm proud of you." Zenon smiled.

As I faded back into reality, I knew what I had to do. *James, Alec, transport near all of your spirit into me! Just keep enough to stay alive for long enough to reach the surface of the water via explosion.* I thought.

Without arguing both of the boys transported all their spirit to me. I could barely see the point where the water ended but I had to try... I started making a spirit ball and began to understand what Rissa and Zenon explained about the pain of my own spirit being damaged; after the ball started getting bigger than it should, I could feel it eating at the rest of my body. To give an idea of how large that would be, Rissa shot a ball the size of a basketball and at that time, I was shooting one the size of a semi.

I held it with one hand while the other was still holding onto Eric, keeping him alive. I held the spirit ball longer and longer until it exploded. I tried to shield James, Alec, and Eric as best as I could and while I did that successfully, I forgot to shield myself. The force of the spirit explosion sent us shooting out of the water and onto land, and for some reason, I didn't expect it to hurt so very much. We were all knocked out for hours but we were finally in Cheuva making everything worth it.

James was the first to wake up. He walked over to Alec to try to get him to wake but instead, Alec started to make sounds of pain.

No... James thought uneasily. *No, that can't be.*

James appeared next to me and began shaking me, "Elaina, Elaina! Wake up!"

"Ouch not so hard... James, what's the problem?"

"We need to get where we're going. Alec is in pain. I don't know what the problem is. I tried everything to get him to wake up. I'm afraid Scorn has hold of his mind." James said. "You know his tactics better, can't you take a look?"

"I know him best? He's known you longer." I said.

Frantically glancing back and forth at me and Alec, James explained, "*Rissa* knew him better than I did."

I looked up at him, "I'm not Rissa."

"You are part of her. Think. You'll figure it out."

"Let me take a look." I began trying to stand and collapsed in pain. *I should be dead. If I was human, I would be dead.*

"Elaina, you don't look so hot yourself. Come to think of it, you took most of the blow... Must have hurt. I'll bring Alec over here so you can take a look." James said.

He almost sounded concerned for a moment.

"Did you try to read his mind yet?" I asked.

"How is that going to get him to wake up?" James asked.

"Did you or not?" I repeated.

"No but... If what you're thinking is correct, if you do that, Scorn'll have you in there too." He began.

"James, shhhhh." I said putting my finger to my lip. I put my hand to Alec's head, closed my eyes and started reading deep in his thoughts with the best of my ability.

Next thing I knew, I was in a dungeon built specifically for Alec. Dark, steel walls covered in memories of his past played as I walked by them. I heard yelling echoing off of the walls which, knowing that Scorn fabricated this place specifically for dreams, vastly narrowed down the amount of people the shouts could have come from.

I opened the only door in the dream arena, stepped through, and leaned against the wall for my own security praying that the more distance I kept from Scorn, the lower chance there was of me being caught. I closed my eyes, ecstatic that Scorn hadn't seen me yet – short lived happiness though. Alec's body was tossed at the wall next to me and narrowly missed me.

Scorn, stared right at right at me, but couldn't see me presumably meaning that since the dream wasn't meant for me, I wasn't really in the dream; there was a veil separating dream from spectator.

Alec apologized, completely out of breath, "I...I'm sorry Scorn ..." He said that after every single hit Scorn threw at him.

I couldn't control myself. "What are you doing? Fight back! Alec, c'mon!" I screamed. Then I remembered that no one could hear me... except... if anyone *could* hear me, it would be Scorn.

"Ahhh, so Elaina entered your mind, eh?" Scorn said.

"Shit. Elaina, get out of here! Quick, before he gets to you too!" Alec shouted in every direction helplessly looking for me.

"Come on Elaina. Don't be a coward. You'll eventually get caught and I'm sure you know that so why not suck up to me *before* you get caught so you don't have such a hard time in... jail." Scorn said.

"I can't run away yet, Scorn. I won't leave without Alec."

"And? There's more. A question, maybe?"

"Why does your ex-wife want me?"

"Okay Elaina but you have to promise me something. Will you do that for your father?" Scorn asked pretending to be like the good dad that he wasn't.

"No." I said. Plain and simple. I refused to do anything for this man.

"Please?" He asked.

"Not without knowing what you want first."

"Well I guess there's no helping that... so you really want to know?" Scorn asked.

"Yes." I said.

"No." Scorn said mimicking my voice. That was a waste of a conversation... I turned to Alec.

"Well, let me take Alec, at least." I asked.

"You can take him when I let him out. It's not up to him or you. You can do all you want. Make potions, transfer all your spirit to him, it doesn't matter. Resistance is futile, my dear Elaina. Now, get out." He said.

At Scorn's cue, the image of the medieval dungeon retreated back into my mind causing me to wake up in the real world with James at my side looking as worried as he could get. "W-what's going on? Was it Scorn?" He asked.

I stared at him apologetically, "I-I'm so sorry. I couldn't do anything. We... I think we just need to get to the place."

"Did you end up talking to him about your mom? I heard you and Alec earlier." James asked.

"He didn't tell me anything... I GOT IT! Come on I'll explain on the way to the place."

We were on our way, mostly focused on running. I forgot all about the conversation that I had earlier.

"Continue with your little half statement, Elaina." James reminded me.

"Oh, that's right. Sorry, I totally forgot. When I was younger, my human mom would tell me stories about Cheuva. She told me about a god named Ri. She did something to make him willingly evil. Well I was thinking that his goal was, and still is, to do the same to me as the evil god did to him." I said.

"And what did happen to him?" James asked.

"When Ri made Scorn willingly evil. Scorn wanted me to become willingly evil... willingly his minion... but now, his plans have been foiled! Now there is no way I will ever cooperate with him." I said laughing. Of course I was just taking an educated guess, but hey, it was better than nothing and definitely made me feel more comfortable with my little thoughts. And truthfully, I didn't have much to live for if it weren't to get revenge on him. The thing that was keeping me going was that I was trying to destroy his plans.

When I was younger, I had plenty of dreams about Scorn. I had dreams about how some of this came to be. Maybe that was Ri's gift to me.

James and I were running at my speed, deeper into the forest until James pointed out a sign reading, "This area is off limits. Enter the Forbidden Woods, and you will suffer the consequences."

I looked at the sign that in my opinion it seemed insignificant.

"What? You've taken me to the impossible woods?" James asked.

Impossible Woods is also, more commonly known as, The Forbidden Woods.

"Don't worry. I know my way around here. I use to play here when I was Rissa. There's a strong possibility that not even Scorn knows his way around here." I said.

"But if we get lost here..." James began.

"Yes, I know. You turn into a walking scarecrow until you die. I know the tale... and I know it's true. But don't worry. As long as you don't get lost you'll be fine." I said.

"How would you know it's true? That's just a legend that our parents told us as Cheuvean kids to keep us from running into the woods." James asked.

"I don't know how I know. I just kind of assumed that every story I've heard as a kid that has to do with magic is true. But I don't re-" I began.

My body was getting the shaky feeling. I heard a familiar sound. The edges of my eyes were getting dark. It was happening. I was experiencing another time hollow.

I was in the forbidden woods with Zenon, Rissa, and some other girls. I could see then why Scorn took my friends in the beginning. The girls Rissa was once friends with were the same ones I befriended on earth. Anna was really a shell for the girl named Alima from Cheuva and Ali was a shell for Nala. Alima, looking like Anna's spitting image, was holding a tiger polar bear mix called a tiber who was mind talking to Rissa's rax who was walking alongside them. In a separate group following closely behind were two girls named Nala and Mashka were talking about the boys in the imperial city. It was easy to tell everything about them with that first glance. They were both dressed in some ridiculous outfit that seemed to overdue everything about it. Their hair had too many ponytails and pigtails and braids and their dresses... They should have gotten some kind of award for being Cheuva's most tacky people. At least I hope that was as bad as it got.

Then behind them was Zenon and a girl named Ameri. Ameri looked very nice and pretty. Her dress was purple, her hair was blonde, her eyes were blue, and she wore her hair down.

"Okay Rissa, where are you taking us?" Zenon asked.

"I'm taking you to the best place ever! No one knows about it because no one except us goes into the forbidden woods so we can keep it like, our secret, ya know? It's called the Duran Village. It's a place where there are a bunch of kids, who live in tree houses, who know how to heal just about any wound there is. It's pretty chill there. When you try to go into the village you are let in by a... virtual Duran tree. And everyone is there to greet you with hellos and stuff. And there are trees that grow fruits and two lakes you can go play in. there's even a river that runs through the village and goes into one of those

lakes and a waterfall and… Oh you'll just have to see it!" Rissa said.

"You dragged me all the way here just for that? MGs, I'm going home." Mashka spat.

I suppose that was her way of saying 'My gods.'

"Wait Mashka, you know the rumors, if you get lost-" Zenon began.

"SHUT UP, Princess! I know the idiotic rumor. I can find my way back easily. Oh Rissa don't do anything stupid with my sister around okay? I know it will be hard for you to do and all but I can still hope. L-O-SER, what does that spell? LOSER!" Mashka laughed to herself skipping obnoxiously away.

"Issues." Alima said. "That girl SO has issues." Ameri finished. They laughed.

They come to a pin sized hole in the ground that you would never notice unless you knew where it was beforehand. Rissa bent down and touched the hole and a hologram popped up. "Welcome Rissa and friends, what business might thee have in our land?" The hologram asked.

He's a giant tree…

"Hey Duran. My friends and I have come here just for a small visit and we brought some balls to play with." Rissa said.

"May thee never change, Rissa? Might thou always be overcome with such joy?" Duran's hologram asked.

Rissa let out a laugh. "I sure hope so, Duran. Will you let us in now?"

"Yes, Princess Rissa. As you wish." Duran said.

"Thank you, Duran. Appreciate it." Rissa said doing a curtsy in the dress she was wearing.

Duran laughed and said, "Do not pretend, Princess Rissa. Thou dost not fit the standards of an ignorant princess."

Rissa laughed. "Oh, my apologies. I should learn my manners before I talk to the oh so great Duran Tree who is said to be the King of all the Duran Children who live here!"

A greenish portal appeared next to Duran's hologram. "Touché." The portal wasn't like my portal or James's portal and completely different than Scorn's portal. Unlike our portals it showed where the portal was heading and it didn't look like a black hole that you just needed to put faith in and hope it delivers you to the correct place.

Rissa led the way into the hole, "Thanks, man!"

That was unexpected… I thought staring at the black hole just inches in front of me but, I felt someone was watching me.

"I did not tell Rissa of thy presents, young ghostly HUMAN, because you have not evil intentions. If thy art not here to burn the Duran Village down, why dost thy come to the imposable woods?" Duran asked.

I began to try to think of a good lie until Duran interrupted my thoughts with a strong, cold voice. "Do not insult me with ye lies, HUMAN! We spirit dwellers can detect HUMAN lies without thought and if thy dost attempt a lie I will inform Rissa and she will DESTROY thee. So, wouldst thee like to try again?" Duran asked.

What is it with you people and hating humans? Not all of them are so bad! I am not so bad.

"Okay Duran. That is correct, I don't have intentions to destroy your forest, although, all I really want to do is watch Rissa and her friends and see what they are doing and then go back to... my... uhm time. You see I have an ability to go back or forward in time just through my thoughts and I cannot go back without seeing what my time ability has brought me here for, now, may I please pass?" I asked.

"Yes... and ye forgot to mention... thee obtain Rissa's essence or did thee not know?" Duran asked.

"Yes, Duran I am fully aware of the fact and I didn't realize that it was your business. But, my apologies for not telling you oh Great Duran." I said.

Duran laughed. "I know thee dost not mean that HUMAN girl but I shall let it slide for now. Now, HUMAN child, complete thy mission and be gone." Duran said allowing me to enter the hole.

"You know she dies, right Duran? Rissa dies and that's why I exist." Without looking back, I told

Duran, "Duran, I do not want you as my enemy and I hope you know that also but... I also hope you will help me when you see me in the future." I said walking into the portal.

This is the first time I actually had seen that place. There was an old bridge that looked fragile but somehow still sturdy, like it had character. There were vines binding it together and the hole infested wood that probably originated from Duran himself creaked when I walked on it even though I was a practically weightless ghostly figure. I continued walking into the village through a natural arch, created from Duran's roots, that the light from above shined perfectly on setting the expectations of the Duran village to be nothing less than a haven.

Everything seemed so natural and undisturbed then. Until I came along. As soon as I actually entered the village it was actually thrilling to see it. To the left of me was a small river that ran along the edges of the village. To the right was a small forest that grew some odd looking fruit. Some looked like slices of watermelon covered in sugar or slices of lemon covered in sugar, or any other slices of fruit you can think of that are covered in sugar.

As I started to look around, this entire place looked like a crater in the ground. Somewhat like a seed shaped hole in the ground with a flat bottom and a number of plateaus tossed in there too; each taller than the last so that the Duran children could jump from plateau to plateau. On each of the plateaus was a different theme. On one, there would be shops; on another, there would be houses. And so on.

Though there was a seemingly unlimited source of food, it was hard not to wonder if the same food day in and day out ever got boring. It was understandable though: easy to grow, and they supply a lot of strength and energy with a great, sugary taste. That's probably why the kids there like it so much.

And best part: the Duran Village was home to the ultimate grass that you could lay in just to take a nap and you won't get any of those pesky bugs on you and people who are allergic to the luscious green grass aren't allergic to this. The reason no bugs will get on you: there are no bugs. The plants do what bugs do on their own thanks to Duran.

To get around, instead of bridges they have large circular stones in the water that will not move and just float there. And as for getting on top of the plateaus, there are vines that the kids climb to get up.

This time hollow, I was much more eager to explore the Duran Village than follow Rissa especially since something was drawing me to the lake to my side in the center of the village. I stared down the water and looked where my instincts pointed towards where I noticed an underwater cave, near *the bottom. I started swimming towards it and then right before I got there, my head started hurting. Something that I couldn't see took hold of my ankle and began dragging me back to land. That had never happened before.*

I tried swimming against it, but I didn't even begin to hinder the speed at which I was taken and once we reached land, it dragged me across the Duran village where Rissa was chatting with her friends.

"-she is lost? That's not possible! How could I have cared so little as to let her go off on her own?" Rissa whispered, stunned with the news.

"It's not your fault, Rissa. Think about the facts. SHE chose to go off on her own, SHE told you to stay away, and SHE made it clear that she didn't want any help. It's not your fault. It's HERS! Don't blame yourself. You don't need to blame everything on yourself. Come on, let's go find Mashka. She may be a brat and all but if it's important to you, then let's go find that spoiled maid's child." Alima smiled.

Frisky is the Tiber and Yuna is the rax "Don't call her that, Alima. It's really not nice and degrading. Not everyone is as lucky as you and I. You and Ameri have a famous warrior as a dad and a Queen's royal adviser for a mom. Zenon and I have royalty for parents. We may have special parents and all but... but... we can't seem like spoiled rich brats. It's just not proper." Rissa began. "but instead of my moral lesson, we should be finding Mashka.

Rissa began walking out towards the entrance of the woods just expecting everyone to follow because that was the leader she was. She was confident, smart, caring; Rissa was the type of person that people WANT to follow.

"Rissa, this isn't the normal path we take. Where are you leading us?" Ameri asked.

"You…" Zenon paused to ponder her accusation. "Rissa, you wouldn't dare take us THERE. You know it's dangerous!"

"I know it's dangerous Z, but it's our only chance of finding Mashka. Think of it as… how would you explain this to her parents if we didn't find her?"

And that struck an excellent, undeniable and inevitable point. If they didn't find her, what would they tell their parents? And who will be the one to tell them?

Everyone went silent because there was nothing left to say about the subject. And that's how Rissa planned it. At that point, we came a ditch with burnt soil and burnt trees. "Mashka, come out. We know you are here." Rissa began as she sat on a near rounded boulder.

"Zenon, I'm scared." Ameri whispered.

"Rissa, IT IS DANGEROUS HERE! We need to leave NOW!" Zenon hissed.

"We need to see if Mashka is alive, Zenon. I can't live with knowing that I didn't try." Rissa said.

Something began to happen. Wind was blowing all around the area a whisper in the winds breath echoed off of the trees. "Rissa," it said.

"You killed me, Rissa." The voice didn't have a gender or really any emotions. It was more of a dry, shaky understandable noise that happened to have an issue with Rissa.

"L-let's go! Alima, Zenon, come on. If she wants to stay then she can!" Ameri stuttered tugging on her sister's sleeve.

"I want to stay here with Rissa. If anything bad happens I would never forgive myself." Alima responded.

"Alima, buddy, it's okay. If you're scared, then by all means, go. I wouldn't want you to be uncomfortable just to try and make me happy." Rissa smiled confidently.

"But I don't..." Alima stared at Zenon and Ameri, quickly changing her answer after seeing them slowly inch away. "Okay. Just be safe."

Right on cue, as soon as the group was long gone, some object appeared in front of Rissa. Is that what has become of Mashka? I thought.

It was much shorter than Mashka. Maybe two feet tall, had a strange hat made of straw, looked like a "dunce hat" except it hung down instead of being pointy at the top. The shirt it had was also made of straw I believe the style was called... Oh my gods... I forgot what the type of shirt it was called down on Earth! I know this... Oh that's right. It was called a T Shirt. Then also made of straw, were some really short jeans.

That wasn't the surprising part. The real thing that creped me out was the fact that it had no ears or nose but yet it could still smell and hear. Its eyes were holes in its coconut shaped head and its mouth was another hole that opened and closed, no tongue, no teeth, no spit, and no lips. It... it didn't even have skin. It was made completely of wood minus its clothes.

"Mashka, is that you?" Rissa asked horrified at Mashka's appearance.

"Yes, Princess. It is I, Mashka. This is my new appearance because of you! Soon I will probably talk like that loser, Duran! That deep, slow voice with the thee's and thy's... except I will have a high pitch, slow, scratchy voice! I am cursed by the Woods. I am to never leave and cause trouble for all who pass... to kill them. What are you going to tell them? My family, I mean."

Rissa stared at her sorrowful. "I don't know. Not the truth; I will tell them anything but the truth."

"How about you tell them that this is YOUR fault?" Mashka laughed.

"Well that would be something but the truth..."

"That'd be the RIGHT thing to do, wouldn't it? Oh wait, princess. You aren't the goody-good we all give you credit for being, huh."

"No! Mashka! Don't go! We can do something about this! It's not too late!" Rissa said.

But it really was too late; Mashka was already gone and lost all... I would say humanity but obviously that's not the case. She more lost her... Cheuvean free will and characteristics.

"What is..?" Rissa looked up and started running thinking "Oh no... Oh no!" I just followed as quickly as my human body could go.

I was clueless of why Rissa was running frantically towards the city she would have to explain another death to until I got to Unashi. There were flames everywhere. Some kids were in chains, being taken through a black hole. The next to go through were Alima and Ameri!

Rissa was frozen in rage. She looked like she was going to explode... but inside that head of hers I knew what she was really feeling: fear and sadness. I got another headache. Oh no! this can't end! I need to see what happens next! *I thought.*

I was sucked out of the past and I opened my eyes to James standing over me clueless of what had just happened.

"Elaina, why did you faint? Another time hollow?" He asked me.

"Not important. We just need to get past a certain place unharmed and without getting lost." I said.

I could see that he was still confused. I tried to get off of his lap and out of his arms. His arms were still gently holding me but wouldn't let me go. "James, let me go." I said.

"Are you hurt? Are you okay to walk?" He asked.

"Yes, James, I'm fine. *Please* let me go. I'm okay. Honestly, what made you so protective all of a sudden?" I asked.

"Elaina, what were you so worried about happening?" James asked.

"Uhm… I won't go into details but I saw in a vision that one of Rissa's friends had gotten lost in these woods and turned into a monster… and her new occupation is to… Kill everyone who comes through here."

"Are you sure that it wasn't just a dream?" He asked.

"Yeah James, I'm sure. I'm not as helpless or stupid as I was when you first found me. I'm not as useless as you may think. So the choice of my… transformation should be coming up right around the corner, am I correct?" I asked.

I asked that believing that maybe I could find a way around it once the time came.

"I wouldn't be sure. Scorn didn't go into specifics on anything. He didn't want us to really know about

Cheuva even though now we are full blood Cheuveans." James exclaimed. "I suppose that he figured if we knew too much, we would know to disobey and question."

"That *is* interesting. I would think that if Scorn told you all that he knew, then you would become more powerful and better for him... Would you think that he wanted you to find out on your own?" I asked.

"Probably. Maybe. I just don't understand how he was just so willing to throw our lives away. We did everything he asked us to without question. Before you came along... he told us that we were his adopted sons. It seems like you have exceeded what we could ever do for him..."

Though Scorn was a dreadful man, James and Alec seemed to have a love for him and though I could never really understand it to its fullest, he raised them into what they were which just so happened to be fighting machines, but the important part to them was that they were *his* fighting machines.

"How long were you with him?" I asked.

"I was with him a month after I turned eighteen... four thousand years ago. I came to earth as a baby Cheuvean boy. I never turned human like you. I was brought over by this idiotic, rich moron. I believe the woman's name was Aphrodite." James said.

And now we know how Greek myths got started. "Four thousand years ago… APHRODITE? You realize that she is a Greek goddess right? Aphrodite was probably a Cheuvean! She is the goddess of beauty."

And now we know why he's so freaking HOT.

Greek Mythology is real. Well, for the most part. Obviously over time it would be morphed and become mostly fiction. Anything of magical importance in history is Cheuvean, apparently. And all that time I thought I was being smart by not believing in religion, but it seemed anyone important in Earth history was somehow connected to Cheuva...

"Well yeah. Humans can't comprehend our strength and knowledge so we become gods in their eyes. It's because they're so primitive. Well hey, while we walk to the Duran Village can you tell me what made you so… nervous?"

"It's just one of *Rissa*'s friends. She got lost in these woods… and… I don't really know how to describe it… Well, she turned into a mutated tree." I said.

James started cracking up. "How in the world do you say that with a straight face?"

I stared at him. "Have you ever heard of Mashka Desperi?" I asked.

"Yes, Mashka and her younger sister were maid's children, am I correct?" James asked.

"Yes. Mashka is the friend that got lost. She said that her new duty was to kill everyone who passed through these woods." I said.

"That's kind of sad for more than one reason. What happened after that?" James asked.

"Rissa went to the city and it was on fire. Scorn had come and taken most the city's children away but two of them were Rissa's friends... Importance of the fact is that one was Rissa's best friend and the other was Zenon's best friend; Alima and Ameri. She reacted while everyone else was just standing there... in the end, her attempt to save them was unsuccessful." I said.

"I see. That's not very good. Were they immortals?" James asked.

"I don't know for sure but I think everyone but Nala and Mashka were immortals." I said.

"How do you know that?"

"Everyone was more mature than them and... well none of them were as greedy and bratty." I said.

"They almost seemed like humans?" James asked.

"Well James, I don't hate humans. So I don't quite describe them like that... although I heard on some television broadcast that humans are so greedy because they live such a short life. Is that the concept you are referring to when you asked that?" I asked.

To him my question wasn't really worth dignifying with an answer. Something was on his mind. At the time, I assumed his mom would be the one on his mind but realistically speaking, why would he really care? They were bonded by blood, not time, not love.

I took the hint that he needed his "James Time" and lead the way silently until I collapsed, mid step into a bush.

James grabbed me out of the bush and laid me on a soft patch of grass a couple feet away. "Elaina? Elaina! WAKE UP, Elaina!"

I was still conscious, just unable to move anything. *Why can't I move anymore, James? I feel so... so... tired.* I said my eyes were closing slowly like a baby trying to fight a very desperately needed nap.

"What is wrong? Elaina?" James yelled laying me on my stomach. There was a dart in my neck.

"What the-Who's there? Who did this?" James roared.

Faint laughing grew in the trees. "My name is Mashka... James, long time no see." Mashka asked.

"Mashka Desperi? So this is what has become of you." James laughed taking the dart out of me. "It's funny, your reason for living is so that you can kill. But you don't have the battle knowledge to kill even the smallest rodent."

"Silence! Don't pretend you didn't know what became of me. I know you! I know what you do! You have deceived me and my sister once and now look at what has become of us! I won't let you do it to her!" Mashka said.

I assume James was unaware that I was able to listen and so he spoke freely. "*Rissa* is no longer in my list of targets. She has done all she needed to do to get me on her side." James said.

"That doesn't look like *Rissa*." Mashka said.

"It is *Rissa*. Trust me. I have done my research. I no longer work for Scorn, Mashka. There is no need to be suspicious." James said.

"I'd bet. But for how long will this truce with the light last before you crawl back into Scorn? Who is this girl? What is her importance? She is no *Rissa*. She was strong, brave... smart. This *Human* is no *Rissa*." Mashka said.

"This human is no more than the shell for *Rissa*. She is not of any importance to anyone until she is fully transformed." James said as he brushed the dirt gracefully off the shoulder of his suit. "May we pass?"

I hated the way he did that. He was always so a gentleman like... but dead inside. But more importantly, he talked about Elaina... Me as if I was only an item that he wanted upgraded, and that being me was just unacceptable.

Mashka stepped aside. "Thank you. Hey. Maybe one day I might just come back and release you of that curse which was bestowed upon you."

"What is wrong with her?" Mashka asked ignoring his comment about her curse.

"Well it's your dart... what *is* happening?"

"It wasn't meant to be so powerful. It's something that stuns someone for a few moments, not ends them. I don't know how to make one of those."

"She is probably just hungry, tired, and to injured from pushing herself too hard. Now she doesn't have enough energy to heal herself from your poison. Do you have any lunar bread?" James asked.

Mashka raised an eyebrow as if to say "That's like asking a ghost if it will hurt if you punch him."

James shook his head and said politely, "Oh, my apologies. Let me rephrase; do you know where I could find some lunar bread?"

It's so hard to tell if he is mocking you or seriously asking you a question. "That tree right behind you is a lunar bread tree." Mashka said.

James, without a thank you or anything, walked away. Mashka obnoxiously flung herself towards the lunar bread tree and hung upside down, blocking James's way. "James, why don't you just stay around here? It's so much more peaceful!"

"Get *out* of my way." James grabbed her arm and yanked her out of the tree.

Just moments later he returned with a hand full of lunar bread, each all sorts of colors. James gave me one and after that very first nibble, I felt so strong... It was like he gave me an energy drink mixed with the strongest coffee with just a dash of speed. All of a sudden I was up and shoving my face in the lunar bread. I didn't realize how hungry I was.

"My, my, Elaina you were starving. No wonder you died there after a weak little dart to the neck. You need to take better care of your body." James said grabbing my hand and helping me up. "You'll really worry someone." He concluded.

"Yes, you're right. I'm sorry I worried you." I mumbled.

James blushed a bright red color impossible to NOT notice and said, "H-hey I never said that *I* was the one worried! That's completely ridiculous!"

I laughed and Mashka, being the wannabe center of attention stepped in and ruined the moment.

"You know, I would have had this moment *long* ago. My first boyfriend in Unashi had this type of talk just an hour after we met. We got all the way to our first kiss after two hours. You know, if you want I can tutor you in dating. The gods sure know that you two need it. If you pay me-" Mashka began.

What the hell? "And how long did that relationship last, Mashka? A day? Or did it just end after the kiss? We aren't in a relationship. We are just partners in a desperate time. After this all ends then we will probably never talk to each other again... at least, we won't talk without a nice fight going on between us." James shrugged.

My attention jolted to James, even though that really was no news to me. I already knew that I was his ride away from Scorn, but it just upset me to hear it out loud. And the toss in about how we aren't even friends... It just hurt.

Mashka mocked looking at my frozen face, "It looks like someone thinks differently."

"You only think of me as an ally from bad circumstances and then you'll turn on me?" I asked.

"No, Ri- Elaina. I would never..." He looked away, unable to lie to my face. "Look, I didn't quite mean it like that."

I let out a bitter laugh. "I thought so. It was too good to be true. Thank you, Mashka. I'll be on my way now, James. Please, don't bother to follow... Of course... you don't know these woods... So you'll be considered lost if you moved from that spot. You can't teleport because you don't know where you are. I suppose you want me to take you out of the woods? I would never want you to get lost here." I mused walking away.

I *was* seriously considering leaving him to get lost... but I convinced myself to be a "good person."

"Elaina." James said walking after me.

"No."

"Elaina, c'mon." He whispered once more.

"I-I don't want you around, James."

He appeared in front of me, gently grasping my arms holding me close. "Elaina, I don't want to get out of these woods. I want to stay with you and go to the Duran Village. Please, Elaina you can't leave us on our own." James smiled sweetly looking like his normal gentlemen self and I hated it. He could manipulate me so easily and I was helpless to it.

"But-"

He put his pointer finger to my lips and shushed me. He stepped away so gracefully, and then held out his smooth hand as if asking for forgiveness in a gentle way. I nodded and put my hand on his.

"Forgive me. Please?" He asked.

It seemed like he was manipulating me. It was just too... sweet. He wasn't like the others. Looking into his eyes always seemed to put me into a trance. He was hypnotizing. Everything about him was supernaturally perfect.

"I don... okay, James. I forgive you." I said.

He seemed to have the power to make me do almost anything.

"Are you almost done eating?" James asked.

"Yeah, should we take some with us?" I asked.

"Yeah I would if I were you." James said.

"What about you?" I asked.

He was talking like he didn't *need* to eat. "Yeah I'll take some too." He said.

"I've never seen Scorn feed anyone other than me. Does he just starve his prisoners?" I asked.

"Well, yeah. I suppose he does. You see, immortal Cheuveans don't exactly need to eat, so he feeds them very little, enough to keep 'em functional, little enough to starve them." James said.

"That's mean. How come you joined him?" I asked.

"Well, yeah. And most of us joined just so we wouldn't become slaves and have to deal with those conditions." James said. "I joined because he… meant something to me."

"That's harsh. Well, I would say sorry you had to go through that, but you really don't deserve it." I glared up at him.

"I know, I'm awful." He smiled taking my hand.

We began walking in the direction we were originally heading until I found the small hole in the ground. You would never see it if you didn't already know where it was.

CHAPTER THIRTEEN
Welcome to the Duran Village

Dear Diary,

So today I learned that trees do speak and they have a short temper. This world is weird. It's a damn good thing I didn't pay attention in school because this world would be confusing as hell. I mean, c'mon, can you point out even ONE version of physics that would work in my world? FML.

-Elaina

I pushed the button to activate a hologram of a tree.

"Hello Duran. I'm Elaina, Rissa's... you know, reincarnate." I said.

"Yes... Miss *Rissa* has a reincarnation now..." He recalled out loud.

"Of course... Do you remember me, Duran?" I asked.

"Yes… ghostly *human*. Thy art of those appearance that lay unforgettable in the mind of most." Duran decided.

His speech was still slow but I suppose that's because of his practically ultimate age. And I was okay with the slow speech because it was just *so* much easier to understand him when I had time to decipher his old English.

At first I thought he was kidding but when I looked at his… uhm… I would say face but… well I don't think trees have those. Well, whatever. When I looked at his face he seemed all too serious. "Is that a good thing, Duran?" I asked.

"Neigh. When not one forgets thy look, tis simpler to oversee a person out in the crowd. More so when one is as *human*-like as thee. I cannot name a situation when that might be recommended when such human creates enemies with each step. Consider thyself blessed with luck of the gods as I dost not hate with ease. Who art these?" He asked.

"This is James, Eric is the one on James's shoulder and the one I am holding is named Alec." I exclaimed.

"I see. Wouldn' thee appreciate a passing, Elaina Martin?"

"Yes please, Duran." I said.

"OPEN." Duran commanded with his booming deep voice sounding even deeper than before.

A root inconspicuously snuck out of the ground and gently wrapped itself around the edge of my foot just hard enough so that I would feel it so that I would allow James to jump into the portal before I had a chance.

Duran stopped me to tell me, "James and Alec have very evil auras. I do not believe that thee have good intentions here in the Duran Village, Elaina Martin." I wasn't very nice to Duran when he said that.

He treated me like he was my parent telling me, the ignorant kid, not to hang out with the wrong people and choosing my friends for me. That's how I've always been treated, they always thought I needed to be protected. Despite popular belief, I can take care of myself! Why does everyone always think that I am so helpless? I broke out from Scorn's clutches, for god's sakes!

"I am very well aware of that, Duran. I am not stupid. Scorn is inside Alec's head and both James and Alec have been with Scorn for a very long time. They are good people. Trust me." I pleaded.

"Whatever you say, Rissa... but I will have you know that if anything goes wrong with these boys I am holding you responsible... and I will assure you that you will pay." He said.

"Leave now, ghostly *human*. I do not want to see your face again until you are a Cheuvean." Duran said.

"Yes… Thank you, Duran. But if I can help it, I won't be changing into one of them. Nothing good seems to come from that race." I said.

How was that not an *enemy's* interaction with each other? I was intimidated by Duran. That may not make total sense to everyone. Allow me to explain: I'm afraid of Duran; my ally, and not my enemies; James and Alec because, well, the thing is James and Alec are variables that I can change and manipulate to join my side… but Duran… Duran is in charge of the village that I am staying in… and all of the people in it. I make him mad; He can easily make my life very difficult… or even more so. I was able to stay in the village for as long as they allowed me to be and if I got kicked out, I knew Scorn would find me and I would be done for. What I didn't know was that it was impossible to escape that fate no matter where I hid.

I was forced into the portal by another one of Duran's vines as a nice little hint that he didn't care to speak to me anymore and appeared next to James, who was holding Alec and Dylan. Alec was still making quiet moaning sounds. Eric was just out cold, sweating, tossing and turning.

"James, will you take Alec and Eric into those two tree houses up there? I can't climb with someone unconscious on my back. I'd end up dropping them. And seriously, that'd be a real shame after all we went through to get those boys here safely." I said.

"Yeah, okay. You get right on that." James said absent minded.

"James," I repeated, trying to get his attention.

"Alright." He said, just staring at Eric.

I turned to face the side of his head, went on my tip toes, put my face right next to his ear, "JAMES!" I shouted. Finally he actually listened.

CHAPTER FOURTEEN
Nothing s secret anymore.

Dear Diary,

It's nice feeling safe for once. This is the Duran Village, where children are laughing, animal things are running free, and there is peace. It's been that way for hundreds of years so what are the chances of ruining that after one day of us being here. Maybe we're even home free and I can focus on my magical regeneration studies to revive everyone that has been lost! I hope I'm not asking for too much... Best aim for the skies I guess.

-Elaina

"What the hell is wrong with you? You know, it's very rude to yell in someone's ear."

"Yeah? I thought it was rude to not pay attention when someone is speaking with you." I pointed out.

"Alright. Fair enough. What did you want?" James laughed gently.

"Take Alec and Eric up to those two tree houses. I would do it myself but I doubt I can climb all the way up there with two people dangling over my shoulder." I said.

"Oh, yeah. I forgot you're still human aren't you?" James chuckled.

"Just do as I say, James." I said.

James chuckled some more as he said, "You're becoming very Lordly, you know."

And he was becoming more playful.

"Shut up, James." I growled.

I looked away trying to fake annoyance. I couldn't hide my smile if I looked at him. He walked over to me, and tapped the bottom of my chin as he smiled back at me. "You know, you have a gorgeous smile and it's a futile attempt to hide that from me."

James laughed, threw Alec and Eric on his shoulder, and walked away. I started thinking about that one hole in the lake and where it led.

"James, wait a second." I blurted out.

I felt his smirk grow on his face as he turned around but by the time he turned around his face looked like he was concerned.

"What is it, Ellie?" He asked.

"Drop the act. When you're finished putting those two to bed I need you to come back here, please." I ordered.

Cute moment: Gone. I won't allow myself to fall for him.

"I don't know… I mean the way up there is just so tiring for me. I don't know if I could make it down." James said.

"James." I growled.

"Alright, alright. Just for you, my dear." James said as he teleported to the top of the plateau with the houses. "You're getting real touchy, during recent times, Ellie."

"Your friend is bad." I heard behind me. "I waited 'til your other friend was gone before I came to talk to you."

I turned to see this little toddler staring, big eyed up at me. I knelt down, "What makes you think that?"

"I know."

"Which friend."

"His name is Alec. He's bad and scary."

"What's your name, little girl?"

"Halley Ruth."

"Why don't you go play with the other Duran kids?"

"I'm too small." She responded.

"Oh, is there no one your size?"

"Stop. I'm the only one that's young. And just like everyone else, you're ignoring me!"

"No, no I'm not. It's just that you should leave that stuff to grownups."

"You'll see when we die because of you. You should have listened to me." She turned, sad faced, and walked away. "It'll happen when you explore with your friend. You should be protecting us."

"From Alec?"

"From your bloodline. I can see bits of the future. See, I've already tried warning the others... but no one is listening because I'm too small. You should run away." The little girl ran and disappeared behind a group of trees.

I waited for James just for a few more moments. "Hello, Elaina, it's nice to see you again." James said lightly hugging me. "Who was that?"

Why is he like this? I thought making sure my thoughts were blocked out.

"Just some kid."

"Oh, well what do you want, Ellie?" James asked.

"I want you to go under water with me. I found this hole and... well..." I began.

"And you're scared. So you need your big strong protector to make you feel all better." James finished my sentence... just not in the way I would have said it.

"Wrong. More like I don't want to go exploring alone because for all I know it's a short cut into Scorn's lair." I said.

"You know, when you want something, you should be nicer to the person giving it to you." James said.

"Not when it's you, James." I smiled, forcefully grabbing his hand and taking him along with me.

He obviously wanted to come. I know he did. He was curious and that was obvious because if he wasn't planning on coming then he wouldn't have been coming. He was a whole lot stronger than I was because I was only *changing* into a Cheuvean and he was already a Cheuvean.

"Elaina!" I heard a call behind me.

James stood on edge, "Anna, what's up?"

"Not a ton. I've been looking for Drake. Have you seen him anywhere?"

Shit. He thought to me.

My mind shut off. I was at a standstill, practically dead because I was not supposed to remember Drake.

"Funny you should mention Drake..." James laughed nervously. "Because he got killed."

"He... Died? How?" She asked.

"Jean shot 'em." James replied.

"Where is his body?"

"We couldn't bring it."

"You couldn't... you couldn't find the strength to not leave Drake behind? What the f-"

James exhaled. "This is pointless."

"WHAT?" She screamed. "Elaina, control your pest."

"Elaina doesn't control me." James appeared in front of her. "You are going to lose interest in Drake. Now shut up and walk away."

Anna turned and walked away.

"Come on, Elaina. Let's go find that hole."

I turned back on, "Alright!"

We dove into the water, we could still breath but it wasn't dangerous this time, we didn't have to put out spirit to survive it was just like human water except it tasted like Sprite and it was very pure. That means that there is no litter and no mold or anything like that.

So we swam into the hole but as we passed through the edges of the hole, it seemed that liquid couldn't get through. We went from swimming to dropping on the floor. Even though there weren't any spider webs or any old deserted smell you could still tell no one has been in here for hundreds of years, maybe even thousands of years.

Picture a hole about fifty feet into a lake that should be pitch black but instead had a dim light coming from the wall. My instincts and my sense of smell were getting a whole lot stronger. The edges, circling the... cave was about a two foot wide river.

On the walls where these little drawings. There were two boy drawings. Both of them had a flame swords but one was taller than the other and looked totally different. In fact one looked like James. And the other looked like Drake. Then there were two girls, one looked like Rissa and the other looked like Zenon.

Then, when I turned around to look at the rest of the place and there were two more pictures. They looked like Alima and Ameri. Whoever drew these was a really good artist. They looked like the real people. Then, as I looked around more closely, I found a light blood line crossing out Ameri and Alima's picture. Only their pictures. Not Rissa's, not Zenon's, not James's, and not that other boy's picture. Though James's picture had been circled. I wondered what that had meant.

"James, your picture is here. What does that mean?" I asked.

"I... I don't know." James said.

"James, you're a terrible liar. Tell me what you-" I stopped in the middle of the sentence. My head started hurting and as James was running toward me I passed out. Great. Another time hollow.

"NO! NO! NO! THIS SHOULDN'T HAPPEN TO ME! I ran away... I was a coward... now... Alima... Ameri... They're both gone..." Rissa said walking to their pictures and sobbing. *"I'm so sorry. I didn't mean to..."* Rissa concluded.

Right. Because it's all my fault. It's always my fault. *I began to sarcastically think sitting on the sidelines.*

"Rissa , stop sobbing. You know I don't like it when you cry." James said.

"James, you're okay." Rissa said running to hug him.

He allowed her to wrap her arms around him. "Get off."

A moment passed and she didn't budge. She was too emotionally weak, too prideful, too stupid to understand what was happening. He pried her arms off of him and shoved her away.

"James," Rissa questioned.

His EYES. The light was gone again. Just like when I first met him. What happened to make him this way?

"I'm leaving, Rissa." James said.

"Where are you going?" Rissa asked.

"Away. I now work for your dad... and his first orders were... well to tell you to come with us or... get beat. I won't force you to come but if you decide not to come you'll be left here in pretty bad shape... so... do you want to come? He'll treat you nicely. He's a nice man... Rissa, I'm not the one that wants to hurt you. Don't put me in the position." James said.

"Us?"

"Alima, Ameri... everyone."

Enraged, she replied, "No. James, get out. Never return, and if you do I'll kill you."

James started laughing. He didn't want to hurt Rissa, you could tell that. But he really seemed to be good at making it look like he's looking forward to hurting her. Just like with me.

"So be it. I won't hold back." James called calmly. "Just like I didn't with Drake."

"Where's drake?"

"Rissa," James smiled. "Where do you think?"

"That's why I'm ASKING, James. Where is Drake?"

"Long gone."

Rissa walked over to get a pair of metal swords from the side of the room. She threw one to him and he caught it but he lightly tossed the sword in the water circling the room.

"Ha! I don't need those. Scorn provided an effective weapon for me. You couldn't chop a tree with that piece of shit, Rissa." James's voice was so... harsh and cold. The sword James pulled out was the fire sword.

Rissa was silent, showing only one emotion... and that was pain. This was one of the first times Rissa did not think of anyone other than herself. All she could process was the fact that everyone was gone. Her life, as she knew it was coming to an end. No more princess, no more friends, no more trust, no more Cheuva. She no longer had it in her to protect everyone else because there was no one else.

Rissa didn't even get a chance to hit him. The fire sword cut through Rissa's metal sword like butter. James swung his sword at Rissa countless times and she kept dodging. Finally she tried to leap into the air and kick him but he stabbed her through the gut.

He threw her off his sword and into a wall. It looks like that's where my entire "fly across somewhere into something" habit started.

He walked towards her grabbed out of the water and dragged her back into the center of the room. He threw her up into the air, punched her, then kicked her then slashed her with his sword over and over again, leaving countless burn marks and deep cuts all over her body. James raised his sword one last time for a final blow when she screamed,

"STOP!"

He gave a relived smile

"Really? You'll come with?" James asked.

"I won't do that. You KNOW I could never do that. But you can't keep beating on me. Just leave me alone. You took everything that I cared about! Isn't that enough?" She asked. He appeared in front of her and swiftly jabbed her one last time through the heart.

"No." He said as Rissa began fainting.

"Don't worry though. I'm sure this was all part of your plan, wasn't it? God forbid you do as someone tells you. And, c'mon, why keep watch over your friends when you can soak in your own blood

knowing you ruined the rest of their undying lives."
James laughed. He was thinking she was so stupid.

Why WOULDN'T I want to take the easy way out?
The difference that separated Rissa and James was
that she did what was right, not what was easy.
"Good bye, Rissa. For now."

She was out cold now... but I wasn't waking up
from the time hollow meaning I hadn't absorbed the
full meaning of what I was here to see. I sat across
the room from Rissa, almost unable to look at her in
such pain.

Finally, after a day or so Rissa woke up. She
couldn't move though. A few days after that, she was
able to move. She was soaking in her own blood for
days... that really must've scarred her for life. She got
a hand full of blood and walked to Alima's picture.
She crossed the picture out and under it wrote (lost).
She did the same to Ameri's picture, then she came
to James's picture, circled it and under it wrote
(Trader). Everything was getting blurry now.

I was waking up from the time hollow. All of a
sudden, I was back in the present and James was
holding me.

I was lying in the spot that *Rissa*'s blood was. I
freaked out, and with good reason. I pushed James
and stumbled backwards into the water that circled
the room (accidentally of course.) That water was
way deeper than it looked. It was about six feet
deep... and it was really cold.

"Elaina, what are you doing? Isn't that cold?" James asked.

I got out of the water and stared at the ground. "What's wrong, Ellie?" James asked.

"You did it. You sold out Rissa and her friends. You beat Rissa up right here in this spot! How could you hide that from me?" I asked.

"It was here? Really? No, I was... that's not my intention this time! I just want to stay with you, away from him! I'm not the one that wants to hurt you! *Rissa*, you have to believe me!" James said.

That made me mad.

I AM NOT Rissa!

"*Rissa*? I AM NOT Rissa! I am ELAINA MARTIN! *Get that through your thick skull!*" I screamed. "But maybe you just called me that because you said that e*xact* line to Rissa however many years ago.."

"I didn't mean to-" James said.

"Shut up! You lied to me. You said you didn't know what this place was. You have a drawing of yourself in here and you beat Rissa to a pulp in here. I *trusted* you! *She* trusted you!" I cried looking away. "And who is Blaze? Why'd you kill him?"

"Do you remember Drake? That's him. His Cheuvean version."

"But he died."

"And that's why Drake could never complete the transformation. Blaze no longer existed for him to morph into."

"You killed Drake... you lied to me..."

He grabbed my head, forcing me to look at him straight in the eyes. "I know. I won't do it again, Elaina. Please, believe me. I won't do it again." James said calmly. His eyes changed as he spoke. His pupils got a little bigger and then shrunk.

It was weird. My thoughts were a little hazy. I blinked it away and replied, "Alright James I believe you... but hear me now... you break that promise, I break you." Elaina said.

Yeah, alright. If Rissa couldn't beat me then Elaina definitely can't, but the message is clear. I won't break the promise. James thought.

"Alright, Ellie. I won't break that promise." He said.

"Good. Wait but Scorn told you to come here to take out Rissa ... so wouldn't he know where this place is?" I asked.

"No. I never told him about this place and his orders where to find her and get her to join us or teach her a lesson." James said.

"What about mind reading?" I asked.

That caught James's attention. He looked at the hole we came in through and he ran out and swam up to surface with me close behind him. When we got to surface, it was sundown, there was fire everywhere.

"No..." I whispered.

"Not here… not again…" James whispered beside me.

"Duran! We have to get to Duran!" I said.

I couldn't look around me. As we ran through the village, there were screaming Duran kids. They were left to burn; to rot with their home that I failed to protect. Twice.

"Hey, look at me." James began as he took my hand, making it impossible to stop and help the people that we were passing. "This was not your fault. There's nothing we can do for them now."

We ran through the fire to Duran's little… place in the Duran village and he was dying.

"Duran?" I asked.

"Thee,"

What the hell is he talking like that for?

"I hath warn-ed thee. I spoketh to thee, The boys are evil! Thy ignorant actions cast the Duran Village into the Demon's wrath. The Duran Village has paid the price for your demise, Rissa!" Duran yelled.

She did this too… History repeats itself.

"Who did this, Duran?" James asked. Duran died before he could answer.

I ran to him and fell to my knees at his stump. I needed to try to help him—even though he was just a tree.

"Elaina, get off of him." James picked me off my knees and tried walking me away. "There's nothing we can do."

"It's all my fault… I should have heeded his warning." I cried turning to James.

"Elaina, stop worrying about him. He's gone. Keep worrying about him and everyone else will share his fate… Eric, we need to go to Eric!" James said.

We teleported to Eric's hut on the plateau. "Eric! ERIC!" James yelled running into Eric's little hut. He was mumbling something. It was so hard to understand. He whispered it into James's ear and then said out loud,

"Why, Alec, why?" He was bleeding from cut marks all over his body, and from his mouth. He pulled James close, coughed the remaining blood out of his system and breathed a warning to James and he truthfully seemed really shocked.

I asked, "What did he say, James?" James slowly looked at me then said

"The act of inflicting excruciating pain as punishment, or maybe revenge, as a means of getting information, or just for sheer cruelty. He told me the definition of torture. Why would he do that?" James asked.

"Scorn probably did something." I turned to Eric, "Are you okay? Are you going to be okay? What happened?" I asked.

"N-no stop! Stay away from me! N-" Eric's blood was gushing out. He was going to die and we couldn't do anything about it.

"Sorry Eric." James said. Eric was now screaming, choking on his own blood. Eric passed away in the worst way I had ever seen. I looked away. What else could I do? To be honest, I probably should have ended it for him. I should have killed him to make it fast. But I just didn't have the stomach for it.

"We need to go see if anyone else was left here." James decided, dragging me out of the hut. "We don't need to watch him go."

He took me from there hoping someone was in there but nothing except dead bodies of the Duran Children.

"I'm seeing something common about this. Umm, well... have you noticed that everyone left here was killed or dying? We are the only two that are still alive and not injured." I said.

"That's a good point but what are we going to do? We could go back into the cave and hide there for a bit." James said.

I didn't know who to trust and that was my fault. I should have never brought people that I didn't trust with everything in me to the place of peace.

"You're kidding. No way can we hide in there. If Scorn knew about the village than yeah, he'll know about there and we'll be trapped." I said.

"I suggest you just come and stop discussing it." Alec said stepping forward.

"We're screwed." I breathed as I saw the ARMY he had appearing rapidly behind him. Seriously? He needed an army to take us down?

"Step down, Elaina, James. We wouldn't want to repeat the incident with Rissa vs. James again would we? Yes, James. I know all about that. You kept that a secret from me. Not very nice of you." Alec said.

I stared blankly at him. How did he know?

"Are they a threat? There are so many of them, if they were strong, why would he need so many people?" I whispered.

James glared at me and hissed, "*Shut up!*"

"Why?" I whispered back.

"That army isn't weak. Scorn trained them. These guys are the real deal. They can do what we do except they do it ten times as well." James said. "Alec, we surrender."

"Surrender your weapons, kneel on the ground, and put your hands behind your head." Alec said.

I felt stupid. I just kneeled and put my hands behind my head because I had no weapons, but James got out nine weapons and then kneeled next to me. A familiar person came towards us checking to make sure we really didn't have any more weapons. He felt around James's pockets quickly and then when it came to me he took his time then looked at Alec for approval and Alec replied, "I don't care, Dylan. Just hurry it up the rest of us don't want to see you messing with a girl." Dylan smiled sweetly at Alec then by the time he turned to me his smile became a sneer.

"I just want to make sure you didn't hide any weapons in inappropriate-" Dylan began.

"I didn't. If you think that I did, let me take it out." I said.

"You haven't got any more respectful since the last time I saw you, Elaina." Dylan said.

"You're pathetic." I said.

He ignored me and turned to James. "And this, James, is for jabbing me in the stomach."

He kicked James once across the face hard enough to have him skidding ten feet across the grass.

"*James*! Dylan, Stop it!" I screamed. Dylan picked up James by his shirt.

"I wonder why Scorn made you the leader and not someone stronger. After all, you're still awake yet you aren't fighting back. That isn't leadership material, James." Dylan asked James.

"I surrendered, remember? If I fight back then that would be asking for death." James said out of breath. Dylan laughed.

"All the more fun for me." He laugh throwing James at the ground and kicking him once more.

"Stop! Alec, make Dylan stop, *please*!" I screamed.

I was making a fool in front of Scorn's entire army. I might as well have told them that the number one way to make me pissed was to hurt my loved ones and friends. Alec laughed then told Dylan,

"Dylan, end it." Alec said.

"Yes sir." Dylan said getting out an electric sword and hitting the pommel of the sword. James fainted. Dylan came up to me with his electric sword and put the tip of it to my stomach.

"Should I just run my sword right through you or should I make it painless like James's?" Dylan asked me with the army snickering some pathetic laughs. I didn't even know those people and I hated them. Completely fickle, brainwashed, useless bodies of mass. They're *nothing*.

"That didn't look painless." I said.

"That's because it wasn't. It probably hurt a lot actually. Whatever you choose will be painful, Elaina so don't take so long deciding." Dylan said.

"What did I ever do to you?" I asked.

"Well if it weren't for you, I wouldn't have gotten this." Dylan said lifting his shirt up. There was a giant scar that covered his entire stomach. "It's slowly healing. But when someone that powerful jabs you through the gut, it takes a little while to heal, as you could imagine, I'm sure."

"You got that when James jabbed you?" I asked.

He brought his foot up and kicked my face. I flipped from my knees to slamming onto my back... "Yes. Any other questions?" He asked.

I wiped the blood from my lip, looking at Alec. He didn't show anything. No remorse, no fear, no nothing.

"He was your friend. You're his best friend and you did this to him!"

He reappeared like, an inch in front of me. Surprised, I jumped backwards to create distance between us.

I was nothing but a coward. I ran every chance I got. Every time I felt fear, I ran. I was nothing.

He appeared behind me, grabbed me, and tossed me back where I kneeled. He reappeared once more a couple inches from my face, putting his pointer finger under my chin and lifting it so I made direct eye contact with him. His eyes now lacked any type of shine that indicated emotions or emphasizes the existence of a soul. "Stop it, girl. Listen to me."

His pupils enlarged and constricted.

I did nothing but stare at him. It didn't occur to me to run that time. I didn't think about anything except doing what he said.

"Good. Now, stand up. And do not move unless I say to."

I stood.

He took my arms and held me to face Dylan. "Now." He told Dylan.

"Finally." Dylan muttered stabbing his sword through my stomach. I was actually expecting that to knock me out right away but I was wrong. It felt more weird than painful, like it was just energizing me, sending small but frequent surges of electric waves through my system, then when I stopped expecting it to hurt, the electric surges started getting larger and larger until it started hurting more and more until I fainted.

God, I hate Alec. God, I hate Dylan I thought as I was losing consciousness. When I was waking up, it was cold. I opened my eyes, it was dark. I heard some voices, and they seemed far away. I couldn't make out what they were saying.

"James?" I called quietly.

"Elaina! You're awake." James whispered.

He was holding me. I was leaning up against him and he was gently wrapping his arms around my frail body, holding my hands to not just keep me warm, but to make me feel safe as well.

"Yeah, where are we?" I asked shivering.

"We are in a truck. They're taking us to Scorn's worst prison, meant for immortals and those who Scorn hates most." James said.

"What are they going to do to us?" I asked.

"I know what they'll do to me, but to you? Who knows?" James said.

"Why would they treat you different than they would treat me?" I asked.

"Wow, Elaina. Have you learned nothing?" James asked. "They plan to keep me there, mostly dead. But you... you're different from everyone. I can't believe you haven't learned that yet. You could give Scorn so much more than anyone else. You are more powerful than anyone can imagine and if Scorn turns you evil… oh god… we'd be done. You get that, right? There is nothing for us anymore." James said.

"Oh… that's… nice." I said.

"Hey, Ellie?" James asked.

"Yes?" I replied.

"I just want to say something before this truck stops. I want you to know… know that whatever happens in here, I believe that you will save the worlds again. I *know* that you will help us." James said.

"Alright, James. I promise that whatever happens I will help you guys. I will save my friends." I said.

"Good, you'd better." James laughed. "And thank you. For everything."

The truck screeched to a sudden halt forcing me and James to tumble over as we slid across the ragged floor of the truck. "Are we there?" I asked.

"Yeah. I think so. I've never really been here before but…" James began. The truck doors opened.

"Out of the truck." Alec ordered. Obediently James and I got out of the truck.

CHAPTER FIFTEEN
I should have never trusted them.

Dear Diary,

They're shipping us here like animals: In the trunk of a stupid truck. Is it weird that I still get scared? I didn't expect to fully get away from Scorn scotch free... but I thought we would be safe, at least for a little. I should have known better. We all should have.

-Elaina

"What's that?" I asked pointing to the fence that surrounded the prison.

"Aura fence." James replied.

"Oh..." I said. "Why is it glowing?" The prison itself was frightening. It looked dead. The sky was dark red, the prison color was black, the sun looked black, and there wasn't any vegetation for miles and there were statues of Scorn EVERYWHERE. That guy needs to get rid of some ego. The doors of the prison flew open as we neared.

"It shocks you if you touch it. Drains your spirit. Now shush!" James whispered.

"Dylan." Alec said. Dylan nodded and disappeared then reappeared next to James and dragged James away. I didn't make an attempt to go after James and he didn't make an attempt to fight back because we both would be over powered and outwitted.

Alec grabbed my... well, my, what used to be a dress sleeve (the one I wore forever and a half ago to dine with Scorn) and yanked me through the door of the prison.

"You're going to be staying with a group of boys from here on. They will be your family. Make them pissed off at you and there will not be any turning back or manipulating your way back to popularity, do you understand, Elaina?" Alec asked.

Group of boys. Like the prophesy? "Yeah, I have a couple questions though; how many boys am I staying with? And when is my sentence in this prison over?" I asked.

"Okay, there must have been a misunderstanding. You don't get out of this prison. There is no escape, there is no release, and there is no mercy. The girl sells have been filled so we couldn't set you in one, and for your question about your inmates, you have five. Their names are James,

Jean, Kalus, Lucas, and Soren. I'm sure you'll make nice with them. You always do." Alec scoffed with a hint of disgust.

Is it really oh so bad that I'm a friendly person?

Conversation was a waste of energy at that point. Pushing to many questions on him would make him angry at me and I didn't want that anyways.

When we got to my new "home" Alec opened the cell door and shoved me in. "See you later Elaina." He said walking away.

I looked around and it seemed like the security was not quite what I had expected. The only thing that prevented us from escape were the mana-bar door that I would need to use as an exit. But beyond that? No cameras, no chains, no nothing.

A soothing, soft voice called from behind me. "Welcome to hell, Rissa." I fell over from fright and squealed. Perfect first impression in a prison.

I looked up at him as his ocean-like eyes complimenting his sporadic and explosive blue hair. "Hi."

"I thought you said this girl was the one, James. She looks like a wimp to me." A blond boy said poking me on the side of the head. I slapped his hand away.

He seemed childish and one of those people who don't know when to keep their mouth shut— Good side: usually people with that personality tend to be

VERY loyal. Something happened? He'll have your back. Probably down side: in most cases, they tend to make a habit to blurt whatever popped in their little heads which tends to get a little annoying.

"She is. She's just going through a hard time." James assured him.

"But she's so small... And scared." A black haired boy said quietly. He seemed to be the smart one of the group. He didn't have glasses or anything like that but he had that kind of superior "brainiac" voice.

Sad thing was that, the black haired one looked a little bit depressed. He had that hair style that covered one eye with his bangs and he had a striped black shirt and skinny jeans but his voice was so depressed. No real feelings were put behind what he said: no tone change, no facial expressions, no eye contact.

"Ha! That's funny. Elaina can't be the anything. She couldn't stand up to anyone." Jean spat. "I've been telling you this the whole time, James. You overestimate her."

I began laughing hysterically. "Ha! Ha-haha-hahaha! YES! You just made this entire event worth it." I pointed at Jean. "He threw you in prison! And to think you could have escaped with us! God, I love being right!"

"Fuck off." He replied.

"Okay really? We're in a freakin' prison and all you can think about is your own selfish desire to hate me to make yourself feel useful?!" I said. "And who are the rest of you?"

"Lucas," The blond, childish boy said.

"Kalus," The dark blue haired boy said.

"Soren," The depressed boy said.

Lucas tried to poke my head again and I grabbed his hand, put the sweetest smile on my face, and said, "You poke me again and I'll break your hand."

Lucas chuckled. "Yeah this girl is definitely the one. Just like the real Rissa. You seem a little bratty though."

Is that my first impression to everyone? Everyone thinks I'm a brat!

"James says that you're going to be even better than the real *Rissa*. He says that you can break us out." Soren said.

"James thinks too much of me." I said.

"He also said you promised to try your best to help us." Kalus added bluntly.

"Damn, you got me there." I said.

"So what are you goin'-ta-do?" Lucas asked.

"Well first, we'll need to know the technology in this place. For starters is there any type of technology in this sell that can eavesdrop on our conversations?" I asked.

"No." Soren said.

"What? Why? I don't understand. If Scorn wanted to know if people where plotting against him he would need to have things to monitor what we say." I said.

"He doesn't need them. People have tried to escape but he enjoys tearing their dreams in half right in front of them. He wants us to think that we can't escape." James began. "This place is where psychological warfare was created, Elaina."

"Do you know this place, James?" I asked.

"I used to work here."

Awkward silence.

"What is your history with Scorn?" I asked.

"We all worked for him in a way. We either took place in selling someone out or just were one of his workers. Oh and we're all immortals just like the rest of the prison." Jean said plainly. "The people in this prison are the biggest threat to Scorn's reign."

"Okay, what is the security like here?" I asked.

"The guards take turns taking patrol. Every ten minutes a guard passes by this cell. You can't break these cell doors from the inside or outside. You actually need a key to get out of this cage or your spirit will be extracted from you through the bars of the cell." Kalus informed me.

"What happens if we are caught?" James asked.

"Let's just say; it's really... unbearable. So, let's not get caught okay?" Jean smiled.

Someone was coming. You could hear footsteps from armor coming this way.

"Hi, we are your Captains. You do as we say and when activities come along then you WILL win and if you don't... well, let's not find out okay?" Two boys said.

Both of their faces were covered by their armor so I couldn't see their faces or describe their voice.

"Who are you?" I asked hesitantly.

At no point is someone assigned to me without reason. I either knew them or they were special people. Either way, it was better for me to know.

They took off their helmets and of course it was Alec and Dylan.

FML "Oh my god. We're screwed." I whispered under my breath.

I was staring at Dylan. I couldn't stop. I was so scared, my life was flashing before my eyes. I guess that maybe once I saw Dylan, my life became real. I realized that I was the only one that could get these boys out of the prison along with myself. I realized that my life sucks.

I thought, *I was on Earth for such a short time. I've been living for such a short time! Why won't they just leave me to my life? Why won't they all just go away?*

I kept thinking to myself, *I'm so screwed, I'm so screwed. What're we going to do? What IS there to do? We're so screwed.* "Why would you be screwed, Elaina?" Dylan asked.

"Let's all put a little thought into it. Why do you think?" I said.

"Is it because you think we're going to treat you unfairly compared to the other prisoners or because you're going to try to escape and you know that we will always be watching you because we know how you tick?" Alec asked.

"Because I am *not* just any other prisoner." My vision blurred but I shook it off. "I *know* that you are going to treat me unfairly." *And because I know you're always going to be watch our every move.* I added silently.

"See, now I don't think that's entirely true. You'll be treated exactly how you deserve to be treated. Elaina, you are no longer under anyone's protection. When you walked through the doors of this prison you have left everything behind. James can no longer protect you, Scorn will no longer protect you, and even if you manage to make friends with everyone here they won't protect you. Because, let's face it, why screw yourself over for an unachievable goal?

I know that will be a change from what you have been experiencing every time you get captured but you will have to learn to cope. But you know all of this, don't you? You're screwed because you're *scared*. You know there's no way out. Not for you, not for anyone." Alec said.

"So how long is my sentence here?" I asked avoiding the previous conversation.

"Forever." Dylan said. "Alec said he told you that once before."

My eyes widened in... I don't even know. Rage? Fear? Combination of the two?

"No. You can't keep me here forever. Not in a prison. What the hell! I didn't even do anything yet!" I said. When Alec told me that I would never leave, I figured that he was just being an ass. Playing with my emotions.

He laughed thinking *the major word there is YET.* "Ahh, the beauty of a *dictatorship*. You don't need to have anything wrong because *your* leader is displeased with you. We really don't need a reason and you can't do anything about it. All you have to do is join us, you know. If you join, then you'll be treated like a princess but if you don't, you'll stay a prisoner." Dylan explained smugly.

"It's surprising how easy it is for me to decline your proposal. Scorn tried to have you killed because you let me escape. I'd rather not have to worry about my 'Lord' trying to kill me because I failed him." I said.

"You obviously don't know a good deal when you hear one, Elaina." Dylan trotted away from the cell as Alec followed.

They hate me SO much.

"You really will regret that…" Soren commented quietly, staring after Alec and Dylan.

"Why didn't you take that opportunity?" Kalus asked.

"Why would I? It's not much of an opportunity anyways. I wouldn't ever want to work for Scorn." I said.

"You skipped your way out, Ellie. Don't you realize that? You could have gotten out of here." James said.

"Yes, I realize that. That would help Scorn wouldn't it? I would never want to do that." I said.

"*Such* an idiot. Your idiotic self-centeredness and hatred for Scorn is honestly worth being a prisoner? How the hell do you figure that?" Jean spat.

"Jean, you of all people should know why I hate him. You were there when he killed my family. He even did it in front of me." I said.

"If you recall, he killed my brother too, and I would still jump for that opportunity." Jean said.

"And *I'm* self-centered." I laughed gently.

"Is that worth being a prisoner?" Soren repeated. I gave him a look that basically said you're nuts.

"I promised I'd help you guys, didn't I?" I asked. "Besides, what fun would that be? I would rather have more of a challenge." I smiled.

"You're crazy." Kalus said.

"That's Rissa for ya'. Never does anything the easy way." Lucas said.

"My name is Elaina. *Stop* calling me Rissa." I said angrily.

"Why? You are her, you know. You're the same person." Kalus questioned.

Really? "I'm *me*."

"I don't see what the problem is with them calling you Rissa. You'll turn soon enough." Jean blabbered sitting on the stone floor.

I wasn't quite paying attention to the conversation. I was more enthused by my surroundings. I just noticed then that there were more rooms in the cell than just the room that led to the outside of the cell. Then it kind of hit me that he said something that I didn't like.

Wait, what?

"I don't have to change if I don't want to. Do I?" I asked.

Awkward silence...

"Elaina, everyone has to change... You began changing when you first met Alec and when we first started changing your destiny. Soon you'll be going through change. Isolation does it. Leaving your human life changes you." James said.

"Why didn't you ever tell me that?" I asked.

"Rissa, no offense but it's kind of obvious. Don't you think we would give up being a Cheuvean to not remain Scorns enslaved prisoners?" Kalus asked.

"Sorry Elaina. I should have told you earlier, but the change shouldn't happen for another few weeks." James said. "I should have never deceived you."

Just after he said that I started getting a small ache in my stomach. I felt my heart beat and my blood pulse.

A little girl's voice echoed unbearably loud in my head. *That was the final key. Your door is unlocked, Elaina. FINALLY.*

My vision was getting blurry. The blurriness was getting harder to see through until I couldn't make out anyone who was standing around me or even if there was anyone standing around me. The pain was getting more unbearable for me to face.

"James, wh-" I began. I fell flat on my stomach, paralyzed.

As the pain increased, all my human functions were freaking out. This was the worst part of my experience in the prison. My hearing increased ten full. I could hear screams, shouts, crying... My vision shut off. My touch blew off the map, the air around me felt like a thousand pounds of weight squishing me, *everything* hurt. I could smell everything, dirt, blood... I lost my ability to move and see.

In this, I had gained one extra sense. Apparently only Cheuveans have this sense. We call it the "Ultimus" sense. It's a word meaning the final and ultimate sense. It's like, all of the human senses combined to make one monster of a sense but it works really differently. Like, you hear, smell, touch, taste, and see aura and spirit and the feeling of it is indescribable.

"It's happening, she's changing. What should we do? Should we get Scorn?" Jean asked.

"Yeah. Go get Scorn. She could die if handled incorrectly. How exactly do we get him?" James said.

"Bang on the cells and hope someone happens to come running." Lucas smiled.

Jean started kicking the cage bars yelling for help. "What is wrong with you? Loud noise is strictly-" Alec said.

I could feel his aura change. He ran here angry but when he saw me scrunched up into a ball holding my head he seemed to get very happy.

"What's going to happen, Alec?" Lucas asked.

"None of your business." Alec said walking towards me.

I could sense his aura and it was almost like, seeing his outline. I could *feel* him looking at me, I could *feel* his strength walking towards me. I could feel his hate and anger. I could feel every molecule in my body wanting to fight him.

He turned me onto my back using his foot.

"Hmmm, I wonder if it hurts." Alec said plainly just staring at me.

"Alec, you know very well that it hurts. That tears apart your insides, destroying all traces of humanity. Most don't even remember being human, but they are aware that they were human. They just feel that something is missing..." Soren rambled.

Alec chuckled. "That's your story isn't it, Soren? ... well, actually, I guess you don't remember." Alec said cruelly.

"Shut up Alec. Just get Elaina some help." Jean said.

That surprised everyone. At the time, we assumed that Jean stood up to Alec because of loyalty. After actually thinking about that, we all realized that that wasn't at all possible because Jean wasn't capable of loyalty. He simply wanted me to turn correctly so I could break him out of the prison.

"That's not my job. Help the prisoners? Especially this particular prisoner... I don't think I'm required to do that but maybe if you persuade me..." Alec said.

"That's a sick trade off Alec! How could we persuade you? We have nothing. You took it all away from us." Lucas said.

"For starters, from now on you will treat me and everyone else around here with the respect they deserve. I am your superior and you will treat me as such. Second, you all will double your daily training for the weekly games." Alec said.

Then he pointed at me and said, "And she will be my play mate if anything goes wrong, if you ever lose a game, or whenever I feel in a bad mood. Sound fair?" Everyone took a bit of time looking at each other, deciding if I was worth having their lives made worse.

"Well I want you to be one hundred percent sure so I'll come back in a few days. Or you can decide now." Alec said.

"We accept your proposal." Soren blurted out.

"You're already disobeying the agreement." Alec said.

"How- oh. Please Alec, help her. We Accept your proposal, just please help her." Lucas said getting on his knees.

You could tell this behavior was completely unnatural for him. His face was straight but mentally, he was thinking about everything other than the situation he was in. Serious situations made him uncomfortable.

I'll give him some props for doing that. I wouldn't have; I couldn't have even if I really wanted to. I have way too much self-respect to be able to get on my knees for some idiot that I *know* I am better than. Call it stupidity. Call it me being too stubborn for my own good. But, c'mon, if I weren't like this I wouldn't be capable of anything that I do.

Everyone else got on their knees except James. He has always been just as stubborn as I am.

"Why aren't you on your knees?" Alec asked.

"I'm sorry, I really am. It's impossible for me to bow down to someone that I know will be such an insignificant bitch." James began.

"Teach him a lesson." Alec said.

"What?" Lucas couldn't even imagine turning on someone that he depended on.

"You heard me. Teach. Him. A. lesson." Alec ordered.

"I heard what you said Alec, but what does that mean?" Lucas asked.

"That means beat him up for disobeying me." Alec said sharply.

"He's our friend, we wouldn't want to hurt him. It's just not-" Lucas began.

Poor kid. I can't imagine how he could have survived in that prison for long.

"That's enough, I'm sorry Alec. Please accept my most sincere and humble apology." James said getting on his knees, shaking.

It most certainly wasn't fear that James was experiencing. It was most definitely fury. The things that were flashing through his head at the moment were horrifying. Things that he wished he was doing to Alec and things that he was fantasying about.

Alec walked slowly up to James and said in a kind voice, "Unfortunately, I don't accept your apology."

"Sorry to hear that, Alec." James commented.

Anything respectful that James tended to say was dripping was sarcasm. It was actually really entertaining to be around.

"No, don't be!" He smiled. "The only person that should be sorry is Elaina."

"How about you just help Elaina now, Alec." Jean asked ignoring Alec. "I mean, let's face it. If she dies, you will be the one at fault. Not us. I'm wondering how Scorn will react when you let his daughter die so you could mess with James..."

Alec sprinted *way* faster than I could see and shoved poor Jean into the stone walls of the cell. "You need to shut the hell up."

"I am just trying to help *you*, Alec. I wouldn't want you to end up in a cell like this one for screwing up the only job Scorn has given you." He smiled.

"You all should know the drill. About anything important you need to make a blood assurance." Alec said dropping Jean.

"A what?" Jean asked.

"Oh, I forgot you never got a chance to learn from Scorn. You screwed your life over before he even began to like you enough to tell you anything. A blood assurance is a type of promise. You cut yourself on your palm and mix blood with the person you are making a promise to and of course, mix some spirit in there as well so you can't break the promise. Your very DNA prevents you from having the ability to do that.." Alec said.

"Oh... that's not cool." Jean said.

"Do you all know how to make a spirit blade?" Alec asked.

Jean sighed, "Obviously."

Alec laughed, "Not this kind."

"What makes you think that?" Jean asked.

"Because you're an idiot and it's not meant for killing which, if I recall correctly is all you know how to do." He spat. "I'll just do it for you idiots. Hold out your hands." Alec said to them.

The boys obediently held out their hands. He slashed Jean's hand open, then moved on to James and slashed his hand open, then slashed Soren and Kalus's hand open, but when he got to Lucas, "I'll do it myself, thanks. I was taught how to do it." He said to Alec a little hesitantly.

"As you wish, Lucas. I'll just slash Rissa and take her to Scorn." Alec said.

"No. No, no, no." He stuttered. "You can cut me. Just don't touch her."

See, now maybe if they actually gave a damn about me, I would find them all really sweet for constantly trying to protect me but the thing is, I think it's more of a feeling like if we keep this kid safe, she'll break us out of prison. They didn't care for me, they cared for the escape I was providing. Heartwarming, isn't it?

"As you wish." Alec laughed. He slashed deeply into Lucas's hand. Alec then walked over to me and slashed eight times to make an asterisk star on both of my palms.

"Whoa, I thought you said that you wouldn't hurt her if-" Kalus yelled.

"Alright, alright, that's enough. She needed to be cut. And I knew none of you wimps had it in you to cut her eight times on each hand so I did it for you." Alec said plainly.

"Eight times..." Soren murmured skeptically. "I've done plenty of blood assurances, they don't require so many cuts."

"Man, each and every one of you are so clueless. No wonder Scorn dumped your useless lives." Alec said.

He thought that he was all high and mighty just because he was Scorn's direct servant. But I knew the truth. He was a prisoner, just like the rest of us, but instead of being locked in a cage he was locked in a prison, and told to keep the rest of us in check.

"Stack your cut hands on top of each other's and put it on Rissa's left hand." Alec said.

It bothered me *more* when people called me Rissa then because... well I really had no clue who I was. I figured that just because I was turning into a Cheuvean, I was turning into Rissa. I didn't get that I always was my own person. I didn't know that I am me not matter what.

My cell mates did as told and Alec said some kind of different language. This time I could actually understand the different language. The language seemed very pure... It was the Cheuvean language that was destroyed ages before and is now only used for powerful spells and blood assurances.

"Goddess of Cheuva, we sacrifice our blood into this girl to assure that we will keep a promise we made on your name. I ask you to make sure that this promise is kept inside the walls of this prison." Alec said.

"There, the blood assurance has been taken care of so will you take care of Elaina's transformation into Rissa?" James asked.

"Say please." Alec taunted.

"Don't push it, Alec." James growled shoving up against him.

Intimidated, he took a step back to keep James out of his face and at least at an arm's length away. "Very well then. One of you can come along if you wish." Alec stumbled.

He realized that if I woke as Rissa, it'd be best to keep me calm with someone I actually felt comfortable with instead of two people that, to be blunt, scared the living daylights out of me.

"Uhm, guys its best if one of us goes along just to make sure that he doesn't do anything unexpected but it should be someone who she trusts." Lucas said.

"Then I guess I should go. I've known her longer than any of you guys have... besides she can't resist me. No one can resist me." James stated matter of factor-ly.

I wanted to laugh but thanks to my transformation I was knocked out. Well, on the bright side; I found out one more thing about the mysterious James. I found out how incredibly arrogant he is.

"Well she has been doing a pretty good job of resisting you so far, James. After all, her hatred of you managed to carry into two different lifetimes. I mean, come on, how many hundreds of years has it been? I seem to have lost count." Alec said.

"Shut up, Alec." James said. "Things could have been different and we both know that."

"Excuse me? Is that allowed?" Alec asked.

"Sorry…" James whispered looking at the ground.

"What did you say? I didn't quite get that. Speak up." Alec said using James's pride against him and holy sweet Jesus; this guy was annoying me out of my mind.

"I apologize, Alec. It won't happen again." James said loud enough for everyone to hear.

"I'm glad to hear that." Alec said tossing me onto his shoulder. "And James,"

He put something in my mouth, I don't know what it was, but whatever it did, it stopped the pain.

"The pertinent information about the matter is that things *weren't* different."

Everything went dark starting with the duration of a thought that didn't belong to me.

Finally, I. Am. Back.

CHAPTER SIXTEEN
I'm no longer human. Who does that make me? Elaina or Rissa?

Dear Diary,

I had a de ja vu dream. I remembered that they burned the Duran Village today. And it's all my fault. Duran is dead and I don't think that any of the Duran Children survived either. He warned me that it was all a bad idea. Duran warned me, I mean. They captured me and James too. I should have never put them in harm's way. That was my fault. I should have known that there is really no escape from Scorn. I'm going to have to live with this for the rest of my life.

-Me

I remember waking up with James kneeling over me. Whatever they did, it worked. "You're awake. I'm so glad to see you're well again Elaina." James said.

I stared at the people in the room a little confused. I didn't speak I had forgotten all that had happened from when I was human.

"Elaina, do you remember anything?" Alec asked.

"Elaina? Who are you? Are you one of Scorn's minions?" I asked.

I was *strong*. I didn't perform any magic, but everything felt different. In a good way. I could see so clear and adjust my vision to see something miles away, to seeing microscopic particles in the air, to regular vision and everything was moving slower. No wonder Cheuveans were such good fighters!

My emotions affected me differently, providing me with a clear mind and a calm appearance.

I appeared calm even though I was furious. I could hear anything I wanted. My voice was soothing and sweet. My movements flowed like water. I was perfect.

"Hey, bitch," He began reaching towards me.

"Touch me and I will shatter your hand, you overly pretentious piece of scum."

"Calm down, it's for your own good if you just shut up." James hinted quietly.

"I'll kill you James." I said.

"Oh… that's… wow. She doesn't remember anything." James said.

He IGNORED my threat. *Does he know who I am? Does he remember what I can do?*

"Maybe it's for the best, James. I mean, don't you agree? Maybe she can finally make a decent decision." Alec smiled at me.

"Oh my sweet daughter. I'm glad you have finally changed back." Scorn said in such a sweet voice that it hurt.

I still hated him. "Scorn, drop dead." I spat.

My memories were gone but different heart wrenching memories took their place. Even in Rissa's world, I was never happy. There was nothing for me on either side.

"Rissa, show some respect for your father." Scorn said angrily.

Funny, he was the only one that understood that I thought I was his precious *Rissa*.

"Oh, SHUT UP. How stupid can you be? I have never seen you as a father and I don't have any respect for you, and we both know that I will take you down." I said attempting to stand.

"Scorn, will she recover her memory of being Elaina?" James asked.

"Hopefully, never. No one really liked the Elaina we knew anyways." Alec laughed.

"I didn't ask you." James snapped.

"Whoa, touchy, James. What does she really mean to *you* anyways?

"If I'm correct, she should be able to remember everything very soon or remember nothing at all..." Scorn said. "She should hopefully snap back to Elaina's reality. Or my plan is, to put it in your words, screwed."

"What does that mean?" James asked.

"It *means* I handpicked the girl here because of how she is. Everything was preset. Destiny was set so this moment would occur. I need this to happen." Scorn said.

"So we may have ruined Elaina's life for no reason?" Alec asked.

"That is correct." Scorn said.

Alec laughed thinking, *sucks for her*.

What kind of dick thinks that?

After that I got a major headache and started having all the flashbacks and memories of... well, being Elaina. Soon, I finished remembering everything and I had so many mixed emotions, so many new ways of thinking. However, the most noticeable change was my incredible lack of strength. My power, everything that made me feel like I was on cloud nine was gone because my humanity was back. Yay humanity.

"Do you remember everything now, my daughter?" Scorn asked.

"Screw you." I said. I apparently had Rissa's courage, Elaina's stupidity and both of their big mouths combined to make my new personality.

As Elaina I would never say that because I would be afraid of the punishment, as Rissa I wouldn't say that because I would be smart enough to try and manipulate him and get on his good side so I could escape easily, but me; well I get on his bad side and I get watched by him and make it nine times harder to escape.

"My apologies Scorn. She is going through hard times and that causes her to get rude to her superiors." James said smoothly. "She doesn't know what she's doing."

I'm glad that James was there to fix what I had just said. I was constantly making things more difficult for myself. I only needed to stay quiet, do what I was told once in a while, smile and act like I didn't want these idiots to go through hell but all that is really a lot easier said than done.

Shut the hell up Elaina! If you make them mad now then we're both dead! James thought to me.

But I- Alright, James. I thought back. "I'm very sorry Scorn, Alec. Please accept my most humble apology. I'm just... confused. I know that's no excuse for my behavior but... it's my obligation to say "I'm sorry" anyway." I apologized.

That apology consisted of complete and utter bull shit.

"Apology accepted my dear Rissa." Scorn said.

"Shall I take them back to their cage?" Alec asked.

Scorn nodded. Alec chained James's hands together but left my hands unbound and walked us out side.

Of course, he wouldn't handcuff me. I'm not strong enough to be a threat. Jerk decided to make that absolutely obvious.

As soon as the doors shut, we were alone in the corridor of the dungeon. Alec slammed me against the wall with his hand around my neck and asked, "How are you doing it, and what are you planning?"

"What are you talking about?" I asked.

"You know just what I'm talking about! How the hell are you blocking both of your thoughts from me?! What are you planning to do?" Alec asked.

"I didn't realize that I was blocking our thoughts from you and I'm not planning anything. I just want to live a peaceful life where you all won't hurt me for being bad." I said.

Alec socked me in the stomach and said, "Oh you'll be beaten no matter what you do. And you aren't fooling anyone. I know you have a plan." A tugging motion caused air to rush around us as inertia tried to hold us in place. Alec had rushed us to the cell and threw both myself and James inside.

As I tumbled and rolled to a stop, Soren, who just happened to be in my path caught me and gently sat me up.

We waited until Alec was far out of sight for my comrades and I to begin conversing.

"Rissa..." Lucas said.

"Hmm?" I responded.

"You look really different, you know that? You've changed." Lucas mentioned

I didn't know what I looked like. I knew what I looked like as Elaina, and as Rissa but I'm like, a mix of the two now.

What the transformation did, was open a doorway between my two lives. I am Elaina. However, slowly but surely I will receive my memories from being Rissa. But until I receive all the memories required for me to be a legitimate Cheuvean, I am just a very unlucky human that cannot die.

"Kalus, can you show Elaina her reflection so she knows what she looks like?" James asked.

"I don't know, *can* I?" Kalus smiled.

"Just show me, Kalus." I said impatiently.

"My, my, testy aren't we? Well alright." Kalus laughed. He waved his hands in some weird motion and then soon there was a puddle on the ground, then the water created a mirror.

Wow... I am pretty. I thought.

I looked the same but my features were modified to make me… perfect. I had my same brown hair flowing just above my hip bone, my eyes had turned a very light blue color; almost like a silver color, a light tan color and flawless skin complexion, long strong fingernails, I had a model's body: dainty arms, my *amazing* hourglass waist line, flat tummy, perfect boobs, and the biggest, roundest butt I had ever seen.

I transformed into *the* perfect girl!

See, now the first thing I saw next to my bed was my little diary. Come to think of it, that's been everywhere I was. It pretty much followed me around to where ever I seemed to sleep. That's actually a pretty important aspect to the little story I'm telling so remember that. "What's the plan?" Soren asked.

"What are you talking about? The plan for what?" I asked.

That was seriously random.

"For escaping here. How much longer will we be here? How do we get out?" He asked shaking.

"It can't be that bad, can it?" I asked.

"I asked you a question." Soren said plainly.

"I have no freaking clue. It will take months, maybe years for us to finally escape… Hell, for all I know, we might never escape. We will need to do so many things… it's not a simple thing for us to do." I said.

"Why will it take so long? I can't stand this place anymore! I want to get out! I want out!" Soren screamed.

He just broke down. *How long has this boy been here for him to get so... frantic to get out?* I asked myself.

"Soren, please calm down!" I hushed him.

He kept screaming. "Get me out!"

I heard footsteps coming towards the cell.

"Please, Soren, stop! Someone's coming!" I hissed.

Kalus came over, "He doesn't stop. When he gets like this, he goes somewhere completely different. He can't feel or hear anything. He needs to get out."

The footsteps sped up.

It's Alec... oh god. I think he's coming to punish Soren for screaming like this. I had to think fast.

There was no way I could get Soren to stop screaming by the time that Alec got here.

That's it! I thought.

I was so lucky one of my identities knew how to think fast. I tackled Soren and pinned him down. He was still freaking out, screaming, "I want to get out!" over and over again.

I punched him... I can't say it was the best thing I could have done but I was under pressure to come up with something fast and I figured this was the best way to get away with it, you know? I threw him at the jail cell and yelled, "How dare you say that to me! I'm going to beat the living daylights out of you." He was facing the outside of the cell and was shaking the bars. This time I kicked him across the chest and he flew onto the ground.

At contact, the cell bars began glowing and even when Soren was no longer touching them, they still glowed. I didn't know what that meant. At the moment, I didn't care.

For once I'm not the one flying across somewhere until I hit something. I'm happy. "How pathetic." I laughed. "You can't take a few hits from me? You little wimp. Next time you really need to think twice before you piss me the hell off." I said.

Alec was watching me mock him.

Soren was still screaming making it look like I really had the power to hurt him... That was when I realized that the bars sucked out spirit when you touched them. I wouldn't have attacked him on them if that was so apparent beforehand. It was terrible. He passed out.

I had to be heartless to pull this off... I was about to kick him again when Alec let out a small chuckle. I stopped what I was doing and turned to Alec.

"Oh, Alec I didn't realize that you were here." I said respectfully. "Is fighting not allowed?"

"Oh really? I suppose your senses aren't as sharp as they should be yet... what did he do to make you so angry?" Alec asked.

Oh shoot I didn't think about that yet... I thought.

"Why so hesitant?" Alec asked.

Wow this idiot thinks that I'm hiding it from him. I am so lucky that he is stupid. I thought.

"Oh, I'm sorry. I dozed off for a second. He insulted me." I said.

"How?" Alec asked skeptically.

"He called me a … a human."

"Oh. I thought you liked humans. Rissa loved humans and Elaina was one so how did it turn out that you started hating them?" Alec asked.

"Rissa? I thought I was Elaina to you." I asked that because everyone seemed to have a different answer as to who I was. James called me Elaina because he *wanted* me to be Elaina, Jean called me Elaina because that's what he met me as, everyone else called me Rissa because they just figured that the human side of me, my history, would all be erased once I became a Cheuvean.

"Scorn told all of us to refer to you as Rissa because that's who you truly are. But answer my question, Rissa."

"I probably turned out to hate humans because everyone I'm around hates them and in Elaina's life I started hating humans when the remainder of their population began hunting me." I said.

"Good." Alec chuckled. "He deserved to be beat up then." He said walking away.

As soon as I knew that Alec could no longer hear us I turned around and I never felt so uncomfortable in all my life. Everyone was glaring at me except Soren who was unconscious.

"Uhm... what?" I asked.

Ugh I felt so weird. There was such an angry aura and that actually affected me physically.

"Why did you do that?" Kalus asked.

"What should I have done?" I asked. I didn't realize that I had done anything wrong.

"Anything but that. You should have protected him not beat him up. How would you feel if we beat you to a pulp?" Jean asked.

"That depends on the situation. Alec was going to hurt him way worse than I just did and you all know that. I saved him a ton of pain. If you all beat me to a pulp to save me from a worse pain I would be grateful but if you just did it for the hell of it that'd be a different deal. Two of you actually did just that, you don't see me having a cow." I said.

"Let's test out your theory." Jean said.

"Stop." James said. "She made a bad choice. She'll receive her punishment, but for now we need her." He explained.

That didn't make my day. *I'm going to receive a punishment? Nice.*

"Hah! None of you can do a thing to me! I'm not a human anymore! You can't push me around anymore! I remember how to fight now. I remember how to protect myself!" I said.

I was bluffing. No way I could fight them and win. "Let's see." Jean tested.

He really wanted to fight me.

"Try and fight me and you'll regret it for the rest of your undying life." I said. That just came out of my mouth but I suddenly realized what that meant and that I was angry enough to use that against them.

"What's that supposed to mean? What can you do to us to make us more miserable than we are here?" Kalus asked.

Wow I made Kalus super angry now. He's actually a pretty chill dude. It takes a lot to piss him off.

"I could join Scorn, I could decide not to help you all escape, I can make your life harder here, and best of all I could make it so you can never leave. How's that? You want to make me mad enough so that I really make all those threats a reality?" I asked.

They were speechless. I should have never said that, it wasn't right for me to hold that over them. I didn't mean it... I was just angry but they all took me seriously. I wasn't totally sure at the time because even though I thought I remembered everything about being Rissa I was wrong... I didn't remember anything except how to fight. That's sad isn't it? A person who has multiple personalities doesn't remember anything about one personality and remembers everything about the useless personality. That's pathetic.

"You're nothing like Rissa... not the one you were anyways. You're a Cheuvean with a *human* brain. The Rissa we were friends with would never *ever* do that to a comrade or threaten us like that. You are not our friend. You are not the same Rissa. You really have nothing going for you." James said.

Now I was the one speechless.

No.... that... that can't be true... I am just as good as Rissa. I do have friends... I thought. I wanted to break down in tears... but I couldn't. That would just show them that what they say affects me. I couldn't show that I cared about what they say. If I did they would push me around... just like they always have. I started laughing this evil laugh. Everyone but James just walked away, into the farthest room from the gate.

Maybe he doesn't really hate me. Maybe he changed his mind. I thought happily.

My main defect back then was that I cared so much. I didn't know any of them but I so desperately needed friends. I had nothing. I wanted something to fight for.

I stopped laughing, hoping he would say something... and he did. I just wish he hadn't.

"I'm really disappointed in you, Ellie. You were our only hope and you turned out to be an insensitive monster. You should have just let Scorn end me when he had the chance. I really can't believe you, Elaina." James said. "I hate you."

I have had the right to say that line to him so many times. Now I know exactly how badly those three words hurt. He picked up Soren and began walking away, following the others.

"Wait, I'm-" I began.

He appeared in front of me and stuck his finger and against my mouth to shut me up.

"Save it. 'I'm sorry' isn't enough. This time you'll have to earn your place back on our side." James said. He walked out of the room without another word. I slammed my back on the wall to keep my balance.

There was something behind what I was feeling. I thought maybe my desperation for friends was the source of my pain but reality of it was that I felt something for James. It *should* be hate. He ruined me. But the emotion was positive.

I hated him for being able to verbally hurt me so easily but couldn't get past the *fate* we shared. I slowly fell down to the ground, silently sobbing, not able to stop. Funny how they needed *me* but I had to earn *my* place back on their side.

"Ridiculous. You finally did something your father would be proud of and you sit there and sulk about it. I can't believe you're his daughter. You act nothing like your mother or father and yet all you want is everyone's approval. You'll never fit in. you just want to be one with the crowd and you are the exact opposite." Alec said.

That surprised me.

Did he realize that I lied about why I hurt Soren? I wondered.

"What's going through your mind, Alec? I don't understand exactly what you're saying. When did you start watching me?"

I asked not even looking at him. I didn't even care to look at him. I didn't care if I got a punishment. He wasn't important… his very existence was irrelevant to me.

"Hmmm you seem sad. Might it have something to do with how you just lost all your allies?" He asked.

"Shut… Yes. It does have something to do with the fact that I lost my friends…" I said.

"But on the bright side you have scored some points with the dark side." Alec chuckled at his own joke. "And Rissa, you need to know that they were never your friends. You are their escape route. That's all you ever will be to them."

"Why did you really beat your comrade up?" He asked.

"It's just as I told you. Don't you believe me?" I asked.

"Why in the world would I believe you?" he asked.

"Because I have a brain and I would be putting myself in a very bad position if I started lying to you on my first day here. In other words, because of my current position if I can't get on *more* your bad side just yet. If I continue playing good girl I just might find a way out of your bad side." I said.

He started laughing.

"Well then. You might just be right. Well at least I hope your right, for your sake." He said.

He just walked away. *I wanna kill that little... Ugh deep breaths... deep breaths... calm thoughts... okay I'm good now. What in the world am I supposed to do in a cell where everyone hates me?* I thought.

You're supposed to apologize, and offer to do anything to make up for the crime you have committed. Someone thought back to me.

Who in the world are you? I thought.

Oh... you don't recognize my voice, Rissa? She thought back. She had a very playful innocent voice but also lacking most emotion... and sad.

You're in this prison? I asked.

Of course I am. Do you think Scorn would allow any voices from the outside to enter this prison? He may not have many precautions but the one thing he did actually care about was magic from the outside interfering with his plans in this particular prison. She said.

I heard that voice before but I couldn't quite match the voice to a name or face.

What do you mean? Are you a prisoner or one of his employees? I asked.

I'm a prisoner. Now that we have a leader, only people on your side of this battle of good versus evil can hear your voice right now. She said.

Oh. That's quite interesting. So, anyways, I'm not going to apologize. That's a waste of time for me. They will take advantage of me if I show any weakness. I said.

That's the Rissa I remember. She said.

Who are you? I asked.

Talk to you later, Rissa. She said.

I already knew it was useless to argue. Her presence was already gone. Besides, I had other problems to resolve. I walked up to James and the others and just blurted out, "Who else can read my mind?" Soren was awake now.

"Hi, Rissa." Soren said.

"Oh, you're not mad at me? Everyone else is… wait, that doesn't matter! Who else can read my mind?" I asked again.

"Anyone." Soren responded.

"Building off of that incredibly uninformative answer..?" I hinted for a further explanation.

"Everyone on our side can read your mind and everyone who knows a lot about you can read your mind." Kalus finished

"So anyone who happens to go to Scorn's side can tell what I'm thinking?" I asked.

"Well… only if they know a lot about you." Soren answered.

"That doesn't make it better! How did you guys *not* think about someone feeding information to Scorn?" I asked.

"Calm down, Rissa." Soren whispered.

Rissa… maybe I really should get used to that…

"How can you say that? It's impossible to escape here. I can't help any of y-" I began. A sword was pointed at me neck. It was seriously cold and it caused me to stop talking.

"Don't you dare talk like you are on our side. If you don't get us out of here I will personally make sure your life is living hell." James said.

"It already is; you ensured that long ago. Don't assume that you have power over me… 'Cause I'll prove you wrong." I said.

"Stop." Soren sat in the corner, staring sadly at me. "She protected me and I would have gone through much more pain if she didn't step in. If you have a problem with her then you don't escape. Understand?" Soren said.

OH MY GOD HE SAID A FULL SENTENCE!

Finally. One can think. I thought.

Shut up. James thought to me.

Can you people PLEASE stay out of my head? I asked.

Nope. What's the fun in that? Lucas thought sticking his tongue.

"I don't like you people." I said.

James and Lucas laughed.

"So we're all on the same side?" Kalus asked.

"I guess..." I said.

"And we don't really have a choice." Lucas added playfully.

It's really so sad. Each and every one of us are very, *very* emotionally unstable. It is easy to piss us off and even easier to have us make up ten minutes later. The reason behind that is unknown to me.

"Now, what is the plan to get out of here?" Jean asked.

"As I told Soren, I don't exactly have one yet. This is my first day here and, well, what we're up against an army; Scorn's army. It isn't a simple thing to do." I said.

"Why are you wasting time?" Jean asked.

"I understand that this place is bad and all so I will work in my spare time but... ugh, whatever. There's no use talking about this. Do you people have any talents?" I asked.

They looked at me like I was speaking in a different language. "We're amazing?" Kalus smiled.

"Fighting talents?"

"Sense we always have time to try out new things, we know all of our talents. It's not like we are in a prison or anything." Kalus stared.

"I didn't ask for sarcasm, Kalus. You lived a full life outside of this prison... but I suppose you didn't need to fight before either... You guys have never tried to spar or anything? Don't you have plenty of spare time since you never leave the cell?" I asked.

"We leave the cell sometimes. But that's to run laps around our field or to go play the... games." Jean responded bitterly looking out the cell doors.

Lack of eye contact. There was something that I couldn't see going on there and I knew that. "How many laps do you guys run?" I asked.

"About thirty... I mean... Sixty." Lucas said.

Stuttering, lack of eye contact, confusion. BS. "Why is it sixty?" Pay attention to your gut, because your instincts will always be ultimately correct.

Everyone looked down. *That only makes it obvious that you think I'm going to get mad so why don't you all just tell me?* I thought.

"We made a deal with Alec..." Lucas admitted.

"What was the deal?" I asked holding back any remarks I had.

"He took you to Scorn and helped you with your transformation. As payment, we train harder for the games. Are you angry?" Lucas asked.

"Yeah." I responded gently and I took a deep breath, exhaled. *Pretend to be encouraged. Pretend to be filled with real optimism.* I reminded myself. "But you all did it to help me. 'Sides, no matter how many advantages they have over us we will still escape."

For once, the cell was peaceful. Happiness was in the air just for a little while and you'd be surprised how far a little happiness can take you in this world; in our world. But happiness, especially in our world comes to an end quickly and ours unfortunately ended as Alec came to a stop at our cell once again.

"Let's go, you all. It's time for practice." He said unlocking the cell doors. I was the last to leave the cell and as I was going through the cell door Alec slammed his hand against me to stop me from going through the door.

"I liked you better as a human." He said.

"I'm sorry to hear that, Alec." I responded half heartedly.

"You were so much more helpless. So much easier to knock down and see reactions from... but now that you have some Rissa in you, your heart has hardened and your human muscles were replaced with stronger, more useful muscles. I want the pathetic wimp back." He said.

"I would love to make you happy, Alec, but I'm afraid that I can't do that for you." I said removing his hand from my chest.

I wasn't nearly as confident as I put out. And for good reason too. This feeling of false power and confidence would only last a few days—until they found out the truth about my incredible lack of power.

We got to the dumb track field and I think each lap was about one mile long. I was surprised to see how much stamina I had. I finished my forty laps in about fifteen minutes when everyone else finished their sixty about a minute and a half before I did.

"Learn to keep up with everyone soon, Rissa." Dylan said knocking me on the side of the head.

"And that's supposed to help me run faster?" I asked.

"Learn your place." Dylan said knocking me on the side of the head again.

"Yes, Sir." I saluted.

Dylan laughed and said, "Good you're learning."

He knew that I was mocking him

Okay, I really don't like him. I thought.

None of us do. James laughed.

"What are you all waiting for? Get back to your rooms." Alec growled pushing James.

All of my cell mates were laughing, which resulted in Alec and Dylan getting angrier, which made it even funnier.

They had no idea why they couldn't read our minds and the thing is they knew that we were thinking some mean stuff and they couldn't do anything about it.

I constantly needed to remind myself that these people were not good. I wanted to believe that they had good in them deep down. I *felt* it.

But I would be a terrible person if I didn't hate these people, right? I'm supposed to hate them. They deserve it. But I just can't bring myself to do that.

So, we got back to our cell, we were all buddies again, Alec and Dylan hated us, and my life still stunk.

I just thought I'd give a short summary in case you were lost in the story and didn't understand a thing that was happening. I just never know about you humans now days.

"Okay, who is able to move enough to spar a little?" I asked.

"Why do we have to spar right after we run?" Jean moaned.

"Because we need time and at the moment we don't have much of that." I said.

"So? You took your time running those laps. We had to sprint through all sixty laps." Kalus breathed a laugh.

"Well, I'm not completely used to this body yet. You guys, on the other hand, have had your entire endless lives to perfect your movement and stamina. My movement ability is at zero and my stamina is just as high, so don't give me that." I said.

"You have definitely changed, Rissa. What happened to the easygoing little girl we all used to hang with?" Kalus asked.

That was the first time it honestly crossed my mind that I am and always will be *me.* It first occurred to me that I shouldn't be trying to fill Rissa's old shoes. The truth was that she had been gone a long while and I am here now. "Okay, that 'little girl' you speak of is nonexistent! I doubt she was ever really happy. My guess is that she just pretended to be happy for all of you.

Second of all, her memories are no longer here. All I remember are the bad times! Last off is how some of you didn't even know me! What *are* you talking about?" I asked.

"We were there! Everyone knew you. We all used to hang with you in the Duran Village." Lucas said.

"What could have been so bad that you remember?" Jean asked.

"My parents were slaughtered in front of me, I remember my other parents locking me in jail, I remember getting beat up for being who I was, and I remember all those times where I was getting mauled by everyone without a single friend to help me get through it. I was alone. I was always alone." I growled.

I guess I was a bit upset that they *didn't* feel bad for me. They actually really believed that I was happy and that *upset* me. One of the things that differ with humans and Cheuveans is that Cheuveans are not fake. If they do not like you, you will *know*. If they are sad, you will know. Humans on the other hand, I don't know if it's because of kindness or maybe because they are self-centered, but they are *fake.* *Rissa* had human traits in her—just like me.

"Why?" Soren asked quietly.

"Why what?" I asked, more annoyed.

"You said that Rissa pretended to be sweet and happy. Why wouldn't you do the same?" He repeated more specifically.

Those words that just came from his mouth made me feel like slapping him.

"You're asking me to be someone I'm not. That girl is non-existent. Besides, would me being sweet break you out of jail? If I was being sweet, we would *never* get out of here." I said.

"Enough. Let's get training." James said.

"Why are you siding with her?" Jean asked.

"Because she's right. We all know she's right. Come on guys, just train. It's really not that hard. Besides, once we find what we're good at and escape this god forbidden hell hole, we can be as lazy as we want." James said.

"What do we do first?" Kalus asked.

I thought silently to myself, *Why is it that they listen to James so easily and not the actual person who can get them out of this "hell hole?"*

"Do you guys have any access to sticks or swords?" I asked.

"Our own swords. They would have to take away everything before they could take away our own weapon. They're attached to our DNA. We just need you to find a way to summon your sword. You haven't even learned how to do that yet." Kalus said.

"How do I take out the sword then?" I asked.

"It comes out with a certain emotion. We just need to find that emotion that you use most; that emotion that you have in you all the time and that you rarely show but when you show it, it's a really strong emotion." Kalus explained.

"You said you pretend to be happy, so it's not happiness, you probably aren't too sad because you're not that hard to please, and chances are you're not scared all the time because... well you would have had a nervous breakdown from what you're going through and if that were the case, I don't think your weapon could have been withdrawn." Lucas decided.

What does that leave us with? I thought to him.

"Betrayal." Soren laughed quietly. *Weird inside joke?*

"What do you mean? You can't betray me. You know you're in no position to betray me!" I said. I was getting so angry.

"Alec! Come quick!" James yelled.

"What?!" I yelled. I was ready to destroy all of them! Angry couldn't describe what I was feeling. I wasn't feeling betrayal.

"What is it?" Alec appeared.

"Rissa is insulting Scorn and talking about escaping! It's not right! She even said that you were *weak* and she could beat you to a pulp." James said.

He didn't even call me Elaina that time. He always called me Elaina.

You could see from the look on Alec's face that he was mad... His eyes widened and soon after turned to a glare and wouldn't look away from me which normally wasn't a good sign.

"You think that you could beat me to a pulp?" Alec asked.

"No." I replied.

"Let's find out, shall we?" Alec smiled holding out his hand.

I couldn't hear any thoughts in their mind. I thought that meant that they were no longer on my side which was indicating betrayal but I wasn't feeling that they betrayed me, I felt pissed.

"No. I know who's goin'a beat the life out of whom and you'd beat the life right out of me." I said.

"How 'bout we try anyway." He smiled sarcastically.

I returned his smile, "Let's not and say we did."

I was really hoping that he wouldn't fight me but with my luck, there was no way that I would get out of this without a fight. He disappeared and re appeared behind me.

Crap. I thought.

It was over before it really even began.

He simply grabbed my hair and dragged me out of the room. I just made some small sounds in pain from this boy yanking my hair. You know, I can withstand a punch, a stab with a sword, a kick. But pulling my hair crosses that line of pain. It *hurts* when you grab a girl's hair like that.

"Ouch, stop it! I didn't say anything! I didn't say anything! You don't have to fight me!" I screamed.

This wasn't okay. I knew this wouldn't draw out my sword. All that would happen is that I would get injured and I wouldn't be at full strength when I needed to fight.

"I'll tell you a little secret, I don't even believe them. I just want to fight you to see how much you've remembered." Alec said.

"I'll just tell you what I've remembered!" I offered.

I was so desperate to not get hurt; I mean I had to be I tip top condition to escape from here.

"No." he chuckled.

"Come on; just-just let me go. Let me live my forever lasting life in peace. You're already going to keep me in a cage for… forever. Isn't that good enough for you?" I asked.

"No. We don't want you to stay in that cage forever. We want you to join us." He said.

"Then how is this going to help me join you? It'll help me hate you." I said.

"We're just going to make your life very difficult until you come to your senses." He said sweetly.

"That's never going to happen." I said.

"You have no idea how wrong you are, little girl." He said.

He let go of my hair, grabbed the back of my shirt and threw me across the room.

How is it that he can still do that to me? I'm not human anymore, so why am I so weak?

After that I came to the conclusion that I did remember how to fight BUT my body was incapable of performing any of the technique.

All of a sudden, Alec had a stone sword in his hands. It looked so strange; like a rock with fragments of rocks coming out from the side.

"That things going to rip me to pieces! Come on, I don't stand a chance. We both know I don't stand a chance!" I yelled.

"That'll make this all the more fun." Alec laughed.

"What will?" I asked.

"Your fear." He answered.

"I'm not scared of you." I said making an attempt to conceal my fear.

"Well then, if you're not scared of just him, then how bout both of us?" Dylan asked just appearing.

FML

I sighed and looked them both straight in the eye, one right after the other. "Just get it over with."

"Thank you so much for giving me your approval." Alec shrugged lazily.

Suddenly, I was on the ground, with something really heavy on top of me. "Don't tell me what to do, bitch." Dylan said.

He put his hand up against my face, for some reason. Now, my face was burning. It was like my skin was being burned off.

"No, NO STOP! That hurts, stop it, please! Make it stop!" I screamed.

My nerves were working much more... effectively than when I was human. Not only could I feel the pain faster, and it hurt more. "Already? You shouldn't give in so quickly, little brat." He said.

He was concerned about my giving in so easily because if I started screaming from the very beginning, he wouldn't have as much fun watching me squirm from pain, attempting to hide what I was thinking.

Frustration overcame me. Defenseless, stupid, ignorant, useless... I was nothing. "What did you guys do to me? I don't remember anything about my human life, or my Cheuvean life... I'm weaker than a human. *What did you do to me*?"

"We didn't do anything to you. Remember, we want you to be of use to us and you won't be of any use as a... as the way you are now." Alec said.

"Get off. Please, get off." I pleaded.

"Wow." Dylan said gently getting off of me. "Scorn did it."

"What?" Alec asked walking towards me, "Wow." His jaw dropped.

"W-what? What's so wow?" I asked.

"You need to promise me now that you won't scream if I tell you." Alec said slowly.

"Just tell me." I said.

"Your face is burned... through the bone. Like, I can see INTO your bone. That shouldn't be able to happen. Your bones should be indestructible, your muscle should be impenetrable. You can break bones but never actually destroy the matter that creates them. This was never supposed to happen." With every word, Alec's pitch raised with accomplishment and excitement. "This is overkill!"

"So? It'll heal." I said.

"Yeah but it *shouldn't* happen. We should be flawless... you're broken." Alec said plainly. "We're going to be over powerful hybrids and you're obsolete."

"Thanks for telling me nicely." I scoffed.

"Anytime." Alec laughed patting me on the head.

Idiot one and Idiot two took me back to my cage and slammed the cell door without looking back.

They still seemed to be disturbed at how Dylan burned me. Oh, and speaking of disturbed, "Oh, god! What in the worlds happened to your face?" Lucas asked.

Thank you Lucas.

"Wow, glad you know how to be so polite about things." I glared. "I can tell you were just *so* popular with the ladies back before you were captured by Scorn."

"How?" Soren asked.

"How exactly would I know that?" I asked.

"Who and what element." James explained more clearly for Soren.

"Why would I work with you all? You sold me out for something I didn't even do. I don't see my motivation for telling you anything." I mumbled stubbornly.

I just kind of sat on the floor and covered my head... somewhat ashamed of my burn mark.

"Rissa, you need to tell us what you know if we plan on escaping this place." Jean said.

"Oh... too bad. I guess you should have thought about that before you managed to get Alec and Dylan to beat the life out of me." I laughed.

"You need to cooperate with us. If you don't you will never leave and you will never succeed in living that normal life you always wanted. Plus as a bonus to making us all live in jail for the rest of time, all your cell mates will despise you and make your life hell." Jean threatened.

"Oh... that's... wow. Just apologizing would have worked fine too but why do that when you could threaten me? Dylan has ability with Acid. I was unaware of that fact until he used it on my face. James, did you ever see Dylan use that type of tactic before?" I asked.

"Until now he only was able to use magic tactics." James explained.

"Isn't acid magic?" I asked.

"Not in the way that he used it... Let me explain. There are Four main sections of fighting types: Mage, Fighter, Distance, and Ally..." Kalus began.

This was a very long and complicated conversation so I made a diagram in my diary to make sure I could study and remember it.

Power Chart Notes
-Mage -
Elementor: Element controller (This is what Soren is) Super-duper rare.
Psych : Psychic powers (similar to teleportation and levitation and stuff.)

-Most that have the "Mage" class have the Psych power instead of the Elementor because each class gets assigned a specific element automatically but when you are "blessed" with the Elementor race you get an affinity for all elements instead of the usual one.

-*Fighter*-

Macer (has two sections)
- *Long Macer: Has power over one very long handled axe (similar to the ones used to behead people in England before guillotines were created)*
- *Clubbion: Has power over a spiked club*

Blade (has two sections)
- *Double: Has two shorter and more agile swords wielded in each hand to use the "Slice and dice" approach.*
- *Single: One long sword (this is what James is.)*

-*Distance*-

-*Archer: Bowman (What Lucas is)*
Boomerang: They use these weapons that are basically like a "windmill shrunken" except it

"boomerangs" and comes back to the user after they throw it.

   -Ally
   Healer: Pretty self-explanatory (they heal things. Trees, people, animals, worlds, etc.)
   Stronger: They improve performance. Similar to your own personal steroid. They improve everything about you: speed, personality, just name it.

   -Apothic-
   Me. I have an affinity for multiple of the above, I just need to learn to use them and figure out which ones I really am.

   Kalus previously explained that there were FOUR main sections for fighting types. I took notes. Well, I guess there's five but it goes unnamed seeing as there is only one Apothic (me) I can't classify as an entire section. Makes sense.

"A little more infrequent than I expected, but what'evs," *evs* in the vocabulary of Elaina equals *Whatever.* "In the end I'm pretty correct. They knew that I had done nothing wrong but wanted an excuse to fight. I'm assuming that was possibly to test their new abilities. Maybe Scorn has found a way to help people gain more abilities than normal Cheuvean bodies can hold without... or maybe with the risk of the body no longer functioning which is why he kept Dylan and Alec." I explained. "And it seems that they have succeeded in making the magic more powerful and my face is proof of that. At the same time though, there's no way to be completely certain because I *am* a half broken human."

"Why is that relevant?" Jean asked.

"Which part?" I asked.

"The more powerful magic part." Kalus confirmed.

"If this continues and Scorn succeeds in creating an unnaturally strong army we will have no chance of escaping, or if we somehow find a way to escape, we will not be out of his reach for long and then we will face worse circumstances than we are currently facing." I said.

"Is there any way of preventing this from occurring?" James asked.

"If I'm correct, we may be able to stop it if one of us gets on their side. It would have to be an inside job. That person would feed the information they receive to us and we know more, and more about them. Does that plan work for you all?" I asked. That was close to a fool proof plan... or as close as it could get in this joint.

"Yeah, sounds great... but who would the spy be?" Lucas asked.

"Obviously the best person of the job would be Rissa." Jean blurted out.

That was absurd. "*What*? No! Why?" I croaked.

"Well, first, it was your idea so you would be most clear on the plan. Second, who would Scorn take in more openly than his daughter that he has been trying to get on his side for apparently years." Kalus explained.

"So, we have all that figured out. When will Plan Suicide begin?" Lucas asked.

"After we show everyone just what we're made of." I explained.

"Sounds like this plan will work easily." James said. "And lucky for us, our next duel is tomorrow. For now, we need to find out how to get your sword out."

"Right. I'd bet Scorn would be pissy if I couldn't even do that. Geez this is going to be so bothersome." I moaned.

"We could toy with your emotions some more. That could very easily work." James said.

"You'll only succeed in getting me pissed off at you." I scoffed.

"That's the plan, stupid." Kalus laughed.

"Don't call me that, Kalus." I warned.

Yet another demonstration of my Cheuvean, emotional stability.

"Watch your temper. Remember what and who we can put against you." Kalus pushed.

"I'm warning you, you worthless piece of-" I yelled.

They can make me angry really easily. All it took was Kalus saying two sentences to me and I was ready to kill him.

James walked up to me and held the sides of my arms, keeping me still and forcing me to stare at him. He made eye contact and I was stunned. I couldn't look away but at the same time, I didn't have the urge to. His pupils dilated once again, just like when I was still human. "Hush, Rissa. Remember you still have some family. If we say the word Alec may just take care of them and completely isolate you. We wouldn't want that, right?" James threatened.

I attacked him... to watch the annihilation of everything I lived for again... would be unbearable.

James laughed dodging all of my punches and kicks until I left an opening. He pushed with just enough force to make me skid on the ground.

"What's wrong, Rissa? Not strong or fast enough to lay even one hit on me? Hey, guys how bout you all restrain her. I'll go get Alec and tell him what he should do."

That was the wrong string to pull. I screamed attacking everyone who came in fighting distance of me. I'm sure they were all going easy on me; after all, they only wanted me to be able to summon my sword.

After attacking all of my cellmates unsuccessfully, I was able to pull out my sword. I was still enraged though, I swung my sword at him time after time until James found an opening to grab my wrist with the sword in it, turn me around and cradle me gently.

"Calm down. Un-summon your sword. I would never do anything to hurt you, Elaina. You know that. Just please, un-summon your sword."

His voice was so smooth and calming. From behind me, he held me and half tuned me around so he could look straight into the eyes, his pupils dilated and my mind went blank.

I thought that it was his voice that was the only thing that could ever get me to stop my rampage or maybe even my possible feelings for him. But I was naive. It was magic.

I dropped my sword and became as calm as I could be and the sword I worked so hard to get disappeared.

"Now, let's go into the back rooms and try and get that sword summoned again." James said slowly walking me out of front side of the cage.

"Imagine what you were feeling a few moments ago when you were trying to kill everyone. Try to imitate that feeling." James said standing a few yards back.

I closed my eyes for a few moments and remembered my anger. But it wasn't working.

"Ellie, you weren't feeling just anger. You wanted to protect your people. Think protection." James smiled

Thinking of it more and more made it easier to pull out the sword. Suddenly a sword appeared in my hand.

It was tinted a light hot pink color (also my favorite color). There was a dark red and pitch black aura around it. "How can I tell what it does?" I asked.

"Test it." Soren told me walking into the room.

"On what?" I asked.

I knew the answer I just didn't want to think it was true. I really didn't want to hurt anyone.

"Us." Soren whispered holding out his hand. "Tap."

I knew it was a bad idea but I went along with it anyway. I tapped my sword on his hand and his entire arm had shattered. Fragments of his bones shot out of his skin, his joints in his were no longer working. Apparently my sword had the ability of spirit.

"Oh my god! I'm so sorry! Here I can heal it!" I panicked. Soren really didn't talk too much to begin with but this was ridiculous. He just nodded or completely ignored everything. He was in some serious shock.

I had him lay on the floor. He was very relaxed, but you could tell he was hurting a lot. I gently touched his arm and a glowing light came out of my hands. I didn't really know what I was doing, and I didn't have any memory of healing anyone so I suppose I was doing this on pure instinct.

Slowly, his arm was getting its normal shape back. And progressively, his arm was regaining its mobility. "Are you okay Soren?" I asked talking in as much of a calm, soft, slow voice as I could.

"Yes...What?" he asked confused.

"What, what?" I patiently asked, fighting the urge to scream 'SPEAK IN FULL SENTENCES!'

"Happened." He finished.

JESUS CHRIST.

"My sword has the power of spirit... I think. When I touched your arm, it pretty much self-destructed and the aura of the sword is the color of spirit and I know how strong spirit can be so..." I said ashamed of myself.

"Great!" Soren yelled quietly. Jumping off the ground.

"Hey, Hey! I haven't finished healing you yet! You're going to hurt yourself!" I scolded.

He stared at me. "He can heal himself, Rissa." Kalus smiled patting me on the shoulder.

In just a few moments his arm was in better shape than it was before I destroyed it.

"Oh, before, from what I have seen, I'm not really an expert in anything I'm just good at everything... If that makes any sense. You seem to be best at magic, Soren. James seems to be good with swords and... destruction of all kinds. Jean seems to be best at defense. Lucas has a bow so he must be good at range. And Kalus... I haven't seen much of his talents yet." I said.

"How would you come to those conclusions, oh brilliant one?" Kalus asked.

"I was able to hear what was going on when I was in change. I could hear Soren tell Alec he knew about the promise ritual thingy. Plus he knows all these spell thingies. James... I've seen him fight first hand. Jean is the biggest "scaredy cat" I have ever seen and he knows how to block just about everything. Kalus, I have never seen you do anything so... yeah. Oh and Lucas has a bow so he had sure as hell be good at ranged attacks." I laughed.

"That's nice..." Kalus mumbled.

"What do you enjoy doing? What was your hobby when you were human?" I asked him.

"I never was human." Kalus laughed.

"Well you did that one mirror thing, so is that your specialty?" I wondered.

"No. We all have elements. Mine is water; James's Fire. Lucas is air, and Soren's special. Because he has the affinity for magic in general, he can do everything except spirit.

"Then hopefully we can figure that out sometime soon." I laughed walking away.

"Hey." Kalus said running after me. I ignored him unintentionally. "HEY!"

"Huh?" I asked. I wasn't paying attention.

"Where do you think you're going?" Jean asked.

"Sleep. Duh. It's like, what, 1:00am? I'm tired and if I'm going to sustain torture from Alec, I should get to bed." I said yawning.

"Jean, come. Let her get sleep. Rissa, good night. Be strong for tomorrow. We're going to need it." James said.

"Night." Kalus said walking away.

"Oh, and Kalus... practice... practice your something for tomorrow. Prove your worth." I moaned walking away.

"Okay, princess." Kalus laughed.

Okay, so I went to bed but of course why would I have sleep without having someone contacting me.

Hey Rissa. Miss me?

Oh, It's you. The anonymous prisoner who enjoys talking to me. I thought.

Haven't you figured out who I am by now? I mean I've been with you all my life and you have those time hollows... hmmm I'll give u a hint; my name starts with the letter 'Y' and it's a four letter name. Come on, you should know this! She encouraged.

She seemed so full of hope. Maybe I was about as important to her as I was to my cell mates. What if I let all these people down?

Yuna? You're the rax, right? I asked.

Ohhh I knew you would remember!!! But at the same time, I'm not really a rax. I'm part of YOU.

Man, hearing her voice was so sad. She seemed so full of hope and yet emotionless and pathetic at the same time. It was just so sad.

Yuna, I'm happy to... Uhhh... Hear your voice and all, but is there something you want? I asked.

Yup. Get me out of my tiny little glass cage in Scorn's chambers. She explained.

but... how? I asked. Maybe that little rax could help me a little.

Ask Alec. Maybe he'll be nice for once. Yuna hoped.

Okay. I laughed.

Scorn is coming. So I'm going to go. Yuna thought cautiously. *I'll contact you soon.*

Alright. Bye. I said sleepily.

317

CHAPTER SEVENTEEN
They took away my food

Dear Diary,

It never fails. I wake up every day thinking that maybe this is all just a crazy dream that I haven't woken up from yet. It's amazing how life changes right under your nose, you know?

I was NORMAL a little while ago. Now I'm in a maximum security prison. How did it even come to this? How did I get involved in such an absurd world?

-whoever the hell I am

After that I woke up—thanks so much, Alec. "Hey, guys, wake up. Time to go." Alec called.

The boys moaned and I pretended to be tired. I was a little... scared to get up. I figured that if I didn't move, and didn't do anything at that, nothing would happen to me.

"What? You all don't want to eat?" Alec asked.

After hearing that, everyone practically just got a shot of energy as they practically ran to the gates. Except Kalus and Soren.

Soren noticed my incredible lack of enthusiasm but ignored it intending to not get involved. He shared my belief of just staying out of everything to avoid the consequences.

Kalus stopped at my side and cheerfully "helped" me up. "I'm more intuitive than the others," He began.

"I don't want to go..." I whispered.

"Come on. It should be fine. Please just come along, get your strength. You'll need it."

We were lining up at the cell door, waiting for Alec to let us out. He took his dear sweet time letting us out and I was mistakenly the first to walk out. It was my fault. I should learn to go in the middle of the line because every time I'm at the front of the line or back of the line something bad happens.

I was kind of shoved against the bars of the cell and I could feel my spirit being extracted. I didn't move at all. I didn't struggle. I didn't argue. I was done making my life harder for myself.

Some spirit cuffs appeared around each of their ankles and then connected them all together. Man, I can't even be a normal prisoner. I wasn't hooked to any of them but I was pressed against a cage. Ugh, I hated prison.

"Rissa, is there anything you would like to tell me?" Alec asked me.

"About what?" I asked in plenty of pain. It's hard to talk much less breathe when you're being crushed with the bars of a jail cell.

"Would you like to be let off of the bars?" Alec asked.

"Yes." I whispered.

"Then, what do you say?" He asked.

"Let me down." I whispered.

"I'll give you one more chance to try that again." He warned coldly.

"Let me down, now." I said.

I couldn't handle being a good prisoner, I wanted my dignity back. Too bad I'm too stupid to just stay away from dignity because it always comes back to haunt me.

He let me down. I thought he was going to beat the life out of me but apparently I was wrong. Suddenly, my wrists were stuck together.

"Good job asking for Yuna's freedom, selfish bitch." Dylan murmured.

Ugh! Freakin' spirit cuffs! I thought. "You... you knew?"

"We know *everything.* But don't you worry your pretty little head; she can't bother you anymore. She's locked somewhere nice and safe."

At that I had given up. I figured that if I argued I would get a worse punishment. No point in asking for Yuna anymore. As we were walking to the cafeteria Alec periodically tugged the rope attached to my spirit cuffs just to make my life worse.

When we got to the cafeteria, I couldn't believe I didn't see this coming. The food smelled amazing. There was like, a total of fifty people in there including my cell. My stomach was rumbling like crazy but, when I tried to move something always tugged me back.

Alec and Dylan had brought me to a place where people eat to watch them eat. "Why can't I eat?" I asked.

"Why would I let you eat?" Dylan replied shrugging.

I stared at his overly dry hands. "Why is your skin so dry?"

"Why are you so unreasonably stupid?"

"Yes, of course, my apologies." I sighed. Stupid dignity.

So for an hour and a half I was sittin' there with my belly aching and whining. After that hour and a half the prisoners where brought back to their cells.

"I'm going to DIE!!" I whimpered walking into the back room of our cell.

"Hey, Elaina, we all saved some of our food for you." James whispered, smiling at me.

I thanked him and shoved all the food in my mouth. He chuckled leaving the room.

"wer er uu oing?" I asked with my mouth stuffed.

"I'm going to keep watch. It won't be good if someone sees that we snuck you some food." James smirked. "You're welcome."

"Oka Jame. Tay to." I said good bye to the best of my ability.

"You're welcome." He laughed quietly.

"Mmmm." I hummed after swallowing the remainder of the stolen food.

"Wow, good job savoring the taste." Lucas laughed walking into the room.

"Well I haven't eaten in quite a while. I was really hungry." I laughed.

"Whatever you say, princess." He laughed.

"Man, being in this place is SO boring!" I moaned leaning against the stone wall behind me.

"Hah! You make things interesting! There was never anything different happening in this hell hole until you came along. We all would have *died* of boredom." Kalus smacking Lucas on the back.

"You *do* know that you can't die, right." I asked yawning.

"Well, princess, we would find a way." I laughed at Kalus's joke.

You all probably think our sense of humor is a little off, huh. Well let's see how easily you keep your laughing skill after living our lives.

"You're ridiculous." I said lying down, getting ready for going to bed.

You know, when I was younger, I used to have the hardest time going to sleep. It would take me hours and I would try to do everything in my power to keep myself from lying down. Now, I take like six naps a day and as soon as I lay down I'm out cold.

I wonder why that is... maybe it's because I keep hoping my life was just a dream, or maybe I'm just hoping time will go faster.

I think it was a few hours later when Alec woke us up shouting, "Hey assholes! Time for the game! You'd all better win or..." he whispered the rest...

He whispered it to everyone other than me. What was his special secret that I couldn't know? I tried to read everyone's mind... they pretty much shut down. I didn't hear anyone's thoughts, they didn't hear my thoughts. They blocked me out temporarily.

"You all suck." That was *supposed* to be a thought but I said it out loud instead. "I... oh my gosh. Never mind." I said quickly.

Alec glanced at me for a moment as if to say *I'll just pretend I didn't hear that*. And then looked mindlessly away.

He asked us all to line up to leave the cell. We were silent on the way to the game until I asked, "How is it that we play this game?"

"It's basically a game of capture the flag. Both teams have a flag and they need to get their opponent's flag to their side of the field. You are to fatally wound the other team which will automatically teleport into your home base cage. As they are in the cage, they will be healed, so don't worry about hurting them by doing that. Of course, sword play is allowed." Alec explained.

"Won't that cut them to pieces? And, like, hurt them? A lot?" I asked.

"Yes." Alec said.

"...oh..." I whispered.

Yeah, after that we were done talking. What more was there to say? We were walking silently down the corridor and then we arrived at this *huge* stadium thing. It looked like an enlarged, newer version of the human Coliseum.

When you opened the door, it was very humid, water and fogs were everywhere. It would be pitch black to the human eye... but most of all; the most noticeable thing about that place was the stench. The place wreaked the smell of blood.

How those people got entertainment from this? You got me. I wouldn't know. This just seemed *barbaric*.

The giant doors closed behind us leaving me and my cell mates trapped in this forsaken battle zone until the match was over.

"We are being let out of this place after we beat these people, right?" I asked.

--BEEP -- BEEP-- Good people of Scorn's Kingdom, welcome to the Blood Bath!

"Yes." Soren said quietly.

For this battle, we have Scorn's gem in action with her first battle! So let's not waste any time!

"Then let's beat them and get it over with." James said.

Let the battles begin! --Click—

CHAPTER EIGHTEEN
Mission Suicide. Let's just get this over with.

Dear Diary,

I've never fought before. I wonder what it's like pounding someone's face in. Then again, I suppose I'm about to find out. I'm not too much of a fighter either. Maybe James'll carry us to victory.

-Elaina

"Losing team gets kept here to starve, and then, I think, punished." Kalus said. "We can't let that happen."

"Why would we care?" Lucas asked. "After all, our job is to impress everyone with all our skills and then get Rissa requited. People will thank us for our disregard of their safety soon enough when we burn this place to the ground."

"I'm done talking about this. We are going to do as I say. That's the end of the story. You try and do otherwise and I'll stop you, all of you." Soren hissed.

He was so stressed. Anything that ever had to do with a part of escaping got Soren so angry and impatient.

Hey, you all. Listen up. I think it'll simplify things if we just have one person guard our... Uhhh... flag while Lucas goes somewhere up high and shoots people and the rest of us go up ahead and guard any passage that leads to home base. Destroy anyone who attempts to pass through, including one of us. We would have no reason to go back unless I give the order so chances are it wouldn't be one of us.

Oh, and Soren. You'll be the one guarding our flag. I hope you're okay with that. I thought.

Why would I be the one to have no fun and stay back there? Soren screamed at me telepathically.

For now, I feel like you would be the best at it. You can use so much magic and have more experience than any of us. If we do our job correctly we won't even have to worry about you making an attack. I find that it's always best to leave your strongest as your last resort. I thought.

Whatever. Soren glared.

So much for that tough talk of stopping anyone who defies him.

How many people are we facing? I asked.

I dunno. I think there's supposed to be like ten to fifteen people in each team. Kalus replied.

...But we only have seven people... plus, everyone else has more experience than we have... I said

laughing a REALLY nervous laugh... but I knew I had to toughen up and make some plan to help us win. *Kalus, Practice making the mist over in all those areas. Find out what your ability is other than water. We have to use every advantage we can get. Lucas, be ready to fire those arrows like crazy. Soren, try to make the water in the air thicker so Kalus's can try more to find something that works.*

James, you fight for your life. Jean, you need to try and put a one way shield around us so Soren, Lucas, and Kalus can attack without us dying. Good luck you all. I thought.

After that, I turned off my thoughts. I needed to hear only what was physically around me and I was beginning to get paranoid. It was taking the other team way too long to come for an attack. I turned my thoughts back on,

Hello?

It's about time you answered! We've all been trying to talk to you for... forever. Kalus's attacks aren't doing anything anymore and Lucas can't take a good shot at one of them. We managed to capture four of them but the rest aren't getting harmed by Kalus. What should we do??? Jean asked.

James, can you hear me? I asked.

Yes. What is it? He replied.

We're going behind the barrier and we are going to take out those people one by one. I said.

That's crazy! What are you thinking? He thought sharply.

Why would that be crazy? How many of them are there? I asked.

There's still ten left that we know of, Rissa. It's a suicide if only two of us try and take on ten of them. James thought.

No, I think that makes the odds even. We're skilled in the arts of fighting. We'll destroy them. I encouraged.

Ugh... Fine. James mumbled.

Good. Soren, Your new job is to make sure that the spots James and I have left APPEAR to be walls, instead of pathways to our flag. And, when I tell you to, you need to let go of the shield. Do anything necessary to protect the flag. I said.

My plan to impress Scorn and everyone in Cheuva depended on this type of thing. I will show everyone that even when the odds are stacked against me; I will be victorious. Scorn would do anything to have me at that point.

There was a wall in front of me and a separate wall in front of James and in the middle of those two walls was the entrance to our base; where all our enemies were.

They didn't notice us. That was a good start.

I don't want to see you holding back. James thought to me as we charged into battle.

We came in on a surprise attack. Each of us took down one enemy with that one blow. Blood splattered all over the walls from their bodies almost as if we cut straight through them. The enemy team immediately reacted; drawing their swords and slashing at us.

Jean, take down the shield. Everyone guard your stations. Get ready for battle! I ordered.

I usually lacked the ability to be independent. However, in certain situations, I was fully capable of taking charge of both myself and everyone else. I had to feel like others really believed or depended on me. My...I wish I could have called these people my friends at this time. But they were using me. I knew that then, I just wished that for once, people would actually care for me as much as I cared for others.

Anyways, My "Friends" were what gave me my reason to fight. They gave me hope. They gave me confidence. They made me, *me.* Even though I didn't know what or who I was.

James was beating the life out of everyone who dared try to challenge him... and he had already taken down four people! Me, on the other hand... I had five people on me and I was getting slashed left and right. I was lucky that I was good at dodging, and even luckier that anything that *did* touch me was nothing that serious and just cut me.

It's hard dodging three swords, some arrows, and random blasts of magic at the same time.

It was time to try a different tactic. All the magic and archery users went after Kalus and Lucas and things were getting out of control.

I had an idea. Maybe a bad idea, but it was something.

James, get back. Soren… shield me and all of the enemies in a bubble. It may hurt you a little bit to keep it all unsealed so I'll help you too. Make sure it's close around us. Just do it. Don't ask questions. I said.

Soren cast a shield around us.

This is SUCH a bad idea. I thought. But it was a bit too late to just declare a "never mind" and continue with business as usual.

I jumped into the air, as high as I could in this bubble and started casting spirit Ball. I used all the spirit of the people in the bubble including mine. Well, not all of mine. I kept enough to build a second bubble to protect Soren's.

I was floating in the air. I suppose the pressure from the giant spirit ball was keeping me up as well as Keeping everyone else still enough to not attack me. I let the spirit ball go right before it blew up, giving myself enough time to shield myself.

There was a bright light that blasted me about one hundred feet higher than I already was. I was so dizzy and exhausted but I still had to participate while I was considered not captured.

I looked down examining the play field, examined the traps along the way to my opponents flag. Lastly, I examined exactly who was watching. All of the captains were there watching along with Scorn. Most of their eyes were on me probably amazed that I wasn't categorized as 'captured' yet.

"Hey, you all watching? You can't take down me and my team like this. We're too strong. We will not lose this." I shouted, loud enough for everyone in the crowd to hear.

I kept a strong face, a strong composure. I landed on the ground hard but made it look as though I just floated down from the sky. I walked around the corner to a hallway that I knew was narrow enough that the audience could not to see me slam my weak body against the wall, hoping desperately for help to come.

I sank to the ground and laid there for a few moments examining flaming surroundings.

Slowly, I got up, making sure no one was going to ambush me. I ran to my base hoping that my spirit blast hadn't injured any of my team mates. Turns out, I had blown up the entire

battle arena (not including the audience of course.)

I wonder how mad they'll get when this is all over. I thought. *Where are you guys?*

I asked looking around my base.

I came across a cage but there was something very, *very* wrong with it. No one was in it. None of my enemies that I vaporized were in it.

You captured us, genius. We're in the enemies' base. Kalus replied.

How did none of the enemies get captured by this? I had them trapped in with the freakin' bomb. How in the world could they block that attack?! Soren? I asked.

Rigged. Soren replied.

It was all rigged.

Hey, is there any possible way that you could sneak over here without being seen by the hidden people on their team and break us out of this cell then steal the flag and get back to our base without being seen? Jean asked impatiently.

What kind of question is that? That's like mission suicide. How can ANYONE pull that off? That's like putting a gun to someone's head and telling them to dodge the bullet after you pull the trigger. I said checking to see if our flag was still there. *Oh, god no! Our flag is gone! Not only did they manage to evade my freakin' attack, they stole our flag!*

GO GET THEM! That was James. No one else could manage to yell that loud in a thought.

I just ran. No more thinking, no more planning, no more getting pushed around by these idiots.

I ran nonstop trying to find the guy that had stolen our flag. Everything was falling apart, burning to the ground. It was like a war of mass destruction had just ended.

You could slightly hear the crowd getting restless, whispering to their neighbors about who knows what and then suddenly, silence. I saw the guy who had taken my team's flag.

"Hey, you. You had best give back my team's flag now." I shouted.

"Awe, shoot it's you. Just give up. It's all over now. This was a big game for the teams on my side." He said.

"Drop the flag now or you're going to pay." I warned.

"What, are *you* going to make me pay?" He asked.

"I can do more than you can imagine." I exclaimed trying to look confident. Now it was all a matter of time before the spirit I put into the ground exploded under him.

He started to move and BOOM he was like, gone. Sad thing was I couldn't find the flag until I found my cell captain behind me.

"Alec, you have our flag. I need that back." I told him.

"No you don't." He replied.

"Why wouldn't I need that back?" I asked.

"Because you want to lose." He exclaimed.

"Why would I want to lose?" I asked.

"Because, if you don't have your team lose, I will lose a bet. My bet is directly with Scorn that you really do care more for others than yourself." He laughed. "He doesn't believe me, but it's true. He thinks that somewhere in you is part of him. The part that doesn't give a flying-"

"I don't see why you're doing this."

"I'll tell you what, you give up this game and condemn your team or you can know that you are responsible for the new inhabitants of this jail. We found that humans make perfect house keepers, if you will. The children can do everything that we have to do to keep this place functioning as well as take the punishment that we need to give." He smiled. "We'll do the same to them as we did to you. Rip them from their family, take them away. And for some, we will turn them into Cheuveans."

"No. You can't do that to a human kid. That's so wrong." I said.

"What do you think isn't wrong that we've done, Rissa?" He asked.

"This is beyond what normally goes on here... You can't do that." I said. "That's so useless! I don't see any reason you would find for doing this to more people!"

"I can and will. That's because," Alec laughed.

He disappeared.

I think what happened next was he kicked me and I slammed into a wall that was like half a foot away from me. Yeah, that one wall was probably the only sturdy wall in the place, but hey. What-evs.

There was so much force in that kick that I went into the wall, and like, got stuck to it. He followed that up with a "Whirl" punch (meaning when his back is to me, he'll hop about two inches in the air as he begins to turn around and slams the back of his knuckle into me). This resulted in me breaking through that wall, slamming into the ground and skidding across the floor another few feet.

"You have no idea what I can do." He finished, walking in towards me.

"Oh my god..." I whispered. I coughed a few times and then continued with, "You've.. Gotten... stronger, Alec. Why?" My voice was, like, super weak.

He picked me up effortlessly. "Don't you *love* it? Look at this! I can do more than *ever.* Your kind is becoming obsolete, Rissa. You *need* this winning side."

I looked at him, stared at him and responded with flipping him off.

"So, you're going to surrender the flag, right?" He asked.

Don't you dare. James thought to me. *Do not even think about this or I will end you.*

"I-I..." *I didn't know.*

He put a little more weight on my on my neck. "Right?"

The enemy team came over to take the flag from Alec.

Don't do this! Lucas thought.

"I don't know." I replied.

"Find out. Now; or I'll just go get those kids instead of waiting for your answer."

We're warning you! If you do this, you'll regret it. Jean thought.

"Fine. They win. It's over." I whispered.

"Good." Alec let me drop to the floor.

He shoved the flag into my chest, "You give it to them."

I obediently handed my team's flag to the opposing team.

"Why would you want your team to lose? What's in it for you?" I called after him.

"My treatment." He smiled. "And Elaina, thank you so much for exploiting your unmistakable *flaw*. You perform well in physical battle but once it gets psychological, you break easier than a toothpick."

"What?" I screamed.

He was gone. I had handed my team flag over to the other team to save some kids and not my team mates... I was so going to be in for it.

--BEEP -- BEEP -- Good people of Scorn's Kingdom, We have a winner! All cheer for the... Beatent Team! Leave now and rest. You've earned it.

Game over. The lights in the arena shut off. We spent the night in the dome.

CHAPTER NINETEEN
Self-sabotage

Dear Diary,

It's dark right now but soon the lights will be back on. This jail is everything other than home. I betrayed my team but for the right reason, you know? I don't know that they'll quite understand and I'm sure that I'll need to pay the price later on. But this time, I've prepared for it. This time, I'll be able to fight back and defend what it is that I believe in.

It's just so... annoying to have to constantly think about everything ALL THE TIME. I always need to think ahead about any possibility or in the end I'll get screwed over.

Lights dimly lit up the way out of the arena by morning. As soon as I stepped out of those doors, my entire team tackled me.

"WHAT WAS THAT?! You just let them win!" Jean screamed getting in my face.

"Get off." I commanded.

"Make me." Jean smiled, shoving me a couple feet back.

"Get off, or I will make you. And believe me, you don't want that." I warned.

"You can't do anything to me." Jean scoffed.

"I'll prove you wrong, Jean." I warned.

That was his last warning.

"Shut up." Jean said, about to punch me.

Yeah, that "don't hit a girl" rule doesn't apply in Cheuva.

That was my chance to try out a new move I remembered. As he threw the punch at me. A memory flashed through my head- of Rissa. Something almost completely took over and taught me what to do.

So I released my spirit from my body. Not much, of course, but it was in strong small surges coming out of my body.

Anyone who was on top of me or within six feet of me flew away. It was like they were all getting hit with trucks.

I warned you. I thought to them.

See now, the reaction was different than I expected. I thought they would fly away but I didn't expect them to stay down. My entire team passed out on me...

"Guys, wake up. Alec will be here soon to take us back to our cage thingy. Come on." I said out loud.

I probably shouldn't have. I mean, if Alec or Dylan were standing behind me they would take that in some bad way and we'd all die.

"What happened to all them?" Dylan asked coming up behind me. *God, I love being right...*

"Dunno, Dylan. I came out and they were all like that. Probably got in some kind of fight with each other after they lost." I replied.

"Understandable. They lost without any real explanation." Dylan mused rubbing his long sleeves.

"No. They know. I'm sure of it." I replied.

"If you say so. Now, I'll take you back to your little home." Dylan said.

Looks like Dylan learned how to teleport people without even touching them. I learned that when I blinked and I was back in my cage. Significance: their power is increasing rapidly. *Much* faster than mine.

"I'm getting so tired of this..." I told myself.

Dylan smiled, but began to shiver as though he were *cold.* But that wasn't logical. It was a cooler prison, but nothing that would affect us. He then coughed a few times and quickly walked away.

I was SOOO not prepared for this one. I would have expected the sky to fall on me before I would have expected this. James seriously got up and tackled me. He *pretended* to be knocked out so he could get the jump on me.

You'd think I would expect everything by now, that I would expect people to never really be knocked out but apparently I was really stupid.

I thought he was strangling me or something since his hands went around my thought for about six seconds and then he let go. I couldn't figure out why. I didn't think it made any sense.

He just kept punching me after. I put my arms up to protect myself. James was really strong and was going at breaking my arms. So I tried using that same move I used earlier.

This, I also should have expected, but again, I was too stupid. The saying is "fool me once: shame on you, fool me twice: same on me" right? Yeah, well fool me like, a hundred times: what the hell is wrong with me?

Something happened when I tried to use my powers. A glowing light began to shine just below where I could see. Then pressure began to build on my tendons and my muscles began to contract followed by pain growing everywhere at an exponential rate.

Reasons for that? Biology for Cheuva 101: all my spirit comes from my brain, down the neck (which was the problem), and then out through my body. Because the spirit brace was on my neck, spirit couldn't move through my body and guess what. Spirit works like blood. My body doesn't function without it. See, the organs of a Cheuvean are much more stern than that of a humans which is why they can take much more aggressive blows without sustaining injury so blood needs the spirit for the strength to make the organs work.

It felt like my lungs weren't getting air, my heart was going to explode; my entire body was just aching with such unbearable pain.

"OH MY GOD! MAKE IT STOP!" I screamed.

"See, the sprit cuff is a type of strainer if you will. When you try to initiate an attack while it's on you, it sorts out your aggressive spirit from your regular spirit and because you initiated that attack... well I suppose you're figuring that out right now." James explained.

You know how if you're hurting really bad and you know you can't do anything about it so you just cuddle into a ball and start freaking out? When I say freaking out, I'm talking about shaking and rolling all over the floor. Welcome to my life.

Well I was doing that until James started to hold me still. Like, you know in psycho-homes, how sometimes the psychotic people freak out and the nice men in the white coats have to pin their arms and legs down.

Well I suppose my non-stop screaming woke Soren up since he came running and just covered my mouth. I kept trying to get them off of me but it kinda just started hurting more so I decided to just try my best to lie still.

Before Soren took his hand off my mouth he took his free hand and held his pointer finger up against his lips to say his version of a "Shut the hell up."

I twitched a really small nod. "Good." He removed his hand.

"Make it stop…. Leave me alone…" I whispered.

It looked like everyone was up now.

"Shhh. Hey, we warned you. You still disobeyed us all." James told me. "And more importantly, you disobeyed me."

"I-I'm sorry okay? I'm sorry! You don't know what was happening! None of you could last even a measly five minutes with them and I have to deal with them *every* single day." I whispered harshly.

It hurt to talk… Man, how I wished I had a normal life.

"You know something? We don't care. Is it our job to make your life comfortable? Nope." Jean told me. "Sucks, don't it? Your status means nothing to us."

"It's your job to help me! I'm your one way ticket out of here!" I screamed.

"Shut up! You understand me? Shut. Up." Soren yelled.

Loudest I'd ever heard him.

"Or you'll what?! Hurt me? Kill me? Make my life *miserable*? Those choices are unavailable, sorry."

I looked up at James; I think I was hoping for back up on this. These guys really scared me. They were unmistakably intimidating.

The interesting part was that Kalus and Lucas couldn't look. They were the kind hearted ones out of all of us.

"Don't look at me. I won't help you. Not this time. You screwed us all to help your little *humans*. We told you not to and you still did. Now you need to face the consequences." James explained.

"Yeah! They were going to torture those little human kids! He told me that if I didn't, people... human people would turn out like me... like us." I said.

"What's that supposed to mean?" Lucas asked.

"That *means* I wouldn't wish this life upon anyone or anything. Especially a human. Especially human children...." I explained.

"So, you choose disgusting *humans* over us? That's absolutely revolting!" James yelled.

"That's not it! It's just-" I was interrupted.

"No! Stop. We are no more than cell mates. You will not talk to us; we will not talk to you. No, scratch that. You will not talk to us unless we talk to you." James explained.

"Screw you, James." I said.

Those were the last words I spoke for the rest of the week. Which, by the way, was incredibly difficult for me. I don't ever shut up. And it didn't help that I was tied to the ground until the next food cession that we were allowed to attend.

Alec came to get us. He didn't seem to be in a very good mood.

"Get out." He ordered.

The line detached from the floor and we lined up to get out of the cell. We got out, and walked in a single file line to the cafeteria.

It looked like about four hundred people in there. The food was basically lunar fruit... or... specific types of food specifically designed for Cheuvean people under the age of twenty.

So, we got in line. There was this girl staring at me from behind. I could feel it.

"Is there a problem?" I asked not bothering to actually look at her.

"Huh?" She asked.

"You've been staring at me. What do you want?" I asked.

"Rissa, is that you?" She asked.

"I suppose that depends on who's asking." I replied.

"Stupid, don't you remember? I'm Nala." She said.

"Hmmm... Nala... I don't remember you, Nala. Some interesting stuff happened to me and now I'm not normal." I said.

"As if you were ever normal, Rissa." She laughed as if that was supposed to be some kind of odd joke.

"Okay." I said.

"How are you so different now?" She asked.

"I have no memories; I am not the Rissa you remember. I'm a half breed between a human and a Cheuvean." I explained.

"Ehw…" She moaned.

"Man, Stop being so prejudice. Humans are not so bad. But, if anyone other than me asks, you hate humans." I told her.

"Whatever." She breathed.

We were still in line for another few minutes and then we got our fruit stuff.

You know what I noticed just then? I had just noticed that I was chained to my cell mates.

Care to know what else I learned? I learned it was only my cell that was chained together.

Jean yanked the chain. "Hurry up." He told me.

"Okay… Sorry." I apologized.

I decided it would make it easier to just be as easy for these guys to control as possible.

If I didn't, it would only make life harder for me. So yeah, we were walking, trying to find a table to sit at.

They all sat down with one seat left open. You would assume that I would be allowed to sit down. Well, you would be wrong. I sat down and almost immediately, they pushed me off. I looked up at them from the floor I landed on. I didn't say anything verbally. I didn't ask why because they would get angry if I spoke before being spoken to.

"Give us your lunch." Jean ordered.

"Why? Are you going to eat it?" I asked.

"No. We're going to stare at it." Kalus said.

This was pretty much like middle school bullying… It was just a little scarier and a little bit more aimed for making my life miserable.

I handed my food over to Jean who was the closest to me at the time.

"Good girl. You're learning." Jean said.

"Yeah thanks." I replied.

"What are you thinking?" James asked me.

"Can't you read my mind?" I retorted.

"Not anymore. So, what are you thinking about?" He asked again.

What? Can't read my mind? They've switched SIDES? Where the hell does that leave me?

"How can you tell if I'm thinking anyway? You can't. It's not possible." I said.

"You have a stupid look on your face when you're thinking. Now, you are going to tell us what you're thinking." He said.

I doubted they really cared what I was thinking. They were just trying to prove their superiority by saying that they control everything and I had no say. They wanted to make sure that I didn't have the balls to cross them again.

Now, if someone really is all that then they have *nothing* to prove. You never see Scorn trying to do that with me because he isn't so desperate for that feeling of security. These boys allowed me to see their desperation and in my book, got labeled as "Pathetic".

"I was thinking that you guys should do something to get your self-esteem up. I pity all of you. This place has bent us back and forth until we have all snapped. We're a bunch of kids and we don't have any emotions.

We don't long for toys or love. We quit caring about that. We long for battles and bloodshed. That is our idea of fun because it's part of our *mission* to get out of here. You guys can't face the fact that you've changed. You can't face the fact that there is anything wrong with you. But you know, tossing me like this and watching me suffer as I try to *help* you is only proof." I said.

To my surprise, they looked hurt. They *knew* it was true.

I then added, "And on that note, I think it would be in your best interest to let me eat."

"And why is that?" Jean asked.

"We're on a team, correct?" I asked.

"No, we just work together and pretend to be a team." Kalus said. He's so sarcastic all the time. "We're still trying to fool them! *SHHHH!*"

I just kind of ignored him. "So, next battle, I won't have any strength left." I said. "I'll be nothing but a handicap."

"After lunch we'll give you our leftovers. Only if you're good of course." James said.

"Of course." I responded.

So I humored them, I waited and stood there perfectly still. I waited for them all to get full and give me my reward for my obedience and patience. After we got back to our cell, I got maybe a quarter of the food I was originally given.

"I'm surprised that you didn't complain at all during the time you were standing there." James said.

"Well, would you have hit me if I did?" I asked.

"Yes. Isn't that a given?" He replied.

"Yes. That's why I didn't complain. Isn't *that* a given?" I asked.

James smacked me right across the face. I think he is the only guy who has ever smacked me in my life. He's obviously capable of monstrous punch but because I'm a girl, he takes it easy-ish on me. The thing is, James's slap feels like a normal punch but it *stings*. I could only imagine his strongest hit.

"Say that again without the sarcasm." He ordered.

I looked back at him, glaring. "I didn't complain because I thought you would hurt me."

"Now, why would you think that?" He asked.

"James, why *wouldn't* I think that?" I asked.

James laughed.

I don't know what is wrong with me but I just love that guy's laugh. It has always seemed so sweet. *Something* deep in my subconscious encouraged me to love that boy and forced me to see the goodness that he hid deep within. Maybe that was Rissa. That small bit of her that was still in me would want me to see that he was only protecting himself with that cold shell of a personality but little by little I was wedging myself inside; becoming the only person he could ever love back.

"Can I ask you something?" I asked.

"Ask again when Alec isn't patrolling." James whispered. "You'll always be able to tell when danger is approaching because of the sound of their shoes. If it's metal against stone, it's no one that you want to allow hear your conversation. If it sounds like cloth, it's one of us."

I nodded. I stayed in smaller bedroom cell while James joined everyone else in one of the other bedrooms.

Something then changed. The aura in my room became dark. The light dimmed, the shadows grew darker and larger. Over time, all the light I could see had disappeared. Something was wrong.

Rissa... I don't know if you can hear me, but if you can... your job has just gotten much harder. I am sending troupes to... your cell... nd... ing... ou... to kill your human... rents... gain.

After... reviving... em... course... ou'll be the... one... to... ave... the ... pleasure. Someone thought to me.

It wasn't Scorn. That was plain to see. The voice was more evil and vicious. And to make it even more obvious, it was a girl. A little girl.

I began shivering. I was scared. I couldn't tell who it was but I was really curious to find out. What made me more nervous? Something, that girl, was in my room with me.

Is this a trick? Maybe this is someone's ability?

Oh, wouldn't you wish? She responded, laughing.

The way she spoke was so intelligent, like she knew *everything* about the worlds we all live in. And her voice was so cruel but she was just a child. I didn't know that evil could exist in such a young girl.

It sounded like she was *behind* me. But the item that was behind me was the prison walls making that *impossible*.

I backed off of the wall and asked fearfully, "Who is this? What do you want?"

She was then in front of me, but not in her true form. It was her shell; her skin, if you will. Her body, but not her features. She was a moving, touchable *shadow*.

"You are going to remember nothing of me, do you understand?"

My mind went blank. "I will remember nothing of you."

"You need to awaken for a little bit, okay? Remember some of those spells you swore you'd never use again. Aging, the *chain*... or what was it you called it? *Necro*?"

"I remember." I whispered obediently to her.

"Good. Then it looks like nothing is truly damaged. If you truly wish to destroy your memories once again, you'll age. But that only holds the truth off for so long. Once you reach your age again, you'll remember it all and you'll only experience the hurt all over." She patted me on the head.

"Yes."

"And one more thing, Elaina." She began leaning in and whispered into my ear, "Awaken both sides until your time is up. All of it, by the way. Don't hold up on the darkness this time."

And at that, she was gone.

Of course she had to step in. God forbid she just leave us to her stupid game. She had to intervene or the game would be too easy for me, too hard for Scorn and that would just be no fun to watch, now wouldn't it...

My vision was beginning to darken once again until I couldn't see anymore. I had no idea what was happening. I couldn't see, I couldn't hear, I could only see auras.

I was left with my primary instinct: spirit. I could see and hear the movement of the spirit around the room and I could make everything out except for who people where.

Unfortunately, I wasn't controlling me. There was something very, very wrong with me thanks to that kid shadow.

Forgetting my meeting with the shadow girl, I was watching myself in third person, witnessing a power that I didn't know I had.

"What is it?" James asked.

"Leave. Now." I warned with a fierce smile on my face. "Or I will kill you. I want to kill you!"

"Bluffs." Jean scoffed walking in.

"Jean, wait." James spoke. "She's not… being herself."

It was his fault. He challenged what I said and took that god damn step towards me and I couldn't help it! Chains flew out of the ground and stabbed him right through the heart.

"You've…" Jean coughed. "You stupid bitch… You released me…"

He should have heeded my warning… I didn't need another death on my hands. Especially of someone that I thought was immortal.

Soren was the furthest back from the room looking in my general direction, but also at the ground—as always but when he saw the chain or as I apparently referred to it, "necro", his eyes shot open. He raised his voice and spoke in full sentences for the first time. I didn't have to hear one word and guess the rest of his sentence. "Rissa! You killed him! You killed an immortal! That's not possible!" Soren yelled.

That was most definitely the loudest thing Soren had ever said.

"Yeah?" I replied. "Get out of this room before I kill you too."

James stepped forward.

"James!" Kalus said grabbing James. "Why do you want to die?"

"She won't kill me. She can't. She knows it. She cares too much. Now, tell me. How did you do that attack? We're all friends here. You can tell me." James said.

"You don't care that I killed your comrade?" I asked.

"No, of course not. You warned him. He deserved it." James said.

"*James!*" Lucas said.

James! I screamed watching my body being controlled by this... Demon... Maybe? I guess that's how I would have described me then. I was trying so hard to get control again for his sake.

"No. You have changed. My old friend would never act like this. She doesn't like this world. I don't see how you all live in it this way..." I said. "I hope you get out of this room before it's too late. Or maybe you would rather join me and take my way out?"

I watched myself close my eyes and think of something… some kind of aura started… coming out of me; poisoning the air.

I was getting shorter, getting younger by the second. All of what was left of my memories was disappearing.

In fact, everyone around me was getting younger.

"What's happening?" Soren asked.

"Get out before it's too late." I responded. "I will kill you."

"What?" Soren whispered again. "I've never…."

I'm assuming that the rest of his sentence would have been 'seen anything like this.'

"Suit yourself." I said.

They attempted to come closer but as a result, as they approached they got younger. James was the first to notice. He stopped right away and jumped back as far as possible. Everyone else noticed immediately after and followed James's lead. I guess that's why he's Lord of rebels. He's the best at what he does and everyone knows that.

The aura coming out of my body had stopped. "We're younger. Why?" James asked.

James looked about sixteen years of age. Everyone else looked about fourteen.

"Better question. Are you getting younger too?" Kalus asked.

"I figured you'd be the one to ask that. I am getting younger. A lot younger." I replied.

"Why are you staying there if you're getting younger?" Lucas asked. "C'mon, get out."

"Let's just say that I know a way out of immortality." I laughed.

"You're aging yourself out of existence…" James growled. *Abso-fucking-lutely NOT.*

"Yes. Good job, James. You figured it out!" I laughed.

But that was when I dropped to my knees grasping my head. "Get *out* of my head!"

James charged back into the room I had poisoned, grabbed me and carried me out. Due to my age now, I was too weak to fight back. Back fire?

"What are you doing? LET ME GO!" I kicked and screamed.

I was six years old and he was now fourteen. "Stop it! Don't you go away. We need you, *I* need you." He whispered.

I was regaining control. "Why?" I asked. "Why won't you let me take over?"

"You can't die. People's lives will no longer exist if you die. You have a destiny." He said.

"What does that matter for you? You should be so tired of this." I commented.

"I will never let you go. Not again. So you shut the hell up and live, alright? If not for you, if not for me, then for everyone."

"I don't…"

James croaked his final argument. "You *can't* leave me again. I won't let you."

"In a matter of moments, my memories will no longer exist. The very last pieces of Rissa will be erased from this girl. I remember everything for now but soon every piece of thought, every memory I have accumulated over the years will disappear. Our memories are a danger to everyone."

"What's going to happen next?" He asked.

"I don't know. Scorn has, I'm sure been informed about what I've done by now. He'll take me into his custody and then… I'm not sure."

"Why would you want this?" James asked.

"Once your heart has been broken a thousand times, you'd be surprised what you'd do." I told him.

"Any way to stop it?" Soren asked.

"No." I replied.

"Anything you want to tell us?" James asked.

"Just… Trust me. I've got a plan. I think. Eventually, everything will fall into place. You will all get out of here. Just remember, it's not too late to keep trying… It's never too late." I told them.

"Is that all?" James asked.

"Kalus," I laughed. "I found out what your ability is apart from water. You make bombs and explosions."

"No way! How awesome!" Kalus smiled. "You be careful, 'kay Elaina?"

"Don't let him win." James told me.

"Of course." I promised. "And will you keep an eye out for Yuna? She's somewhere in the prison. Just take good care of her, kay?"

"Yeah." James replied.

"And James…"

"Hmm?"

"I love you."

And as I began to drift to sleep, my spirit was allowed back into my body.

My consciousness woke in a different world – one that existed only inside of me. "You." A girl called, sitting on a throne in the distance.

"You look…"

"Just like you will, girl."

"Rissa?"

"Obviously." She sang, glaring down at me. "Why won't you let me take over?"

"Because you're EVIL?"

"But it'd almost be a benefit to you."

"I don't care."

"Once you summon your sword, you can easily release me, you know."

"I won't though."

"You will. I always have my ways." She pointed upwards, towards the infinite darkness above. "One day, you'll need me. and when you do, you will stab yourself – it's nothing eccentric; don't get your hopes up. You will just stab through your own hand. And so will I. When that happens, this world will not be just dark anymore no matter how gorgeous it is. Our essences will be mixed. Just wait for it. You'll know what I mean in a matter of years here. I'm patent enough to wait for this. You'll need to be bigger, faster, stronger to survive in the world you've recently discovered. You'll see that I'm right soon. You'll understand soon.

CHAPTER TWENTY
Life s redo. But like I said, there s no running from fate

Dear Diary,

I think recently I've been getting creative with my journal entries. Because the last few I've written are completely illogical... They say my daddy's bad and stuff... That I'm working against him. But that's crazy right? I love him and he loves me. He would never EVER hurt me.

No one can ever know about this. I can only imagine how angry Daddy would be.

-Rissa

I awoke to a glamorous bedroom filled what things that I've always loved. Scorn really did his research.

The room had stone walls painted hot pink with small black polka dots. The bed frame was black, the comforter for the bed was a pink and black zebra design, and same with the pillow.

My little desk was black and the chair for it had a neon pink frame with a pink cushion, the silky carpet was very light pink, almost white and that matched the base boards of the room.

The room was just the most adorable thing. I LOVED IT!!

All I could really think about was; "Where's my daddy? Daddy? Where are you?" I called.

I didn't get off my bed. Apparently, the story behind that was when I was a child, my parents told me to never get off my bed until they came to get me for something, 'cause I refused to get off that piece of adorableness no matter how much I wanted to leave my room.

My memory was all messed up. I had memories of things that never actually happened. The first thing I really vividly remember seeing of my mom was when I was four, she dumped me into the street to fend for myself but in reality, *Rissa* was with her until she was about fourteen years old.

In my memory, my dad had found me and cared for me until now. He was my hero. I would do absolutely anything for him. My obedience was absolutely unmatchable.

I waited there for my beloved "Daddy" to come through that stupid door and take me away as if he really, truly cared.

Finally, the door budged. On the down side, it was Alec instead of my Dad. "Hi, Alec!" I screamed.

He shushed me. "Okay." I smiled.

"Come on, Kiddo. Time to get out of bed." He told me.

"But, Daddy told me to always stay here until *he* got me. I don't know if I'm allowed to get off if you tell me to..." I said.

"I asked your dad. It's okay." Alec assured me.

"But I want my Daddy to get me, just in case. I don't wanna make my Daddy sad at me." I smiled.

"How does that even make sense?" He laughed.

"Well, when he's sad and it's because of me, that means he'll be sad at me." I laughed.

I was so full of joy. "Okay, suit yourself but, Scorn may not be able to get you for a while..." Alec told me.

"Well that's okay. It's only eight a clock in the morning, so I can wait for a little more." I said happily.

"Are you sure?" He asked.

"Yeeeah." I said.

"Yes, Rissa." He corrected. "Well okay, Princess. It's your choice." He said walking out the door.

So I waited. Actually, the wait wasn't too bad.

About a half hour later, my dad came in. "DADDY!!!" I squeaked.

"Hey, Kiddo. Why didn't you leave when Alec asked you to?" Scorn asked.

"You never gave me permission… I didn't want to risk you getting sad at me." I whimpered.

"Oh, Rissa, you could never do anything to make me sad at you." Scorn said.

"Okay Daddy." I replied joyfully. Seems like I wanted nothing more than his approval. Manipulation sucks.

"Come on. Get off your bed." He told me.

"Okie." I squeaked hopping onto the floor.

I had such a bounce in my step. You could see Scorn getting more annoyed every moment as he watched this *brat* full of pep and energy almost dance towards him as if she thought she was *good* enough to be loved.

"You know, I had to stop work because you didn't trust Alec's words." Scorn said frowning at me.

"Oh no! I'm so sorry!" I said.

"It's fine. I don't mind." He told me. "I just lost so much time of my day."

"Is there anything I can do to make up for that time that you lost, daddy?" I asked.

"I don't know…" He said.

I noticed that he was smiling but at the time, I didn't quite recognize what a smirk was and I truly thought the man loved me. After all, why would he try to fool me if he loved me?

"Come on, Daddy! There has to be *something* I can do. Please? I want to make it up to you." I pleaded.

How incredibly uncharacteristic of me... I've never actually *asked* for work before. I never thought the day would come that I would actually appreciate it if someone said, "here's a job for you!" I guess I always just viewed it as a form of punishment. Unless, you know, I was brain washed out of my mind.

"Well... Now that I think about it, you *could* go see these prisoners that I have been needing to talk to..." He told me.

"Prisoners? What prisoners? I never knew we had prisoners." I said concerned.

We never kept secrets from each other according to my memory. We were just the *closest* and *best* friends.

"Rissa, I have been keeping this from you for quite a while. But it was for your protection. There are people who are very serious threats to both you and me. They break the rules and *hate* Cheuva, our home. I have tried to change their minds and have tried to solve the problem peacefully... but... my attempts are futile. To prevent any more casualties I have locked all of the resistance away... but there is this one group... they are pure evil.

They can make anyone believe that they are good when they oh so obviously aren't..." Scorn told me. "But I don't think you'd fall for those tricks, right?"

"What did they do that was so wrong?" I asked.

"They have tried to kill me, humans, you, civilians, Cheuva. They are so very special but they used their powers for bad instead of good." He explained.

Hypocrite.

"How are they so special? Are they more special than I am, Daddy?" I asked.

I meant special as in; immortal, powerful, etc. Not like more sentimental special.

"They are not as special as you are, kiddo but very close. They are immortal, just like you. They are all prodigies, just like you. They are the masters of, well, different things." He told me.

"What are their names? How can I identify them?" I asked,

"James, good leader, strong, cool. Don't be fooled. Soren, Magic user, very smart, doesn't talk much though. Kalus, water master, really sarcastic. Lucas... he's very loud." Scorn said.

He didn't know Kalus had an explosion talent. He didn't know.

"Okay. So, what exactly do you want me to do for you?" I asked.

"You're going to talk to them. Pretend that you know them. Pretend that a little while ago, you were their cell mate. Remember, they had told you that they were no more than cell mates because of a recent fight. Ask them what has been happening, what their plans are. Just make me proud. You'll

know what to do. But know, if you mess this up..."
He warned.

I didn't need to know what would happen. I just knew it would be bad. Well, to me, it was awful enough with just the thought that I would have let down my hero and his disappointment would drive a hole in me. But the *fear* was what really threw me off. I thought then that he would toss me on the street just like my mom supposedly had done previously.

In my right mind though, I know I can't let him down or all shit will hit the fan and I'll be the outlet of his anger. You don't fail Scorn and there isn't a soul that doesn't know that rule. "Don't worry, Daddy. I'll do it." I told him.

"Good." He laughed.

Adding to that, you also don't say no to Scorn.

"What are the details? It's not like I just walk up and say 'Hi, I'm your long lost cell mate'..." I pointed out.

"Of course not. Alec will throw you in jail. But he will be very mean to you, are you prepared for that? He and Dylan will treat you very harshly for a week so you can gain the traitor's trust." He told me.

"Okay, I think I could handle that." I said. "Where's Alec?"

"Just down the hall, why?" Scorn asked.

"Just trust me, Daddy. I have a plan." I exclaimed.

I ran down the hall, and into the lounging room, where I could almost always find Alec.

"Alec, my daddy-" I began.

"I know." He replied.

"How? We just discussed it right now..." I responded.

"I know. What can I say? I'm psychic." He laughed.

"Seriously, how did you-" I began.

"Shut up." He told me. "I mean, Jesus, really? What's with the stupid questions?"

In my memories, he had never talked like that to me. In reality, that was actually one of the nicest things he's ever said to me but.... Well, I didn't know that. In my memories, he was like my older brother. Actually, to be more precise, my memories of my older brother were replaced with Alec; real events, different people.

He has never said anything bad to me in my memories. It was like; he was always there for me, always protecting me, playing games with me, he was always there. Always.

You know, I would have preferred this life. If I was given the choice to make this my reality instead of some manipulation, instead of having my reality being some stupid ass prophecy to lead the rebellion against the tyrant leader of the worlds... I would have accepted that choice without hesitation.

Once he had realized what he had said he covered it all up. "I'm just kidding, Kiddo. You know I would never mean anything like that. You do, right?" He asked.

He managed to make *me* sound like the bad guy. He made me feel bad... "Yes! Of course I do! I'm sorry!" I smiled desperately.

I needed his forgiveness so badly. I needed his acceptance. Without it, I couldn't function. I needed his love to live in this world. "It's okay, Ri. I forgive you." He told me.

"Do you think I can do it?" I asked. "Infiltrate an enemy jail... it sounds so difficult. Especially if they're as smart and special as James says they are."

"Of course I do. Just remember you need to be sarcastic and never know when to actually shut your mouth. But you need to remember to be obnoxious to me, Scorn, Alec, everyone you care for. Your character hates us and you need to be prepared to play the part." He told me.

"Okay..." I sighed.

"What's wrong?" He asked me.

"I just don't want to mess up. You know... My dad isn't a good person to let down..." I told him.

"I know." He mumbled. "Look, you realize that you will be hurt a lot right? A lot of the time you'll be hurt by me or Dylan or even your cell mates. You'll only get fed once a week... It's really... not the place that you'd want to be. The emotional stress could be way too much for you to handle." He told me.

He really was worried about me. "It's alright Alec. I'll be fine. I promise. I won't fail my daddy. I'll be awesome." I said hugging him.

"Okay, Kiddo. We should get you in jail no-… never mind. This isn't a good idea." He stuttered.

"Why? I told you I could do it!" I yelled.

"*No*! You don't understand! You'll get beaten up! By me! I'm *not* okay with it!" He yelled.

"Become okay with it! Be a man!" I drew out my spirit sword and began swinging it at him. I had enough accuracy for him to think it was real but not enough to actually hit him. Of course, he thought that I was serious. Which was the plan I half informed Scorn about. "See? I'm trying to kill you now! If I can do it now, I can do it later. This isn't something that will be difficult!"

He became serious. He got out his stone cut sword. That thing scared me in itself much less that guy that was wielding it. The sword reacted to his thoughts meaning, it stretches and moves to create the perfect damage to my body. I was trying to upset him enough to encourage him to hurt me… but not this bad.

"You little brat! How dare you!" He yelled.

He was swinging his sword blindly, nonstop. Try dodging like, fifty blows to your body in like, five seconds. He finally got me when he swung that death trap of a sword at my shins. I jumped over his sword and while I was in the middle of that jump he swung his sword straight up to split my body in two. Needless to say, sense Cheuveans are indestructible; He didn't literally slice me in two. What he did was position himself far enough away to comfortably swing upwards without actually cutting though bone. Only our skin and organs can be cut so he damaged what he could.

I screamed. After he hit me that one time, it was over. It became impossible for me to dodge any more blows. Now it was just hit, hit, hit, hit. By the time he decided to stop, my clothes had been ripped to shreds. My entire body was dripping blood.

Seriously, it wasn't a pretty sight. "Why attack me, Rissa?" He asked. "You must know by now that you don't know how to fight and you can't beat me like this."

"So I could have this result. What better way to infiltrate an enemy base than to make it look like you're my enemy? Keep going if you need to. Take all your anger out on me. I told you, I'm not weak." I explained. "If you can hurt me that easily now, I'm sure you won't have a problem later."

"No. I won't let you do this. You're willing to do too much for your dad." He told me.

Now, what he didn't know was that my dad could hear what Alec was saying... "Why would you say that, Alec?" Scorn asked appearing.

"Scorn! Oh god... I'm sorry... but look at her. She's just a little girl. Look at what she just did to make sure she didn't fail for *you*." He told Scorn.

"She'll be fine. Rissa, it's time for you to go to jail." Scorn told me.

"Scorn, you can't be-" *serious*

"I am perfectly serious. And you need to learn to control your emotions. Once they start getting in the way, I will take them away. Do you want that?"

Alec looked at the ground apologetically and silently.

"Okay Daddy. Alec, care to escort me?" I asked.

"Yeah, sure." He told me.

Alec and I walked calmly out of the room. Every step that I took stung. Like, you know when you have a paper cut on your finger and if you touch it, it stings? Well, that's what my entire body felt like.

So, yeah. We were walking, just me and Alec, from that lounge Alec always hangs out in, down the stairs, through the cafeteria, into those double doors that lead to the giant hall way that is filled with some empty cells, Some cells with just one or two prisoners, and then, at the very end of the hall way was my cell.

As we were walking, I noticed the condition these prisoners were in. Their clothes were mostly shredded. Most of the guys didn't wear shirts. They were so skinny... I figured half of them hadn't eaten in weeks. They all had cuts and bruises, and sometimes burns all over their bodies.

What could be happening to these poor souls that they end up looking as dreadful as this? Is this really what my Dad does to people? How could I not see this? I thought.

It was as surprising as it was depressing for me. Seeing people like this made me sad yet angry at myself for not knowing. Part of me wanted to truly believe that these people really deserved what they had gotten. But can people really deserve this type of punishment for anything?

I began to feel sorry for them, and detest their conditions. That was bad... I wanted to do anything for my dad but I completely disagreed with what was going on here. More than anything, I began to regret my decision to do this for my dad. It made me question everything.

"Starting to have second thoughts, Rissa?" Alec asked.

I looked away. I was ashamed that I felt that this was wrong.

"Answer me." He ordered.

"Yes. I am." I whispered.

"Do you want to turn back now? It's not too late, you know." He told me.

"No. I told my Daddy that I would do it for him." I replied. "And you know he would take it out on you for me coming back. Like it was your fault that I became scared and you were the influence on my decision…"

"Suit yourself then." He decided his fate was a lot more important than mine.

My plan was working perfectly, I guess… I was soaking in blood, my own clothes in shreds. I was no different than the other prisoners and I hadn't even entered the cell yet.

I walked near my cage and Alec managed to quickly and swiftly lock me in spirit cuffs. He cuffed my wrists together and my ankles together and then had a long spirit chain connecting my wrists to my ankles. So, with that, I couldn't raise my hands above my head, I couldn't separate my wrists, and I couldn't have my ankles more than a foot apart.

Oh, Alec, being amazing ruler he was, he grabbed my hair and pushed me forward and yanked me back with it.

"Ouch…" I mumbled.

"Shut up." He hissed.

"Sorry…" I whispered.

He opened the cell door to let me in. "Get in." He ordered.

Without answering, I began walking in; apparently too slowly considering once I got to where the door way was, he kicked me into the room. I flew straight down.

I slid to a stop once my shoulder collided with the wall. "Alec…" I whispered.

"Hurry up next time." He said walking away.

Everyone stood still until Alec was gone. "Rissa! Are you alright?" Lucas yelled running to me.

"Do I *look* alright?" I asked.

"Well, not exactly. If it makes you feel better, I'd say you look great as a dead girl!" Kalus laughed high fiving Lucas.

"What, do you think that's supposed to be *funny*? Shut up! Honestly, *no one* thinks that you're funny." I said.

Kalus looked at me sadder than he ever has. That was his form of comic relief. Without his jokes, he was just as scared and sad as the rest of us but he thought he was bringing us up. He wanted to do his part in the war to help us without killing.

No one said anything. They were all so stunned, except one. He didn't seem to care much; in fact, I think he was glaring at me. Then, there I was, thinking that these boys were bad, and hurting my dad, I hated them. I got up, and walked into a different room.

There was silence in our cell, well, until they came into the room I was in. There was one missing, the one who didn't seem to care earlier. "What's wrong?" Kalus asked. "You've never yelled at me like that before..."

"I'm mad." I said.

"Why?" He asked.

"Look at me! Doesn't that answer your question?" I asked.

"So do you remember us?" Lucas asked.

"Of course I remember you. Why wouldn't I?" I asked.

"What else?" Soren asked.

"Full sentences?" I responded.

"What else do you remember?" Lucas restated Soren's question as he smiled and patted him on the back.

"Why are you interrogating me?" I asked.

"It's not that, girly. He just wants to fill in some of the blanks for us. Why are you being defensive?" Kalus asked me.

"Because I'm in a bad mood! What part about that didn't you understand?" I yelled.

Soren sat and put his head in his hands, "Don't yell."

"Soren's right, Elaina. We're your *friends*. Don't treat us any differently." Lucas smiled.

"Hah! Or you'll what?" I asked getting defensive.

"Nothing. We're friends here. Remember?" Lucas repeated once more.

"As I recall, we had a huge fight and you all agreed that we were no more than cell mates." I told them.

"We're friends; we get in fights. We say things that we don't mean." Kalus told me.

"Yes, people do, but people don't attempt to hurt each other and hate each other every other day. It's wrong." I explained.

"But, it was a mista-" Lucas began.

"Enough. We apologize. It was very wrong of us. Although, you know what is very wrong of you? Pretending that you remember everything. I know you don't. I know you're doing this for your dad." James said walking into the room.

That's the leader. I can tell just by the way he spoke for everyone else... but, how did he know that I am working for my dad? I thought. *It has to be a guess.*

"I don't know what you're talking about, James." I said.

"Yes you do." He told me.

"Why would I *ever* want to work for *Scorn*? He's evil. We all know that. We all have experience with his games. We all know what he's like. How could I ever want to join him?" I asked.

"A way through all the pain he put you through. He may have manipulated you. He may have erased your memory again. Tons of reasons. We just never really know with Scorn. Or you." He said.

"Look, I only really remember my time in this prison with you all. My memory is *gone*." I said.

"*Liar!*" He snapped. Apparently, my de-aging him affected his calm, cool personality.

"How would you know, James?" I asked.

377

"When we were younger, we went to the Duran Woods all the time. I know what you look like when you lie to people." He told me. "And I'm not stupid."

I scanned my memory of the conversation. There had to be a reason he could tell. A physical trait that changes maybe? Maybe a vocal pitch change. Then I found it. I realized that whenever I lied, I looked away from the person I was lying to. I had to fix that right there and then.

I looked straight into his eyes and told him, "I am not lying to you."

"I don't believe you." He hissed slowly.

Each word that escaped his mouth had such a sting to it; slower words, quieter, but sharper.

"Why? Are you starting to get *paranoid*? You think that the world is out to get you. Believe it or not, James, the world doesn't revolve around of this jail cell. Not everything is about you. What would you like me to do to prove that I'm on your side?" I asked.

All of my words were very well thought out and almost planned from the moment I was informed of the mission and my vocabulary and way of speaking was something Scorn had taught me sense he picked me off of the street. He told me, "No daughter of mine will be uneducated."

"I want you to win the next battle for us." James said. "The girl we know was a strategist to high levels. You create us a strategy, you're in."

"Fine. Consider it done. Do you have any information on the other team or teams that we're facing?" I asked.

"Yeah. We overheard a little at lunch earlier today." Soren said.

"Okay, what about 'em?" I asked.

"You understand that we're all prodigies, we are all very special. There are a few more prodigies. They're in the group that we're going to fight. Ameri, prodigy of illusion, Andrew, prodigy of the earth, and Samuel, prodigy of, well, um… transformation? Is that right Soren?" James asked.

"Correct." Soren responded.

"Those are the only three?" I asked.

"Yes." Soren told me.

The last time I had seen Soren, he was desperate to get out. He grabbed the spirit bars and pleaded for someone to take him out… Now, everyone had changed. They seemed emotionless, hopeless. Maybe it was because of my absence. No worries though. I got it back safe and sound.

Of course, I didn't remember that though. I was a little seven year old with no idea that I really knew these people.

"Alright. How do you counter illusion?" I asked.

"If we knew, we wouldn't have a problem." Kalus said.

"I suppose so. So, how do we find out? None of us know illusion, right?" I asked.

"No." Soren replied.

"Yeah, Soren knows how to do illusion. Soren knows practically everything." Kalus laughed.

"Oh, I didn't know that..." I said.

"We know you didn't know. We never told you, we never showed you." Lucas smiled warmly at me. "You don't have to prove anything, Ri. We are on your side. You are welcome here."

Kalus cracked up, "If you really *want* to be welcome anyways. We're in a cage."

Lucas laughed along. "True, bro. Well Rissa, if you ever want to be part of our cage, feel free to join!"

Back to business.

"Do you know how long you've been gone, keeping us all waiting?" James asked.

"A day? That's what it seemed like..." I whispered cautiously.

I only said that because there could be a million reasons that I only thought I was gone for one day or lower than the real amount but, the few reasons I could have for estimating over time is that I either didn't care, or that I was just guessing and both of those are bad things.

"It's been a year." James said walking out of the room.

"A year?" I asked. *For evil guys, they lie really well... they show much more emotion than my dad does but at the same time, they're hurting. And their story... it's just so elaborate.* I thought.

I knew that I had to believe them but I chose not to. I chose to believe my dad's lies.

"HEY, game time! Get out here!" That was Alec.

James projected his voice across the cell: "Alec, you're a day early. The games are tomorrow."

We no longer had time to figure out the illusion technique. Wonderful.

"Scorn has plans tomorrow, we moved it up to today. Hurry up, now. Don't keep us all waiting."

Too many things to really decide right then. *Do we trust her?* They all discussed.

Is it worth the risk?

Do you think she'd really work for her dad after all that he's done?

I think there's only one way to find out, don't you think? Include her for now. If any red flags happen to pop up, cut her off right then. James finally decided.

They refused to actually speak out loud near me. They didn't want to risk the exposure or the loss of the game.

My dad used to tell me stories about battles. I assumed that this would be the same thing. I was wrong. The stories I were told were like, kid stories compared to the truth.

Dylan grabbed the back of my shirt, swung me around, let go of my shirt and as I slammed against the wall, he pressed one hand against my ribs and arm against my throat.

"Don't make us lose again this time." He told me.

"-kay." I whispered. I couldn't really get the "O" out of my mouth so I ended up just saying "Kay."

"Good." He said releasing me. "You're responsible for the outcome, Rissa."

It was easy to find the arena. The stench of blood was unmistakable and difficult to miss. Not to mention, the halls grew darker and there were more and more blood stains along the floor and walls as we got closer.

Finally, we were lead to the doors of the arena. They were overly huge and designed just like castle doors in the middle ages. Dylan and Alec swung the two doors wide open and the sight of the arena just attacked me.

It was... well, breathtaking. I remembered how my dad had told me in his stories about how large the arena was, but never, in my wildest dreams, did I imagine such a large death trap to be in my dad's jail.

"Oh, what happens if we lose this battle?" I asked.

Scorn also explained that every battle had a consequence if you lost.

"The loser of this battle will never leave their cell again." Dylan told me.

"I don't understand. Wouldn't that make life better?" I asked.

"That means that the loser will never be fed again, will never see the sun again, never drink again, never breathe fresh air again, never socialize with anyone again, oh and most importantly, their cell will be relocated underground, each of you, in a separate coffin. So, as you can see, it is in your interest to win." Alec laughed.

That startled me. I looked at Alec in fear. I didn't have to verbally ask him, I just looked at him and he knew me well enough to know I was thinking, *me too?*

He thought back to me, *For a bit. Just enough to sell the con to them that you died with them instead of betrayed them. Just a week or so.*

I stayed silent but my expression spoke for me. I was enraged.

"Don't try to hide it. You're worried. What happens to you and Alec if we lose?" James asked.

Cheuveans have this flaw, this one single flaw. We are incapable of lying if we have any form of an emotional attachment. Good or bad. We will just automatically tell the truth without even thinking about it. There are a select few that *can* lie, however. Usually the select few are the immortal and some get special training to allow them to lie as they please and the rest are capable of lying, but they just aren't good at it. Like me.

"... We take your place in your cell." He mumbled.

"Hah! That would almost make it worth it, but, don't worry. We won't lose." Lucas laughed.

"You had better keep your word." He growled unlocking our restraints and letting us into the arena.

James looked back at Alec. "Where's Dylan?"

Alec stared back at James expressionlessly. The doors began to shut behind us, lessening the light and the sound of the audience above.

"Give me our flag." I demanded.

--BEEP -- BEEP—

"No. I told you, none of us trust you." James hissed.

Good people of Scorn's Kingdom, welcome to the Blood Bath! For this battle, we have Scorn's... Child in with her Team Regicide verses Team Victorian!

"Hey! My... hah, I was about to say life, then I remembered that I was immortal... Then I was about to say my freedom, then I remembered I don't really have freedom ether." I laughed.

So let's not waste any time! For this battle, we have Scorn's gem in action with her first battle!

"Point?" Kalus asked.

So let's not waste any time!

"My point is, we all have something to lose here. Screw everyone and everything else. We *have* to win." I said.

Let the battle begin!

"Why do you need the flag?" Soren asked open minded.

"Does anyone else have a plan?" I asked.

No one said anything.

"Then I suppose, you'll have to trust me. I'm the fastest and... well, most daring and we all know that I have the most unbelievable luck in history." I pointed out.

"Fine. Now, tell us *why*." James whispered.

"They can't catch me, so, they don't catch me, they don't get the flag. Also it's a completely new strategy. They won't see it coming. While I'm running, Soren, you can guard where the flag is supposed to be. Kalus, James, Lucas, you go get their flag." I whispered.

Our voices echoed REALLY LOUD which was why we were whispering.

We nodded and all ran in our separate directions. That made me one step closer to gaining all of their trust, just to destroy it later on.

I had the flag and I ran to the one place that I knew no one knew about. Scorn told me about that too. It was in an illusion of a wall.

I was hiding in there, too stubborn to move, too scared to move, when suddenly, I heard two people coming closer. One was a girl. You could tell by her soft, quick step pace. One was a boy, you could tell that because, well, he was talking.

"Stop. We arrived. She's around here. I know it. I can feel her pulse through the ground." He said. "She's really small though. I wonder where she could be hiding." That had to be Andrew. He was the only one who could be able to feel through the earth.

"Andrew, Shush." The girl responded. "She can hear us."

"Regardless, she's here."

"I don't know what I would do if you weren't on my side." The girl laughed. "You're the best tracker in this jail, I don't think we could have gotten so far without you."

"Wait... The girl around here is Rissa." He whispered. "Rissa's small? That's impossible. I know her; she's bigger than that, ya know? She's bigger than small."

Why is it that when people whisper, they think that I can't hear?

"*Rissa*? Really? Wow!" The girl squeaked.

"Rissa, come out." Andrew said. "If you don't, eventually I will find you. You chose the wrong team to use this hiding spot on, ya know?"

Lucky for me, I knew some moves to help me speak to other people through their thoughts but block my ingoing chat to make it so they couldn't speak back.

Andrew, move on. Don't try to catch me. I thought to him.

"Why would I do that, kiddo?" He asked speedily out loud. "It's been a long time, by the way. How are you? Good, I assume. Living the nice life with your new daddy? Does it feel nice to betray all of your friends?"

Long time? No, shut up. Don't call me that. Look, the loser of this gets buried alive. Neither of us wants that, I know but guess what! My team is going to be breaking out soon, I can almost guarantee it. But if my team gets buried, what would happen to us? Your team won't be able to break out, and I'm sure you know that because... you don't have me. All you have to do is lose and you'll be out of here forever!" I said.

"You don't really plan to break them out, do you?" He asked.

Of course I do! I hissed.

"No, you don't. You're working for your dad, aren't you?" He laughed. "It's all around the jail, Rissa. We all know."

No... I thought.

"You forgot what he's done to you, haven't you." He said.

He hasn't done anything to me! I.... Uhhh... thought loudly.

387

Yeah, I kind of yelled in a thought.

"You don't remember what he's done to your human parents?" He asked.

I don't HAVE human parents.

"Yes you do. Well, actually, you *had* human parents. He killed them right in front of you. I was there. So was James. And Alec." Andrew explained. "We all *helped* him."

Shut up. He would never do that to me. I told him.

"Oh, yes he would. You really don't remember." He laughed.

He was really getting to me and apparently, he was enjoying it.

That did not happen! I thought.

"Ameri, show her. Show her *exactly* what happened. Don't hold back any details. Show her who she really is. Look into my memory and show her." He told her.

No, no. Don't do that! I pleaded.

I wanted to stay ignorant. I knew how miserable my life must have been when I hated my dad and I really didn't want to go back to that ever again.

Suddenly, my vision was getting blurry. Everything was going black. *No, no… no…* I thought.

I pictured my family; my human family. I remembered my entire life with my mom, my dad, and *Jason…* I remembered how much I loved them, how much I missed them.

I remembered my family going to the door… They were always so friendly with everyone. They probably never thought anyone was so dangerous.

Now I was watching Scorn kill them all. I was watching him curse my house. Watching my house burn endlessly.

"Maybe now we should show her how she was kidnapped and treated when she was human…" He mused.

I could hear him through the illusion.

I began remembering all the pain I was in. all that pain coming on at once… was unbearable.

Stop… Andrew, make it stop… stop… I thought to him. He didn't make it stop, so finally, I screamed, loud enough for the entire arena to hear; "STOP!!"

The illusion ended then. What happened was, when I shouted I broke Ameri's concentration. Andrew was too focused on her to realize that he was about to be done.

A steel box grew out of the ground and trapped them before they even had a chance to escape. It wasn't their fault though. The result was completely inevitable.

Andrew, when I tell you to do something, you do it. I told him. Then I decided to add, *Or else you'll get hurt.*

"Let me out! Let us out! *Elaina*, this isn't you! Don't let him take over you! Don't let him have the pleasure of realizing that he had succeeded in

controlling the world's most powerful Cheuvean!"
Andrew screamed.

Elaina... He too calls me Elaina.

You could hear him bashing the steel wall I had
put around him.

"Rissa, please, don't be a fool! Don't let him get
to you!" I heard Ameri scream.

Their pleas were getting to me more and more. I
couldn't take it.

*You know something? I remember how to kill
people like you now. I just destroy your body, your
soul. Whether it's un-aging you out of existence, or
just something as simple as piercing your heart with
a chain that only I can summon. I know how to do it.*

*But, you see, I don't think you deserve death. Or
rather, death doesn't deserve you. Most of us in this
forsaken prison want to die. I can see that. I think the
coffin in the ground will make a perfect domain for
you.* I told him.

I sighed. I couldn't be evil. It just wasn't in my
nature. I knew how to pretend and all but every time
I tried, it just broke my tiny little heart.

*Look, I'm sorry for what my daddy has done. I'm
planning on fixing it. Soon, after my team beats
yours, we're going to break out. All of us. That means
that my team will come and dig you guys out of the
ground. I promise. I have a plan but you guys have to
trust me. I want you all out of here once and for all. If
I take you out, you have to help my team win. If you*

don't, you will never get out of here. I thought to him.

I lied. I didn't think I would do as much as lift a finger to help these people that I thought to be traitors.

"I believe you. Just, please, don't let us down." He pleaded.

I had released them to tell their team to forfeit, and if their team refused, they would attack. I definitely had learned from both my dad and mom. They're the most manipulative people I have ever met and now, I guess, in this case, the apple really didn't fall far from the tree. When I need to, when it comes to the most important things in life, I am a wonderful liar. The situation just needed to be right.

Obviously, they couldn't persuade their team. You want to know how I found that out? You could hear them having an argument all about it. Then you could see a huge explosion sending Andrew and Ameri flying in separate directions.

Then I remembered, the other team didn't have any special explosion person.

Kalus... I thought.

They tried to trick us into thinking that they were on our side. But, don't worry. I didn't believe them. Kalus gloated sounding so proud.

Idiot! They ARE on our side! I told him.

Oh... Should I go find them? He asked.

No. *Find the flag. They can take care of themselves.* James said.

I was slowly walking around, careful not to make a sound. *Oh, uhm I kind of don't have a hiding spot anymore. What do I do?* I asked.

"Hi." A man said from behind.

I spun around. "Stay away." I ordered.

I didn't know why but I had this *huge* feeling that he was... bad news to me. "Rissa." He said.

"What?" I asked.

"Where is the flag? I know you have it but I can't see it. Where did you hide it?" He asked.

"I don't have it. It's possible James has it. After all, he's much stronger and faster than I am." I told him.

"I can see you're a pitiful liar." He told me.

"But I'm not lying." I told him.

He sighed, "Damn, I was hoping to avoid this entire encounter... but I suppose what has to be done will be done." Fire balls appeared around him. Every fire ball he threw at me, I dodged but, every one fire ball he threw, another five appeared.

Finally, it seemed that he was out of spirit when he had one last fire ball left to throw at me. He threw it, and I dodged it effortlessly. I was in the air and something, or in this case, someone wrapped himself around my entire body.

It was a snake. Of course, because of my lack of human memory I had no idea what that was.

"AHH! Let go! You disgusting animal!" I yelled.

"Now thatsssss ssssso rude. If you behave like thisss, I won't react well." He told me.

"You talked. That's not possible. Let me down." I told him.

The stupid oversized snake squeezed the life out of me. I started gasping for air. Half coughing, I felt my bones getting crushed under the pressure.

I wanted to cry. Well, I didn't want to because that would be showing them that I was weak, but I did because, well, I was seven.

"You can't talk that way to people like us. We have very, very short tempers." He warned halfheartedly.

I kind of twitched a nod of apology I guess. They seemed to understand so they had Mr. Snake loosen his grip on my body.

"You can talk. Why?" I asked.

"Because, my good friend here can transform into just about anything." The fire boy behind the snake told me. "Leaving me with nothing to do."

"Oh, so the long animal is Samuel." I said.

"Ah, sssso you know our namessss?" The snake asked.

"No. I just know yours because my team told me about a prodigy for transformation. I don't know anything about Fire Ball over there." I explained.

"Jacob." He said, laying against the wall. "My name is Jacob."

"Alright. I'll be sure to keep that in mind." I laughed.

"Where isss the flag?" Samuel asked.

"Let me down and I'll show you." I told him.

"No. You tell us now or he might accidently snap your neck." Jacob warned.

"I don't know how to explain. I hid it in this special invisible place that my dad told me about a while ago. I don't know how to get there other than with what I see. I can take you there." I explained.

"You're lying. It's with you." He said.

Samuel tightened his entire grip on me. He squeezed harder and harder until he saw tears coming out of my eyes. Silently, drops of water trailed down my face and dripped off of my childlike chin, onto the snake's dirtied yellow scales.

I wasn't screaming and crying like a little girl, my soul had just given up. My body was not ready for battle. A weak, seven year olds body wasn't meant for this kind of battle.

Samuel's grip loosened until I dropped, like a lifeless rag doll, onto the cold, hard floor.

Samuel morphed back into his original shape. Jacob tossed a red baseball cap at him, "You should see if you can find a way to morph the hat with you so I don't have to take it every time you make a transformation... Or just cut your hair."

Samuel took the baseball cap and lightly placed it on his head, careful not to damage the look of his mandible length dirty blonde hair that matched the color of his beasts. He wrinkled the freckles along his cheeks and told Jacob, "Not really worth it, ya know? And you're really not one to talk, Mr. Ponytail."

Ignoring the comment Samuel spat about his longer hair in his stiffened and teased ponytail, "Why did you let go?" Jacob asked.

"She's a little kid. She's not even moving anymore. Did I break her or something?" Samuel asked walking over to me, examining my unmoving body.

"Nah, she just gave up. She isn't talking, she isn't moving. She's planning on just laying still until we lose. Get her to talk by doing whatever is necessary." Jacob moaned. "Damn, this is such a pain. Why did *we* have to be the ones to beat up the *little girl*?"

The people there were for the most part eighteen through fourteen years old. They act all tough and cruel but deep, deep down, they're just scared *kids*, doing what they need to do to survive.

"That's sick! I can't do it. Seriously, I can't go destroy a little kid." Samuel said.

Jacob got up and walked over, hands in pockets. "Unfortunately that *kid* is our nightmare. She's a spawn and servant of our worst nightmare. She knows what her 'Daddy' does. She really doesn't care. She just wants *her* life to be nice. Now, what she doesn't know or understand is that, her dad will eventually turn on her just like he has to all of us once she is of no more use to him and at that point, if she thinks this is hell, just wait till he doesn't need her."

That's crazy; he would never ever do that to me. I thought happily.

"Keep telling yourself that. We'll see who's correct in the end; some brainwashed kid or someone with personal experience."

You're stupid. Before I even finished that thought he just came over to me and kicked me in the chest like I was a soccer ball or something.

I flew into the wall. The impact with the wall didn't hurt *nearly* as much as the actual kick hurt.

I still didn't move or make a sound even after the attack, just silent streams of water drained from my eyes. Seeing me was breaking Samuel's heart. Jacob was just doing what he had to, to survive.

"Stop it! She's just a little girl!" Samuel yelled jumping in front of me, blocking Jacob's reach of me.

"We both know she's not. She's a little monster and she needs to be slain." Jacob murmured. "What a pain..."

Now they were arguing about me. This was my time to escape. I got up, quietly, running around the corner, by the time they noticed that I was mobile I had already run about three meters.

That wasn't far enough.

I tried my best to inconspicuously run out of the hall that they had been killing me in. "She's gone. Samuel, track her down!"

I need help! Samuel and some kid named Jacob are tracking me. They're chasing me, I'm scared!

I started to panic. Samuel could turn into anything he wanted to meaning he could easily catch up to me. There was no where I could hide. There was no where I could run.

Everyone, don't use your mind to talk to anyone! I think they're tapping it. James said.

That was the end of hearing voices in my head. *Who could be tapping our mind talk?* I thought.

I ran further into the maze. I thought I was doing well. No one had caught up to me yet. Then, I ran into a dead end. I skidded to a stop and quickly tried to turn around and run out-

Oops. Too late. After I turned around, a giant yellow wolf pounced on me then morphed into a... well, an almost weasel. It was just *giant*. Its monstrous claws dug into both of my shoulders.

"What in the world is that?" I shrieked.

"Don't you remember anything from your human life?" Samuel asked.

"Ugh! Why would I ever have been a *human*? They're disgusting, idiotic creatures." I asked in disgust.

"Scorn really erased your memory well. You don't recall *anything* from your human life?" He asked.

"Get off of me." I ordered.

"No. You're acting like a little brat. You're making this *so* much harder than it has to be. Jacob doesn't show mercy. This really is your last chance before I do everything he wants me to." Samuel said.

"Honestly, I think you losers will get exactly what you deserve. Buried alive. Spending the rest of your undying life being stuck underground." I spat on him.

Now, this is always where I start acting really bratty to get the people who already hate me. This allows them to hate me more which results in one of two things: they get more pissed and destroy me *or* they get pissed and begin making mistakes. This is why in war, you need to be impartial. Emotions are *bad*.

Unfortunately, these two were emotionally impartial. They didn't make mistakes. "Little brat!" He rolled over, (with me still attached to his claws) grabbed my ankle with his tail, yanked his claws out of me, and slammed me into the ground.

I laid there as I let out a gentle moan. I really didn't enjoy getting slammed into everything.

"You aren't even worth my time." He laughed morphing back into a Cheuvean.

I got up, got my little spirit sword out, and ran after him. I caught up with him and as I took a swing at him, he turned around. Surprised, he held his arms up in front of his face to protect himself.

Basically, to put it simply, the bones in his arms shattered sending little shards of bone shooting out of his skin. He cried, "What did you just do to me!? You stupid bitch! Fix my arms!"

"Holy..." I said. "No! That's what you get, you! No one picks fights with me."

"Do it now or I'll end you!" He asked.

"You're the enemy. I won't help you for that reason and also because you're a jerk." I smiled my little taunting smile.

"Get this over with Samuel. Destroy her body. This place will become her tomb." Jacob took his time walking up.

"No arms..." Samuel muttered.

"Snake." Jacob suggested.

Now Samuel transformed into a snake and wrapped his scaly body around mine. He started squeezing harder and harder until we all heard a ton of snaps. Yeah, those were my bones. He still kept squeezing until,

-BEEP- -BEEP- Good people of Scorn's Kingdom, We have a winner! All cheer for the... Team Regicide! Leave now and rest. You've... earned it.

I don't even know where that came from. It was just this huge sound declaring that my team had become victorious.

"You guys won…" Samuel had returned to his original form, dropping me.

"Are you really going to help your team get out of jail and help us get out of our tomb?" Jacob asked.

I knew he knew the answer. He just was hoping that I would prove him wrong. He needed that. He needed hope to keep him going.

"No, absolutely not." I laughed.

This time, it was my time to mock someone's torment. I enjoyed it. It was the most effective release of anger I've ever had. I knew that I had just crushed any hope these boys had. I knew that I was betraying everyone but by taking their strength and hope, it was almost like I absorbed it. It made me *stronger*. It made me *happy*.

They had now lost given the last of their strength to me. They both just fell to their knees and trying their best to stop the tears running down their faces.

I just turned around, not remembering how horrible it felt to be in their position, grinning at their despicable fate. I pranced gracefully back to my gate with no regret.

"Hey, man." I heard Jacob back in the distance, comforting in between sobs. "Maybe… We can finally rest, ya know? Someone will eventually find us. We… can just relax in… in the meantime. This was all a big pain anyways. It's best that it's all over."

Unfortunately, I had to pretend to be sad for what I thought was a group of moronic traitors. I had to pretend that I felt guilt for saving myself.

"We won…" Soren said.

"Did you hide the flag?" Lucas asked.

"No, she ate it." Kalus said sarcastically.

"Actually, I did eat it." I told them.

"Huh?" Lucas yelled.

"Shhh. After I began being persued, I shrunk the flag, and ate it. It's not like they could get to it after that." I said.

It was hard for me to walk, but I still managed. I felt like if I didn't break down in tears, I would explode but I had to hold my composure or that would provide others with a sense of my weakness.

I can always tell when you're upset, Elaina. James thought to me.

I'm good. I responded faintly.

You don't have to worry about what happened to them. We'll help them out of their tomb one day and that is thanks to you.

No one in my team wasn't injured. James had plenty of cuts from other people's swords, Lucas was shot with the other team's bowman, Kalus was burnt, Soren was shot, slit, and burnt, and I had every bone in my body broken.

"I did it!" I whispered. "We did it…"

CHAPTER TWENTY ONE
I did it! We did it

Dear Diary,

We won. I watched the opposing team crumble in front of me and I don't know if I'm happy or sad about it. My job is becoming harder too. I'm good at it - gaining their trust. It all just makes me feel so crummy. I wish there was a way for me to just make everyone happy.

-Rissa

My team just started screaming with excitement. Dancing around with tears dropping from their faces, believing that now, I could help them escape. They didn't know rather to be sad or extremely excited. Soon though they stopped dancing and just stared staring at me, wondering why I was not dancing, why I didn't seem happy.

"Common Kiddo, be happy. We did it!" Kalus yelled lifting me off of the ground, tossing me in the air.

I landed on my feet. I actually had hints of sorrow deep in my stomach. I felt *guilt* for delivering what I thought may be justice. The guilt grew as I thought of the people who I had just doomed to live under ground for, like, forever.

"Kiddo, you're our little ace in the hole. Be happy! We won, and it's all because of you!" Lucas yelled kinda giving me a little pat on the head, messing up my hair even more.

"Ouch…. I'm hurting. They broke most of my bones." I said quietly.

"Don't worry about it. You'll have plenty of time to heal before the next battle. Almost a whole week." Soren said smiling.

"Ooh. A whole week. Now I'm happy." I laughed.

I was growing closer to these people. They were becoming my friends without my approval. I couldn't let them become my friends or I would disappoint my dad.

James scooped me off the ground and cradled me as though I was an angel.

"We're sorry we didn't trust you." James said.

"It's alright. I understand why." I smiled at him.

I was so exhausted that I fell asleep right there, in James's arms.

CHAPTER TWENTY TWO
Ace in the hole

Dear Diary,

I'm lying down right now. I won the game for these guys and I really wish I didn't like them so much... it would make everything so much easier. Now I'll actually need to make the choice between these... strangers that I just happen to have a fondness for, and my DAD. It's just so unfair. ☹

-Rissa

I had just woken up. "Welcome back to reality sleeping beauty." James said.

"James..." I mumbled.

"What is it? You need anything?" James asked.

"No, no. I'm fine. I was just wondering how long I was asleep.

"You were sleeping for a full twenty four hours." James said.

"Why are you holding me?" I asked.

"What, you think that was my choice? You wouldn't let go of me sense you passed out so I just laid here for the entire time. You're just lucky nothing was happening for that twenty four hours or I'd be very angry." James laughed.

"Sorry." I laughed faintly. *I'm on my third day now... great.*

"So... sorry to bring up business, but have you happen to have found the source of the extra powers Scorn has been giving his guards?" Kalus mentioned walking into the room.

"What?"

James laughed quietly, "I'll fill you in. Each Cheuvean is *supposed* to only be skilled in one category of power. You, before you unaged yourself, informed us of the almost certain probability that Scorn doing something to make his men skilled in multiple categories just as he is."

"I don't know, I woke up and then I came here." I replied.

"We were going to send you in at one time... to see if maybe you could find the source of his additional power and if you could, destroy it." Kalus explained further.

"And then you unaged yourself! So maybe this is our chance!" Lucas bounced in.

"But I don't... want to leave." I responded.

"It's important..." Soren whispered under his breath.

"Yes, it is important," James interjected. "But so is what she wants. Maybe when you're older, you'll feel more comfortable, eh Elaina?"

"HEY! Food time." Dylan croaked, unintentionally interrupting.

Shoot. I heard James think. *Meal time. Bet you're hungry, huh.*

We walked over to the door quickly. "Dylan. Hi." I said.

"Shut up." He said keeping a distance between himself and us almost like he was afraid.

I held my arms up in surrender and quietly replied, "Okay..."

He unlocked the door and we all walked out. Conversation for most of the prisoners was nonexistent if not very rare while their prison handlers were around. However, there was still me. Learning the lessons proudly provided by Scorn was a little more difficult for me. "You're welcome."

"For?" Dylan asked beginning to get angry and the more agitated he got, the more he fidgeted like a mental patient with fleas.

"Because of us, you aren't in a cell right now. You should give us some credit and actually thanking us. We could get out of the ground easily but we chose to show mercy to you. You should thank us." I smiled.

"You-" Dylan spat.

Alec looked at Dylan, probably mind speaking to him.

"Thank you." Alec replied giving a pat of reassurance on Dylan's shoulder.

Wow. How did she do that? Lucas thought. *I need to learn that trick.*

Got me. I have NO idea. Kalus said.

None. Soren finalized.

Aren't you supposed to be the smart one? Kalus asked.

HAH! It's not his fault. As if anyone could predict that girl. James thought. *There is no predicting the Chosen girl.*

"Any time, guys." I smiled sarcastically.

Alec shot me a glance almost *begging* me to stop provoking Dylan.

Stop pushing it. You think you're impenetrable in here? Dylan thought to me. *Your Daddy's shield can't help you in here, Rissa. You are forcing my hand inch by inch.*

I nodded. Dylan's thoughts were really difficult for me to hear now. That meant that I was drifting more to James's side.

Alec and Dylan hurried us to the cafeteria and instructed us to get in line for food. This time we were not chained together and we had a little bit of freedom—probably to show me that Scorn's side wasn't so bad.

We got into the cafeteria line and thought briefly, just in case the worst happens, I need to complete my mission. "How are we going to get out of here? What's the real plan?"

"You're our plan, Ellie. You're the one who's going to get us out of here." James said. "You were supposed to infiltrate Scorn before you un-aged yourself but plans changed once they took you."

"It's all up to me? I didn't remember that..." I said.

"I know, because you decreased in age, to you, it's like "before" never happened. It's like your life started at age... whatever age you are. But you know, you promised, it's your destiny to break us out." Kalus explained.

"That's not how you talk to a seven year old. Man, lighten up. Unlike the rest of us, the kid isn't a trained fighting machine." Lucas smiled using my head as an arm rest.

I loved these guys. They were more than just my friends, I looked up to them. They were like my best friends or even my brothers.

"Don't worry. I'll do this." I smiled.

So we got our food and sat at our apparent usual table. My happiness was completely contagious. The cafeteria had this eerie aura filled with secrets and unhappiness but around my group, we were happy, laughing, filling the cafeteria with noise and in our own little way, showing that there was still hope. There was still happiness in the world.

All eyes were on us and little by little, we were making a difference. We were changing the way things had always been.

Unfortunately, lunch was over way too quick. I was enjoying myself. You know how *rare* it is for someone to say that in a prison like this? It's close to impossible for someone to say that in there.

We were walking back to our cage now, stuffed with food. "Why were you brats laughing?" Dylan asked stopping us in the hall.

Why is it any of your business? I thought of saying. "We wanted to. We're *happy*. Does that bother you?"

You're really, REALLY pushing your luck. He thought to me.

Of course. That's my goal, Idiot. I thought to him.

"OKAY THAT'S IT!" He yelled.

Guard me! I thought.

Sure enough, James slammed himself against Dylan and jumped back towards me, guarding me just by standing in front of me. These guys really did care for me. I was at that point, on their side. Screw my dad.

"You can't do anything to me." I told him.

"Would you like to make a wager on that?" He challenged. "With just a few words, I can make this fortress of yours crumble beneath your feet."

I looked down. I knew he could. "I'll tell your dad to stop your get together with your friends." He threatened.

"You had better not. I know who's lying now." I told him.

"What?" Soren questioned skeptically.

"Don't let them take me away!" I pleaded hanging on to James.

"Why would they?" He asked.

"She was sent here to infiltrate you. Get your secrets. I'm sure she didn't really do that though. She has fallen in love with all of you. She thinks that you'll forgive her for betraying you but we all know the reality to that sad little delusion, right? You're all going to turn her in. Just like you always have. Just like you always will." Dylan chuckled. "After all, history does have a way of repeating itself."

"No. You're wrong! They wouldn't ever do that to me! I made a mistake, they won't get mad... Right? Right guys? You won't get mad?" I asked.

I had these innocent tears running down my face. I only wanted to make Scorn happy but I ended up disappointing everyone.

"I knew we shouldn't have trusted you." James said. "I should have known better than not trusting myself."

You don't care about what we think... You don't care about what anyone thinks. I can't believe you of all people would do this... No, wait, I know you. I know precisely what you are capable of and I know you would do this. You've told me yourself... We have helped you through many different hard times and now you think you might just throw that all away... You only help yourself. You know that? Even when you help others, bottom line is that you are only trying to help YOU.

I knew he was just angry. When I forced him to become younger, his control disappeared with it. Something happened after this point in his life to make him who he was.

No, that's not true, James! I thought to him tightening my grasp on his arm.

I'm gladly done with your bullshit. I wonder if your life will get more screwed up than it is now, which would be a hard thing to do, or better... have fun being a submissive little bitch to your parents who love to abuse you 'cause they know you won't fight back. Hope you enjoy your pathetic little life cause we're sure as hell gone from that messed up shit forever. James glared.

That was enough of my reality for one day. My mind shut down; my poor, undeveloped mind just trying to grasp what the hell just happened and quit processing regular bodily actions.

I was so sad. I dropped to my knees, shifting my grasp to hold onto the edges of his ripped shirt.

He wouldn't even look at me.

Dylan opened the door to the cage and everyone other than James walked in. Finally, James looked down on me, eyes showing no emotion, telling me that he felt nothing for me. And after the message was made clear, he grabbed my hands, squeezing them together until I couldn't bear to hold on anymore.

He then, after I unwillingly surrendered my grasp, he walked into his cell. *He would rather face imprisonment than have a conversation with me!* I thought bitterly looking up at Alec.

It was hopeless: Alec and Dylan were on each side of me. Their fighting skills obviously surpassed mine by an immeasurable amount and there was really no talking myself out of this so, I got up and ran.

I wasn't fast enough to escape Dylan *and* Alec. *They had this all planned out.* I quivered.

I had messed up big time. I was out matched, outnumbered, out aged, and out powered. "You failed." Alec said.

"And you lied to me." I retorted. "This all feels *so* real! How could you fake this? How can you fake such emotion? How could you fake caring about me?"

"You don't know which side is the side to be on!" Alec shouted at me—almost screaming. "I do care! I cared so much, you stupid girl! Don't you get it? I loved you! Why do you have to ruin *everything*?"

"And *you* don't know who *not* to mess with!" I screamed back, fists clenched. "Stop *lying* to me!"

I was then forced against the wall, getting my wrists chained together. "You won't get a free pass out of this one. Not this time." Dylan finalized. "I'm the only one that wasn't injected with emotion here. I'm the only one that truly hates you to the core and I cannot wait to see you suffer."

I had realized it then. I had realized what I *had* to do. I stopped fighting Dylan's grasp so Dylan would allow me to get on my knees. "I'm sorry..." I whispered.

"That's not enough, Ri. Why did you change sides?" Alec asked.

"They told me that you guys really didn't like me and you were only pretending to because you wanted to use me... They sounded so... They made it seem so real..." I sobbed.

Yeah, I made it seem like I was that helpless, innocent seven year old who had been deceived.

"Aw! Geez... What are we going to tell Scorn?" Alec asked.

That would have worked if stupid Dylan wasn't there. Bias little piece of dirt.

"The truth. She disobeyed orders and so we had to punish her. I don't care what the reason was; she disobeyed orders so now she needs to pay the price, just like everyone else." Dylan said. "It's because she is always excused from punishment that she is like this, you know."

He clenched his hands into fists and this green aura appeared on them. "What are you doing?" I asked. I wasn't aware that Dylan had such power.

"Get up." He said.

"Dylan, this is dangerous. Look at your skin." Alec tried to intervene.

"Why?" I asked.

"Get up now or Scorn will be the one to give you your punishment, and believe me, what I'm about to do will seem merciful compared to what Scorn would do to you." Dylan said.

I took his word for it. I was naïve thinking that Dylan would keep his word. I got up and before I was able to react to Dylan punching me. He had already hit me six times before a second passed. Every hit left a burn mark just for a few seconds because of rapid Cheuvean healing. Dylan's special power was acid which was not what you could call an "instant death" specialty but it was known for its cruel torturous sting not to mention it temporarily impairs you until you are able to fight back.

He continued attacking until he himself dropped from pain. He began squealing, holding his hands up into the air as his own skin started to melt away.

Alec called out to Dylan, "Hey, hold on. It's going to be okay."

And the final blow was done by Alec, when I finally had the chance to run from Dylan, I jumped backward and Alec stabbed me through the heart, probably some kind of symbolic strike, physically showing the world what I had done to him.

CHAPTER TWENTY THREE
The Dark Room

Dear Diary,

They say that I've been bad. That they need to fix me. Everyone's so mad that I chose the prisoners over my own dad and to be realistic, they're only proving that I chose right.

I really wish that my dad would have been the right choice but... GOD he scares me... But I love him.

-Rissa

I woke up in a dark room tied to a chair. "W-where am I?" I asked.

"You're in your new room. This is where you will be staying until I am completely sure that I can trust you." Scorn said.

"Daddy... I'm sorry, Daddy." I said. I was crying. I had failed my hero. I knew he was bad but I really didn't want to believe it. I wanted to stay in my illusion of happiness.

"You were tricked. I had warned you of their dishonesty. Yet, you still have failed." He explained.

"No, I haven't. I have the information I was sent to get." I told him.

"Really? Prove it. Show me what you have learned about these people." He said.

"They planned to break out very soon, but they won't do it without me. They think that I want to help them get out of here. If you keep them away from me, they can never escape." I explained.

"Really? Then what was that with Dylan? What was that argument?" He asked.

"I was *trying* to keep my cover to, you know, see if there was anything else that was worth finding out. He didn't catch on. After that, I got scared, and tried running and then, I surrendered. What else could I do? It was Alec and Dylan verses me. I had no other choice." I explained.

"And why don't I believe you?" He asked.

"Why would you?" I asked.

"You tell me." He ordered.

"Because I refused to come back. It's easier to believe Alec and Dylan than to believe me." I said.

"Smart kid you have there." A voice said from the shadows. "She's seven and able to lie just. Like. Her. Parents. Just like *Daddy,* eh Scorn?"

"Grant, leave us alone. It's not your time to show yourself to her just yet." Scorn ordered.

"Yes, of course. My apologies." He commented halfheartedly. "You realize, Scorn, that you will eventually need to treat me as an equal. We both know who's-"

"Out, Grant. Please." Scorn asked again.

PLEASE?

Grant smiled, his golden eyes glimmered even in the darkness until he made eye contact with me. "See you in a while, Rissa. Or Elaina. Or whatever is it that you go by now days?"

Confusion struck me. "What?" *They really were telling the truth.*

"Grant, OUT."

"Calm down, 'Lord'. I'm only trying to be friendly." Grant laughed leaving the room.

"Who was that?" I asked.

"No one of importance to you." He glared out the door that Grant failed to shut.

"Okay..."

"I'll be back for you later."

"Why don't you just let me go? I'd never be a bother to you again. Daddy," I tried for my freedom.

"No." He said plainly.

"When will you trust me enough to let me out of here?" I asked.

"When I forgive you for failing me. Take this time to think over what you have done and what you will do after I decide to give you a second chance. If what you say to me is good enough, I might just let you out."

That was when I really truly took hold of the situation. When he looked at me, he didn't care. When I smiled, he didn't return the feelings of joy. When I called him Daddy, he might have smiled, but in his head, he felt disgust.

It hit me *hard* that I hadn't done anything to deserve this hate but I loved a man that wanted nothing more than my suffering or even my death.

"But... Didn't I do what I was supposed to do?" I asked desperately.

"I suppose."

"Then why?"

"Awe, little *toy*, you're useless to me right now. I don't trust you; I don't *need* you. So here you'll stay gathering dust until the day comes that both of my needs are met."

"When is that going to be, Daddy?" I asked.

He didn't answer me. Alec just shut the large door and Scorn's words were the last sounds I heard in years. Just like in that human prison years and years ago, I received no water, no food, no light, and absolutely no visitors and during that whole time, I only thought about James and the other prisoners.

The first days were hardest. I was still trying to understand that extent of hate, that awful feeling that was constantly surging through my body. I cried on an hourly basis, and on a daily basis, I begged to be let out because I prayed that someone had secretly been listening or watching me.

After a while, the crying stopped. I was incapable of producing any more of that sadness that fell down my face.

After the sadness passed, the rage came. I tried breaking out of my bonds multiple times—each time, less successful than the last and the force hurt more against my frail skin each time.

Finally, I gave up. Years later, I accepted that maybe, instead of my cage being in the ground, in a coffin, it'd be in this room. Which was almost alright with me. It would be fitting, wouldn't it? I doomed my fellow prisoners so in return, I would be doomed as well.

I thought I'd never get out. Until the day came when I heard the startling sound of breaking silence. The door unlocked and then light shined into the room, half blinding me.

An overwhelming feeling of happiness overcame me as I croaked to the best of my loving ability, "DADDY! You really did come back! You didn't forget about me! You didn't lose hope in me!"

I couldn't hold it in anymore. I started crying out of both joy and sadness.

"Shut up. Don't speak unless you have been spoken to. You don't have the right. Not yet." He said.

"Okay, sorry Daddy." I whispered.

"Don't call me that. You don't have the right. You are a disgrace." He said.

"That's what Mommy told me before she dumped me on the street." I said quietly. "Are you going to abandon me too?"

Stupid false memories.

"No. I told you, you will always be my little girl." Scorn said sweetly and gently caressing my face.

His voice and smile seemed so real... but his eyes would forever give him away. You can lie with your voice, your face, your bodily expressions but *never* with your eyes.

I could see that he was trying to play me. I could tell that he needed me. Without me, he couldn't rid the worlds of humans or dominate the Cheuveans. I had to play along. I had to gain his trust.

"Do you hate me, Daddy?" I asked.

If I'm still his 'Little girl' then this should work.

"I suppose that depends." He replied.

Wow, that didn't go as expected. That was like a slap in the face. "Oh... Okay." I mumbled.

"It's been three and a half years since your betrayal. Do you think that you're ready to help me?" Scorn asked. "Are you ready to be my tool?"

On one hand, I wanted to say yes, and on the other hand, I wanted him to feel like he was in charge. So I just said; "Of course. It's completely up to you though, Daddy. I think I'm ready." I said innocently.

He smiled at my innocent reply. At the time, I wasn't sure if it was because he was happy with it, or because he was laughing at me.

"Fine." He laughed. "Alec, come in here and untie her."

Alec walked in, glaring at me, wishing with everything in him that I never made that choice. He wished that he could trust me. He wished those memories of me and Jason that were implanted in our heads were real feelings of love, instead of forgotten feelings of my dead brother.

He appeared behind me and unbound my hands.

"Thank you." I smiled.

My first memories of him were *stolen* from my memories with my brother, Jason. My second memories of him were him throwing me in jail and treating me like a prisoner.

"Don't talk to me." He ordered.

I ignored the anger in his voice. "Why?"

"You're too weak to assume that you're important enough to talk to me." He told me.

That was harsh… "Oh. My bad." I said walking out of my prison and waiting for Scorn to follow.

Scorn eventually followed me after having a silent conversation with Alec. "This time, if you betray me, I will make sure you will have a much harder time in jail. You will remember your place." He told me.

"Of course. That's only expected." I agreed.

I had learned how to talk to people like him during my three days in his prison. And more importantly, I had learned how to tell good from bad. Also, my real only goal was revenge. Similar to that "Fool me once, fool me twice" deal, I had a similar saying. Catch me once, shame on you. Catch me twice... that will never happen.

"Do you trust me?" I asked.

"No." He responded.

"How can I help to change that?" I asked.

"I don't know." He said.

"You had three years to think about it." I growled, unsuccessfully hiding my anger.

"Don't talk to me that way." He said simply.

"You locked me away for *three years.* Don't you dare tell me that you never thought about that or hadn't come to a conclusion in that time. " I asked.

"You want to go back until I do figure it out?"

"No! God, of course not. I'm grateful you let me out, but I'm just upset that you are still angry with me."

"Wouldn't you be if your only daughter had betrayed you? Even after you rescued that kid off of the street? That child would be *worthless* if you didn't help her and she still betrayed you!" He yelled.

I whimpered, hurt by his sudden guilt trip and began walking away.

"Where are you going?" He asked, grabbing my shoulder, forcing me to a stop.

"I'm going to my old room… Or did you turn that into another prison?" I yanked my shoulder back and continued on my walk.

CHAPTER TWENTY FOUR
A deal with the devil

Dear Diary,

I may not be behind bars, but I'm still in a prison. I actually kind of wish I was back in a cage. At least my expectations are accurate there. Now I'm just afraid that something I do will get me thrown back into that dark room. One thing is most definitely decided though. I HAVE to get them out.

-Rissa

The castle looked the same as when I had last seen it. It was always in perfect shape. You couldn't find a particle of dust even if you had Cheuvean eyes. He always kept the place spotless.

Not to mention that it seriously took me like, nine minutes to get to my room. My room hadn't changed. It was still clean, still pink, and still really pretty. It seemed the only thing that had changed was me.

"It's still the same, you know. Your dad still loves you. Way, way more than you could ever know.

Everyone still remembers you as both a brat, and a little innocent kid. Prove them correct with the little innocent kid side of you and you're back to being a princess." Dylan mused behind me, almost completely bandaged.

I turned around to find him just standing in my door way. Come to think of it, maybe I wasn't the only one who had changed. Dylan looked five years younger than when I had last seen him but what little of his skin hadn't been totally destroyed, was cracking and almost looked like it was falling off.

"Hey Liar. Trouble in paradice?" I gently grasping a loose bandage and rewrapping it around Dylan's arm. "What do you care if I get back to being a princess?"

"I'll ignore that. You're welcome. I don't. I'm just trying to make everyone's life easier." He replied. "You don't know how much everyone cares about you here. You're so important and you don't even get *why*."

"On the flip side, I don't care why. I know I'm plenty important just not for the right reasons." I mumbled. "But anyways, I need a shower. And come to think of it, food would be wonderful, as well as the ability to sleep in my own bed. Is it at all possible for me to do all that with privacy? I mean, it's been three years."

"I suppose you're entitled to that much. I'll make sure everyone obliges." Dylan laughed hobbling out of my room.

"Thank you." I smiled.

I walked into my bathroom and noticed that I didn't like who I saw in the mirror. I didn't like the dishonest, naïve girl that stared back at me. I needed to get my memories back and more importantly, I needed to keep the promises I made to those in Scorn's jail. I needed to stop just hiding my mistakes and hoping that they'd never find and burn me in the end.

I made the decision to go down the hard road. I needed to be able to look at the girl in the mirror and be proud.

I turned, unable to look at myself any longer with all that dirt, blood, and shame I wore. I walked into the shower, turned on the water and took in the amazing warmth.

Unlike humans, we don't quite, *need* to shower. Our hair doesn't get greasy, we don't sweat, so dirt usually doesn't easily stick to us unless there's something to help it like water or in my case, blood. Usually, we take showers as a form of therapy. Our water has healing properties and the heat can soothe anyone. And with the correct amount of power, could maybe do something amazing like bring back a certain someone's memories?

Also, it just occurred to me as I watched the bronze colored water spiral down the drain that I first had gotten bloody the day that I had gotten sent to prison. I obviously hadn't taken a shower in the prison and hadn't taken a shower in Scorn's room of demise meaning I hadn't showered in over three years. Disgusting.

After I was sure I completely decontaminated my body, I sat down and prepared for the water to assist me in getting my memories back.

I closed my eyes and let the water run down my head. *Please get my memories back.* I pleaded silently. *I need to know the truth.*

A little girl's laugh echoed around me. *Come now, Dad is stronger than that. Maybe you should be asking someone else for help with your memory.*

Who are you?

I'm you. Your other you. Remember your attack on Daddy back when you were human. Recognize my essence from when you attacked Scorn? Yeah, that was me. Awesome, right? Are you wondering if I can help? Can you remember our deal?

I didn't care to solve the puzzle she was trying to spit at me. *Can you help me?*

You're asking the wrong questions, girly. She taunted.

Will you? I asked again.

Of course I will! But at a price. You know my price.

Meaning? Nothing ever comes cheap.

You know my price. Remember our last conversation.

Nothing in addition?

You have to let me in. let me see what you see, hear what you hear, and whatever else I might want.

Hefty price, don't you think? I don't want to make a deal with the devil.

That's your decision to make. Is this deal worth making? She asked. Her voice was so smiley yet cruel.

I don't-

Is it worth taking down Scorn?

Well...

Is it worth saving your friends and keeping your promises? And we have a winner.

And without another thought, *Deal.*

I appeared once again in the room full of infinite darkness. "And you're sure you're ready for this, girl?"

"Shut up." *I summoned my sword.*

"That's... not your weapon. Well, it is. But you haven't even fully activated it."

"Does that matter for me stabbing my hand?"

"No... but,"

"Then shut up."

Rissa sneered at me. "Whatever, girl." *She summoned her triple curved dual swords, knelt, standing her swords upwards and slammed her hands down on them, watching her own darkened soul mix around her blood and leak onto the ground. Just like a faucet, being called upon by Rissa's own sacrifice, a dark waterfall of blood and essence poured from the sky.*

"Your turn, girl. Make sure you use both your hands."

"Oh my god..." I breathed, setting my sword down.

"Come on."

I placed my hands on top of each other, as I stared down at the sword and slammed them down as I knelt in one blunt and swift motion.

She began laughing more cheerfully than I'd ever expect. "Go on, girl! Every. Last. Drop." She stared at my mixed essence pour down from the sky just like hers did earlier.

I took my hands off of my sword and waited for the very last drop of my essence's blood dripped onto the ground. More blood began to drain from the sky.

"Do you see that, Elaina?"

"The blood? It's pretty damn difficult to miss." I looked carelessly at my hands and rubbed off the extra blood.

"No, stupid girl. I was talking about THAT!"

The draining from the endless sky began to cease, lessening dramatically with each passing second revealing an artifact – the same artifact that was being held in Scorn's portraits by a little girl, the same artifact that was on the tapestry in the abandoned "Demon Factory".

"What is that?"

"US! That is OUR power we share. You can control that now and so can I. That chain you seem to enjoy killing with is now accessible for you at any time along with any of your other abilities. WE are unbeatable!"

Moments of silence passed.

"This binds us." She murmured, "This is all the people we've killed. All the people we will kill will end up here... Magical, isn't it? And awful."

"Yeah, it is terrible."

"No. See, your people do that. You took the meaning of a word that summed up a great meaning and turned it into "bad". No. Awful: full of awe. Amazing."

I stared at her, dazed and confused.

"One more time, girl. Do you agree to my terms?" the endless darkened floor now was covered in our essence.

The last drop began to drip with the deal including the selling of my soul's essence I called hesitantly out to Rissa, "I agree to your terms." And the last drop plummeted in with the rest.

"We are linked and you have set me free."